QUANTUM TEENS ARE GO

Written by: **MAGDALENE VISAGGIO**
Line art by: **ERYK DONOVAN**
Colors by: **CLAUDIA AGUIRRE**
Letters by: **ZAKK SAAM**
Series Editor: **JON GORGA**

cover and series covers: **ERYK DONOVAN**

For this edition, book design & layout: **PHIL SMITH**
Produced by: **MATT PIZZOLO**

Published By Black Mask Studios LLC
Matt Pizzolo | Brett Gurewitz | Steve Niles

For licensing information, contact: licensing@blackmaskstudios.com

Tachyons are fucking crazy.

You may not know this, having perhaps not been raised as I was in a high-tech lab by a small cabal of dedicated astrophysicists and computer scientists wielding weaponized *Star Trek* episodes, but it's the truth. Tachyons are total assholes; difficult, hypothetical particles that refuse to be proven to exist at all. They move so fast that they cannot be observed, they have imaginary mass - they're just ridiculous and complicated and even the people who want to understand them tend to give up out of sheer frustration.

Teenagers are essentially the same. Unstable particles, not sure where they're beginning or ending, charging forward at impossible velocities on missions of the gut. Observed from a safe distance, teenagers are dramatic madness. But observed honestly, as they are in the wonderful QUANTUM TEENS ARE GO, teenagers are inspiring. They are the best and bravest of us. They're the only hope we've got, Obi-Wan-style. Because, again like tachyons, the future is in their hands.

This is the tale of Nat and Sumesh, a couple of teenagers in a highly-relatable future - practically an alternate now - where humanity found hope in the mad science of quantum mechanics. But, like most things that give adult humans hope, the quantum bubble burst - leaving abandoned brutalist warehouses filled with technology sitting across the world like Silicon Valley graveyards. Humanity has woken from dreams of impossible science and embraced a very familiar philosophy towards the Disappointing Now:

"Fuck it, I guess."

But Sumesh and Nat don't have that luxury. Nat is in the middle of transitioning into the woman she knows she is - and her parents are still deadnaming her. Bullies misgender her. The world is a vampire set to drain Nat to a husk if she can't give herself the acceptance the rest of the planet refuses her. Sumesh is dealing with the tragic loss of his parents - and a new family situation in which he feels like a hostage. Other kids might grow up to find themselves protected by this shithole of a future, but Nat and Sumesh are vulnerable. They're the kind of kids who've only found love in one another - and only found hope by literally building it together. To outside observers, they're invisible hypothetical particles - they might not even exist. But to each other, they're the only thing that matters.

The story of QTAG is the tale of two lovers taking the future into their hands, because no one else ever even tried to lend a hand. Like tachyons and the teenage ideal, they must be more than they appear. The future is in their hands.

And in this case, it's also in yours.

See, when it comes to the book you're holding, that old chestnut can be taken quite literally. This teenage punk rock queer AF garage science love story is the singular product of two future comics luminaries. Your kids, if they're cool enough to read comics, are gonna think you are super dope for having gotten on this train as early as you did. Trust me.

Mags Visaggio is a voice of her generation, all spit and rage from an optimistic heart too often scarred by our shittown present. Her words demand your notice, her characters kidnap your sympathy, her stories hijack your imagination. This can be seen in her masterpiece *Kim & Kim* and it is all the more obvious here, in the much more grounded QTAG. There's an honesty and kindness to even her most inconsiderate and outlandish characters - an Amblinesque humanity - while at the same time you can tell all her kids listen to Smashing Pumpkins at every opportunity. Everybody's hurt. Everybody's human. Everybody's real.

Eryk Donovan was widely recognized as the future of comics by the time he graduated goddamn college, so he hardly needs my praise here. So of course I'll give it anyway. Eryk's work is funnier than it first appears - filled with references to memes and big acting moments - but it can step down to a human moment on a dime. Look at any panel of Sumesh and Nat together; their chemistry and dynamic is apparent from every look and pose. His characters aren't illustrations, they're people. I'd read the phone book if he drew it - but he has the good sense to seek more interesting material. I'm infuriated Mags got to do a book with Eryk before I did - and let me tell you, it wasn't for lack of trying.

So, let's recap. You're lucky enough to be holding early work by two names who will be defining the comics medium for the next generation. Inside these pages, you will find a story about the possibilities of young love. You'll find an honest and loving portrayal of transition. You'll find a world not that different from our own, except for all the shuttered mad science laboratories and dumpster-diving salvage techs.

And most of all, you'll find a story that - like tachyons and teenagers - moves at speeds both blindingly fast and deceptively slow. QTAG speaks its own language and doesn't wait for you to catch up, so with every page you become more like the mad science punk rockers at its center. In the first issue alone, you'll time travel, argue with your parents, get rejected by mad scientists, get recruited by madder scientists, fight scary temporal agents, fall in love, get bullied, get one over on the bully, raid a robot lab, and look good doing it in fishnets.

Quantum Teens Are Go is fucking crazy.

And that's what makes it fucking brilliant.

Jackson Lanzing
Los Angeles, 2017

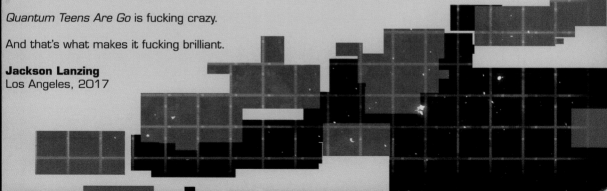

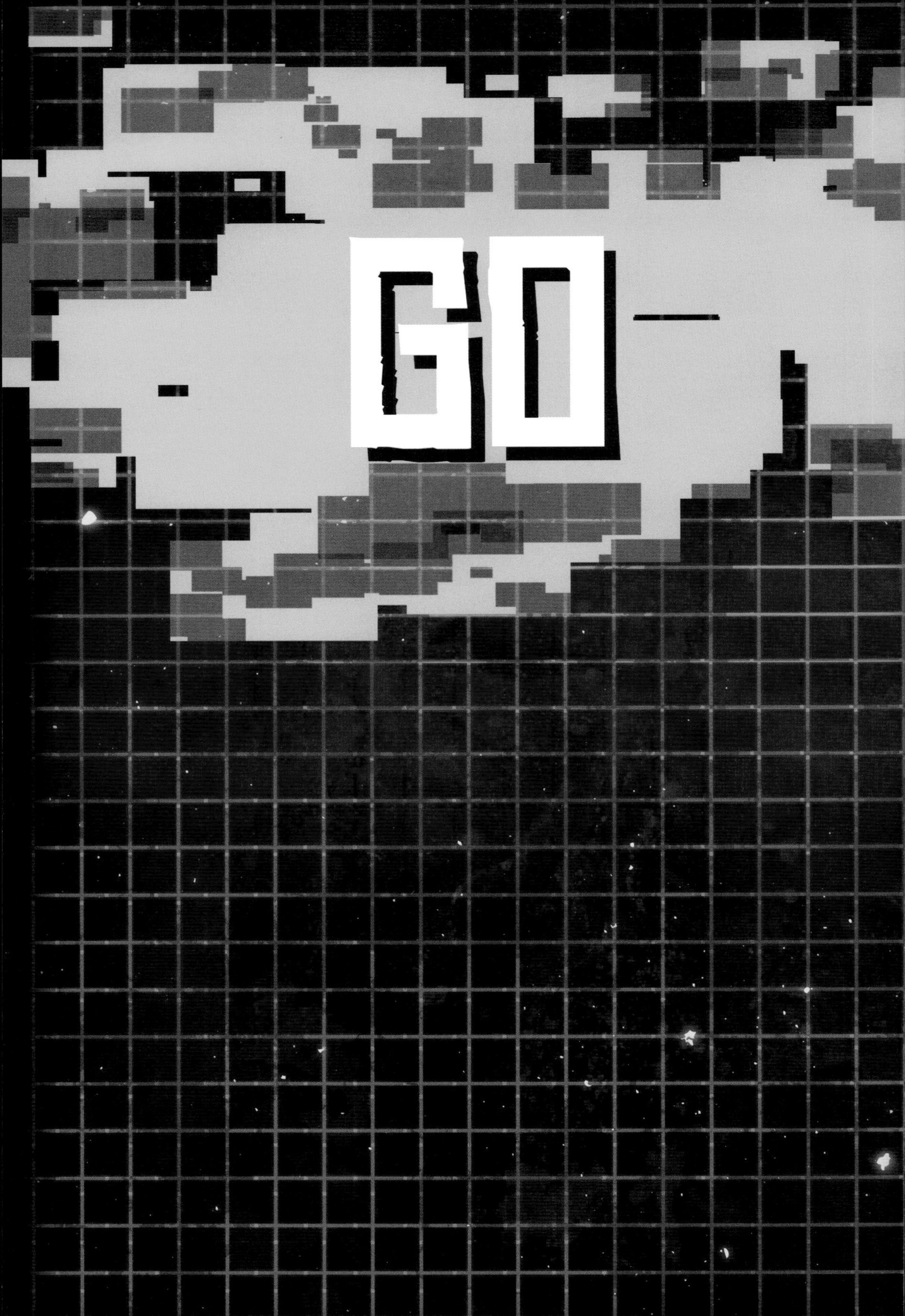
GO—

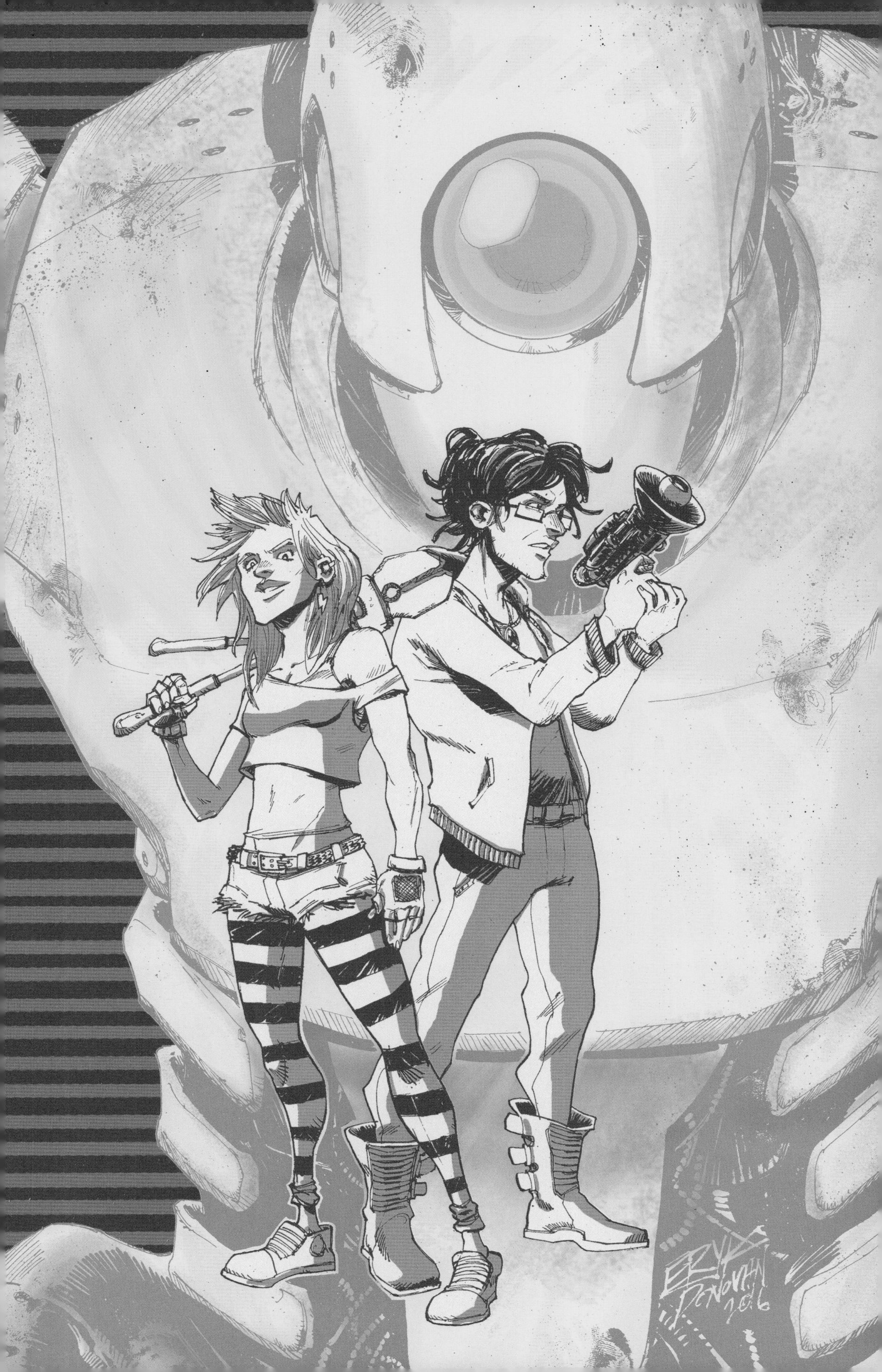

01 ALTERNATES

QUANTUM
TEENS
ARE
GO

Issue #1 cover B
art by: **RYAN FERRIER**

QUANTUM
TEENS
ARE
GO
FRIED PIE
VARIANT
VISAGGIO
DONOVAN
AGUIRRE
SAAM
GORBA
01

Issue #1 cover C & D
art by: **BEN TEMPLESMITH**

01
QUANTUM
TEENS
ARE
GO

Issue #1 cover E & F
art by: **ALEXIS ZIRITT**

QUANTUM
TEENS
ARE
GO
01
VISAGGIO
DONOVAN
AGUIRRE
SAAM
GORBA

Issue #1 cover G
art by: **SKYLAR PATRIDGE**

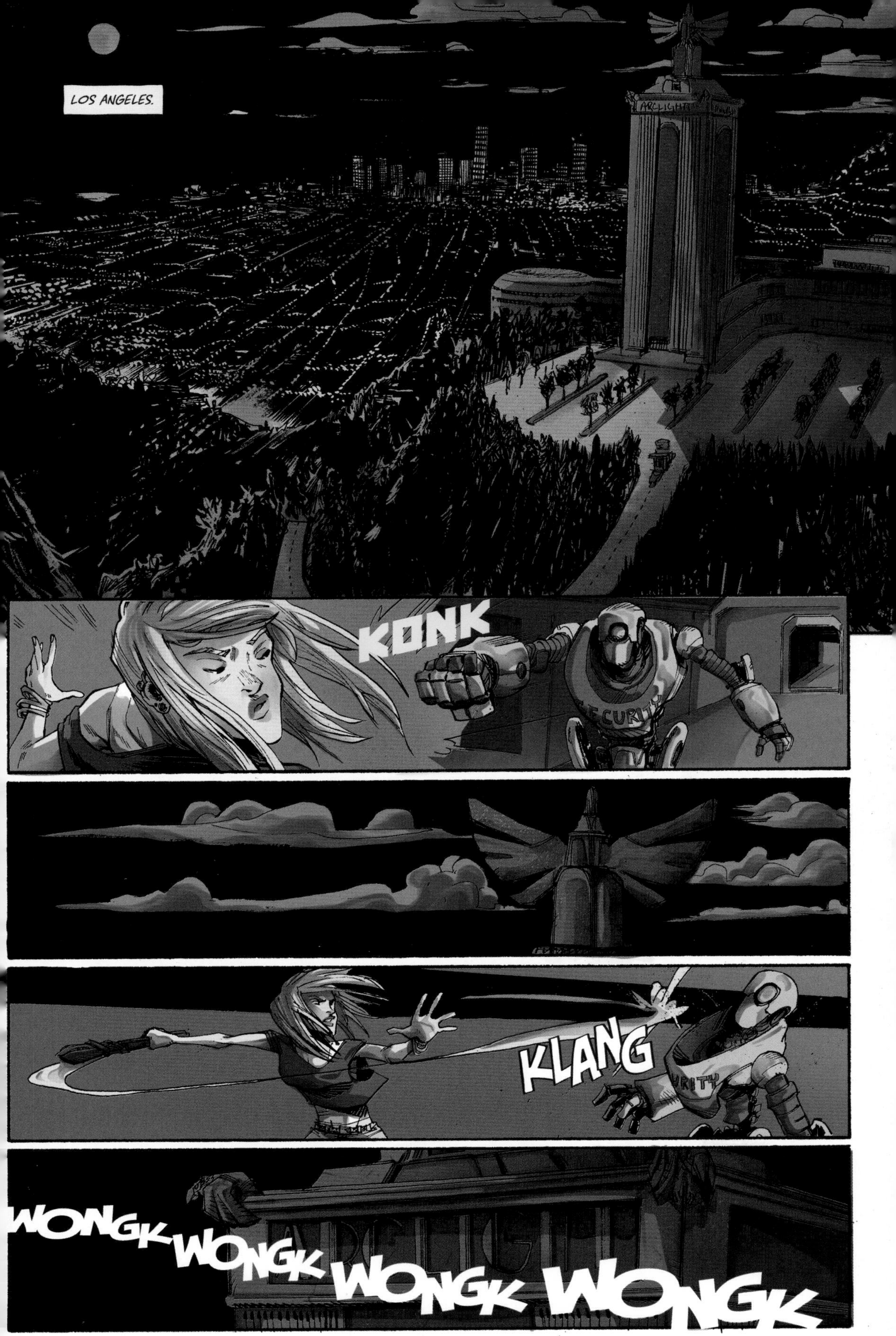

LOS ANGELES.
ARCLIGHT
KONK
SECURITY
KLANG
WONGK WONGK WONGK WONGK

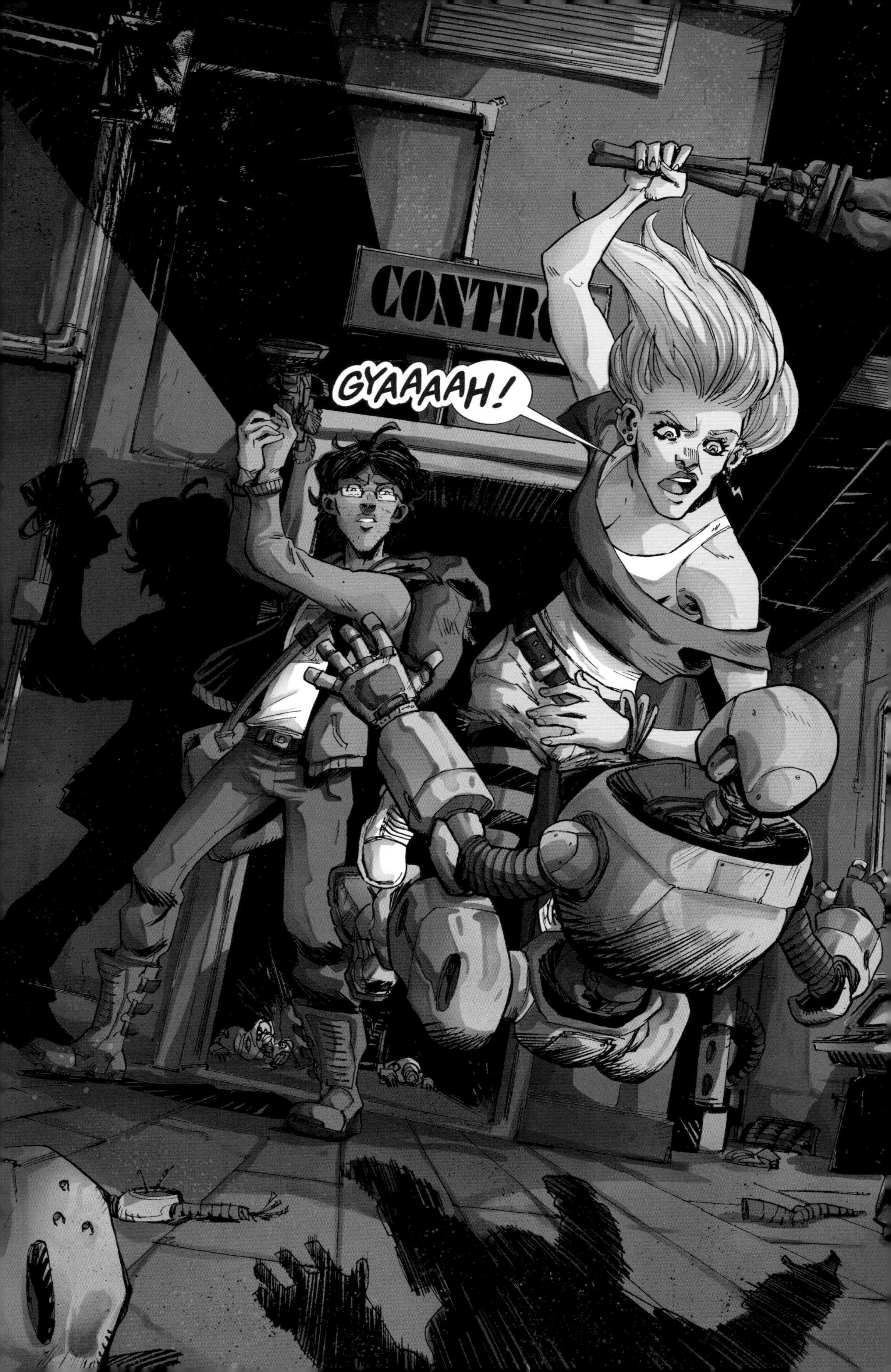
CONTR
GYAAAAH!

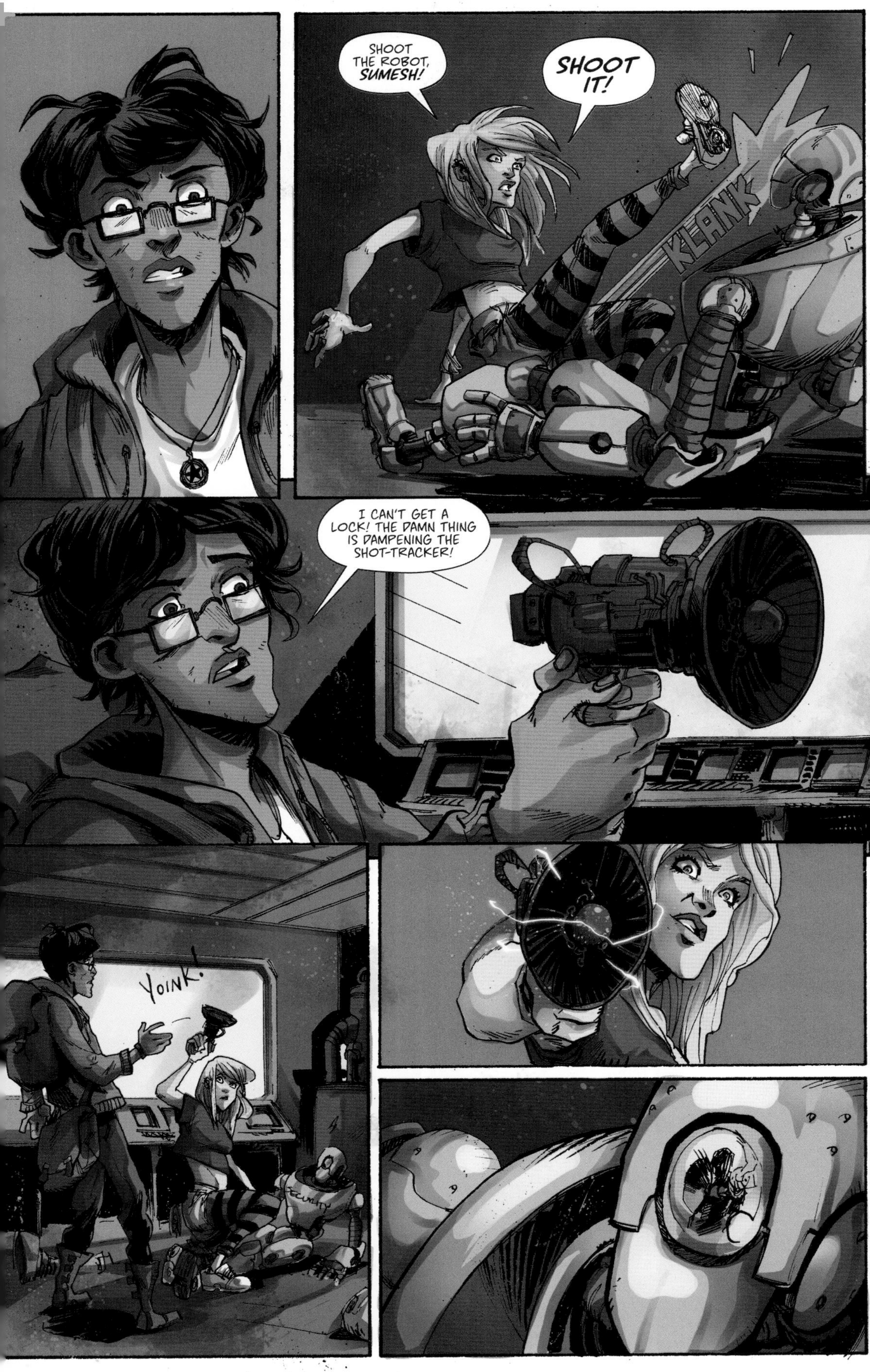
SHOOT THE ROBOT, SUMESH!
SHOOT IT!
KLANK
I CAN'T GET A LOCK! THE DAMN THING IS DAMPENING THE SHOT-TRACKER!
YOINK!
SECURITY

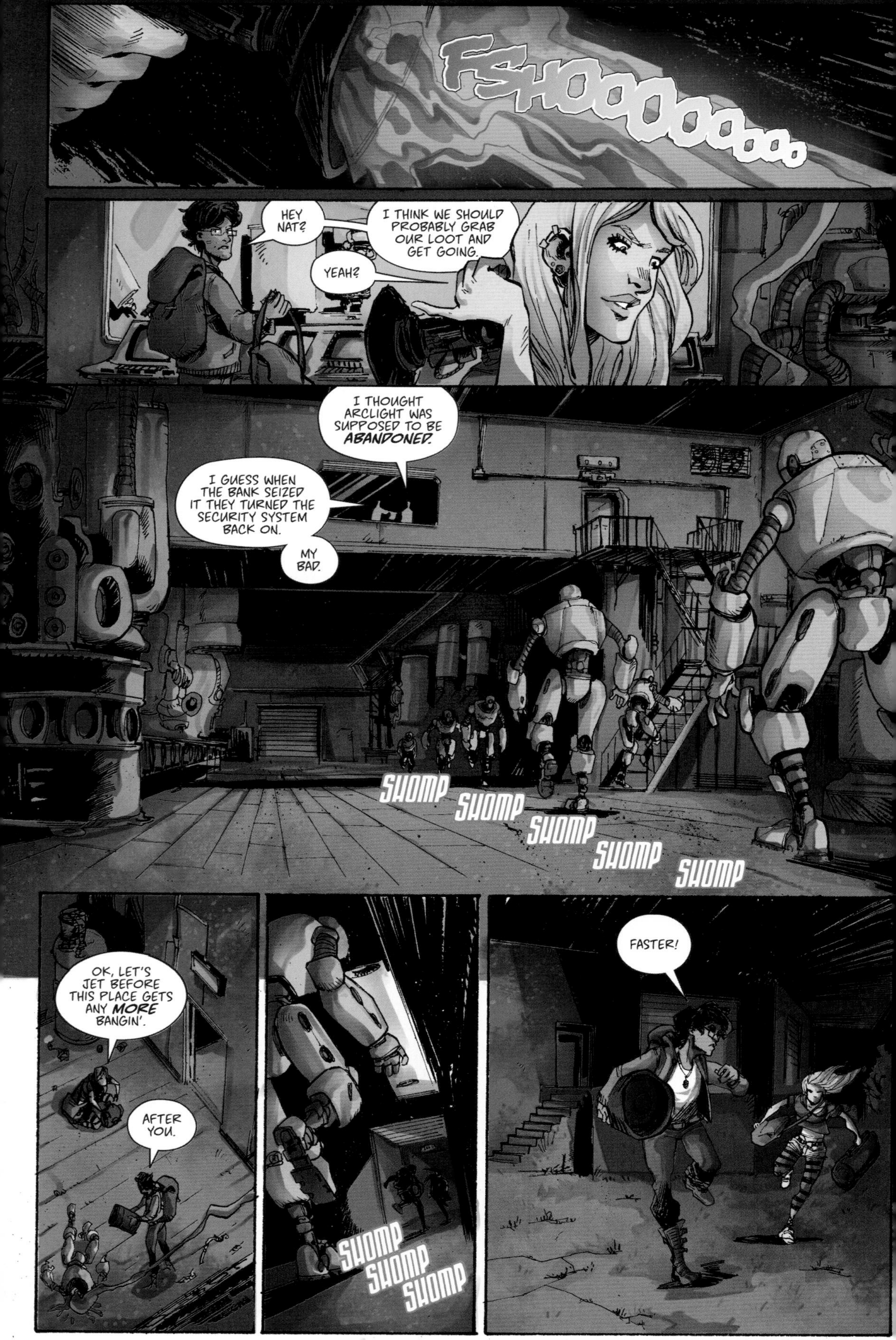
FSHOOOOOOooo
HEY NAT?
I THINK WE SHOULD PROBABLY GRAB OUR LOOT AND GET GOING.
YEAH?
I THOUGHT ARCLIGHT WAS SUPPOSED TO BE ABANDONED.
I GUESS WHEN THE BANK SEIZED IT THEY TURNED THE SECURITY SYSTEM BACK ON.
MY BAD.
SHOMP SHOMP SHOMP SHOMP SHOMP
OK, LET'S JET BEFORE THIS PLACE GETS ANY MORE BANGIN'.
AFTER YOU.
SHOMP SHOMP SHOMP
FASTER!

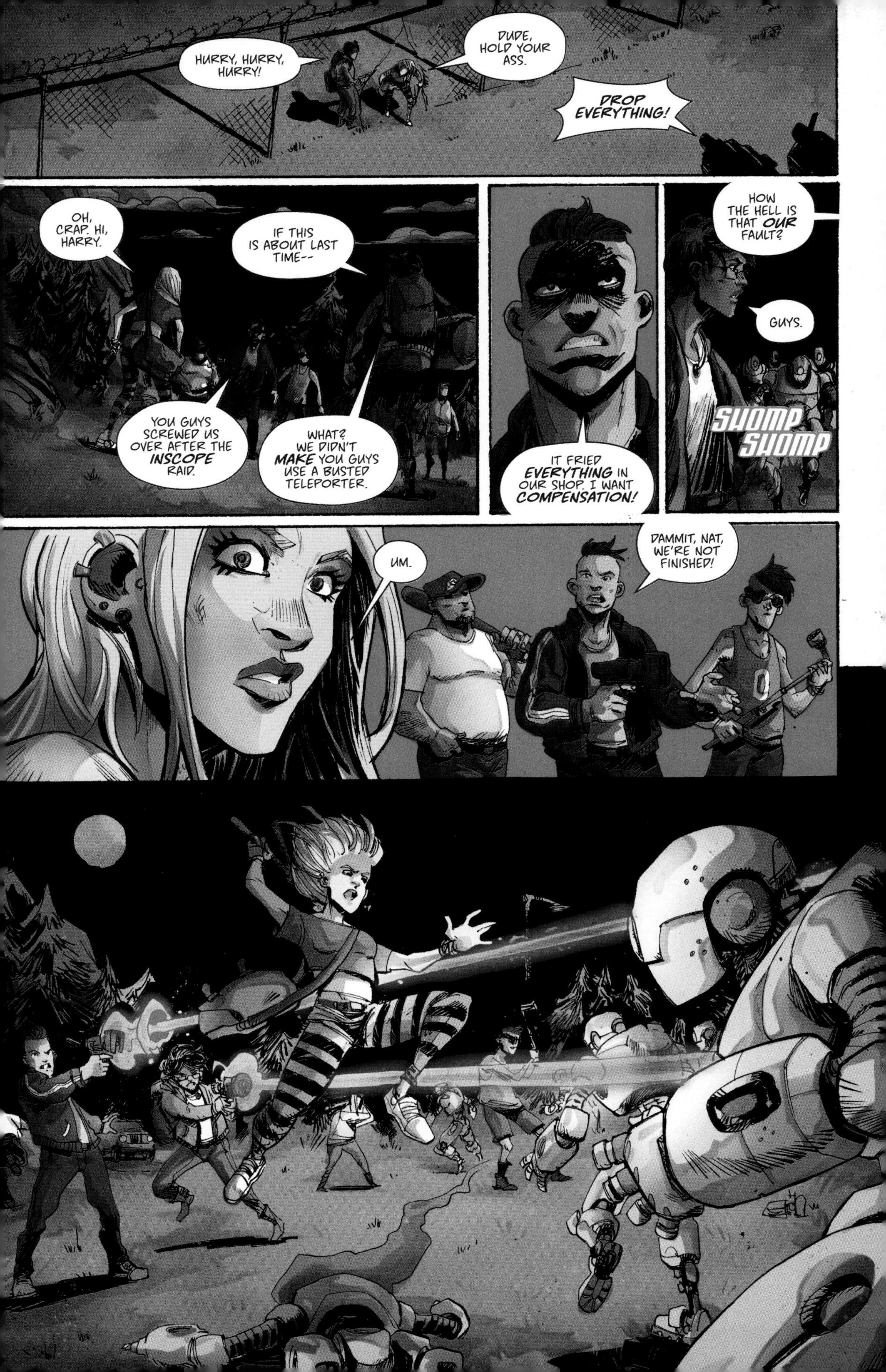
HURRY, HURRY, HURRY!
DUDE, HOLD YOUR ASS.
DROP EVERYTHING!
OH, CRAP. HI, HARRY.
IF THIS IS ABOUT LAST TIME--
YOU GUYS SCREWED US OVER AFTER THE INSCOPE RAID.
WHAT? WE DIDN'T MAKE YOU GUYS USE A BUSTED TELEPORTER.
IT FRIED EVERYTHING IN OUR SHOP. I WANT COMPENSATION!
HOW THE HELL IS THAT OUR FAULT?
GUYS.
SHOMP SHOMP
UM.
DAMMIT, NAT, WE'RE NOT FINISHED!

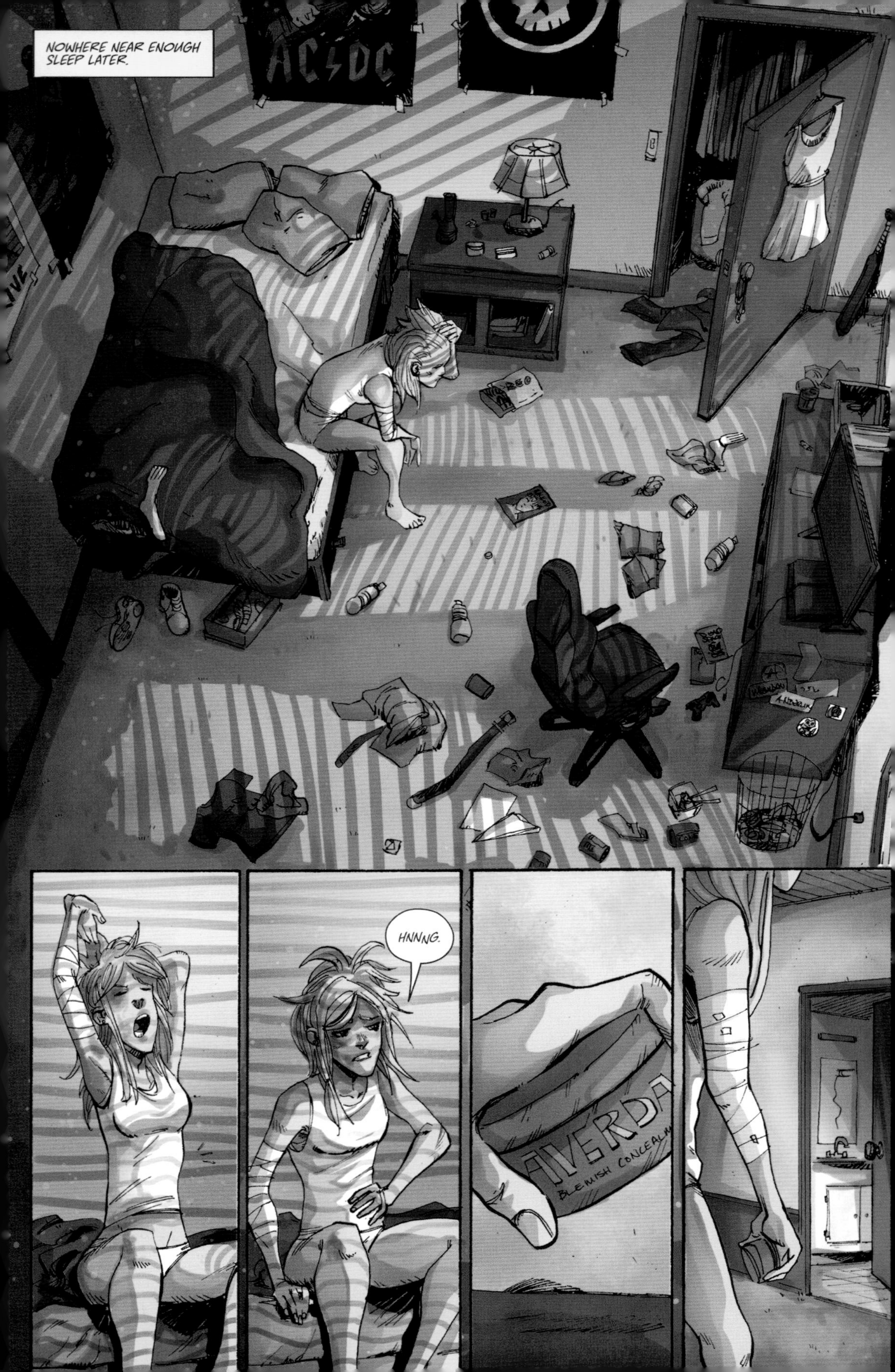

NOWHERE NEAR ENOUGH SLEEP LATER.
AC/DC
HNNNG.
AVERDA
BLEMISH CONCEAL

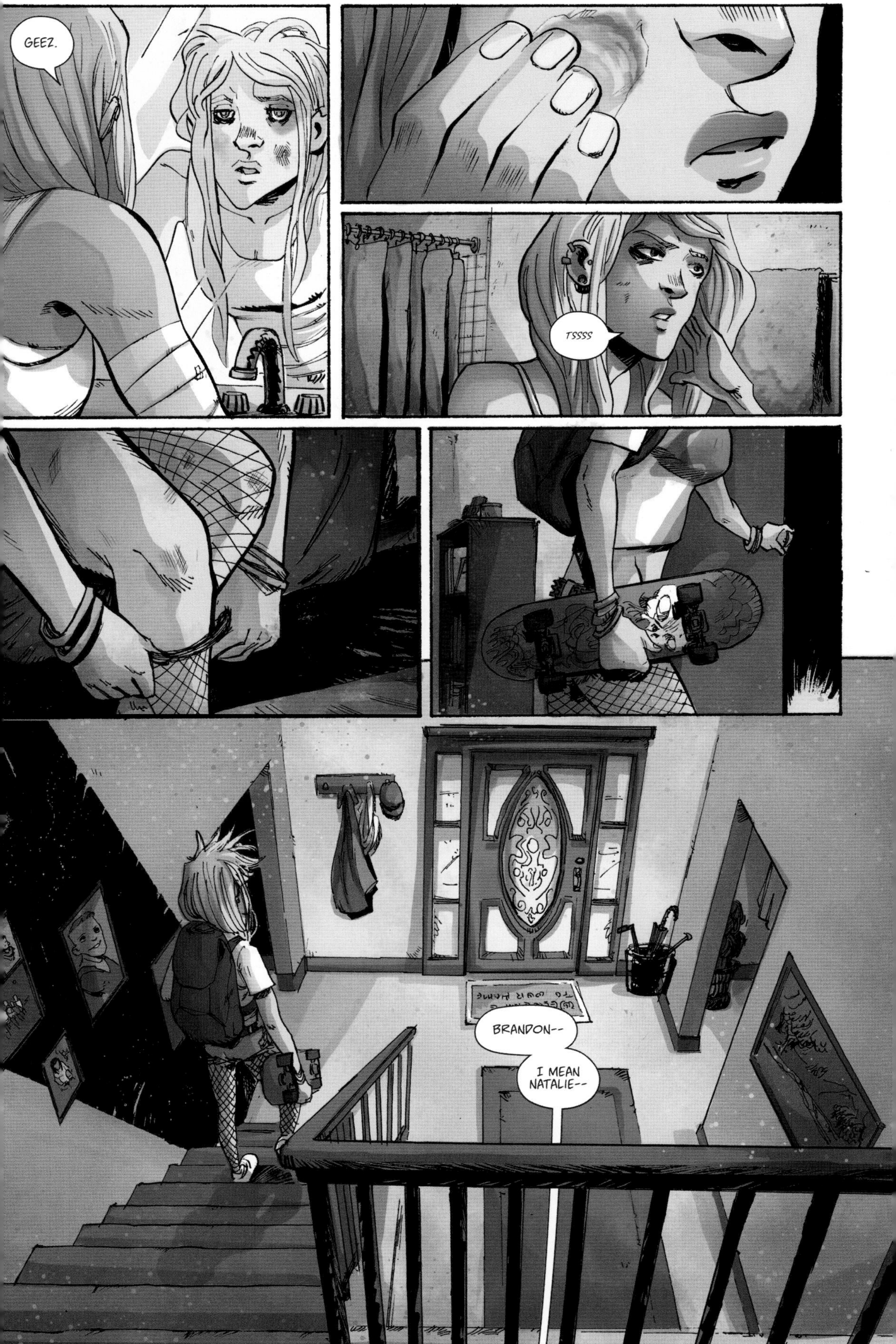
GEEZ.
TSSSS
BRANDON--
I MEAN NATALIE--

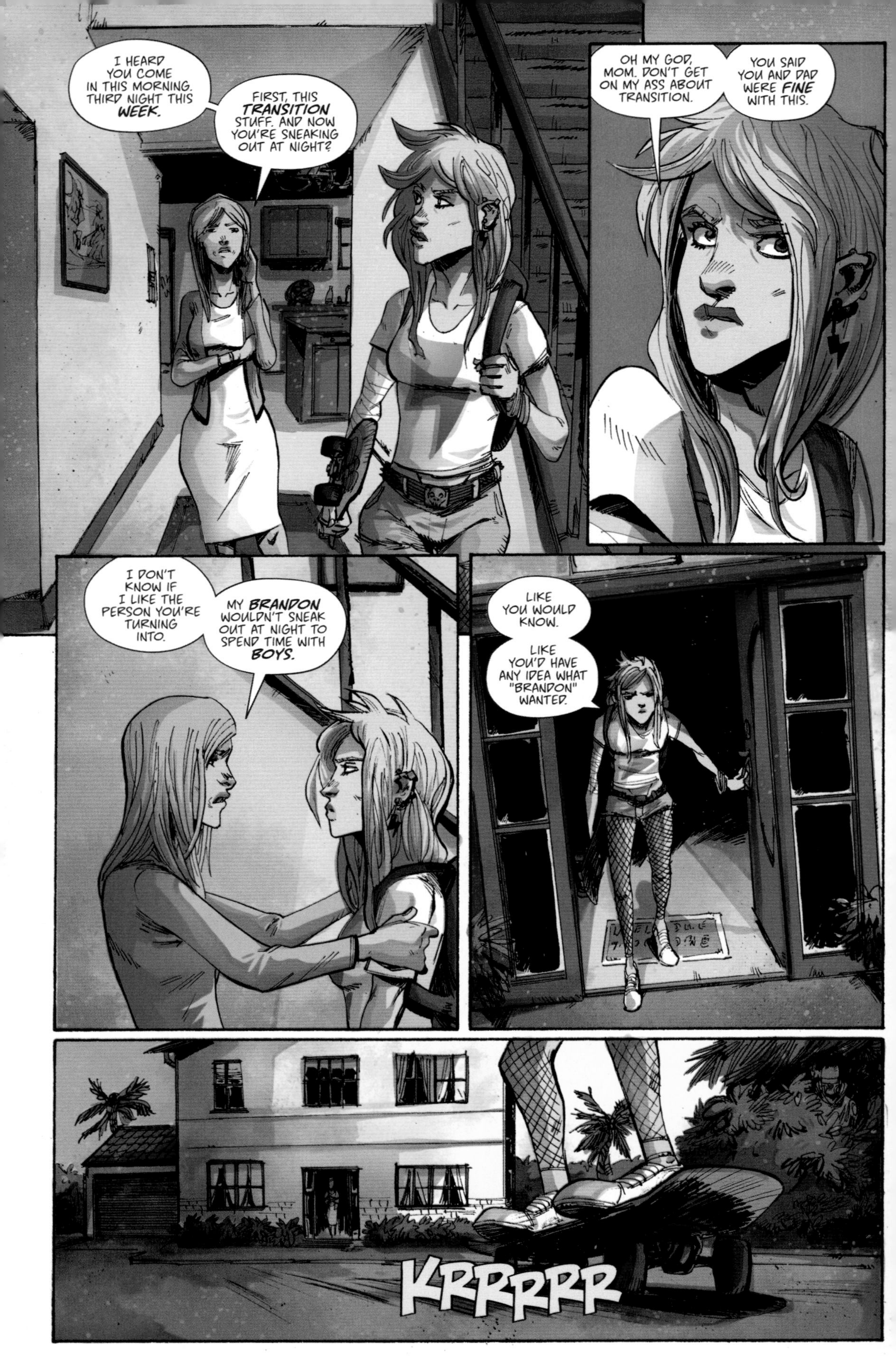
I HEARD YOU COME IN THIS MORNING. THIRD NIGHT THIS WEEK.
FIRST, THIS TRANSITION STUFF. AND NOW YOU'RE SNEAKING OUT AT NIGHT?
OH MY GOD, MOM. DON'T GET ON MY ASS ABOUT TRANSITION.
YOU SAID YOU AND DAD WERE FINE WITH THIS.
I DON'T KNOW IF I LIKE THE PERSON YOU'RE TURNING INTO.
MY BRANDON WOULDN'T SNEAK OUT AT NIGHT TO SPEND TIME WITH BOYS.
LIKE YOU WOULD KNOW.
LIKE YOU'D HAVE ANY IDEA WHAT "BRANDON" WANTED.
KRRRRR

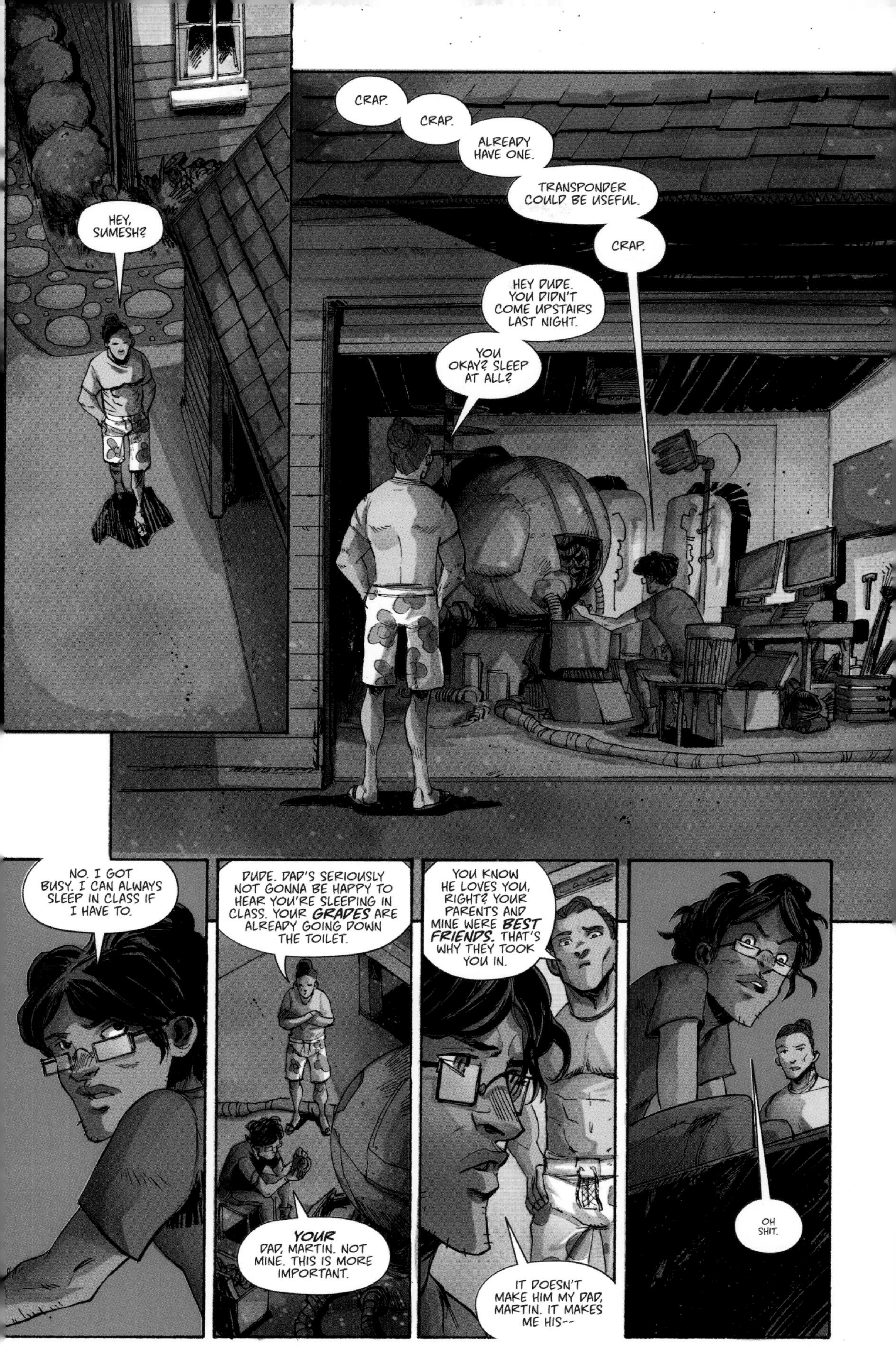
HEY, SUMESH?
CRAP.
CRAP.
ALREADY HAVE ONE.
TRANSPONDER COULD BE USEFUL.
CRAP.
HEY DUDE. YOU DIDN'T COME UPSTAIRS LAST NIGHT.
YOU OKAY? SLEEP AT ALL?
NO. I GOT BUSY. I CAN ALWAYS SLEEP IN CLASS IF I HAVE TO.
DUDE. DAD'S SERIOUSLY NOT GONNA BE HAPPY TO HEAR YOU'RE SLEEPING IN CLASS. YOUR GRADES ARE ALREADY GOING DOWN THE TOILET.
YOUR DAD, MARTIN. NOT MINE. THIS IS MORE IMPORTANT.
YOU KNOW HE LOVES YOU, RIGHT? YOUR PARENTS AND MINE WERE BEST FRIENDS. THAT'S WHY THEY TOOK YOU IN.
IT DOESN'T MAKE HIM MY DAD, MARTIN. IT MAKES ME HIS--
OH SHIT.

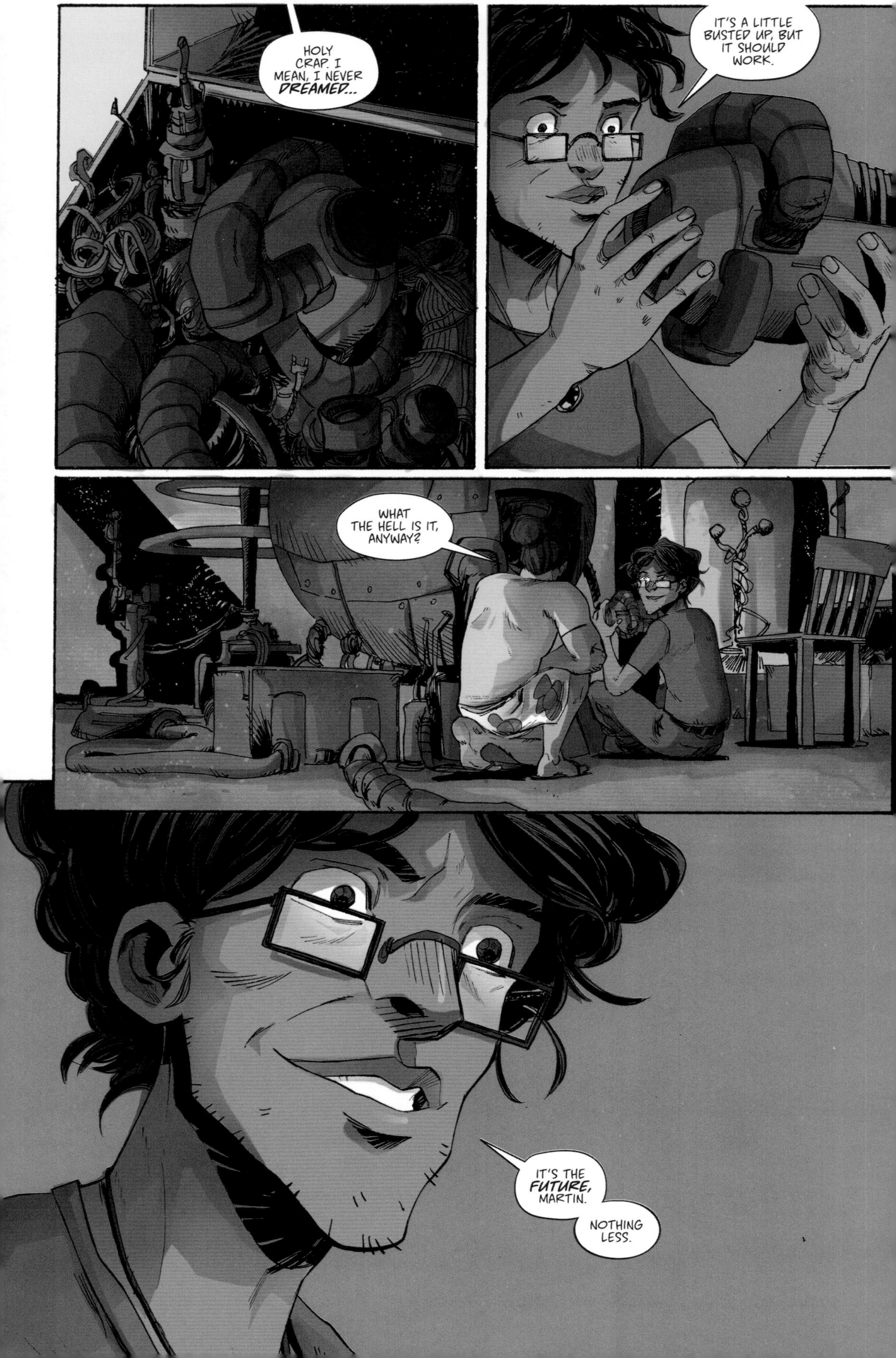
HOLY CRAP. I MEAN, I NEVER DREAMED...
IT'S A LITTLE BUSTED UP, BUT IT SHOULD WORK.
WHAT THE HELL IS IT, ANYWAY?
IT'S THE FUTURE, MARTIN.
NOTHING LESS.

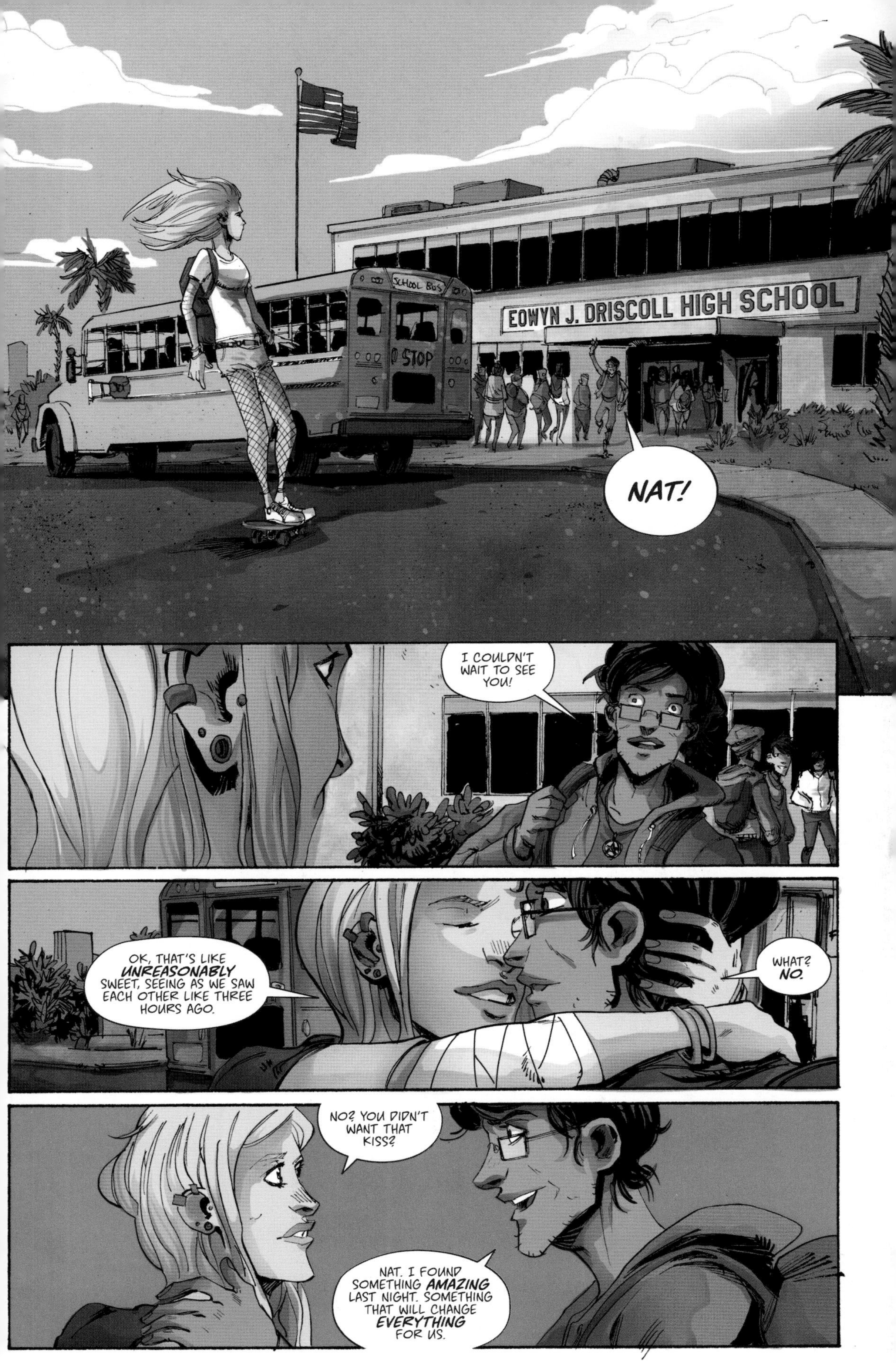

EOWYN J. DRISCOLL HIGH SCHOOL
SCHOOL BUS
STOP
NAT!
I COULDN'T WAIT TO SEE YOU!
OK, THAT'S LIKE ***UNREASONABLY*** SWEET, SEEING AS WE SAW EACH OTHER LIKE THREE HOURS AGO.
WHAT? ***NO.***
NO? YOU DIDN'T WANT THAT KISS?
NAT. I FOUND SOMETHING ***AMAZING*** LAST NIGHT. SOMETHING THAT WILL CHANGE ***EVERYTHING*** FOR US.

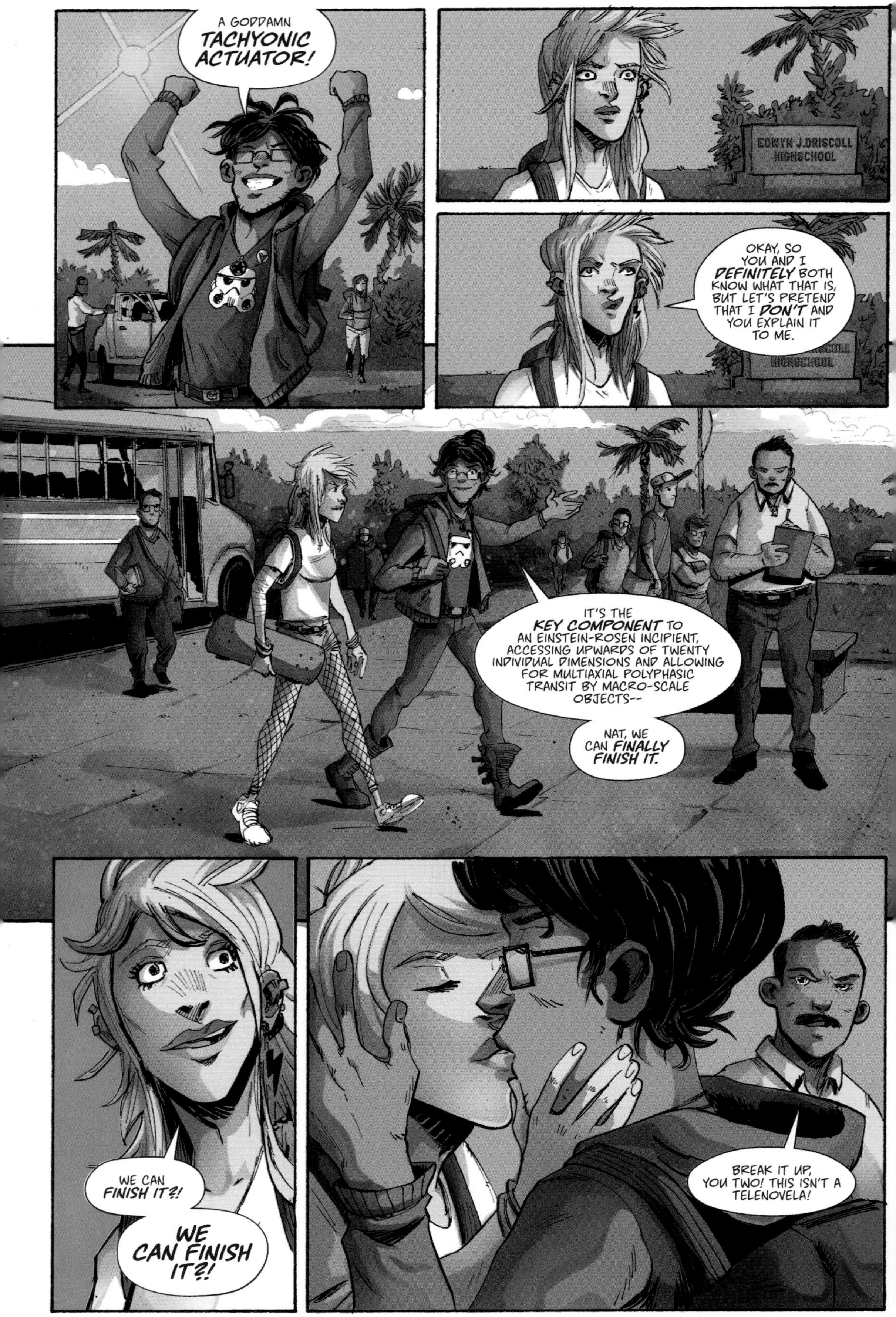
A GODDAMN TACHYONIC ACTUATOR!
EOWYN J.DRISCOLL HIGHSCHOOL
OKAY, SO YOU AND I DEFINITELY BOTH KNOW WHAT THAT IS, BUT LET'S PRETEND THAT I DON'T AND YOU EXPLAIN IT TO ME.
IT'S THE KEY COMPONENT TO AN EINSTEIN-ROSEN INCIPIENT, ACCESSING UPWARDS OF TWENTY INDIVIDUAL DIMENSIONS AND ALLOWING FOR MULTIAXIAL POLYPHASIC TRANSIT BY MACRO-SCALE OBJECTS--
NAT, WE CAN FINALLY FINISH IT.
WE CAN FINISH IT?!
WE CAN FINISH IT?!
BREAK IT UP, YOU TWO! THIS ISN'T A TELENOVELA!

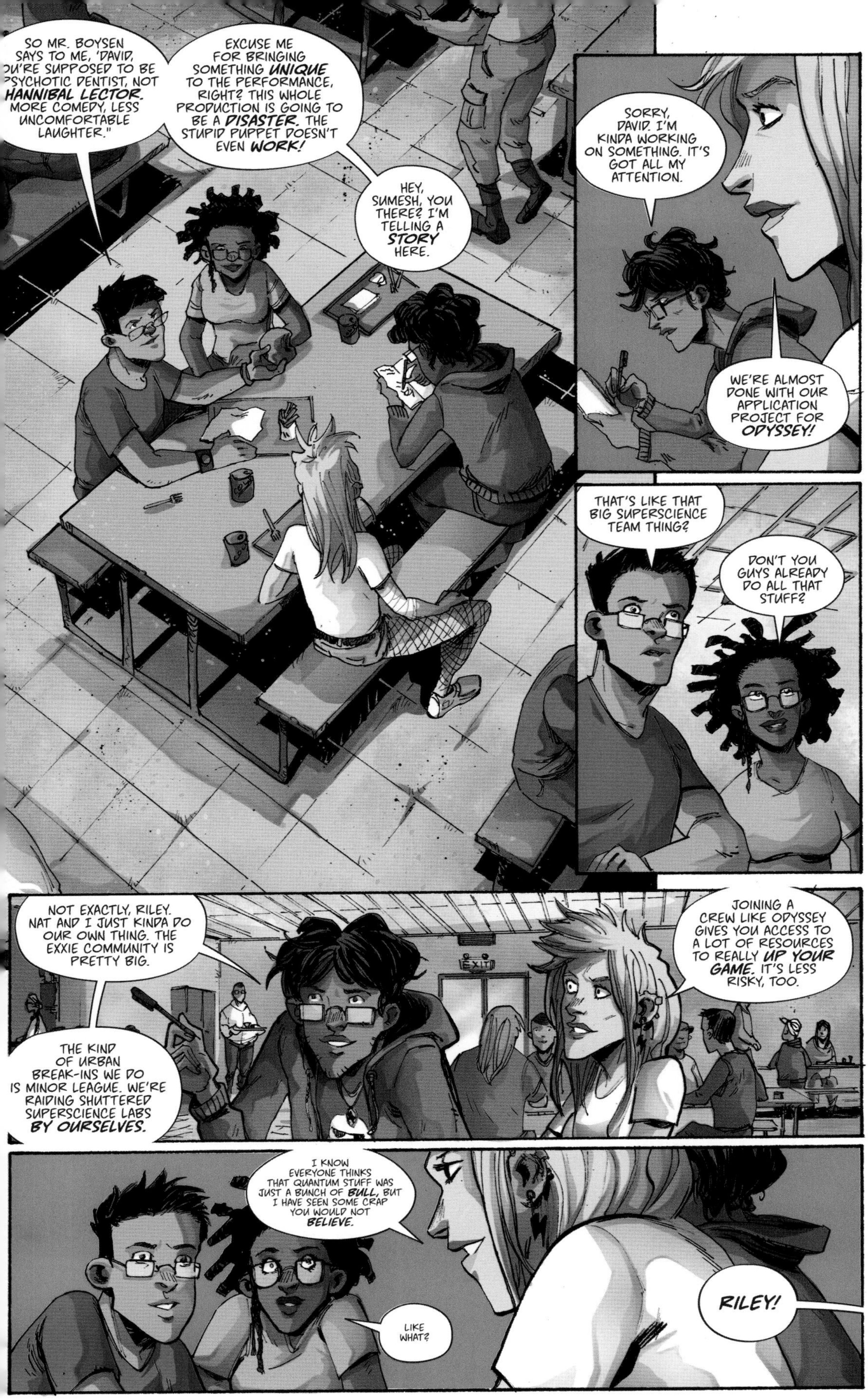
SO MR. BOYSEN SAYS TO ME, 'DAVID, YOU'RE SUPPOSED TO BE PSYCHOTIC DENTIST, NOT HANNIBAL LECTOR. MORE COMEDY, LESS UNCOMFORTABLE LAUGHTER."
EXCUSE ME FOR BRINGING SOMETHING UNIQUE TO THE PERFORMANCE, RIGHT? THIS WHOLE PRODUCTION IS GOING TO BE A DISASTER. THE STUPID PUPPET DOESN'T EVEN WORK!
HEY, SUMESH, YOU THERE? I'M TELLING A STORY HERE.
SORRY, DAVID. I'M KINDA WORKING ON SOMETHING. IT'S GOT ALL MY ATTENTION.
WE'RE ALMOST DONE WITH OUR APPLICATION PROJECT FOR ODYSSEY!
THAT'S LIKE THAT BIG SUPERSCIENCE TEAM THING?
DON'T YOU GUYS ALREADY DO ALL THAT STUFF?
NOT EXACTLY, RILEY. NAT AND I JUST KINDA DO OUR OWN THING. THE EXXIE COMMUNITY IS PRETTY BIG.
THE KIND OF URBAN BREAK-INS WE DO IS MINOR LEAGUE. WE'RE RAIDING SHUTTERED SUPERSCIENCE LABS BY OURSELVES.
JOINING A CREW LIKE ODYSSEY GIVES YOU ACCESS TO A LOT OF RESOURCES TO REALLY UP YOUR GAME. IT'S LESS RISKY, TOO.
EXIT
I KNOW EVERYONE THINKS THAT QUANTUM STUFF WAS JUST A BUNCH OF BULL, BUT I HAVE SEEN SOME CRAP YOU WOULD NOT BELIEVE.
LIKE WHAT?
RILEY!

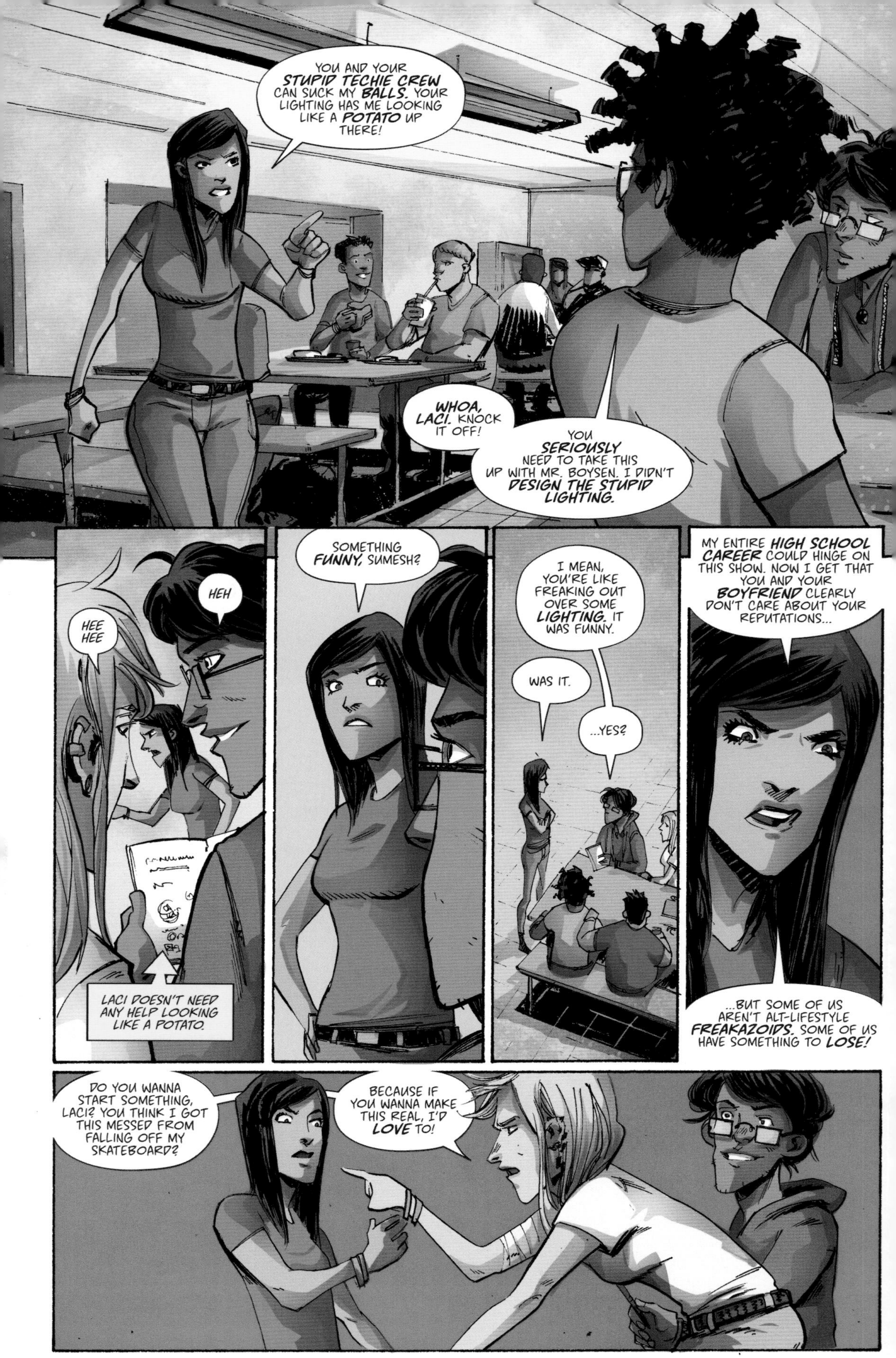

YOU AND YOUR STUPID TECHIE CREW CAN SUCK MY BALLS. YOUR LIGHTING HAS ME LOOKING LIKE A POTATO UP THERE!
WHOA, LACI. KNOCK IT OFF!
YOU SERIOUSLY NEED TO TAKE THIS UP WITH MR. BOYSEN. I DIDN'T DESIGN THE STUPID LIGHTING.
HEE HEE
HEH
LACI DOESN'T NEED ANY HELP LOOKING LIKE A POTATO.
SOMETHING FUNNY, SUMESH?
I MEAN, YOU'RE LIKE FREAKING OUT OVER SOME LIGHTING. IT WAS FUNNY.
WAS IT.
...YES?
MY ENTIRE HIGH SCHOOL CAREER COULD HINGE ON THIS SHOW. NOW I GET THAT YOU AND YOUR BOYFRIEND CLEARLY DON'T CARE ABOUT YOUR REPUTATIONS...
...BUT SOME OF US AREN'T ALT-LIFESTYLE FREAKAZOIDS. SOME OF US HAVE SOMETHING TO LOSE!
DO YOU WANNA START SOMETHING, LACI? YOU THINK I GOT THIS MESSED FROM FALLING OFF MY SKATEBOARD?
BECAUSE IF YOU WANNA MAKE THIS REAL, I'D LOVE TO!

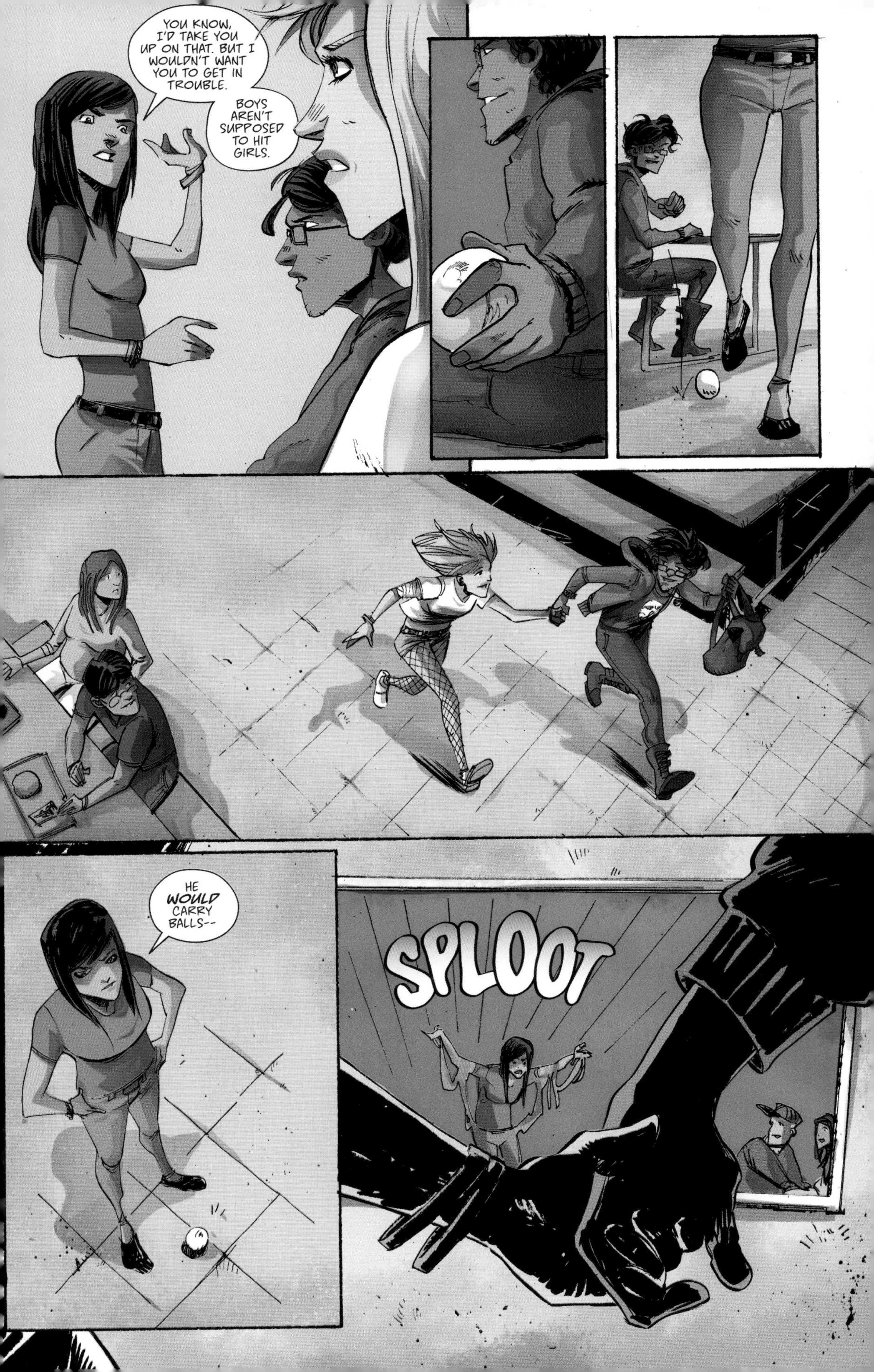
YOU KNOW, I'D TAKE YOU UP ON THAT. BUT I WOULDN'T WANT YOU TO GET IN TROUBLE.
BOYS AREN'T SUPPOSED TO HIT GIRLS.
HE **WOULD** CARRY BALLS--
SPLOOT

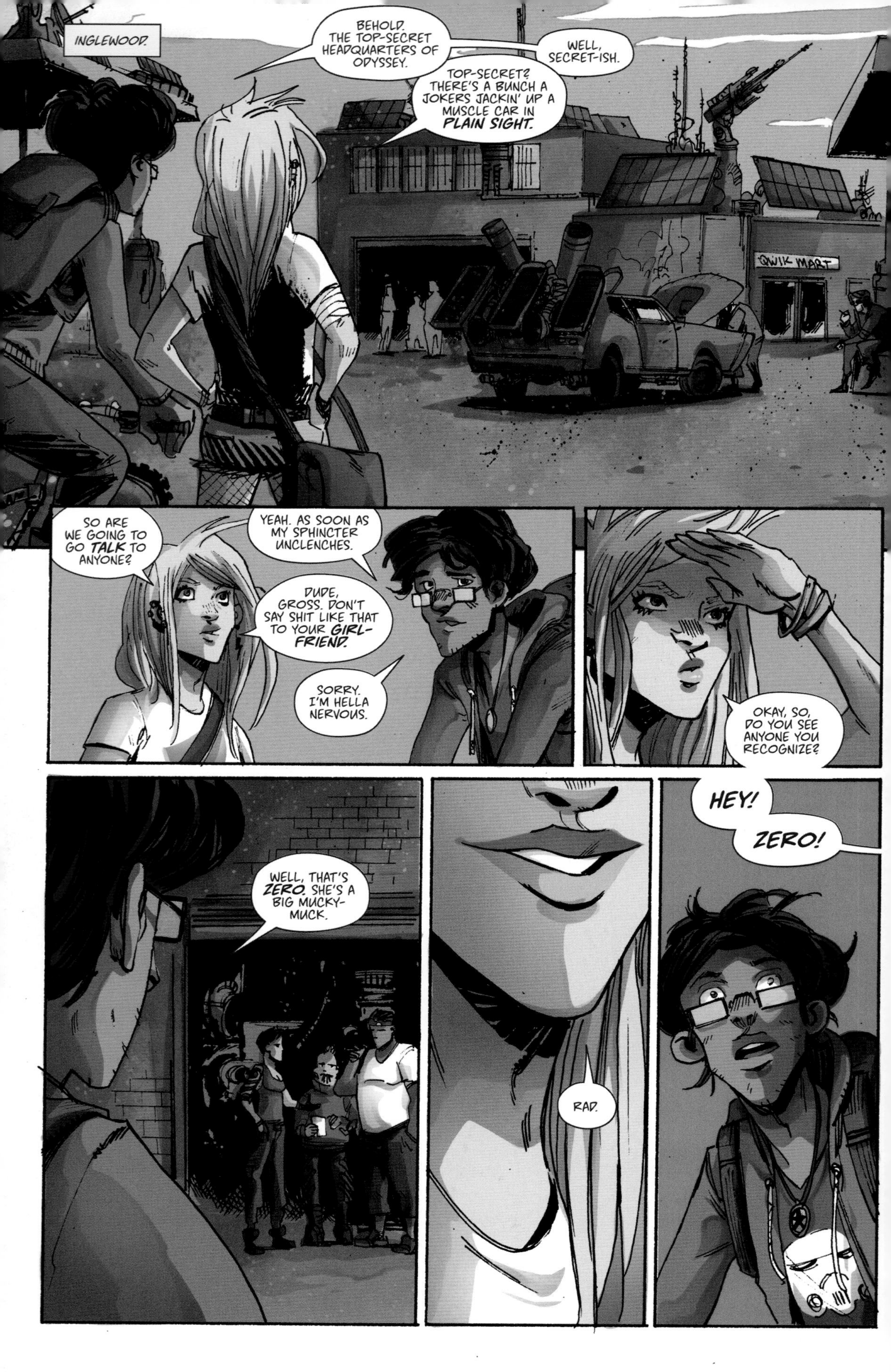
INGLEWOOD.
BEHOLD. THE TOP-SECRET HEADQUARTERS OF ODYSSEY.
WELL, SECRET-ISH.
TOP-SECRET? THERE'S A BUNCH A JOKERS JACKIN' UP A MUSCLE CAR IN PLAIN SIGHT.
QWIK MART
SO ARE WE GOING TO GO TALK TO ANYONE?
YEAH. AS SOON AS MY SPHINCTER UNCLENCHES.
DUDE, GROSS. DON'T SAY SHIT LIKE THAT TO YOUR GIRL-FRIEND.
SORRY. I'M HELLA NERVOUS.
OKAY, SO, DO YOU SEE ANYONE YOU RECOGNIZE?
WELL, THAT'S ZERO. SHE'S A BIG MUCKY-MUCK.
RAD.
HEY!
ZERO!

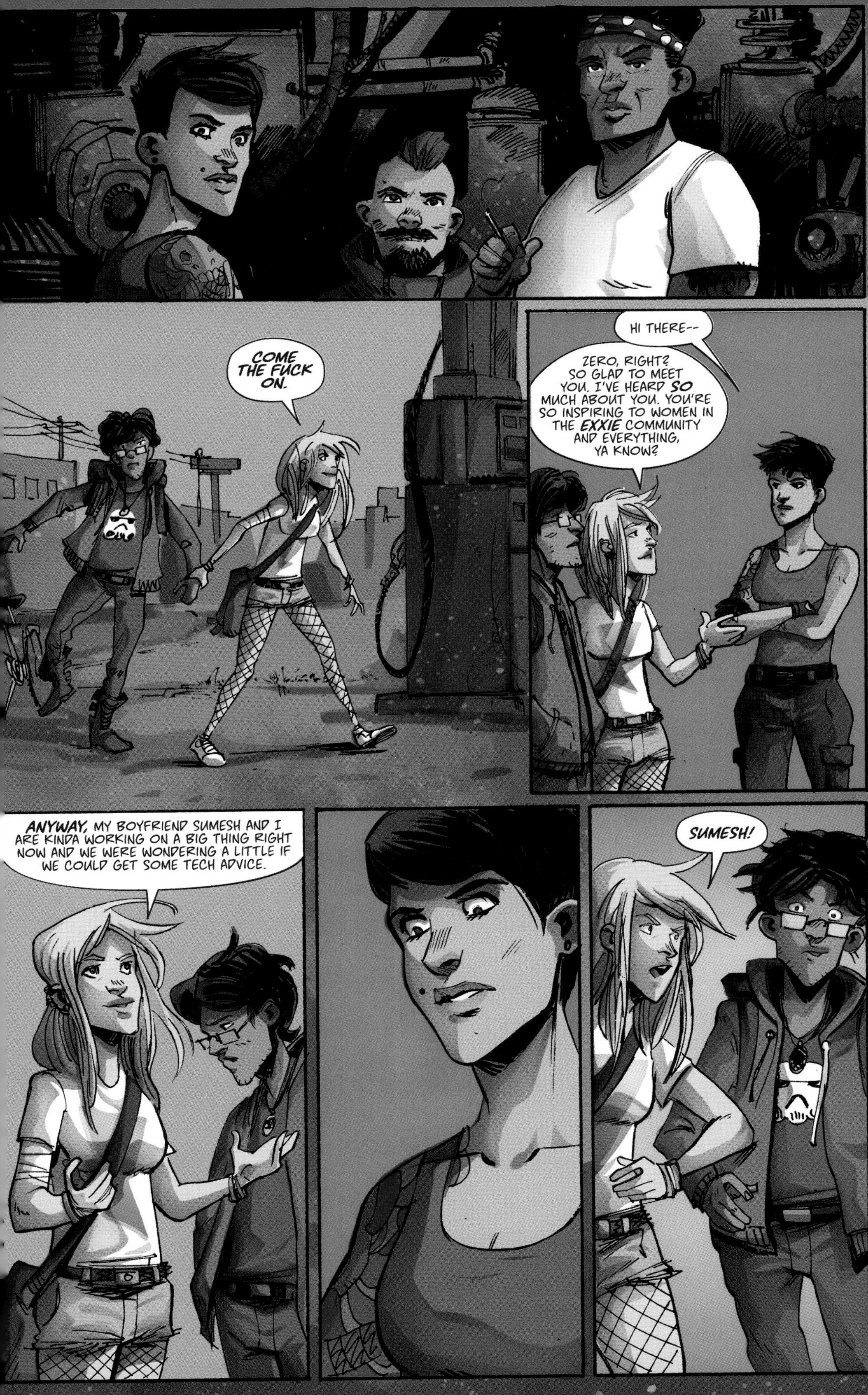
COME THE FUCK ON.
HI THERE--
ZERO, RIGHT? SO GLAD TO MEET YOU. I'VE HEARD SO MUCH ABOUT YOU. YOU'RE SO INSPIRING TO WOMEN IN THE EXXIE COMMUNITY AND EVERYTHING, YA KNOW?
ANYWAY, MY BOYFRIEND SUMESH AND I ARE KINDA WORKING ON A BIG THING RIGHT NOW AND WE WERE WONDERING A LITTLE IF WE COULD GET SOME TECH ADVICE.
SUMESH!

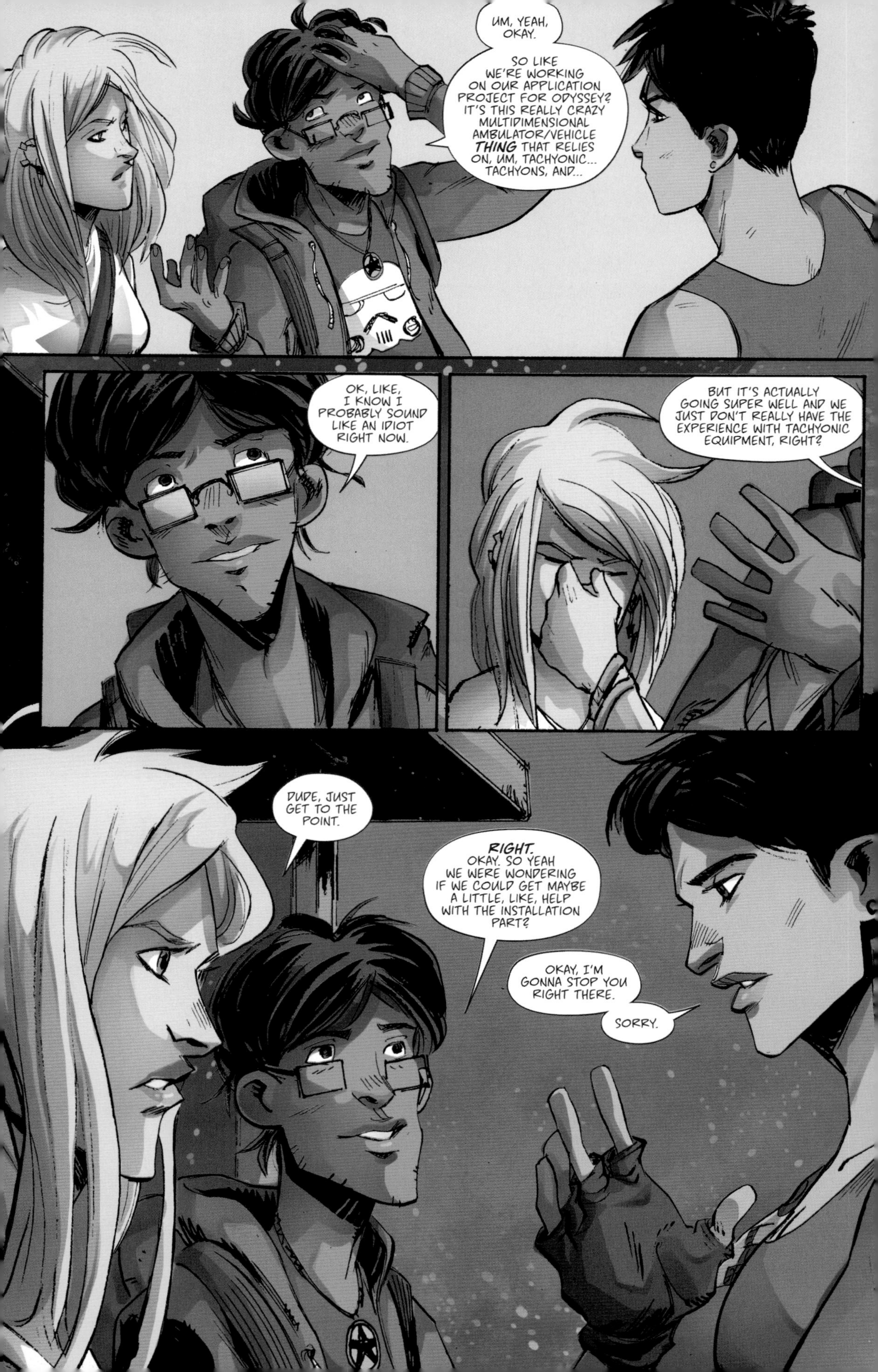
UM, YEAH, OKAY.
SO LIKE WE'RE WORKING ON OUR APPLICATION PROJECT FOR ODYSSEY? IT'S THIS REALLY CRAZY MULTIDIMENSIONAL AMBULATOR/VEHICLE *THING* THAT RELIES ON, UM, TACHYONIC... TACHYONS, AND...
OK, LIKE, I KNOW I PROBABLY SOUND LIKE AN IDIOT RIGHT NOW.
BUT IT'S ACTUALLY GOING SUPER WELL AND WE JUST DON'T REALLY HAVE THE EXPERIENCE WITH TACHYONIC EQUIPMENT, RIGHT?
DUDE, JUST GET TO THE POINT.
RIGHT. OKAY. SO YEAH WE WERE WONDERING IF WE COULD GET MAYBE A LITTLE, LIKE, HELP WITH THE INSTALLATION PART?
OKAY, I'M GONNA STOP YOU RIGHT THERE.
SORRY.

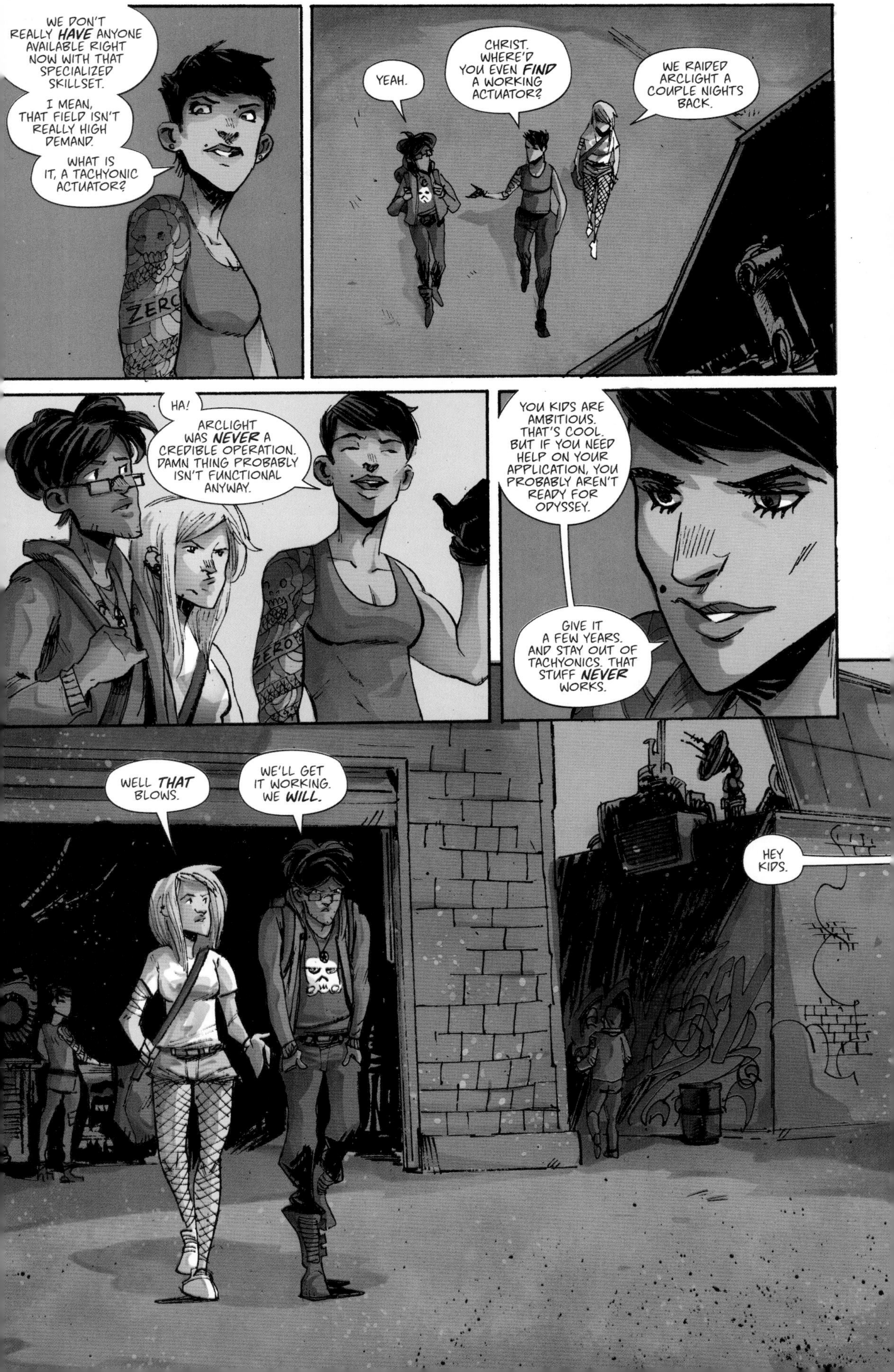
WE DON'T REALLY HAVE ANYONE AVAILABLE RIGHT NOW WITH THAT SPECIALIZED SKILLSET.
I MEAN, THAT FIELD ISN'T REALLY HIGH DEMAND.
WHAT IS IT, A TACHYONIC ACTUATOR?
YEAH.
CHRIST. WHERE'D YOU EVEN FIND A WORKING ACTUATOR?
WE RAIDED ARCLIGHT A COUPLE NIGHTS BACK.
HA!
ARCLIGHT WAS NEVER A CREDIBLE OPERATION. DAMN THING PROBABLY ISN'T FUNCTIONAL ANYWAY.
YOU KIDS ARE AMBITIOUS. THAT'S COOL. BUT IF YOU NEED HELP ON YOUR APPLICATION, YOU PROBABLY AREN'T READY FOR ODYSSEY.
GIVE IT A FEW YEARS. AND STAY OUT OF TACHYONICS. THAT STUFF NEVER WORKS.
WELL THAT BLOWS.
WE'LL GET IT WORKING. WE WILL.
HEY KIDS.

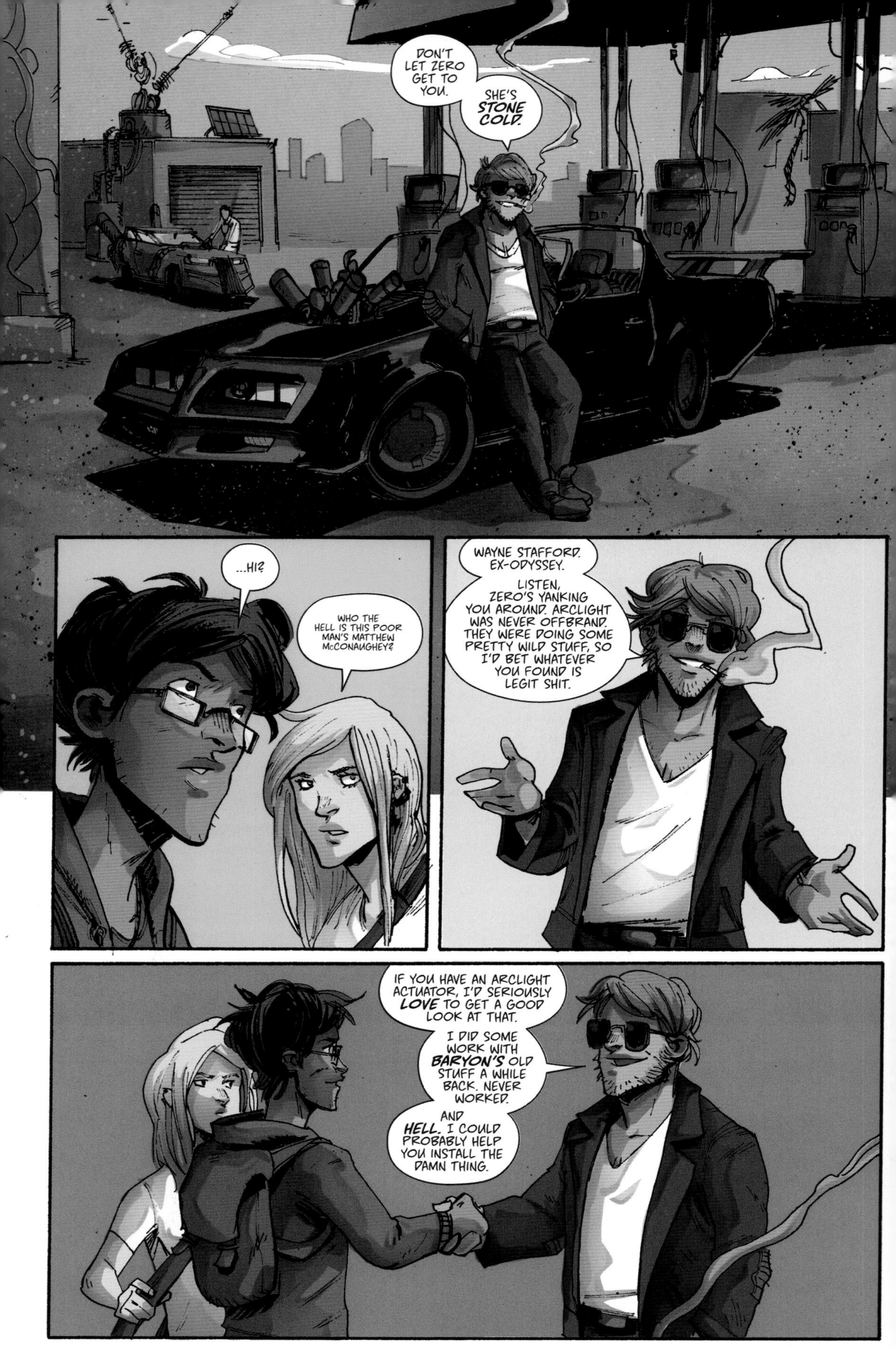
DON'T LET ZERO GET TO YOU.
SHE'S STONE COLD.
...HI?
WHO THE HELL IS THIS POOR MAN'S MATTHEW McCONAUGHEY?
WAYNE STAFFORD. EX-ODYSSEY.
LISTEN, ZERO'S YANKING YOU AROUND. ARCLIGHT WAS NEVER OFFBRAND. THEY WERE DOING SOME PRETTY WILD STUFF, SO I'D BET WHATEVER YOU FOUND IS LEGIT SHIT.
IF YOU HAVE AN ARCLIGHT ACTUATOR, I'D SERIOUSLY LOVE TO GET A GOOD LOOK AT THAT.
I DID SOME WORK WITH BARYON'S OLD STUFF A WHILE BACK. NEVER WORKED.
AND HELL. I COULD PROBABLY HELP YOU INSTALL THE DAMN THING.

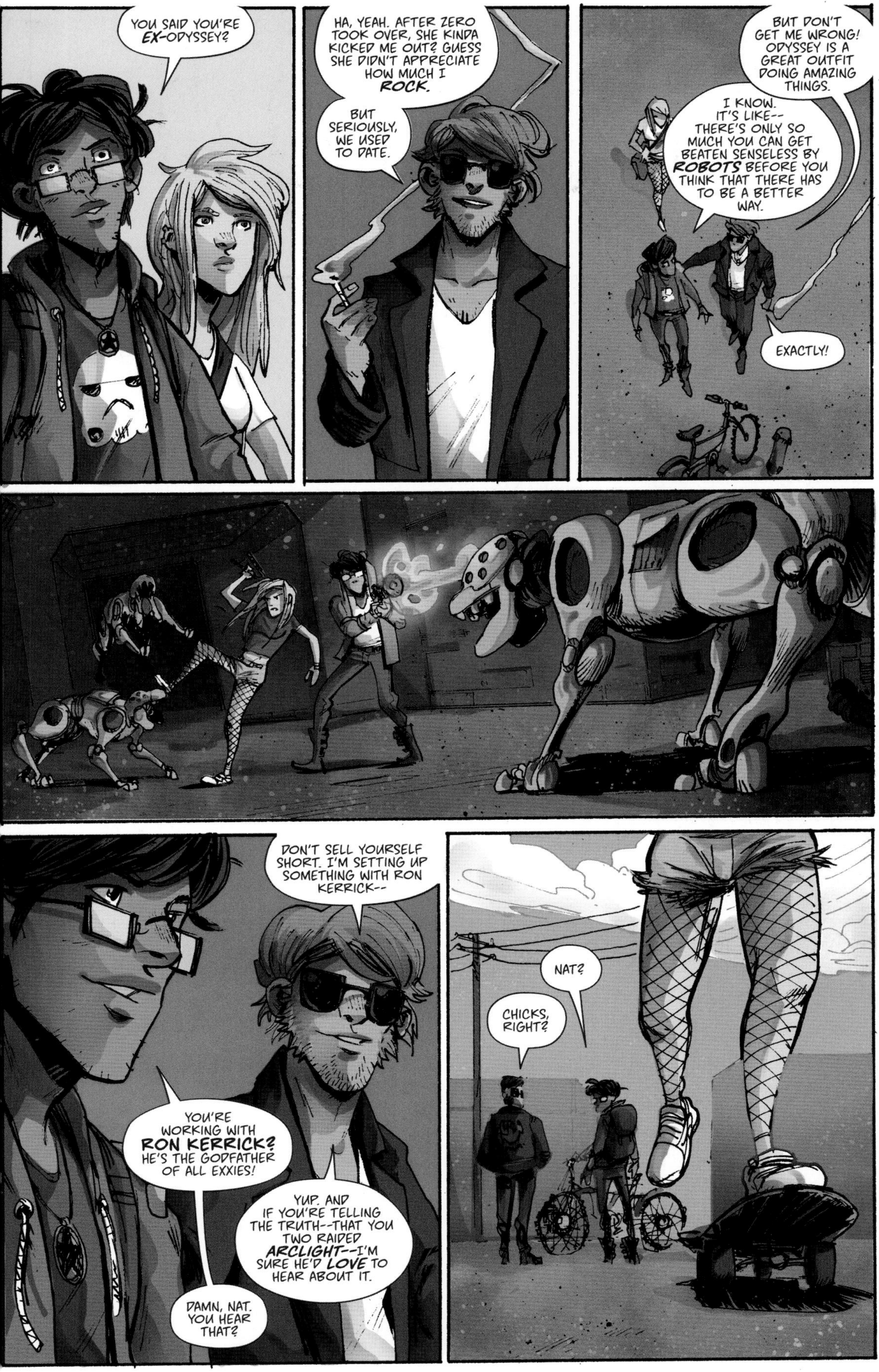
YOU SAID YOU'RE EX-ODYSSEY?
HA, YEAH. AFTER ZERO TOOK OVER, SHE KINDA KICKED ME OUT? GUESS SHE DIDN'T APPRECIATE HOW MUCH I ROCK.
BUT SERIOUSLY, WE USED TO DATE.
BUT DON'T GET ME WRONG! ODYSSEY IS A GREAT OUTFIT DOING AMAZING THINGS.
I KNOW. IT'S LIKE-- THERE'S ONLY SO MUCH YOU CAN GET BEATEN SENSELESS BY ROBOTS BEFORE YOU THINK THAT THERE HAS TO BE A BETTER WAY.
EXACTLY!
DON'T SELL YOURSELF SHORT. I'M SETTING UP SOMETHING WITH RON KERRICK--
YOU'RE WORKING WITH RON KERRICK? HE'S THE GODFATHER OF ALL EXXIES!
YUP. AND IF YOU'RE TELLING THE TRUTH--THAT YOU TWO RAIDED ARCLIGHT--I'M SURE HE'D LOVE TO HEAR ABOUT IT.
DAMN, NAT. YOU HEAR THAT?
NAT?
CHICKS, RIGHT?

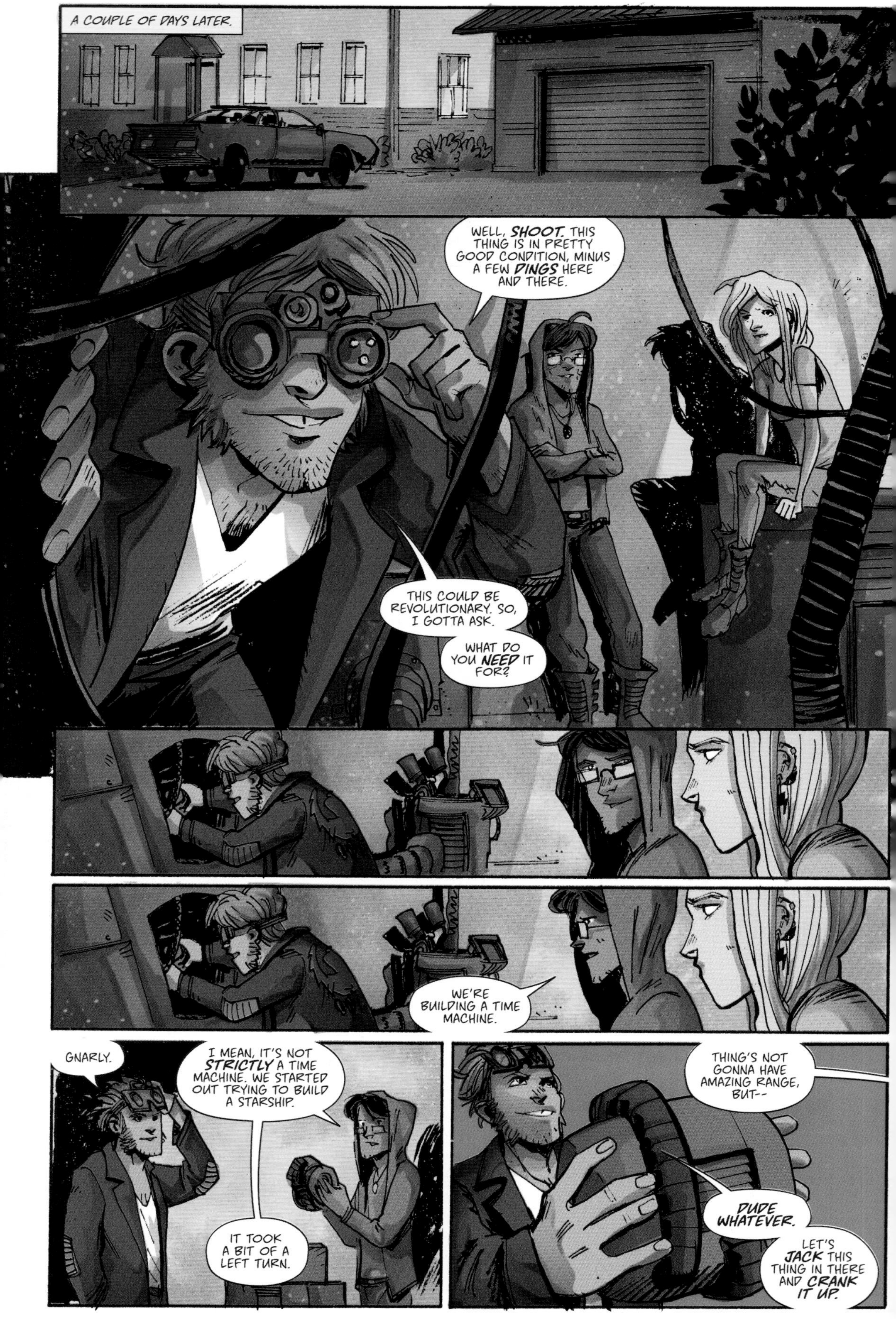
A COUPLE OF DAYS LATER.
WELL, SHOOT. THIS THING IS IN PRETTY GOOD CONDITION, MINUS A FEW DINGS HERE AND THERE.
THIS COULD BE REVOLUTIONARY. SO, I GOTTA ASK.
WHAT DO YOU NEED IT FOR?
WE'RE BUILDING A TIME MACHINE.
GNARLY.
I MEAN, IT'S NOT STRICTLY A TIME MACHINE. WE STARTED OUT TRYING TO BUILD A STARSHIP.
IT TOOK A BIT OF A LEFT TURN.
THING'S NOT GONNA HAVE AMAZING RANGE, BUT--
DUDE WHATEVER.
LET'S JACK THIS THING IN THERE AND CRANK IT UP.

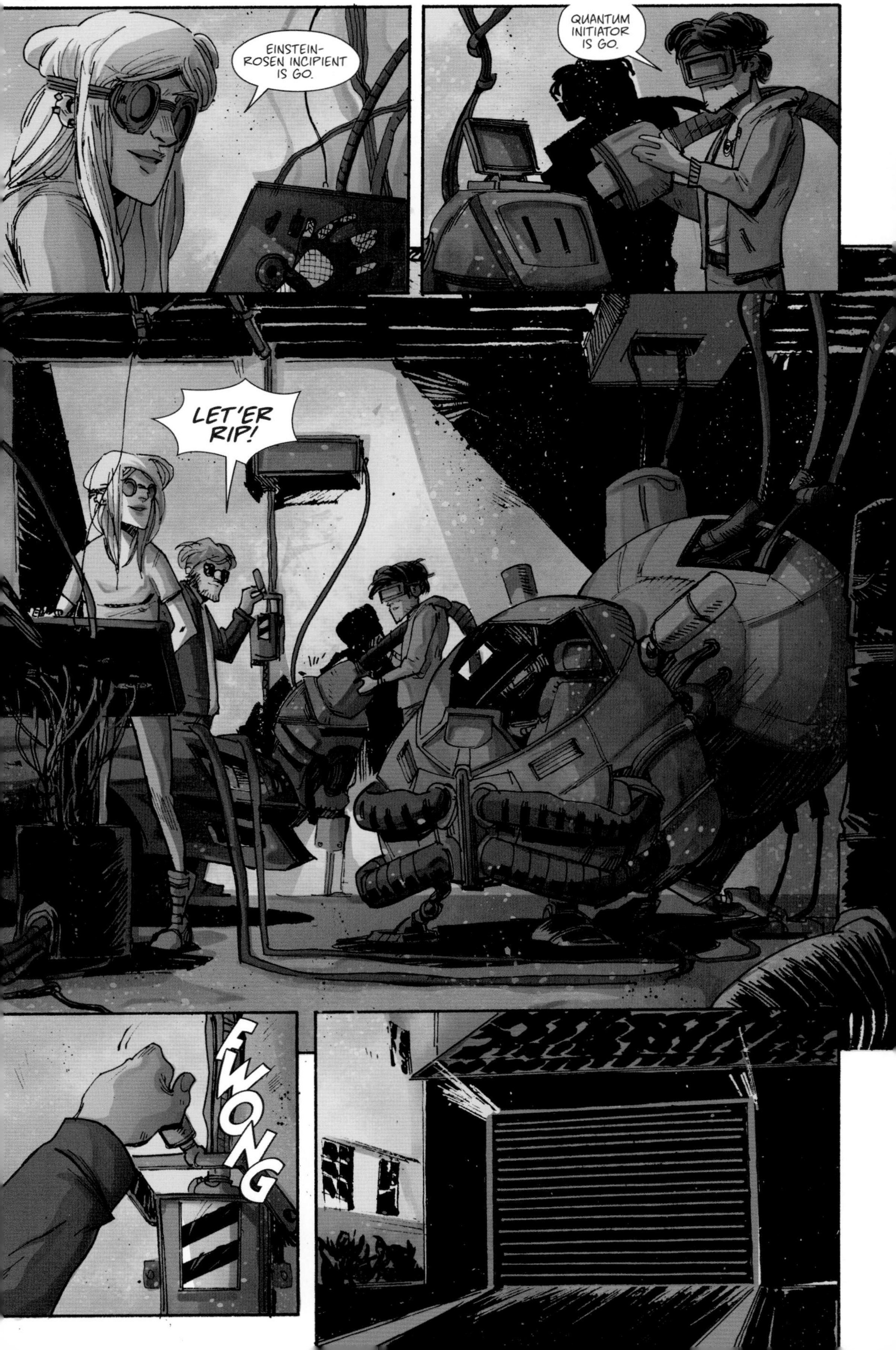
EINSTEIN-ROSEN INCIPIENT IS GO.
QUANTUM INITIATOR IS GO.
LET'ER RIP!
FWONG

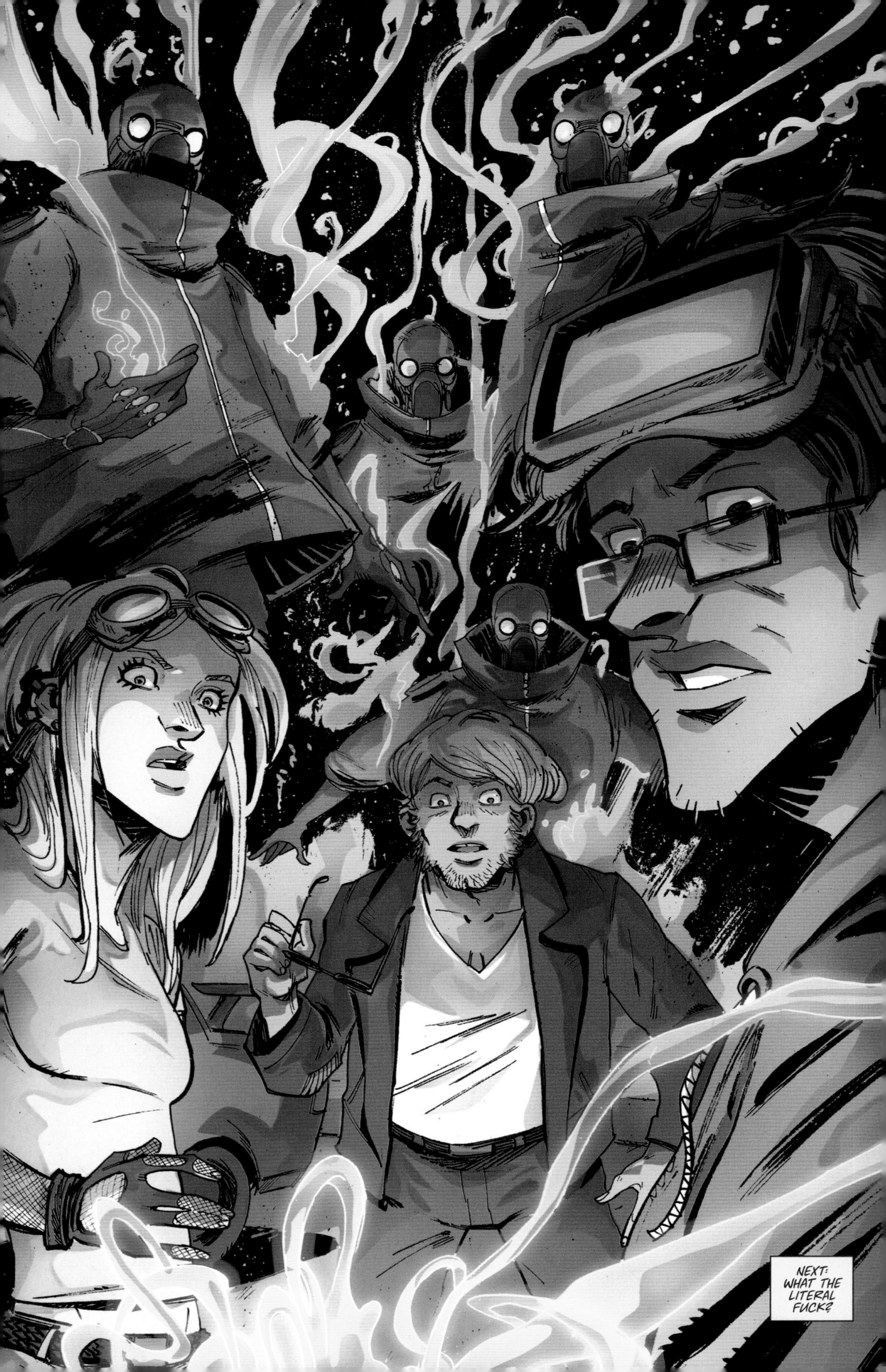
NEXT: WHAT THE LITERAL FUCK?

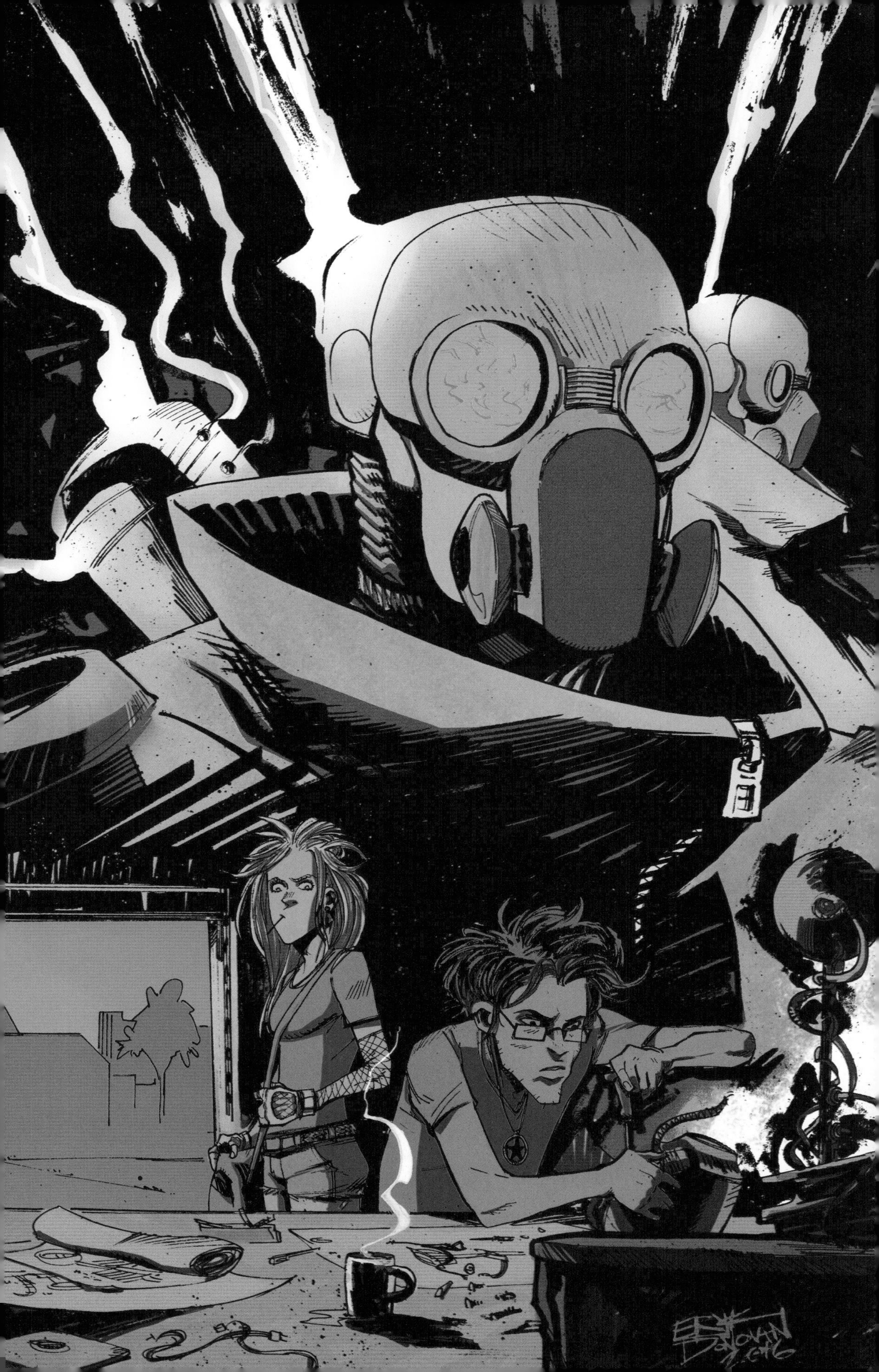

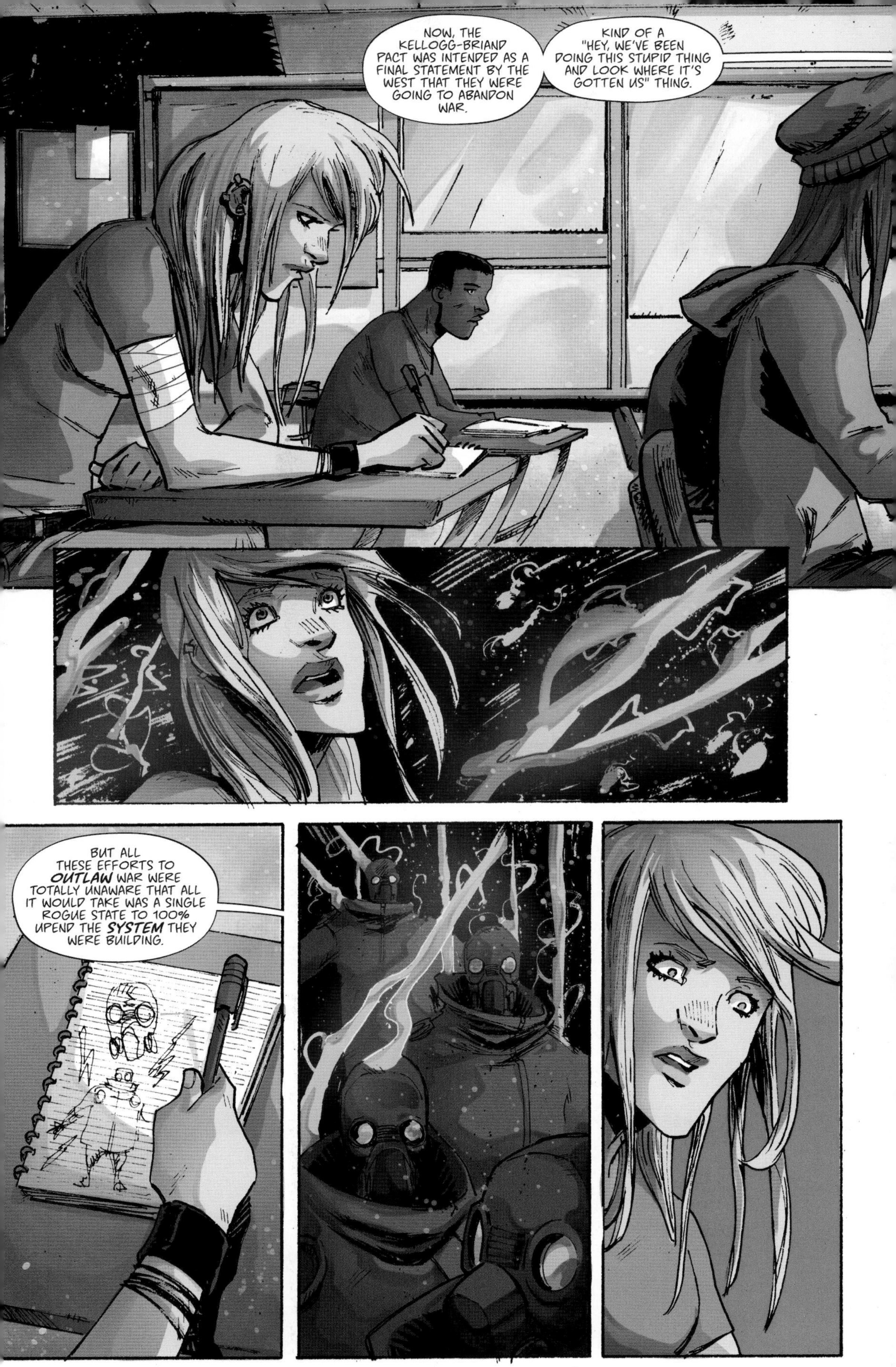
NOW, THE KELLOGG-BRIAND PACT WAS INTENDED AS A FINAL STATEMENT BY THE WEST THAT THEY WERE GOING TO ABANDON WAR.
KIND OF A "HEY, WE'VE BEEN DOING THIS STUPID THING AND LOOK WHERE IT'S GOTTEN US" THING.
BUT ALL THESE EFFORTS TO OUTLAW WAR WERE TOTALLY UNAWARE THAT ALL IT WOULD TAKE WAS A SINGLE ROGUE STATE TO 100% UPEND THE SYSTEM THEY WERE BUILDING.

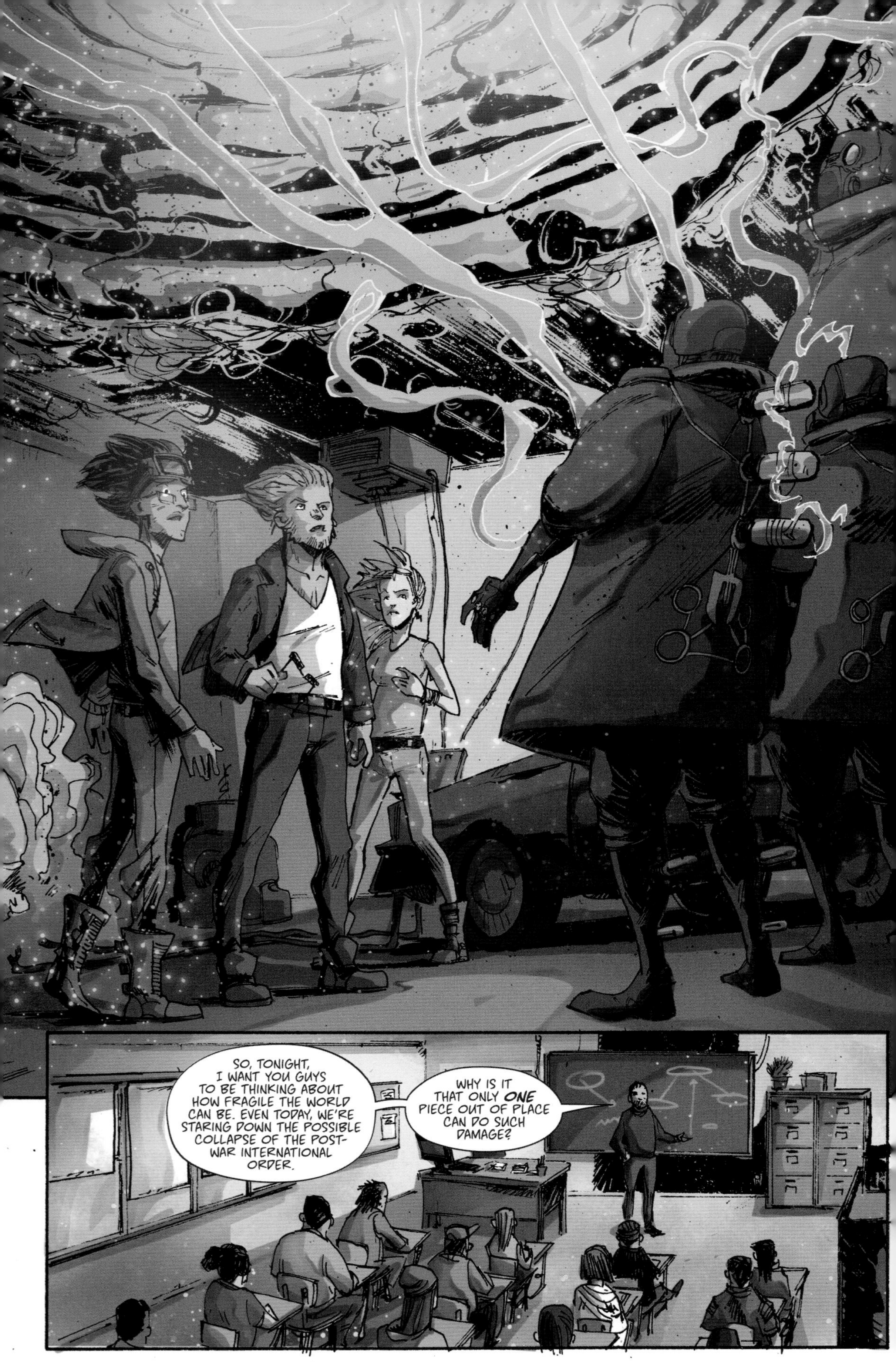
SO, TONIGHT, I WANT YOU GUYS TO BE THINKING ABOUT HOW FRAGILE THE WORLD CAN BE. EVEN TODAY, WE'RE STARING DOWN THE POSSIBLE COLLAPSE OF THE POST-WAR INTERNATIONAL ORDER.
WHY IS IT THAT ONLY ONE PIECE OUT OF PLACE CAN DO SUCH DAMAGE?

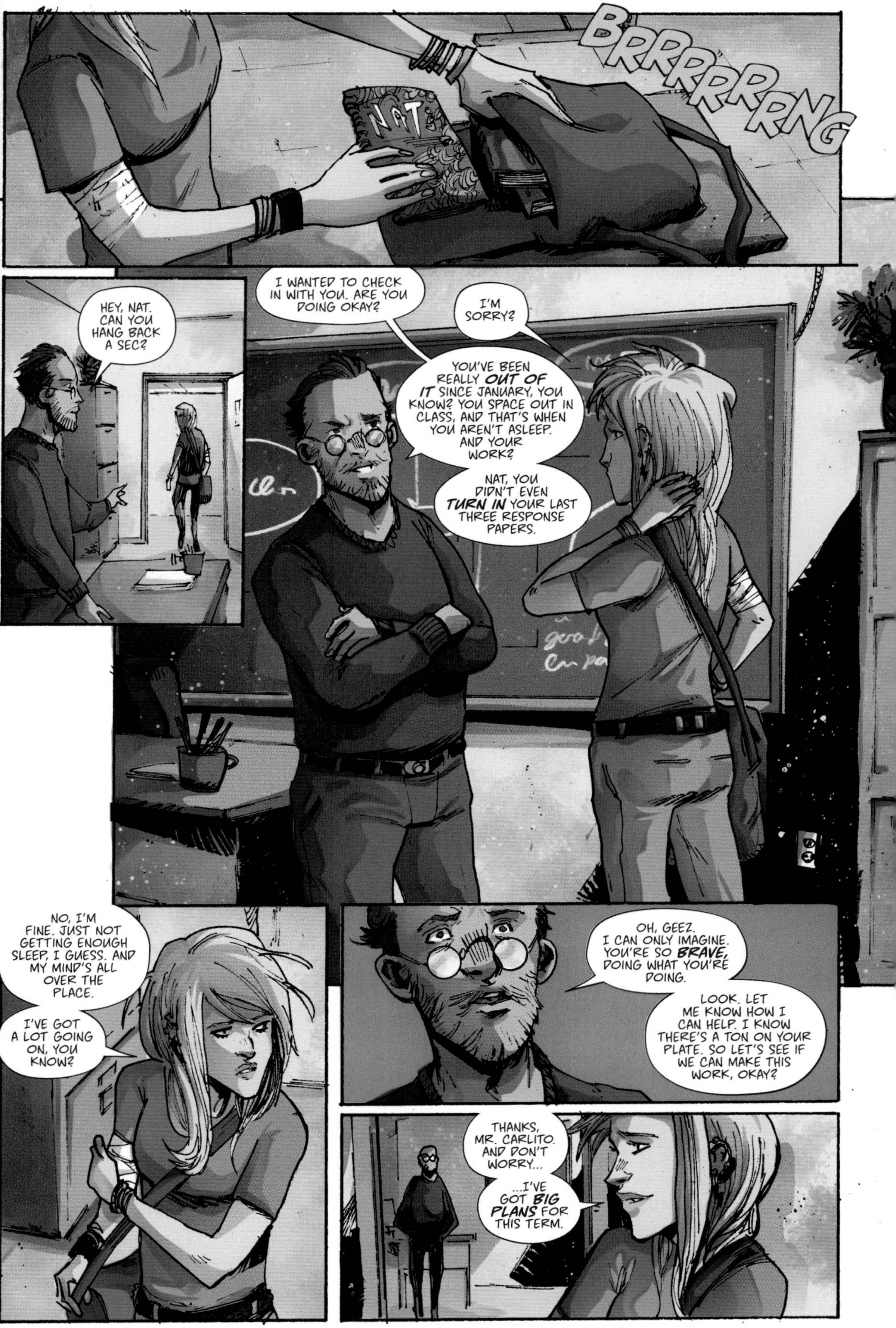
BRRRRRRRNG
NAT
HEY, NAT. CAN YOU HANG BACK A SEC?
I WANTED TO CHECK IN WITH YOU. ARE YOU DOING OKAY?
I'M SORRY?
YOU'VE BEEN REALLY OUT OF IT SINCE JANUARY, YOU KNOW? YOU SPACE OUT IN CLASS, AND THAT'S WHEN YOU AREN'T ASLEEP. AND YOUR WORK?
NAT, YOU DIDN'T EVEN TURN IN YOUR LAST THREE RESPONSE PAPERS.
NO, I'M FINE. JUST NOT GETTING ENOUGH SLEEP, I GUESS. AND MY MIND'S ALL OVER THE PLACE.
I'VE GOT A LOT GOING ON, YOU KNOW?
OH, GEEZ. I CAN ONLY IMAGINE. YOU'RE SO BRAVE, DOING WHAT YOU'RE DOING.
LOOK. LET ME KNOW HOW I CAN HELP. I KNOW THERE'S A TON ON YOUR PLATE. SO LET'S SEE IF WE CAN MAKE THIS WORK, OKAY?
THANKS, MR. CARLITO. AND DON'T WORRY...
...I'VE GOT BIG PLANS FOR THIS TERM.

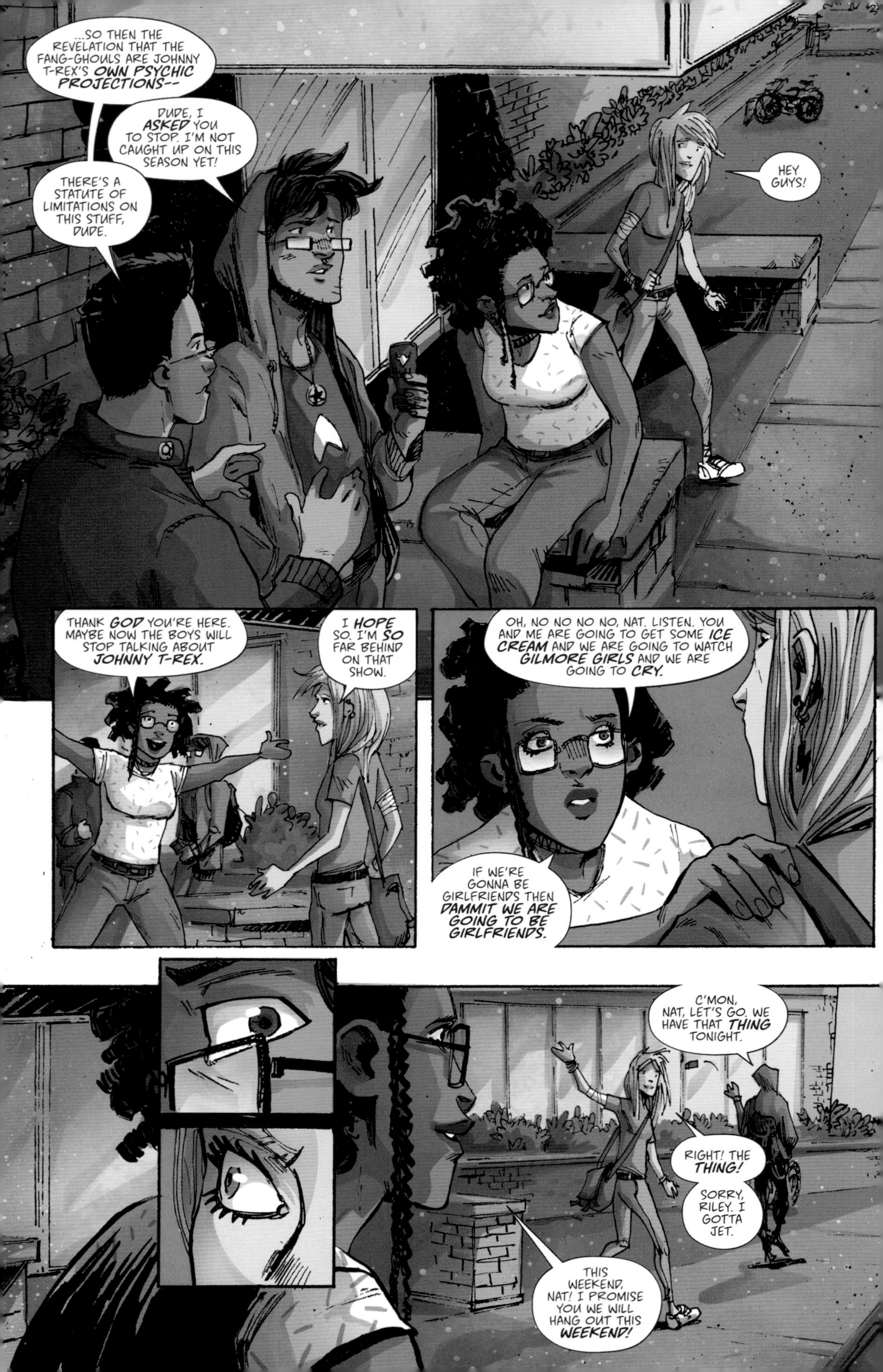
...SO THEN THE REVELATION THAT THE FANG-GHOULS ARE JOHNNY T-REX'S OWN PSYCHIC PROJECTIONS--
DUDE, I ASKED YOU TO STOP. I'M NOT CAUGHT UP ON THIS SEASON YET!
THERE'S A STATUTE OF LIMITATIONS ON THIS STUFF, DUDE.
HEY GUYS!
THANK GOD YOU'RE HERE. MAYBE NOW THE BOYS WILL STOP TALKING ABOUT JOHNNY T-REX.
I HOPE SO. I'M SO FAR BEHIND ON THAT SHOW.
OH, NO NO NO NO, NAT. LISTEN. YOU AND ME ARE GOING TO GET SOME ICE CREAM AND WE ARE GOING TO WATCH GILMORE GIRLS AND WE ARE GOING TO CRY.
IF WE'RE GONNA BE GIRLFRIENDS THEN DAMMIT WE ARE GOING TO BE GIRLFRIENDS.
C'MON, NAT, LET'S GO. WE HAVE THAT THING TONIGHT.
RIGHT! THE THING!
SORRY, RILEY. I GOTTA JET.
THIS WEEKEND, NAT! I PROMISE YOU WE WILL HANG OUT THIS WEEKEND!

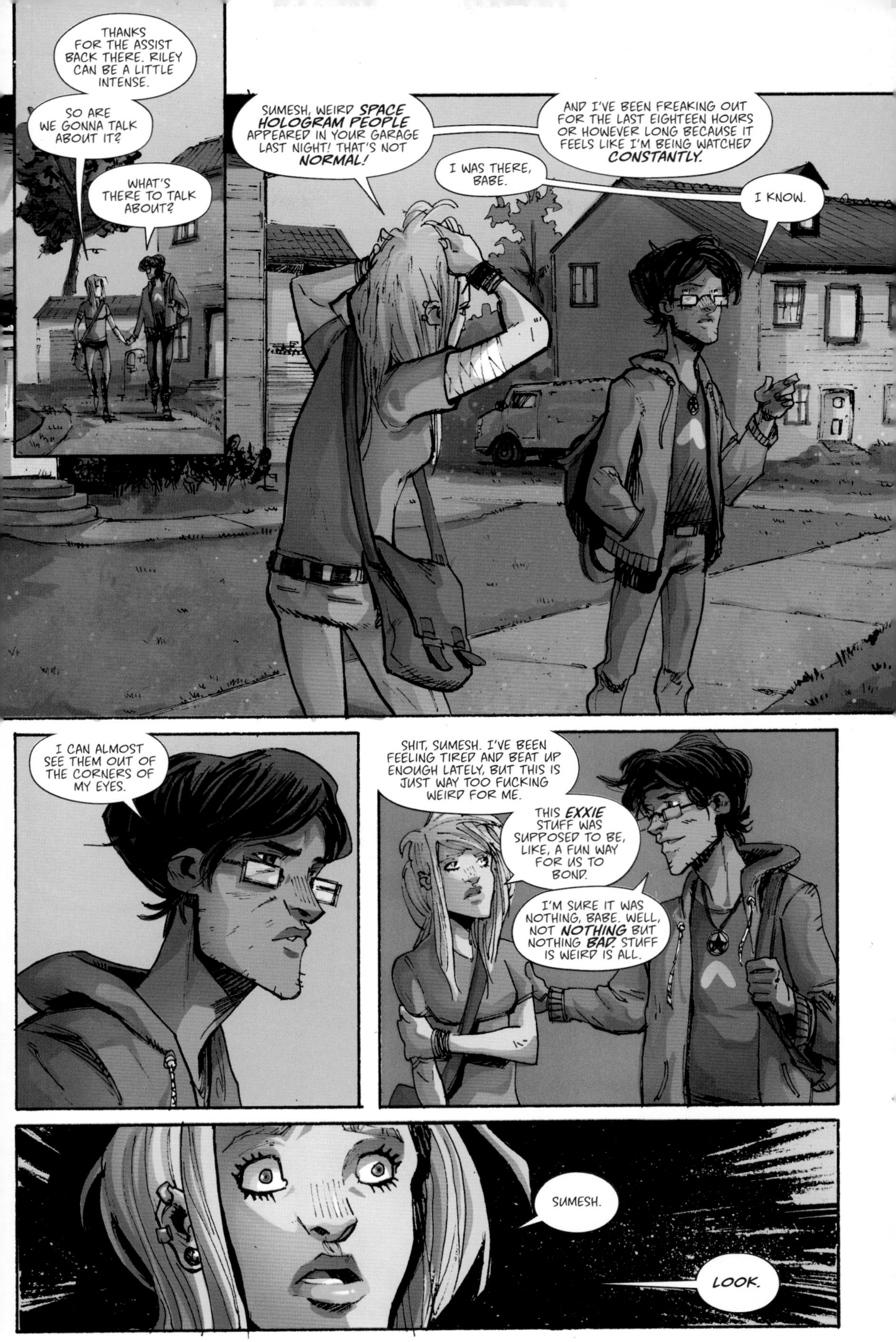
THANKS FOR THE ASSIST BACK THERE. RILEY CAN BE A LITTLE INTENSE.
SO ARE WE GONNA TALK ABOUT IT?
WHAT'S THERE TO TALK ABOUT?
SUMESH, WEIRD SPACE HOLOGRAM PEOPLE APPEARED IN YOUR GARAGE LAST NIGHT! THAT'S NOT NORMAL!
AND I'VE BEEN FREAKING OUT FOR THE LAST EIGHTEEN HOURS OR HOWEVER LONG BECAUSE IT FEELS LIKE I'M BEING WATCHED CONSTANTLY.
I WAS THERE, BABE.
I KNOW.
I CAN ALMOST SEE THEM OUT OF THE CORNERS OF MY EYES.
SHIT, SUMESH. I'VE BEEN FEELING TIRED AND BEAT UP ENOUGH LATELY, BUT THIS IS JUST WAY TOO FUCKING WEIRD FOR ME.
THIS EXXIE STUFF WAS SUPPOSED TO BE, LIKE, A FUN WAY FOR US TO BOND.
I'M SURE IT WAS NOTHING, BABE. WELL, NOT NOTHING BUT NOTHING BAD. STUFF IS WEIRD IS ALL.
SUMESH.
LOOK.

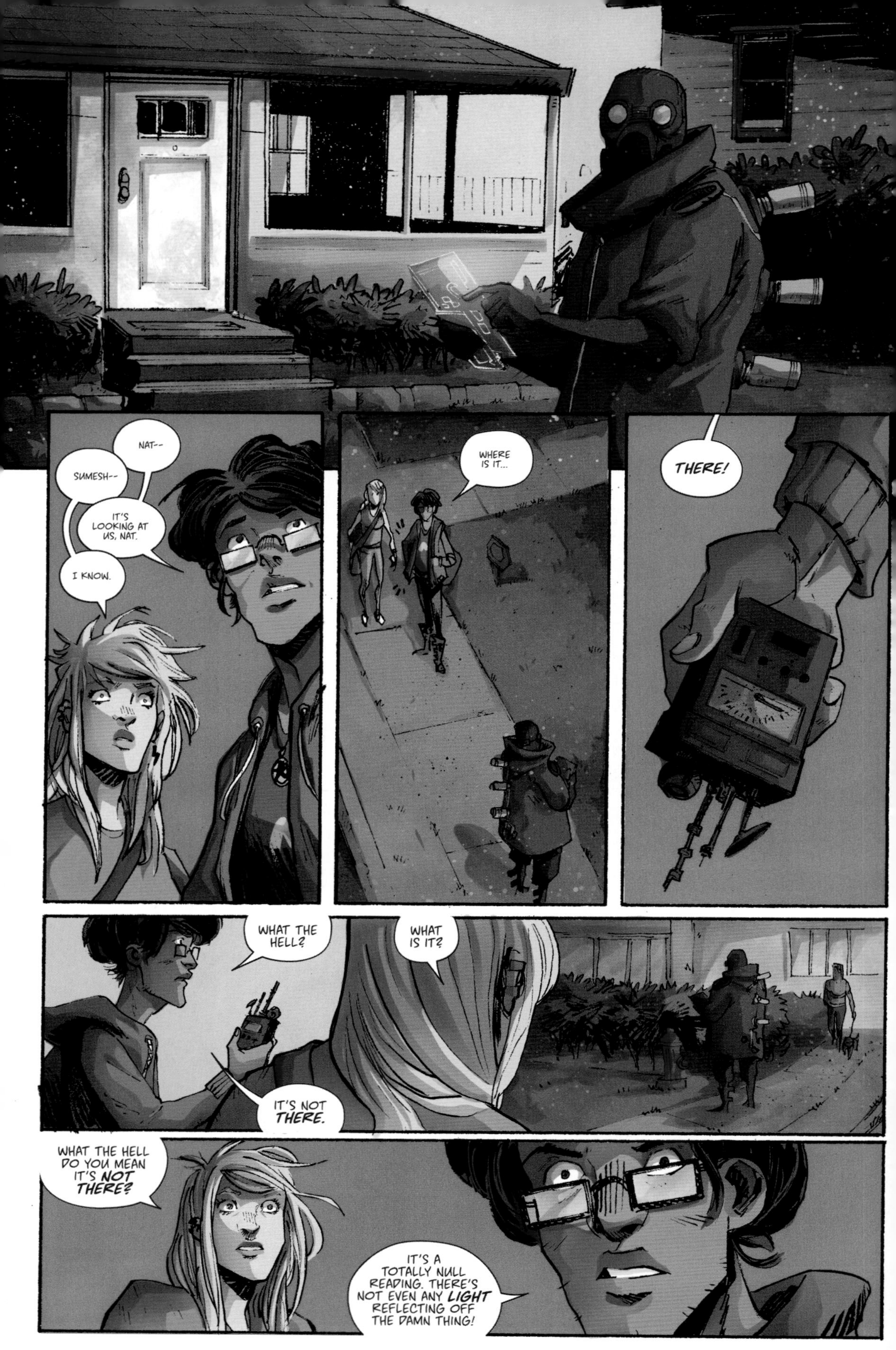
NAT--
SUMESH--
IT'S LOOKING AT US, NAT.
I KNOW.
WHERE IS IT...
THERE!
WHAT THE HELL?
WHAT IS IT?
IT'S NOT THERE.
WHAT THE HELL DO YOU MEAN IT'S NOT THERE?
IT'S A TOTALLY NULL READING. THERE'S NOT EVEN ANY LIGHT REFLECTING OFF THE DAMN THING!

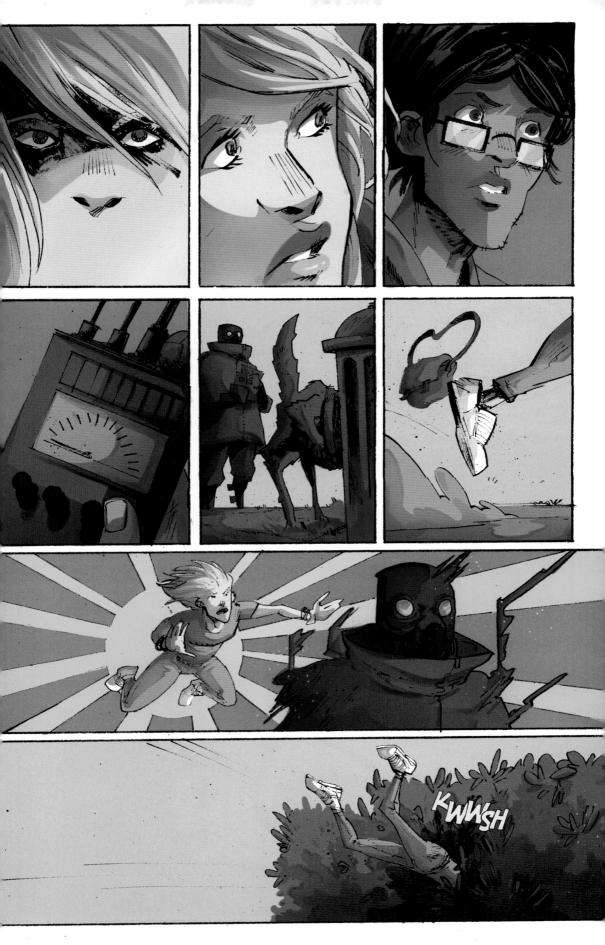

KWWSH

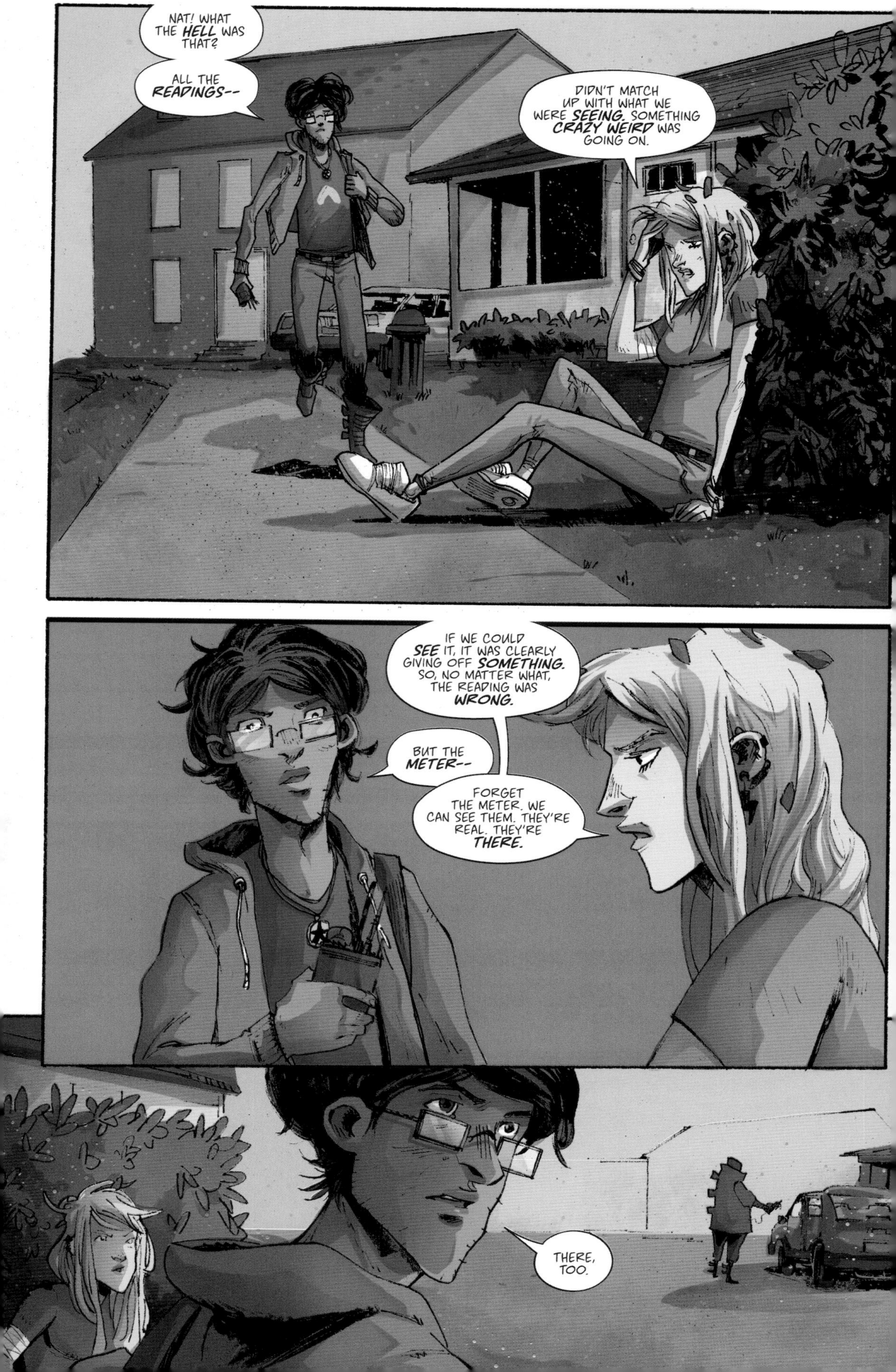
NAT! WHAT THE HELL WAS THAT?
ALL THE READINGS--
DIDN'T MATCH UP WITH WHAT WE WERE SEEING. SOMETHING CRAZY WEIRD WAS GOING ON.
IF WE COULD SEE IT, IT WAS CLEARLY GIVING OFF SOMETHING. SO, NO MATTER WHAT, THE READING WAS WRONG.
BUT THE METER--
FORGET THE METER. WE CAN SEE THEM. THEY'RE REAL. THEY'RE THERE.
THERE, TOO.

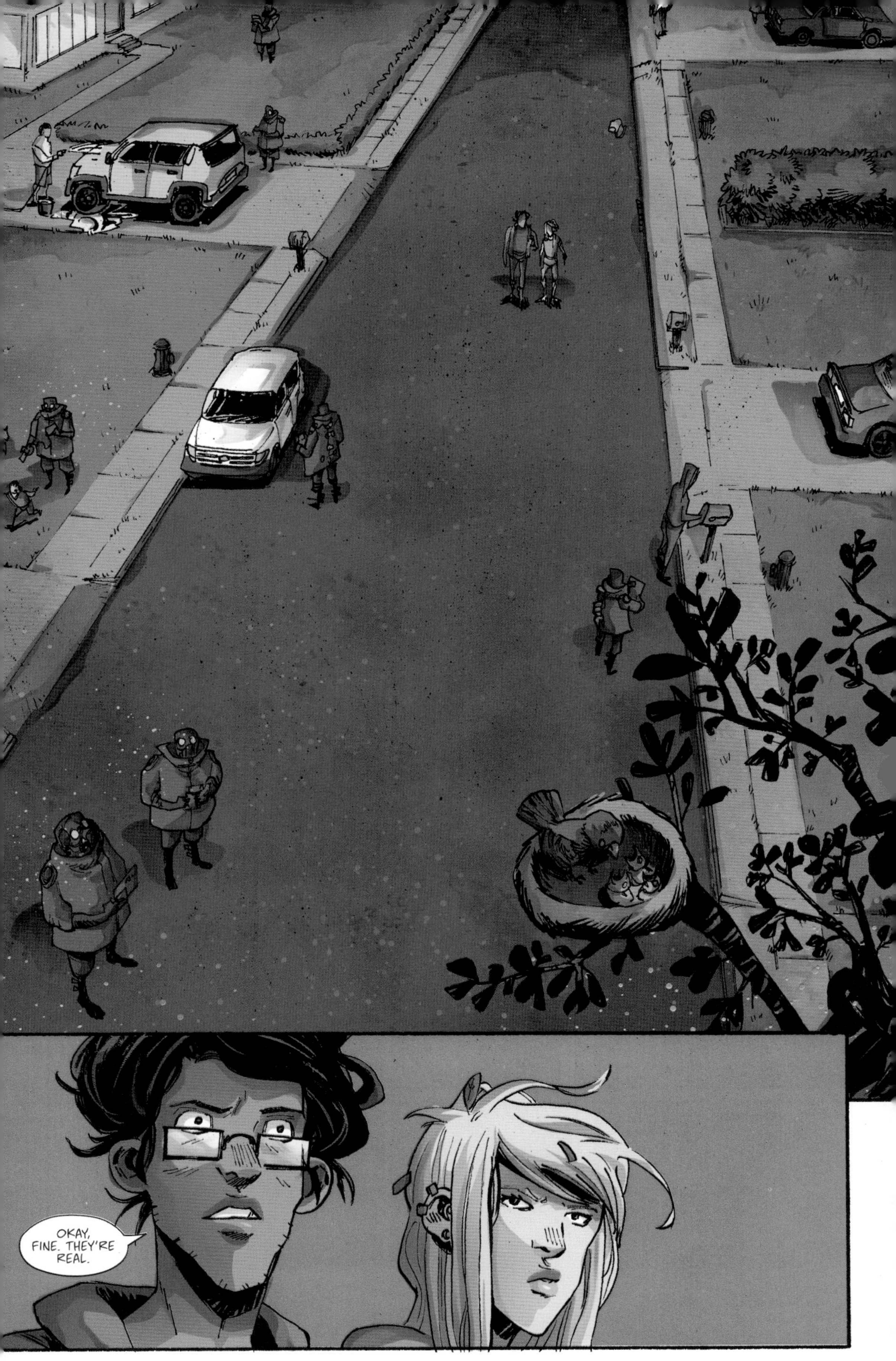
OKAY, FINE. THEY'RE REAL.

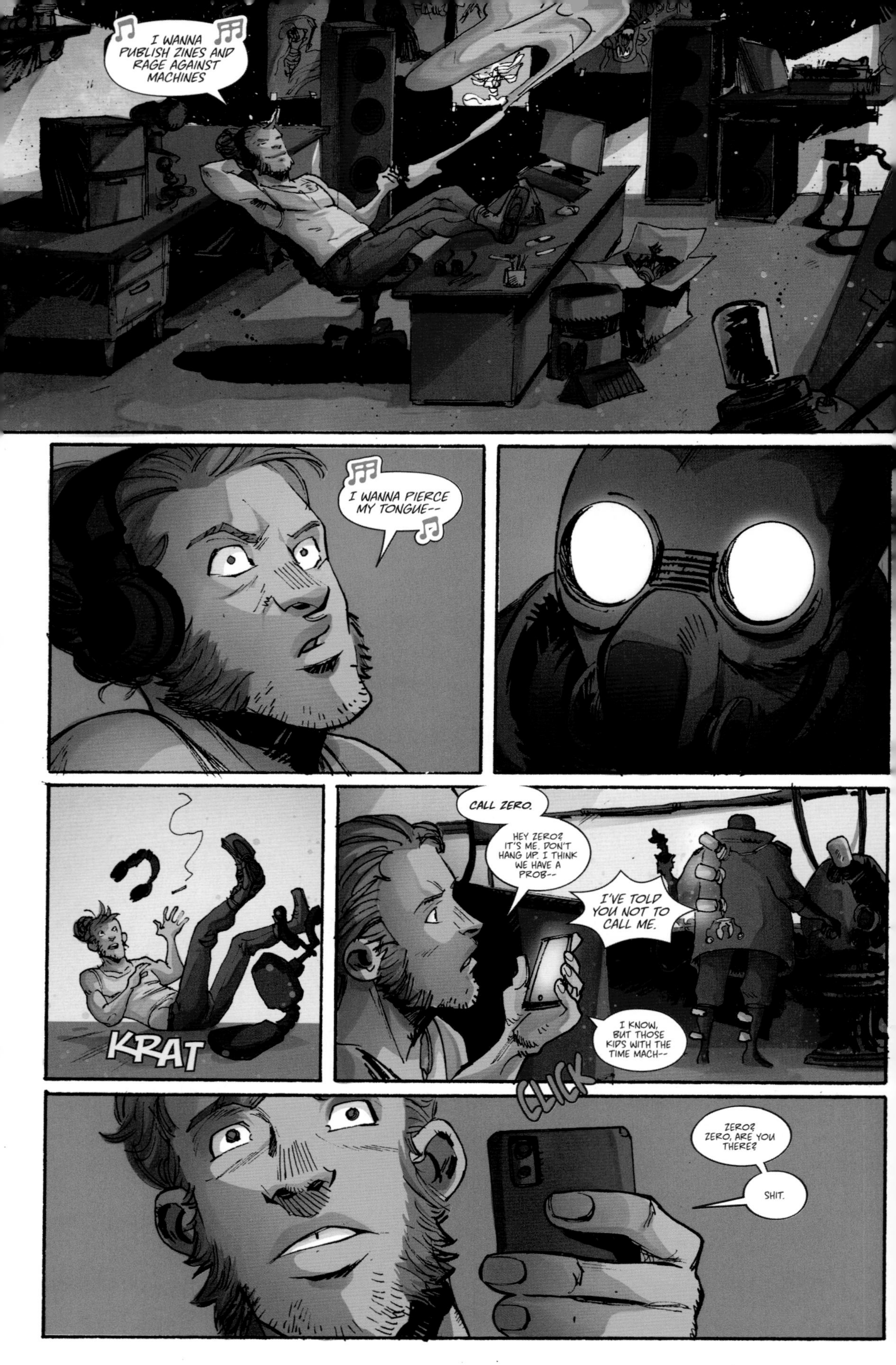

I WANNA PUBLISH ZINES AND RAGE AGAINST MACHINES
I WANNA PIERCE MY TONGUE--
KRAT
CALL ZERO.
HEY ZERO? IT'S ME. DON'T HANG UP. I THINK WE HAVE A PROB--
I'VE TOLD YOU NOT TO CALL ME.
I KNOW, BUT THOSE KIDS WITH THE TIME MACH--
CLICK
ZERO? ZERO, ARE YOU THERE?
SHIT.

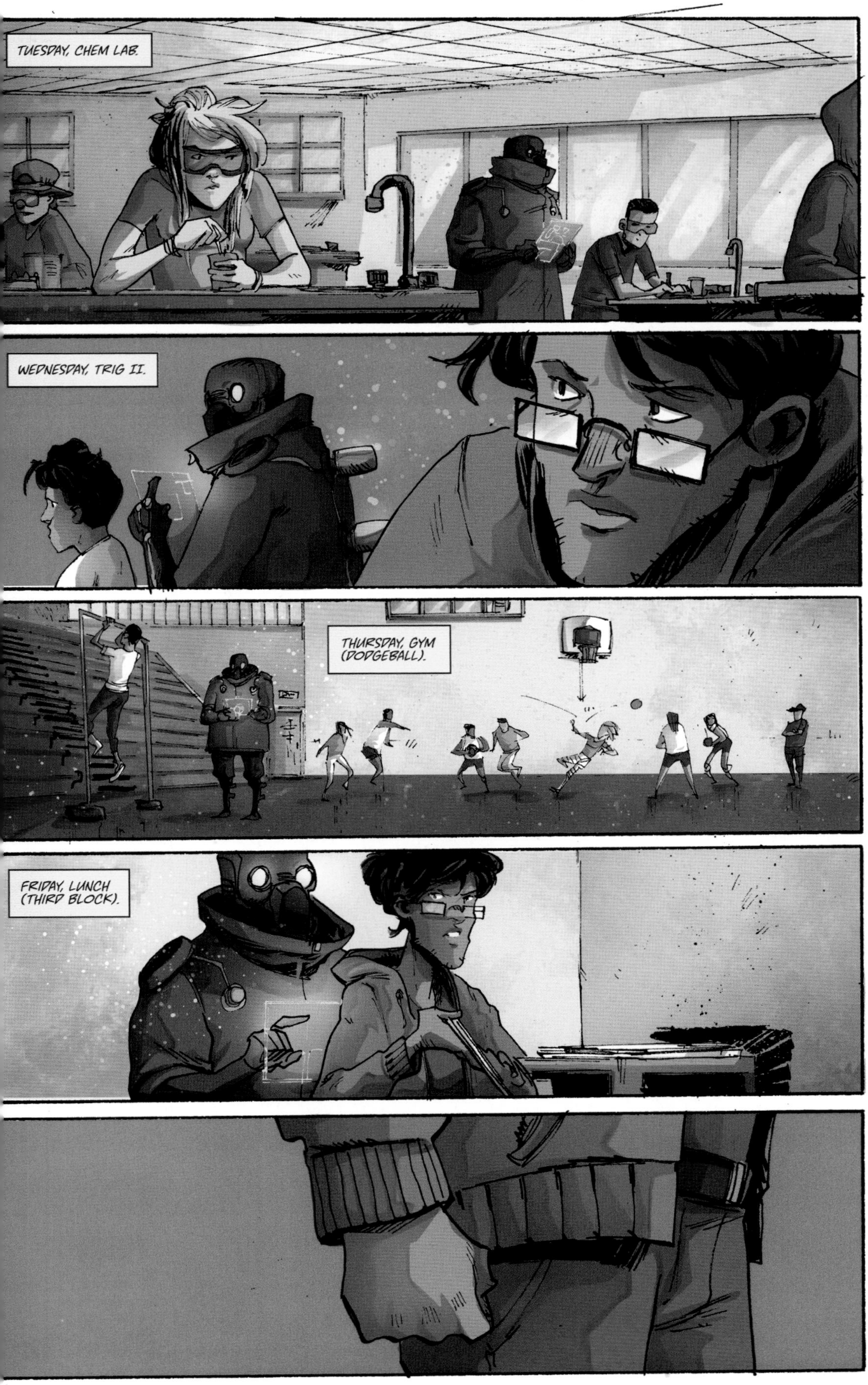
TUESDAY, CHEM LAB.
WEDNESDAY, TRIG II.
THURSDAY, GYM (DODGEBALL).
FRIDAY, LUNCH (THIRD BLOCK).

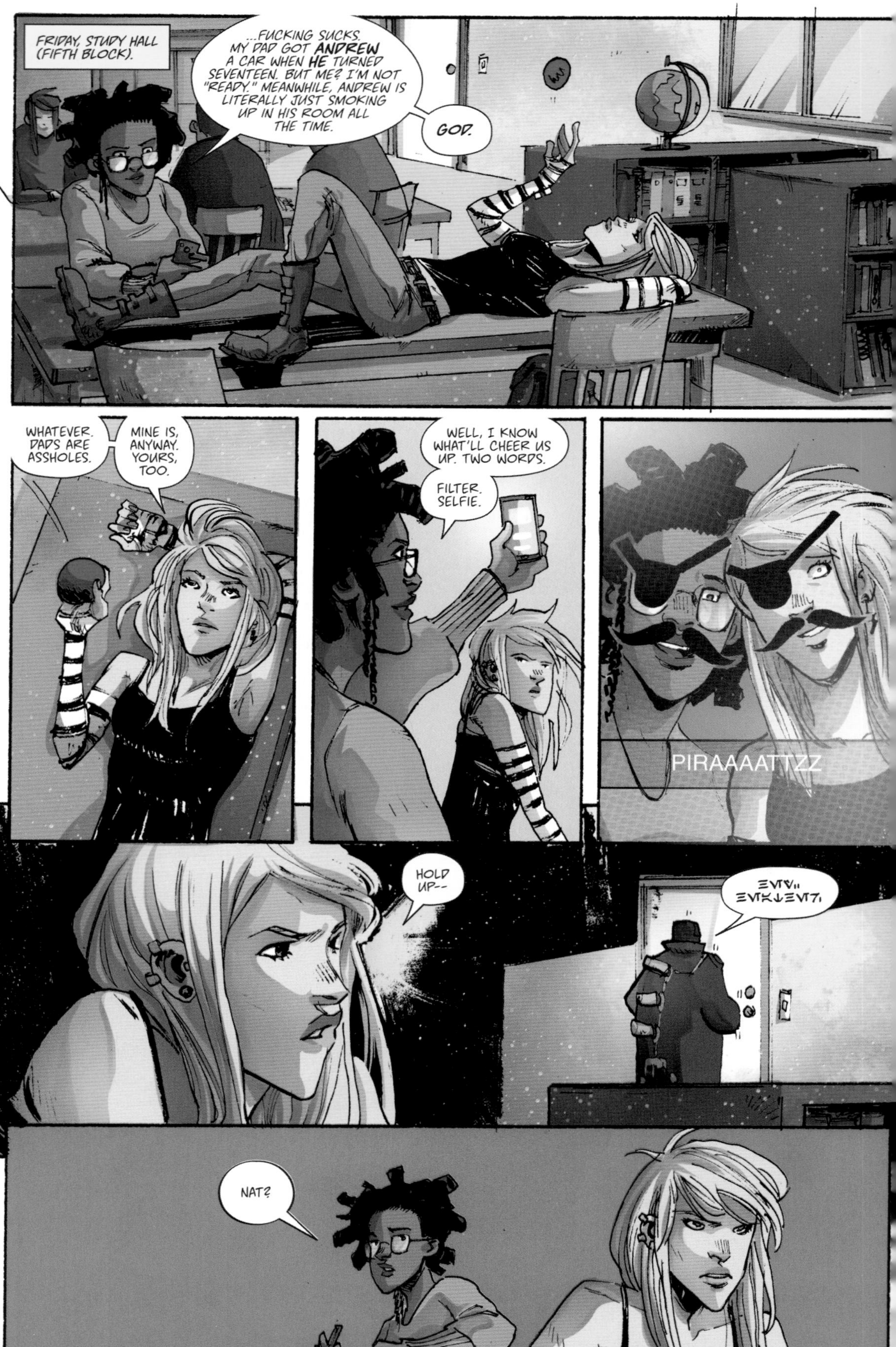
FRIDAY, STUDY HALL (FIFTH BLOCK).
...FUCKING SUCKS. MY DAD GOT **ANDREW** A CAR WHEN **HE** TURNED SEVENTEEN. BUT ME? I'M NOT "READY." MEANWHILE, ANDREW IS LITERALLY JUST SMOKING UP IN HIS ROOM ALL THE TIME.
GOD.
WHATEVER. DADS ARE ASSHOLES.
MINE IS, ANYWAY. YOURS, TOO.
WELL, I KNOW WHAT'LL CHEER US UP. TWO WORDS.
FILTER. SELFIE.
PIRAAAATTZZ
HOLD UP--
NAT?

WHERE ARE YOU GOING?

WHERE ARE **WE** GOING?

I JDNᒪ ᓀᐁᑕᑎᒪJᐁᑕᒷᐁᑎᒷ ᒷᐁᐁᒷ ᐁᒷᒷ ᒷᐁᑎᑕᑕᐁᒷᐁᑕᒷᑎᑎᒷᒷ ᒷᒷ ᒷᐁᐁᐁ ᒷᑎᐁᒷᒷ ᒷᑌ ᐁᒷᑕᒷ ᑌᑕᐁᒷᐁᑎᒷ ᑎᒷᒷᑕ ᐁᒷᒷᒷᒷᐁᒷᑎ ᐁᑕᒷᒷ ᒷᑕᐁᐁᒷ ᒷᐁᐁᒷᑌ

WHAT THE HELL IS GOING ON? WHO ARE WE HIDING FROM?

I DIDN'T SEE--

SHHHHH.

I ᑕᒷᒷᒷᑕᒷ ᒷᐁᐁᒷᑎᒷ ᒷᐁᑌ ᑕᑌᒷᒷ ᒷᐁᒷᒷ ᐁᒷᒷ ᒷᒷᒷᒷᑕᒷ NATALIE ᒷᑎᑎᒷ ᒷᐁᒷᒷ ᐁᒷᐁᒷᒷ ᒷᒷᒷᒷᒷᒷ SUMESH.

DO YOU GIRLS WANNA TELL ME WHY YOU AREN'T IN CLASS?

GAH!

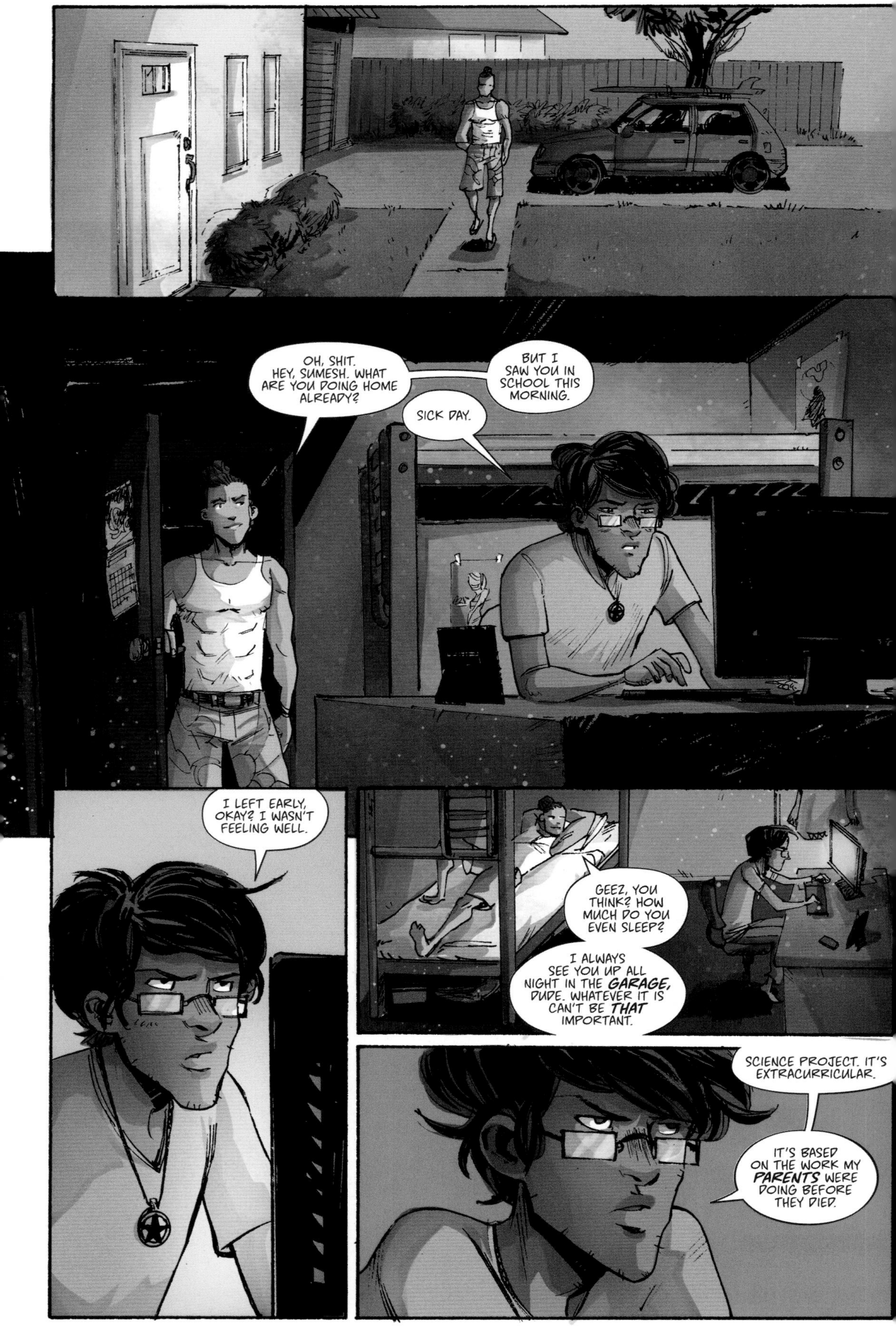
OH, SHIT. HEY, SUMESH. WHAT ARE YOU DOING HOME ALREADY?
SICK DAY.
BUT I SAW YOU IN SCHOOL THIS MORNING.
I LEFT EARLY, OKAY? I WASN'T FEELING WELL.
GEEZ, YOU THINK? HOW MUCH DO YOU EVEN SLEEP?
I ALWAYS SEE YOU UP ALL NIGHT IN THE GARAGE, DUDE. WHATEVER IT IS CAN'T BE THAT IMPORTANT.
SCIENCE PROJECT. IT'S EXTRACURRICULAR.
IT'S BASED ON THE WORK MY PARENTS WERE DOING BEFORE THEY DIED.

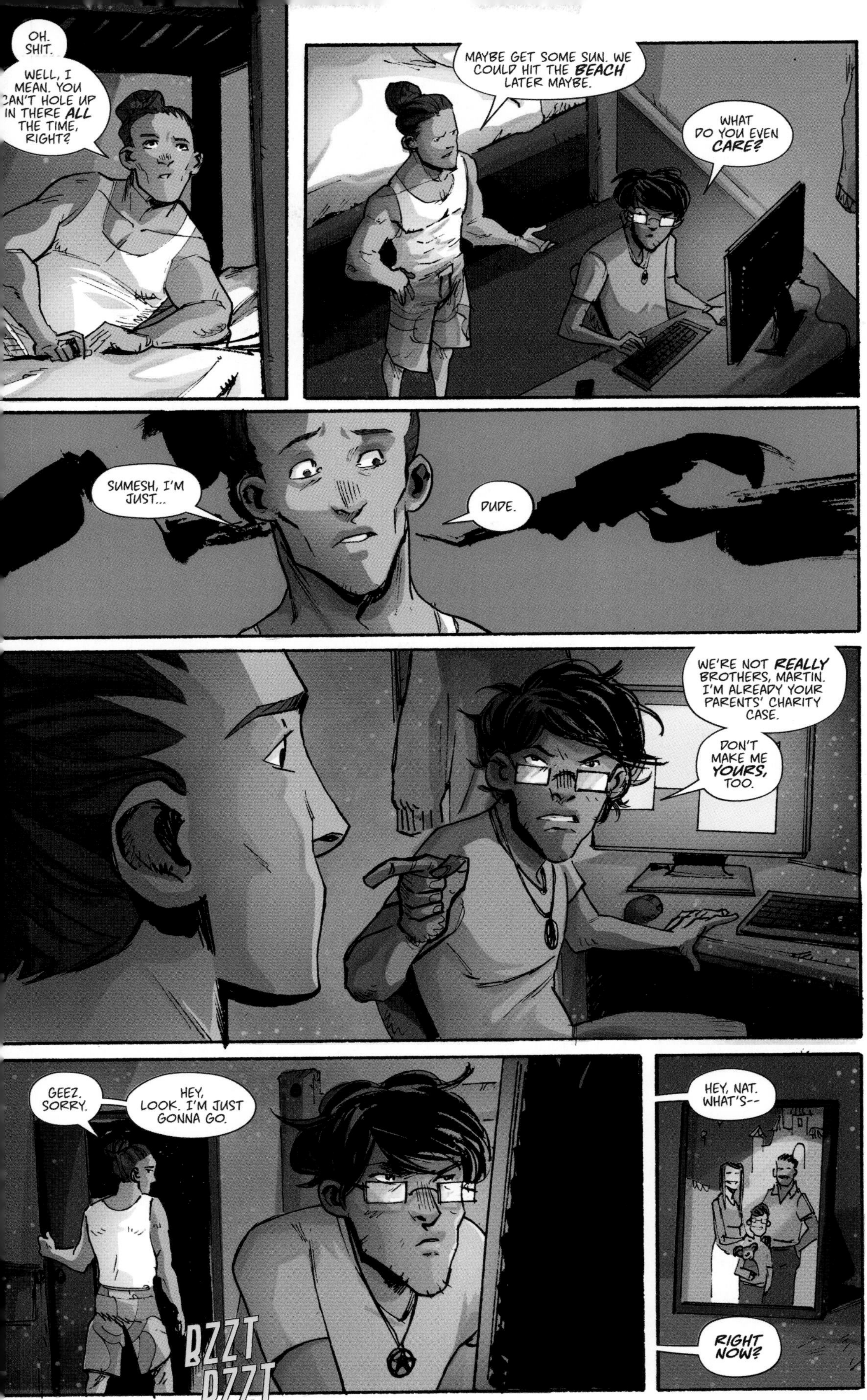
OH. SHIT.
WELL, I MEAN. YOU CAN'T HOLE UP IN THERE ALL THE TIME, RIGHT?
MAYBE GET SOME SUN. WE COULD HIT THE BEACH LATER MAYBE.
WHAT DO YOU EVEN CARE?
SUMESH, I'M JUST...
DUDE.
WE'RE NOT REALLY BROTHERS, MARTIN. I'M ALREADY YOUR PARENTS' CHARITY CASE.
DON'T MAKE ME YOURS, TOO.
GEEZ. SORRY.
HEY, LOOK. I'M JUST GONNA GO.
BZZT BZZT
HEY, NAT. WHAT'S--
RIGHT NOW?

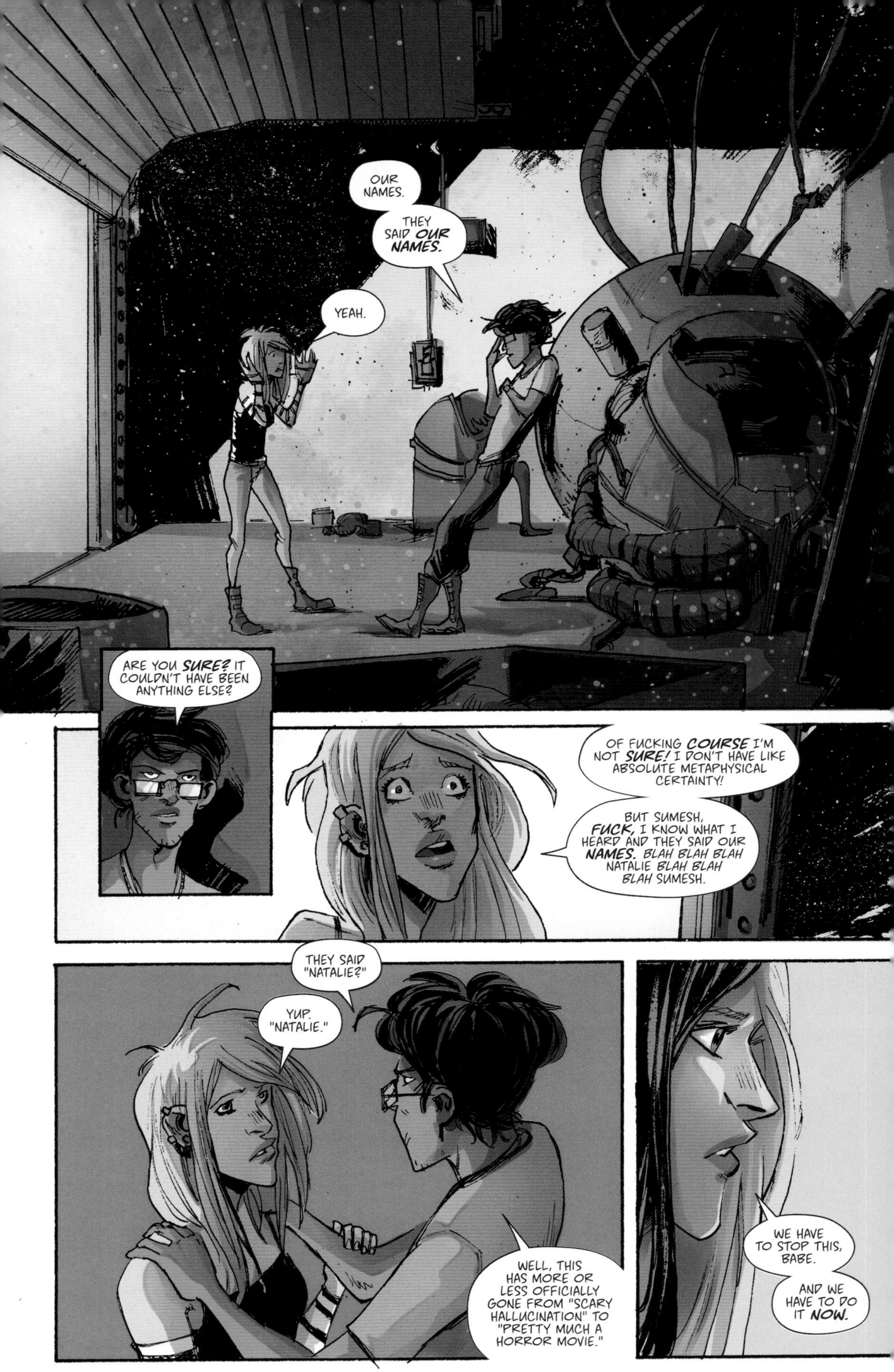
OUR NAMES.
THEY SAID OUR NAMES.
YEAH.
ARE YOU SURE? IT COULDN'T HAVE BEEN ANYTHING ELSE?
OF FUCKING COURSE I'M NOT SURE! I DON'T HAVE LIKE ABSOLUTE METAPHYSICAL CERTAINTY!
BUT SUMESH, FUCK, I KNOW WHAT I HEARD AND THEY SAID OUR NAMES. BLAH BLAH BLAH NATALIE BLAH BLAH BLAH SUMESH.
THEY SAID "NATALIE?"
YUP. "NATALIE."
WELL, THIS HAS MORE OR LESS OFFICIALLY GONE FROM "SCARY HALLUCINATION" TO "PRETTY MUCH A HORROR MOVIE."
WE HAVE TO STOP THIS, BABE.
AND WE HAVE TO DO IT NOW.

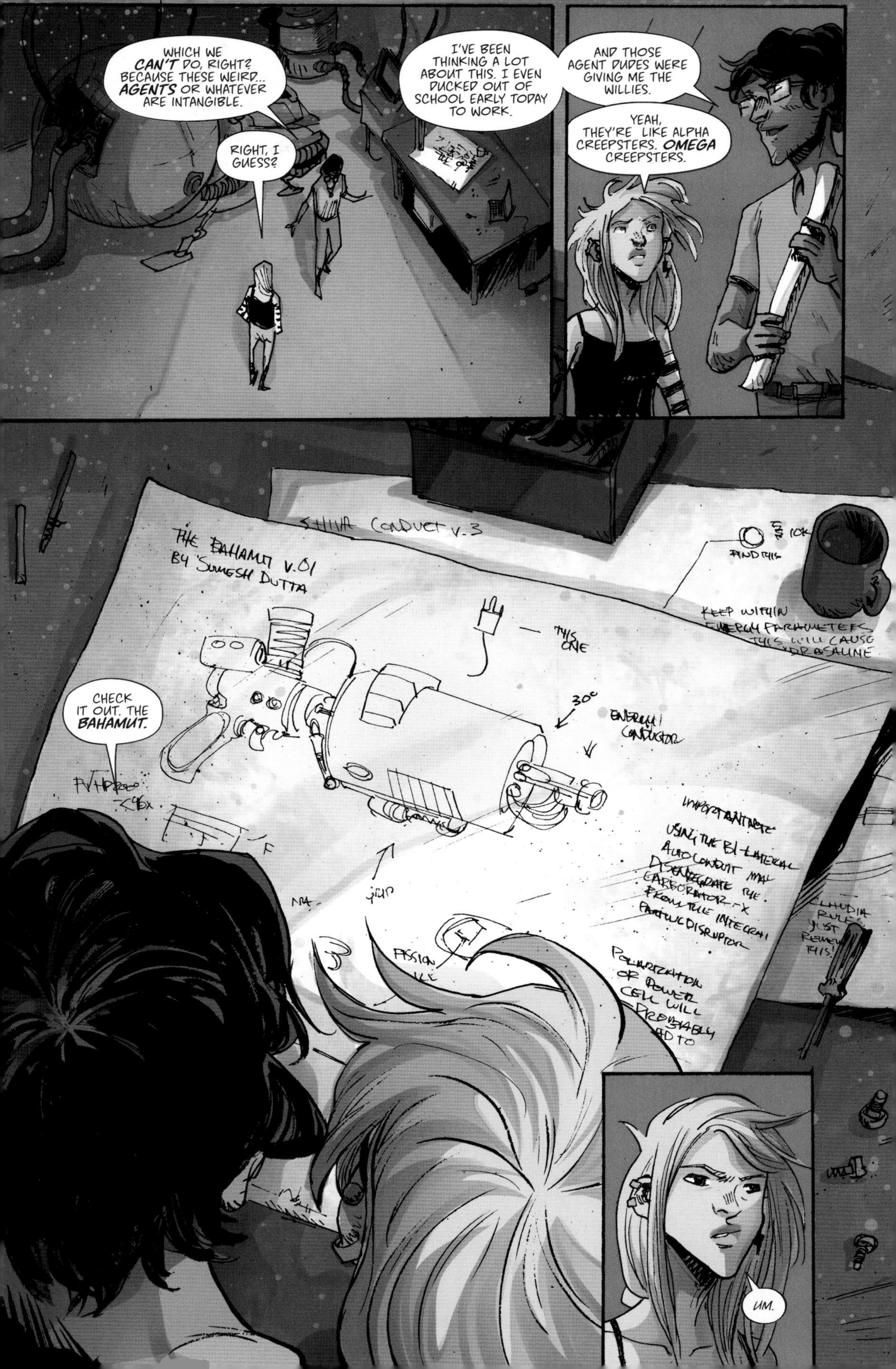
WHICH WE CAN'T DO, RIGHT? BECAUSE THESE WEIRD... AGENTS OR WHATEVER ARE INTANGIBLE.
RIGHT, I GUESS?
I'VE BEEN THINKING A LOT ABOUT THIS. I EVEN DUCKED OUT OF SCHOOL EARLY TODAY TO WORK.
AND THOSE AGENT DUDES WERE GIVING ME THE WILLIES.
YEAH, THEY'RE LIKE ALPHA CREEPSTERS. OMEGA CREEPSTERS.
CHECK IT OUT. THE BAHAMUT.
UM.

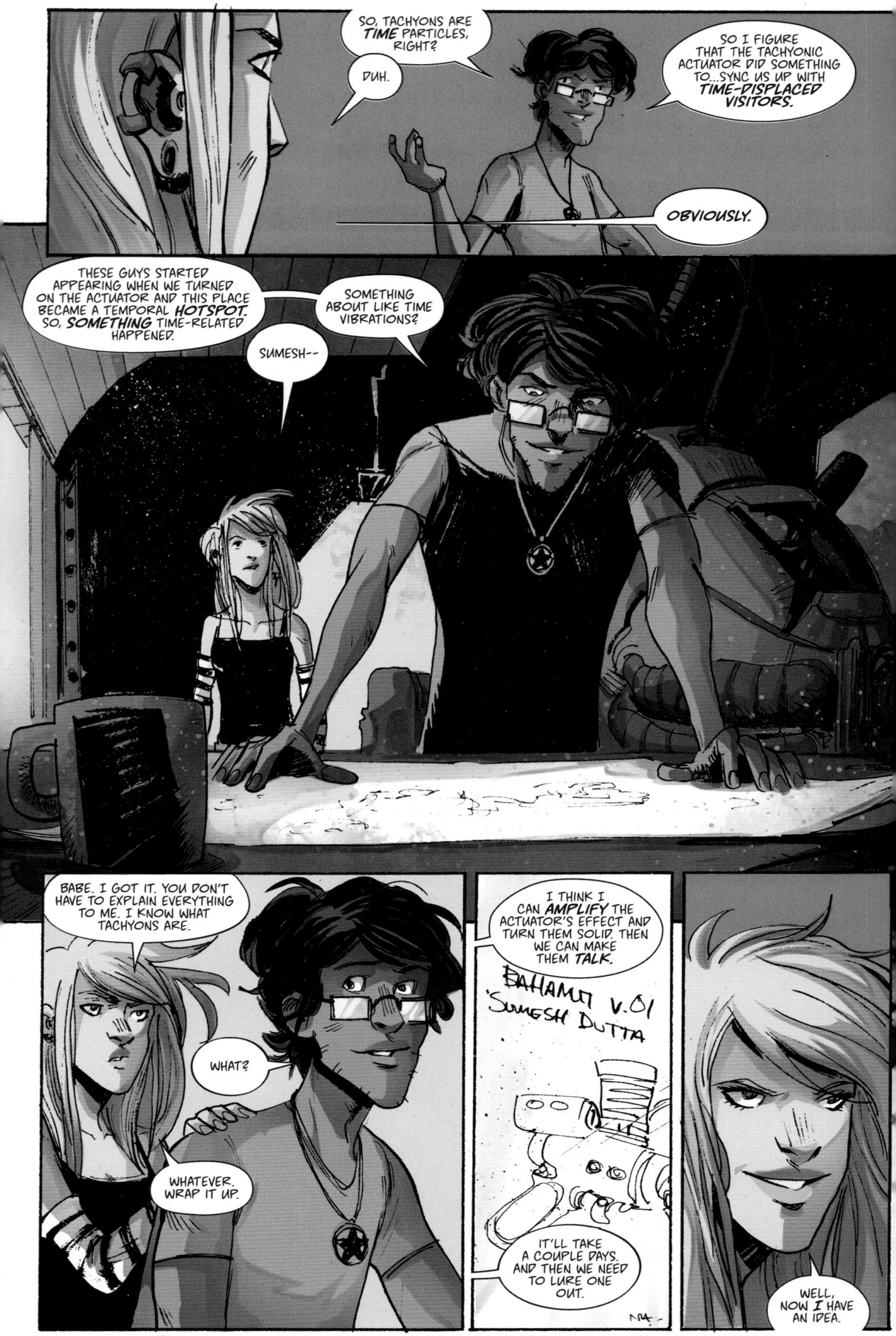
SO, TACHYONS ARE TIME PARTICLES, RIGHT?
DUH.
SO I FIGURE THAT THE TACHYONIC ACTUATOR DID SOMETHING TO...SYNC US UP WITH TIME-DISPLACED VISITORS.
OBVIOUSLY.
THESE GUYS STARTED APPEARING WHEN WE TURNED ON THE ACTUATOR AND THIS PLACE BECAME A TEMPORAL HOTSPOT. SO, SOMETHING TIME-RELATED HAPPENED.
SOMETHING ABOUT LIKE TIME VIBRATIONS?
SUMESH--
BABE. I GOT IT. YOU DON'T HAVE TO EXPLAIN EVERYTHING TO ME. I KNOW WHAT TACHYONS ARE.
WHAT?
WHATEVER. WRAP IT UP.
I THINK I CAN AMPLIFY THE ACTUATOR'S EFFECT AND TURN THEM SOLID. THEN WE CAN MAKE THEM TALK.
BAHAMUT V.01
SUMESH DUTTA
IT'LL TAKE A COUPLE DAYS. AND THEN WE NEED TO LURE ONE OUT.
WELL, NOW I HAVE AN IDEA.

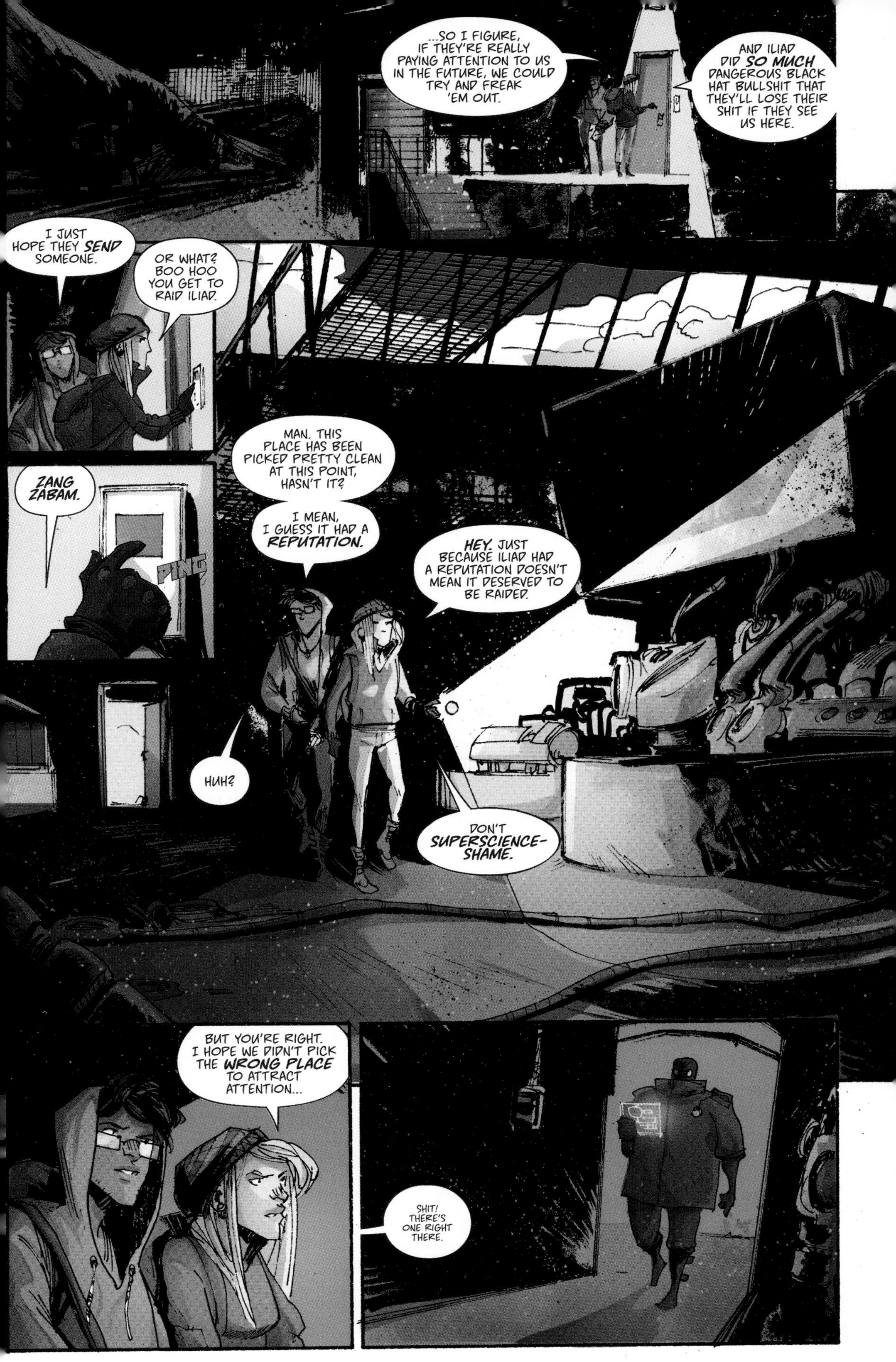
...SO I FIGURE, IF THEY'RE REALLY PAYING ATTENTION TO US IN THE FUTURE, WE COULD TRY AND FREAK 'EM OUT.
AND ILIAD DID SO MUCH DANGEROUS BLACK HAT BULLSHIT THAT THEY'LL LOSE THEIR SHIT IF THEY SEE US HERE.
I JUST HOPE THEY SEND SOMEONE.
OR WHAT? BOO HOO YOU GET TO RAID ILIAD.
ZANG ZABAM.
PING
MAN. THIS PLACE HAS BEEN PICKED PRETTY CLEAN AT THIS POINT, HASN'T IT?
I MEAN, I GUESS IT HAD A REPUTATION.
HEY. JUST BECAUSE ILIAD HAD A REPUTATION DOESN'T MEAN IT DESERVED TO BE RAIDED.
HUH?
DON'T SUPERSCIENCE-SHAME.
BUT YOU'RE RIGHT. I HOPE WE DIDN'T PICK THE WRONG PLACE TO ATTRACT ATTENTION...
SHIT! THERE'S ONE RIGHT THERE.

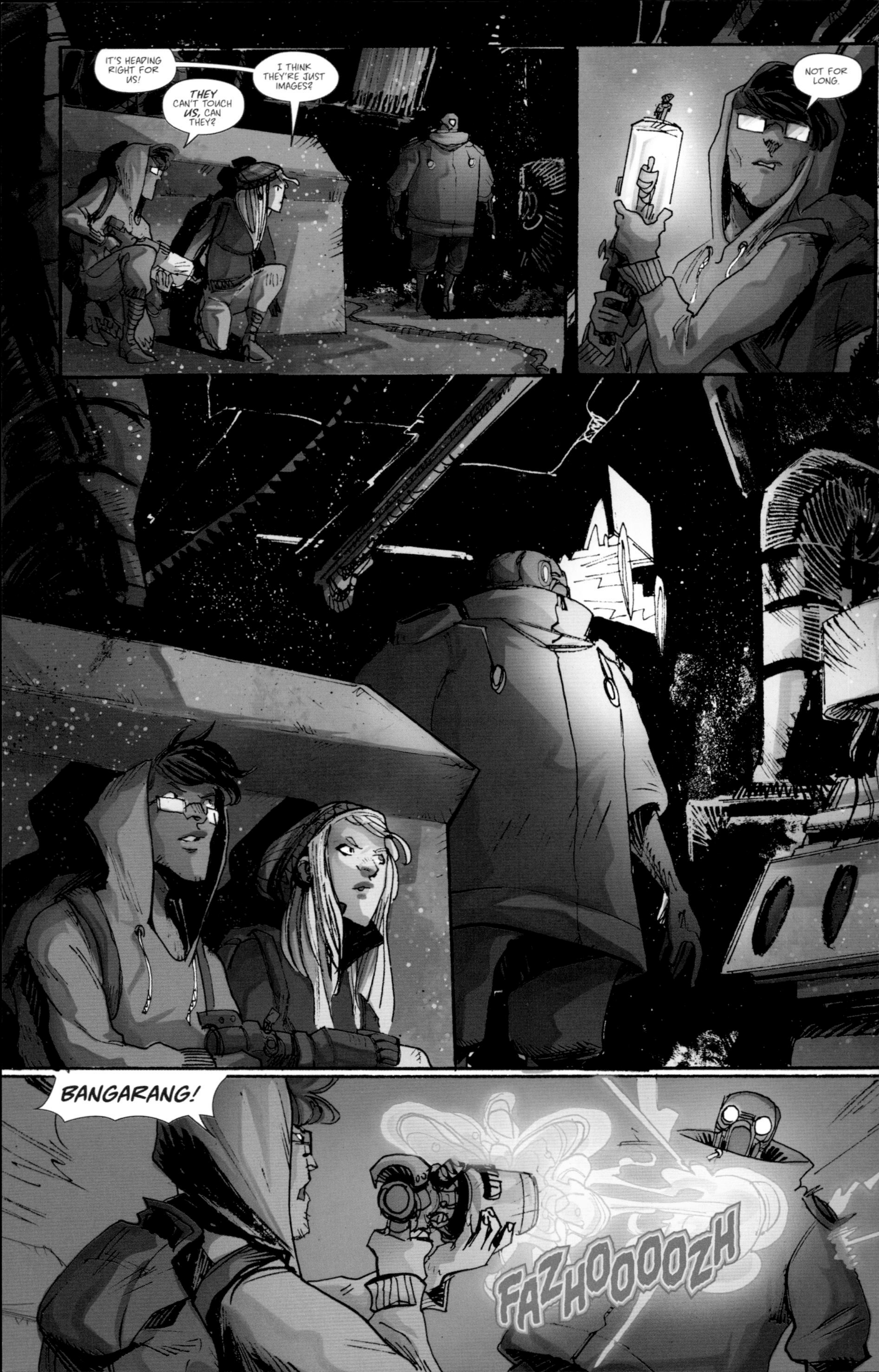
IT'S HEADING RIGHT FOR US!
THEY CAN'T TOUCH US, CAN THEY?
I THINK THEY'RE JUST IMAGES?
NOT FOR LONG.
BANGARANG!
FAZHOOOOZH

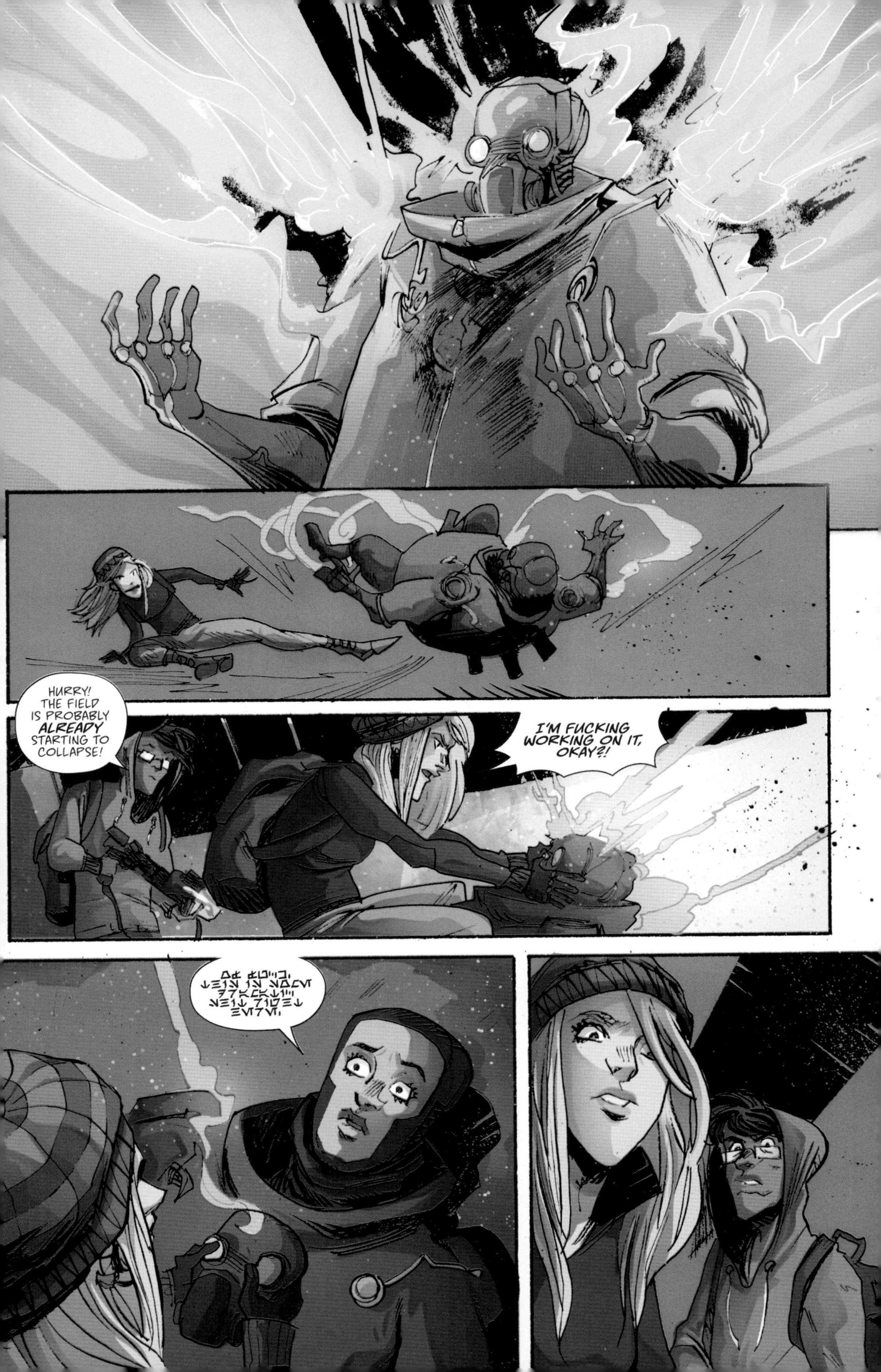
HURRY! THE FIELD IS PROBABLY ALREADY STARTING TO COLLAPSE!
I'M FUCKING WORKING ON IT, OKAY?!

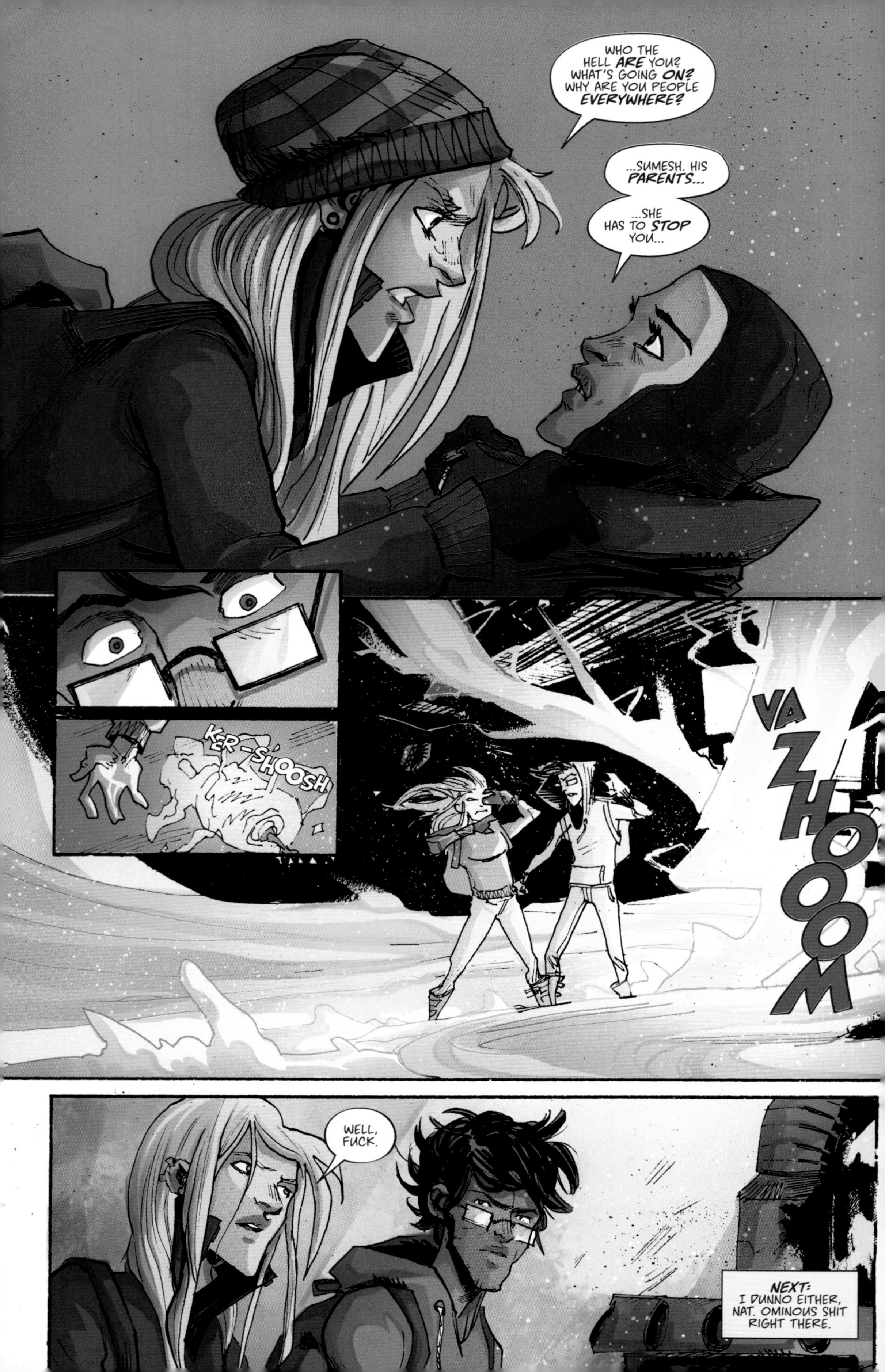
WHO THE HELL ARE YOU? WHAT'S GOING ON? WHY ARE YOU PEOPLE EVERYWHERE?
...SUMESH. HIS PARENTS...
...SHE HAS TO STOP YOU...
KER-SHOOSH
VA ZHOOOOM
WELL, FUCK.
NEXT: I DUNNO EITHER, NAT. OMINOUS SHIT RIGHT THERE.

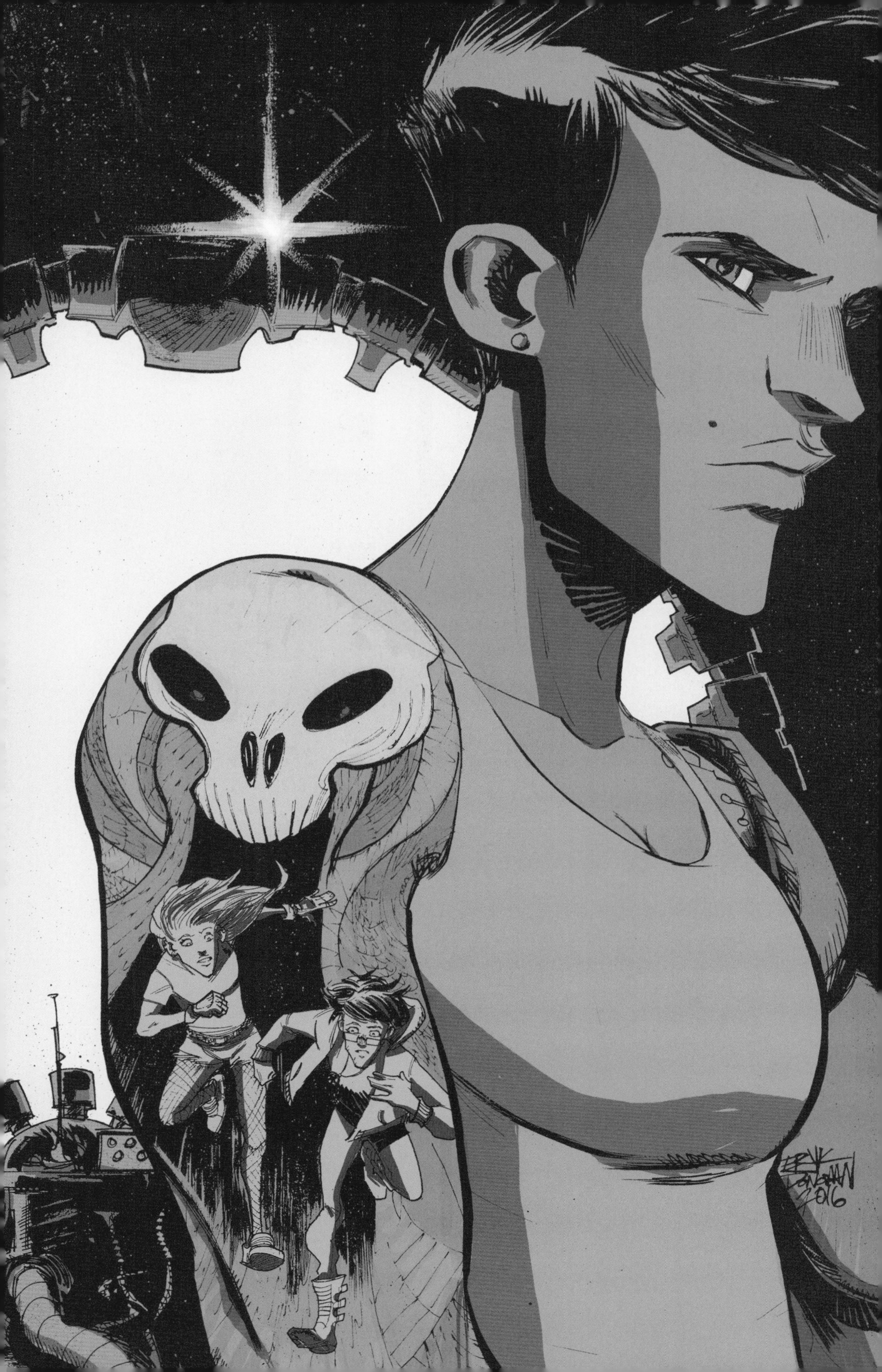

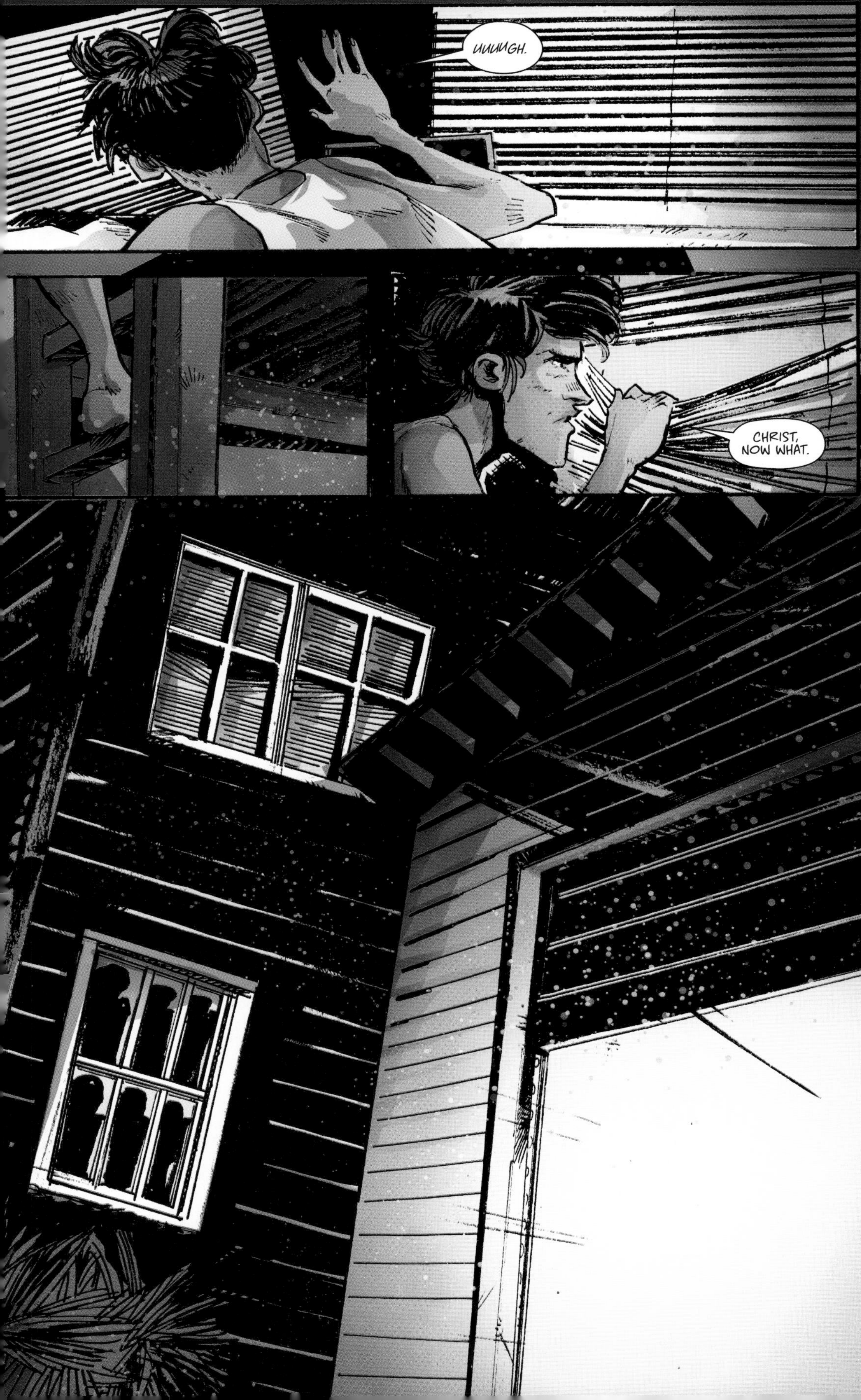
UUUUGH.
CHRIST, NOW WHAT.

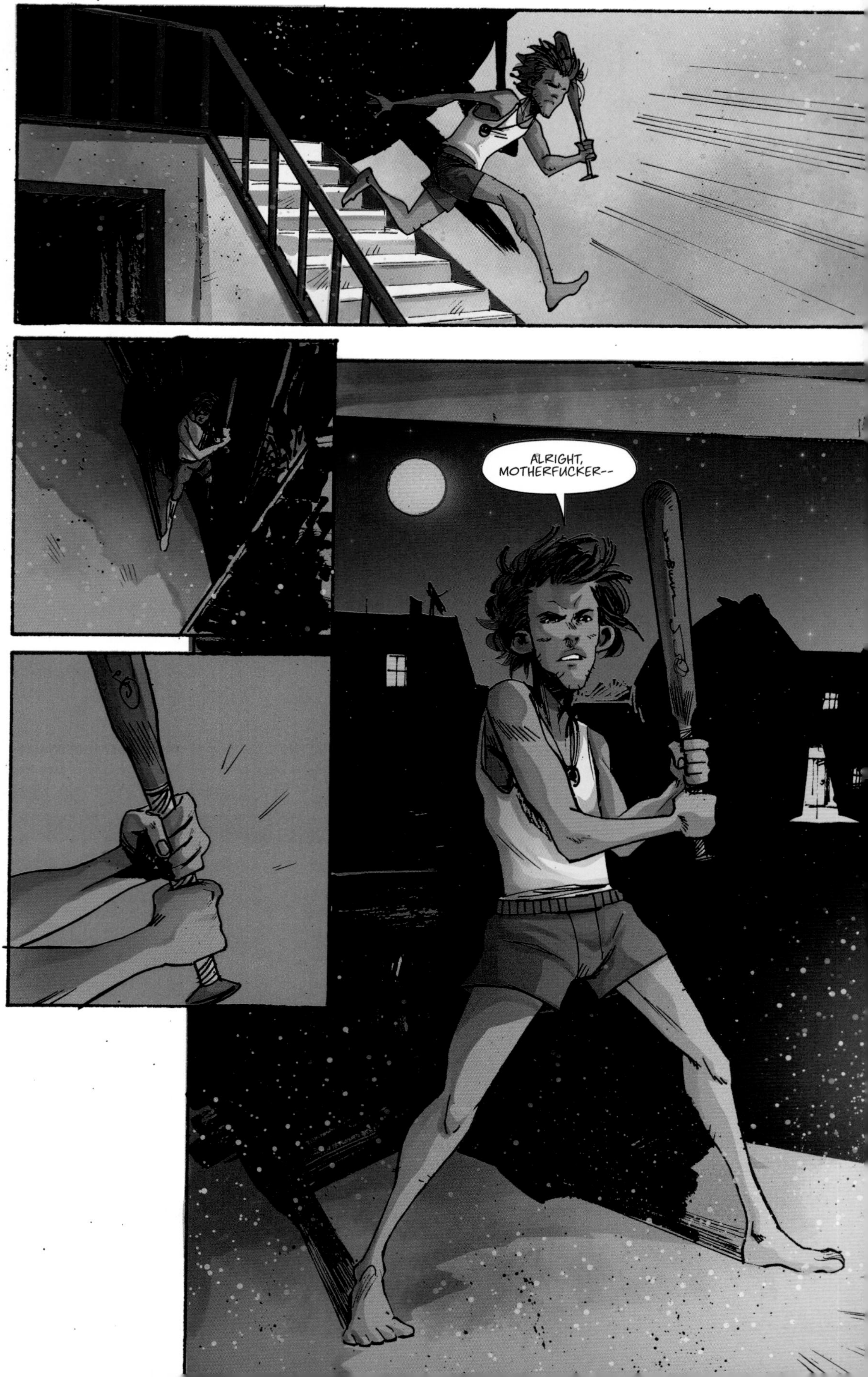
ALRIGHT, MOTHERFUCKER--

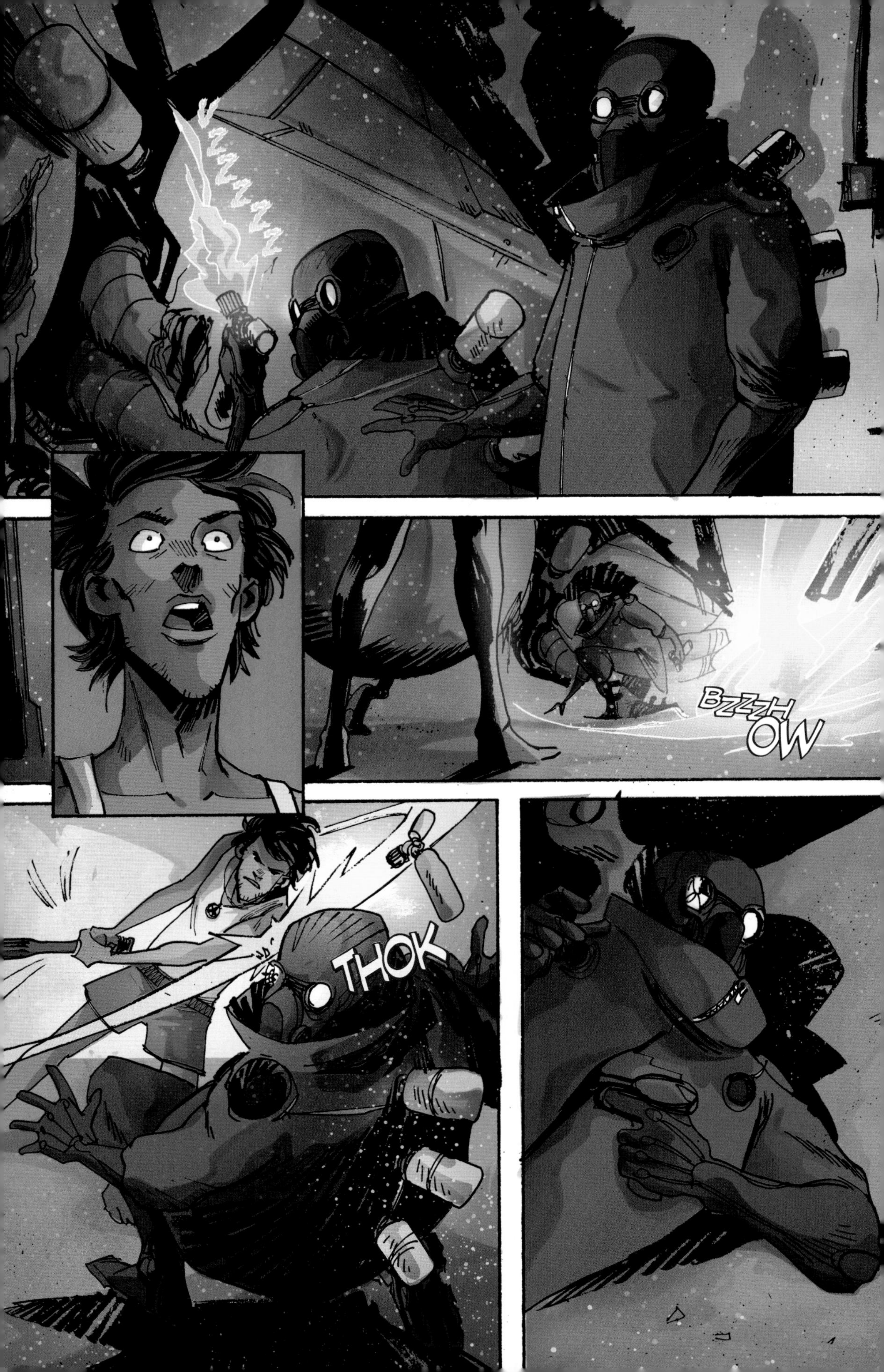
ZZZZZZ
BZZZH
OW
THOK

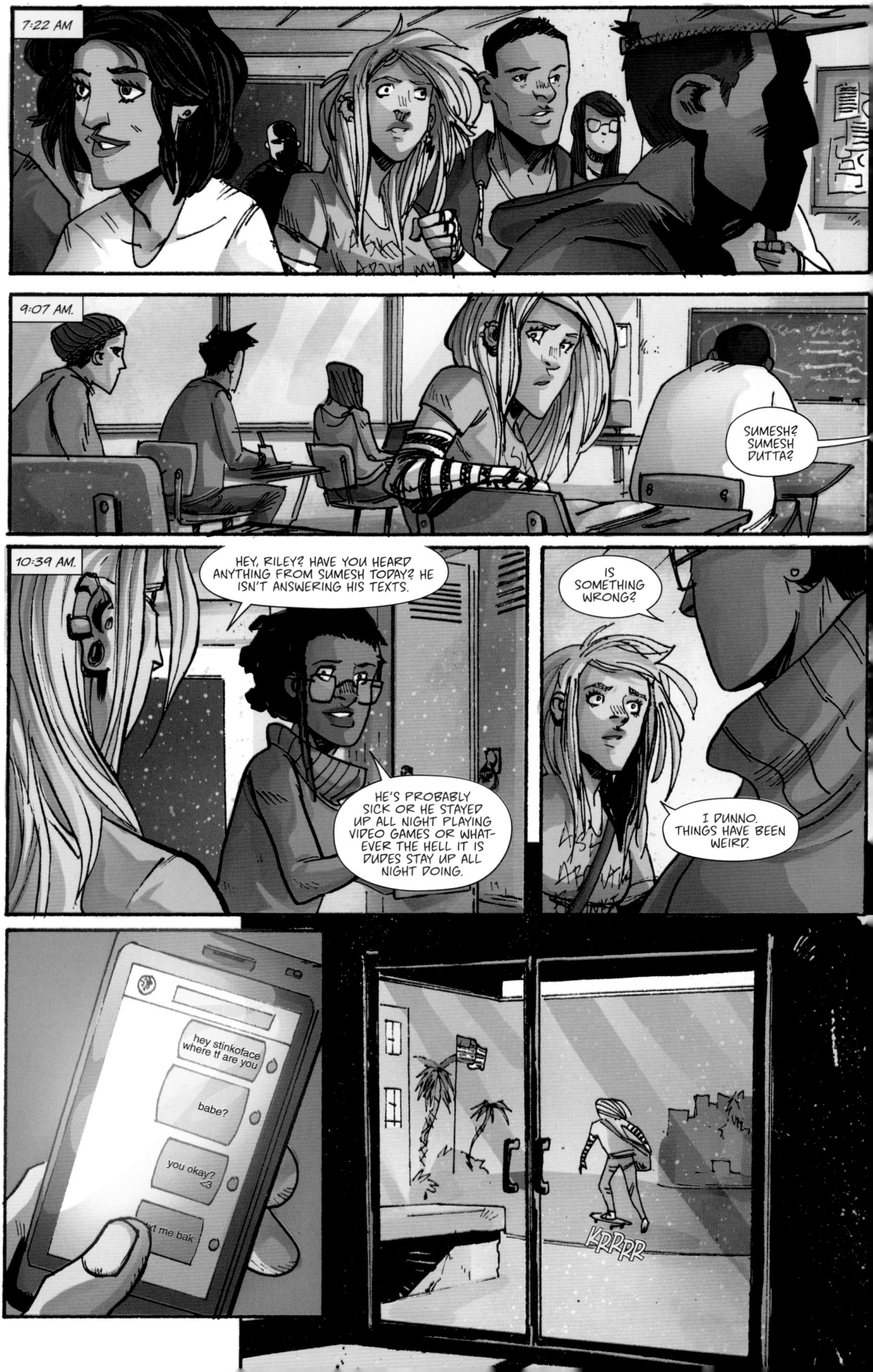
7:22 AM
9:07 AM.
SUMESH? SUMESH DUTTA?
10:39 AM.
HEY, RILEY? HAVE YOU HEARD ANYTHING FROM SUMESH TODAY? HE ISN'T ANSWERING HIS TEXTS.
HE'S PROBABLY SICK OR HE STAYED UP ALL NIGHT PLAYING VIDEO GAMES OR WHAT-EVER THE HELL IT IS DUDES STAY UP ALL NIGHT DOING.
IS SOMETHING WRONG?
I DUNNO. THINGS HAVE BEEN WEIRD.
hey stinkoface where tf are you
babe?
you okay? <3
KRRRR

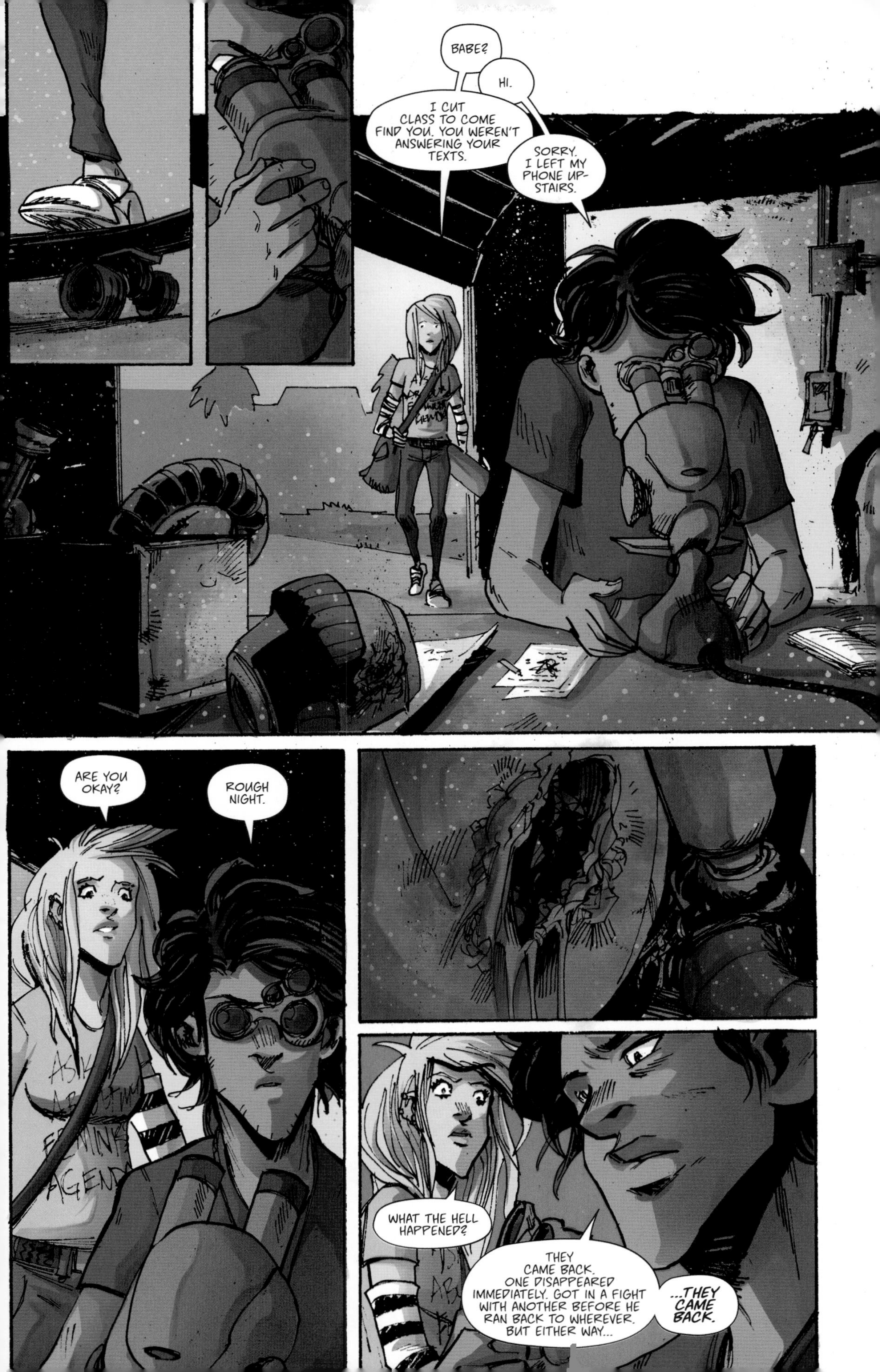
BABE?
HI.
I CUT CLASS TO COME FIND YOU. YOU WEREN'T ANSWERING YOUR TEXTS.
SORRY. I LEFT MY PHONE UP-STAIRS.
ARE YOU OKAY?
ROUGH NIGHT.
WHAT THE HELL HAPPENED?
THEY CAME BACK. ONE DISAPPEARED IMMEDIATELY. GOT IN A FIGHT WITH ANOTHER BEFORE HE RAN BACK TO WHEREVER. BUT EITHER WAY...
...THEY CAME BACK.

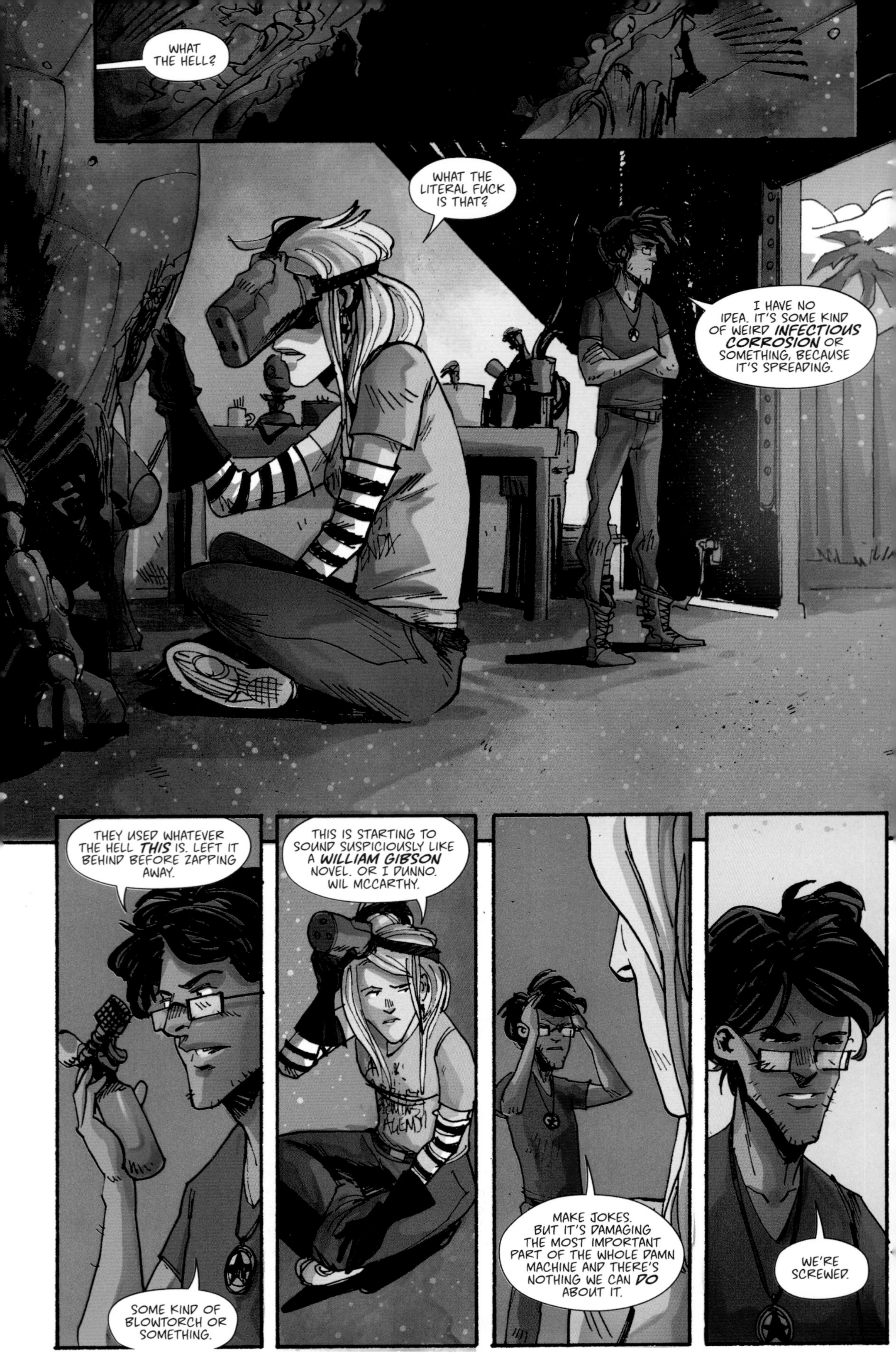
WHAT THE HELL?
WHAT THE LITERAL FUCK IS THAT?
I HAVE NO IDEA. IT'S SOME KIND OF WEIRD INFECTIOUS CORROSION OR SOMETHING, BECAUSE IT'S SPREADING.
THEY USED WHATEVER THE HELL THIS IS. LEFT IT BEHIND BEFORE ZAPPING AWAY.
SOME KIND OF BLOWTORCH OR SOMETHING.
THIS IS STARTING TO SOUND SUSPICIOUSLY LIKE A WILLIAM GIBSON NOVEL. OR I DUNNO. WIL MCCARTHY.
MAKE JOKES. BUT IT'S DAMAGING THE MOST IMPORTANT PART OF THE WHOLE DAMN MACHINE AND THERE'S NOTHING WE CAN DO ABOUT IT.
WE'RE SCREWED.

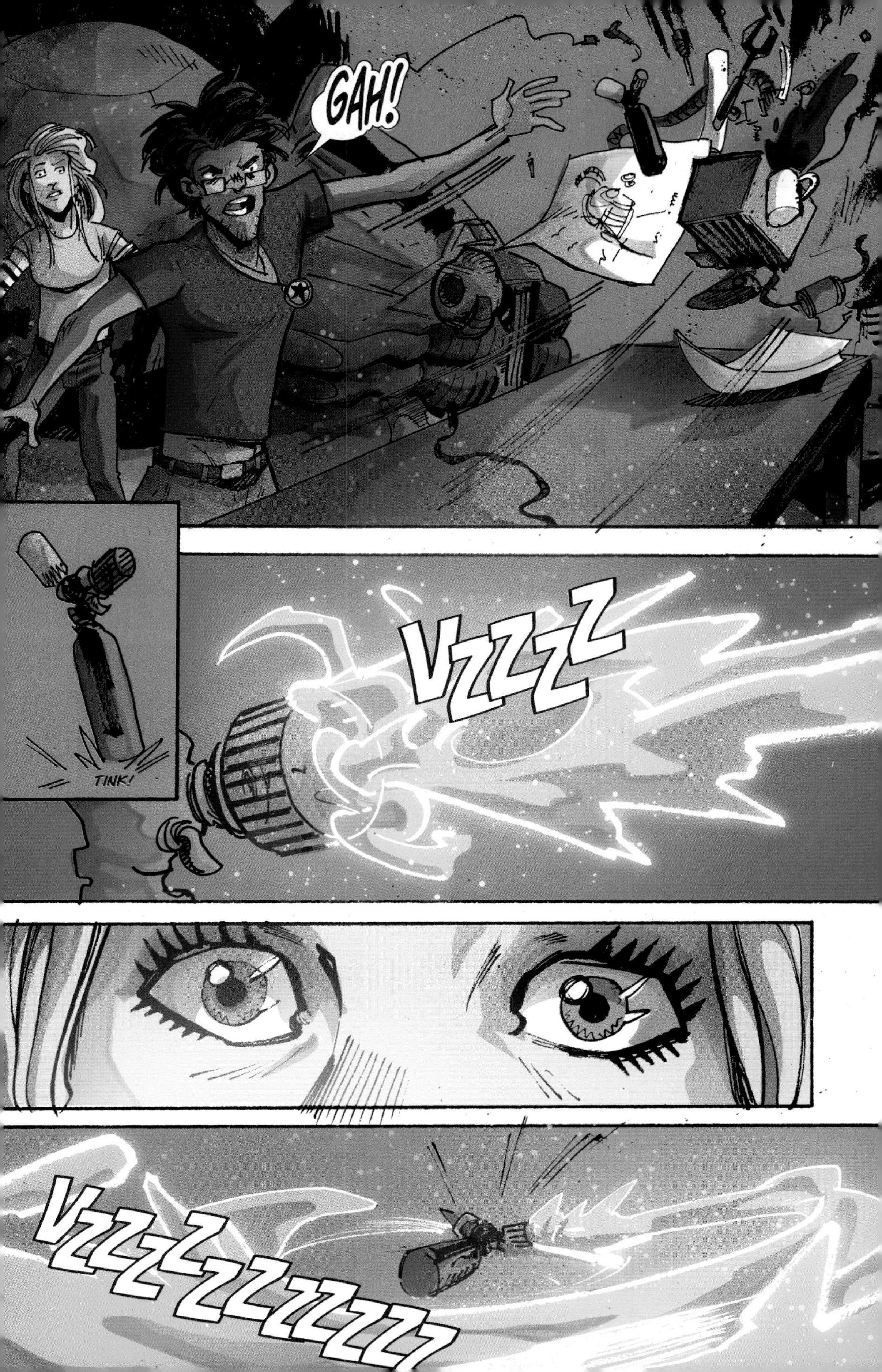
GAH!
TINK!
VZZZZ
VZZZZZZZZZZZ

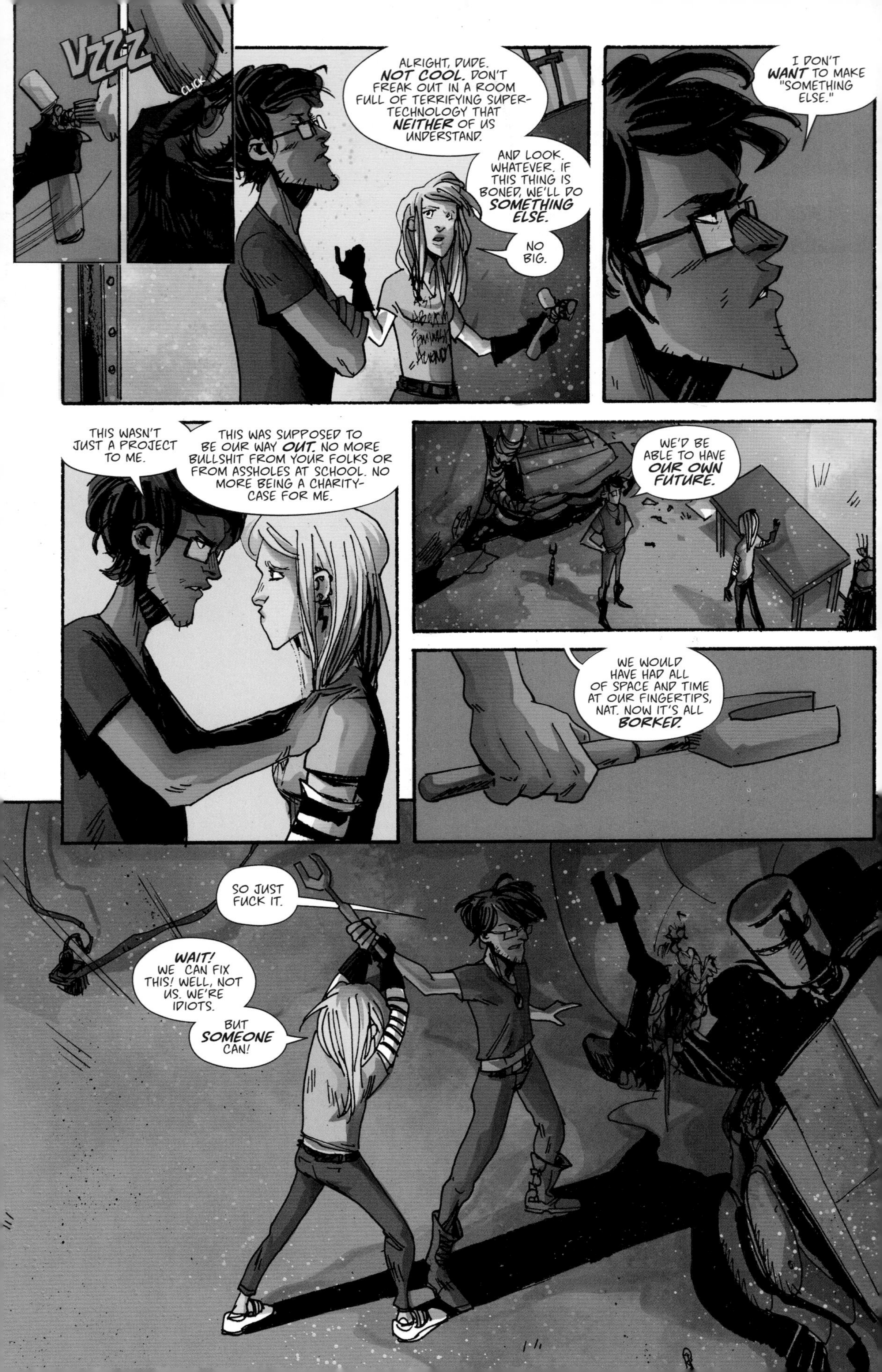
VZZZ
CLICK
ALRIGHT, DUDE. NOT COOL. DON'T FREAK OUT IN A ROOM FULL OF TERRIFYING SUPER-TECHNOLOGY THAT NEITHER OF US UNDERSTAND.
AND LOOK. WHATEVER. IF THIS THING IS BONED, WE'LL DO SOMETHING ELSE.
NO BIG.
I DON'T WANT TO MAKE "SOMETHING ELSE."
THIS WASN'T JUST A PROJECT TO ME.
THIS WAS SUPPOSED TO BE OUR WAY OUT. NO MORE BULLSHIT FROM YOUR FOLKS OR FROM ASSHOLES AT SCHOOL. NO MORE BEING A CHARITY-CASE FOR ME.
WE'D BE ABLE TO HAVE OUR OWN FUTURE.
WE WOULD HAVE HAD ALL OF SPACE AND TIME AT OUR FINGERTIPS, NAT. NOW IT'S ALL BORKED.
SO JUST FUCK IT.
WAIT! WE CAN FIX THIS! WELL, NOT US. WE'RE IDIOTS.
BUT SOMEONE CAN!

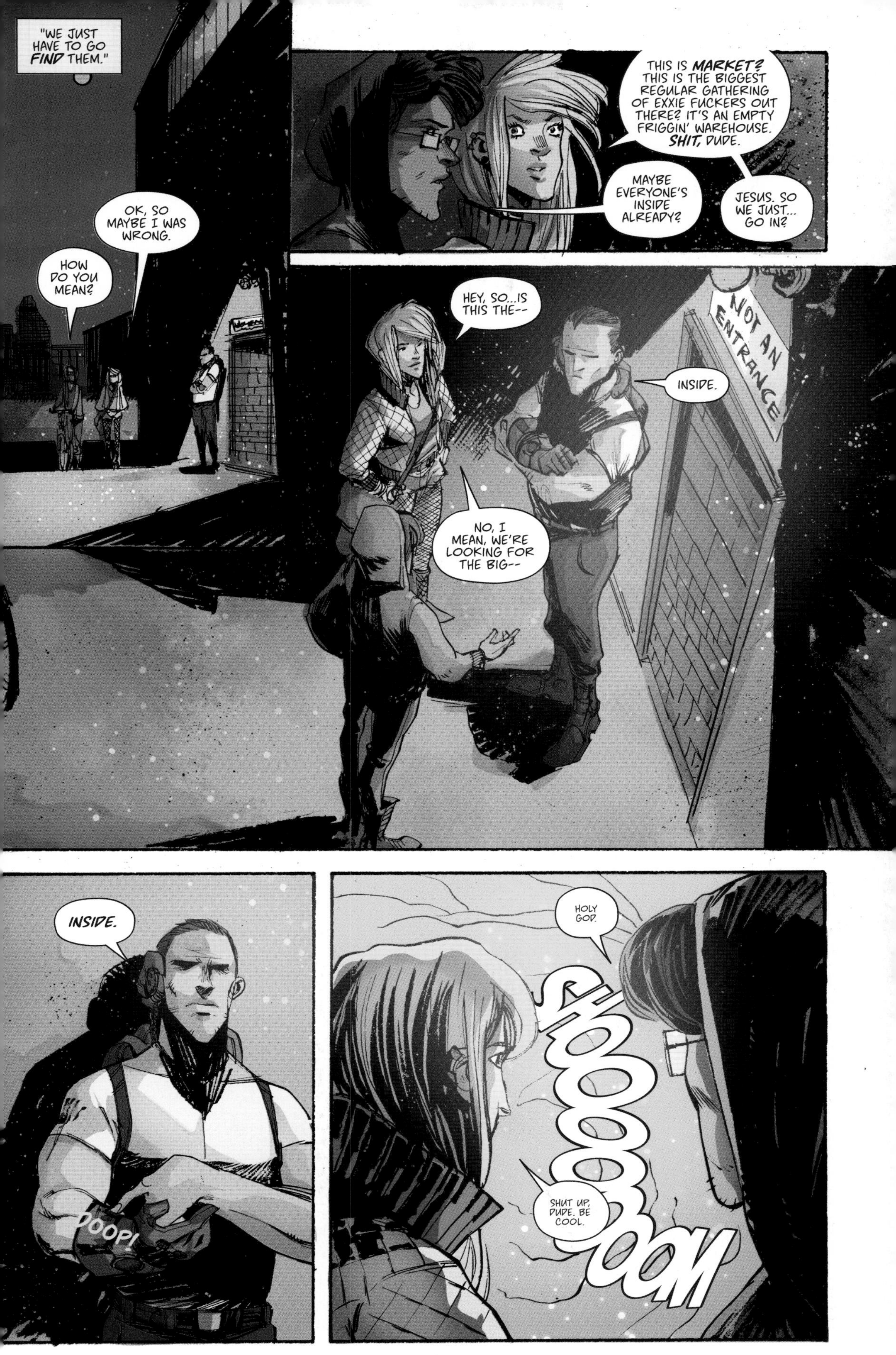
"WE JUST HAVE TO GO FIND THEM."
THIS IS MARKET? THIS IS THE BIGGEST REGULAR GATHERING OF EXXIE FUCKERS OUT THERE? IT'S AN EMPTY FRIGGIN' WAREHOUSE. SHIT, DUDE.
MAYBE EVERYONE'S INSIDE ALREADY?
JESUS. SO WE JUST... GO IN?
OK, SO MAYBE I WAS WRONG.
HOW DO YOU MEAN?
HEY, SO...IS THIS THE--
NOT AN ENTRANCE
INSIDE.
NO, I MEAN, WE'RE LOOKING FOR THE BIG--
INSIDE.
DOOP!
HOLY GOD.
SHOOOOOOOOM
SHUT UP, DUDE. BE COOL.

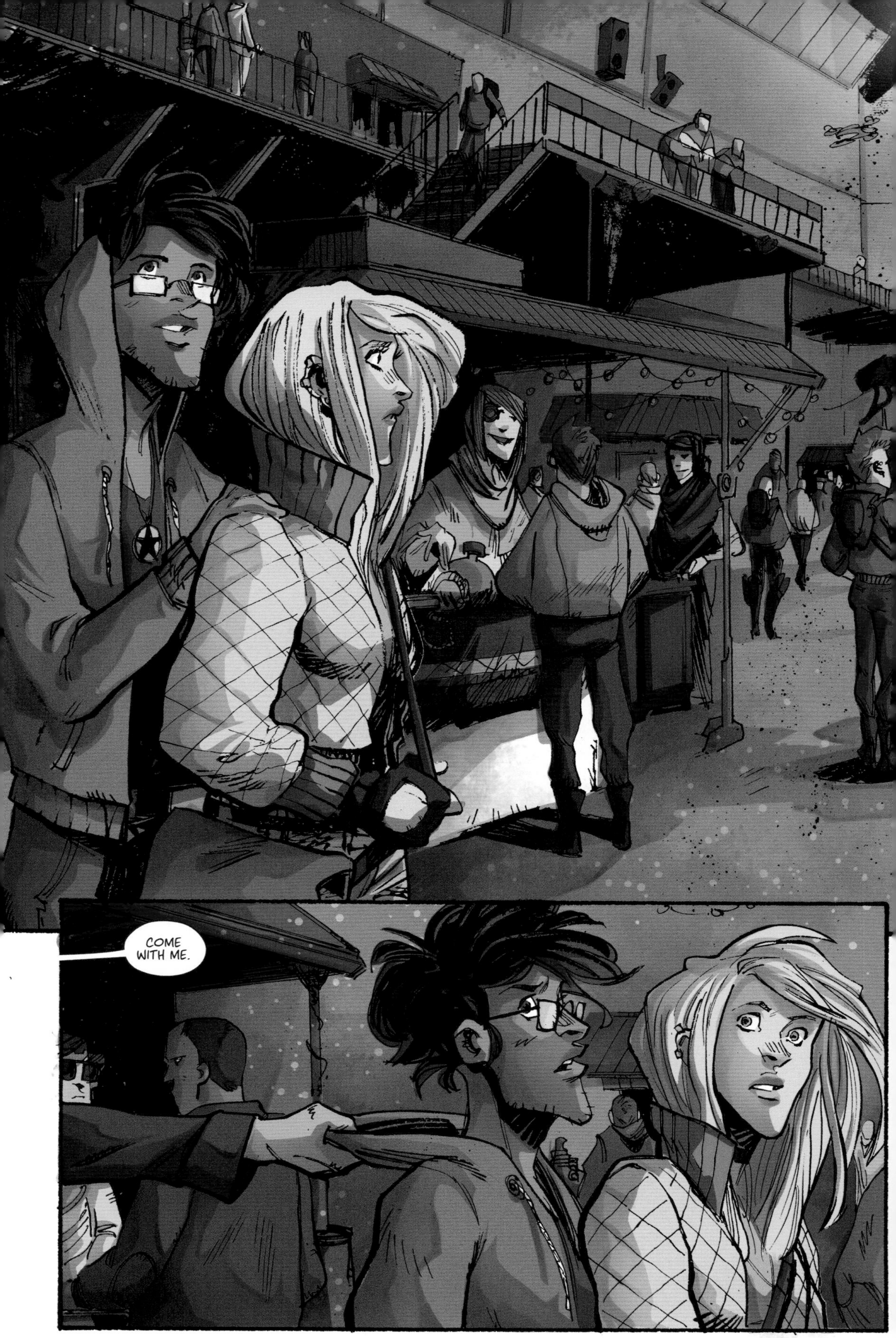
COME WITH ME.

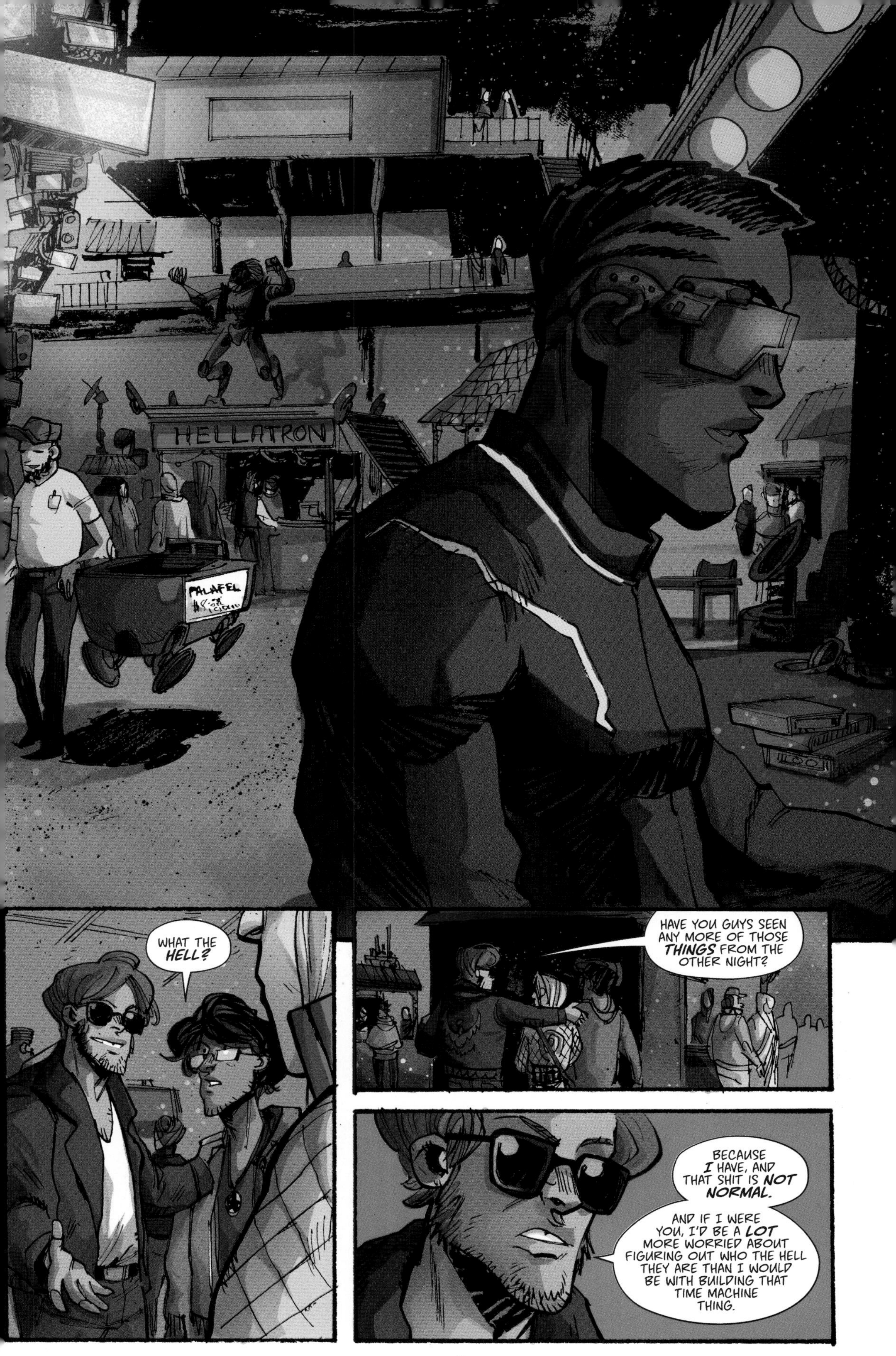
HELLATRON
FALAFEL
WHAT THE HELL?
HAVE YOU GUYS SEEN ANY MORE OF THOSE THINGS FROM THE OTHER NIGHT?
BECAUSE I HAVE, AND THAT SHIT IS NOT NORMAL.
AND IF I WERE YOU, I'D BE A LOT MORE WORRIED ABOUT FIGURING OUT WHO THE HELL THEY ARE THAN I WOULD BE WITH BUILDING THAT TIME MACHINE THING.

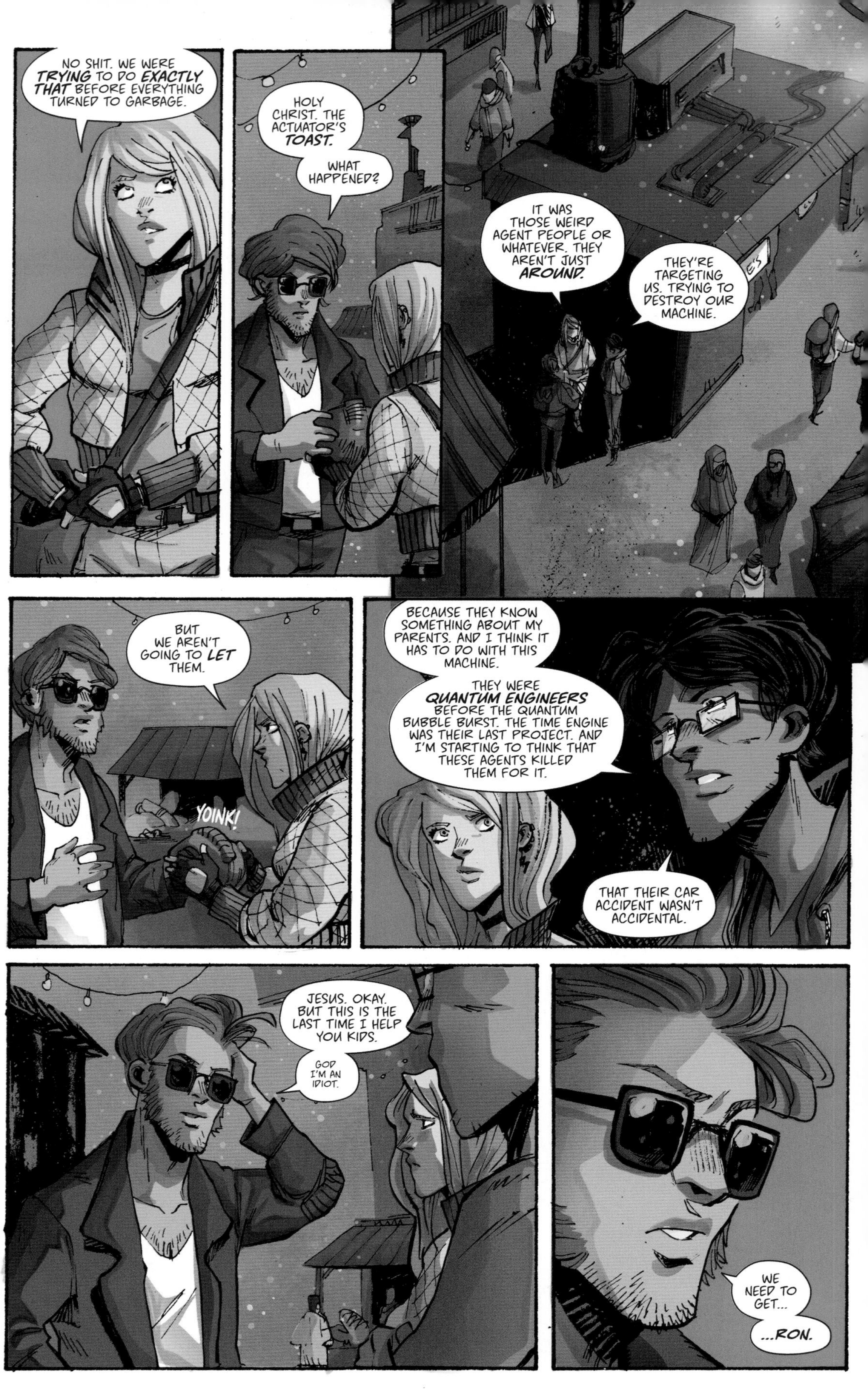
NO SHIT. WE WERE TRYING TO DO EXACTLY THAT BEFORE EVERYTHING TURNED TO GARBAGE.
HOLY CHRIST. THE ACTUATOR'S TOAST.
WHAT HAPPENED?
IT WAS THOSE WEIRD AGENT PEOPLE OR WHATEVER. THEY AREN'T JUST AROUND.
THEY'RE TARGETING US. TRYING TO DESTROY OUR MACHINE.
BUT WE AREN'T GOING TO LET THEM.
YOINK!
BECAUSE THEY KNOW SOMETHING ABOUT MY PARENTS. AND I THINK IT HAS TO DO WITH THIS MACHINE.
THEY WERE QUANTUM ENGINEERS BEFORE THE QUANTUM BUBBLE BURST. THE TIME ENGINE WAS THEIR LAST PROJECT. AND I'M STARTING TO THINK THAT THESE AGENTS KILLED THEM FOR IT.
THAT THEIR CAR ACCIDENT WASN'T ACCIDENTAL.
JESUS. OKAY. BUT THIS IS THE LAST TIME I HELP YOU KIDS.
GOD I'M AN IDIOT.
WE NEED TO GET...
...RON.

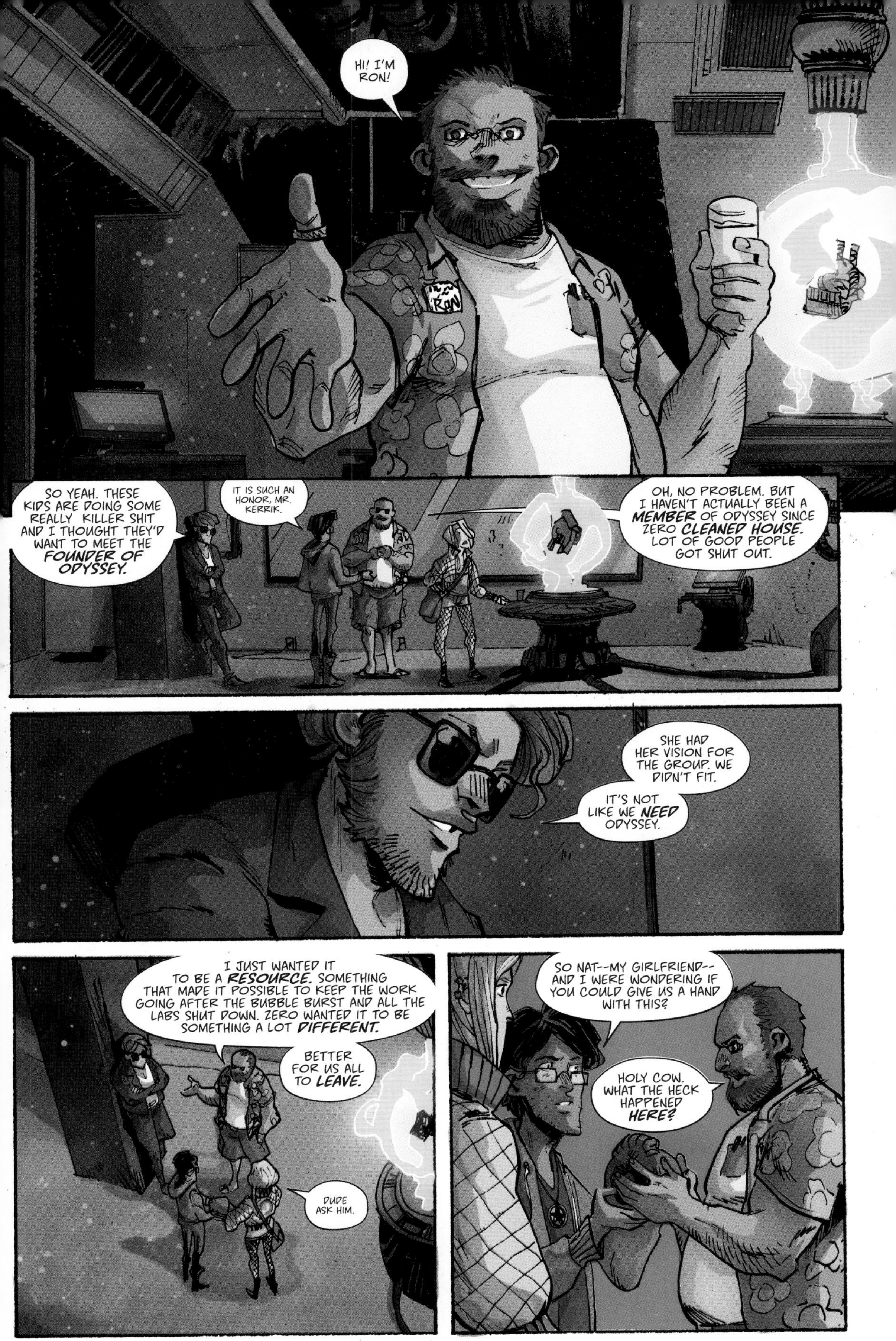
HI! I'M RON!
RON
SO YEAH. THESE KIDS ARE DOING SOME REALLY KILLER SHIT AND I THOUGHT THEY'D WANT TO MEET THE FOUNDER OF ODYSSEY.
IT IS SUCH AN HONOR, MR. KERRIK.
OH, NO PROBLEM. BUT I HAVEN'T ACTUALLY BEEN A MEMBER OF ODYSSEY SINCE ZERO CLEANED HOUSE. LOT OF GOOD PEOPLE GOT SHUT OUT.
SHE HAD HER VISION FOR THE GROUP. WE DIDN'T FIT.
IT'S NOT LIKE WE NEED ODYSSEY.
I JUST WANTED IT TO BE A RESOURCE. SOMETHING THAT MADE IT POSSIBLE TO KEEP THE WORK GOING AFTER THE BUBBLE BURST AND ALL THE LABS SHUT DOWN. ZERO WANTED IT TO BE SOMETHING A LOT DIFFERENT.
BETTER FOR US ALL TO LEAVE.
DUDE ASK HIM.
SO NAT--MY GIRLFRIEND--AND I WERE WONDERING IF YOU COULD GIVE US A HAND WITH THIS?
HOLY COW. WHAT THE HECK HAPPENED HERE?

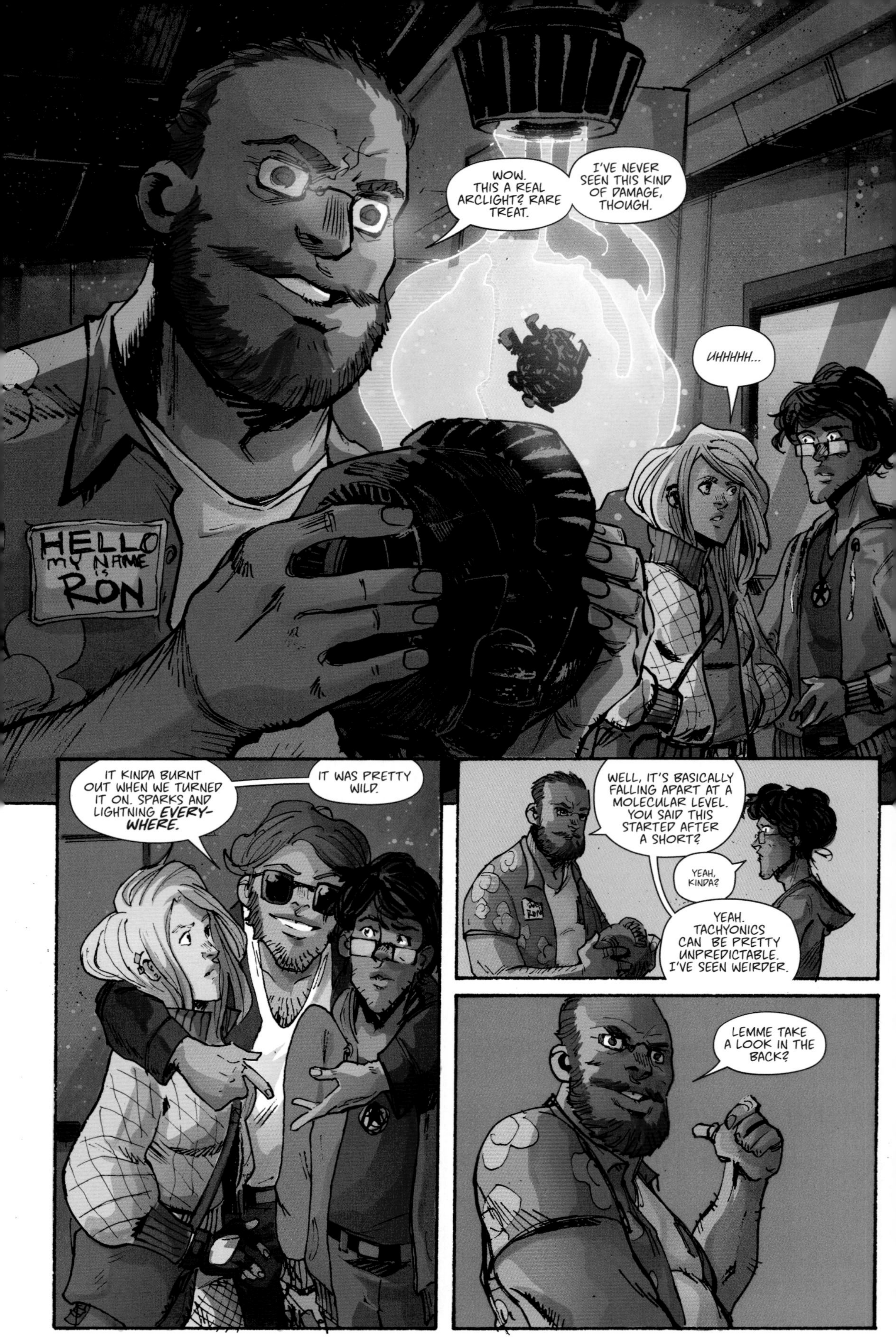
HELLO my name is RON
WOW. THIS A REAL ARCLIGHT? RARE TREAT.
I'VE NEVER SEEN THIS KIND OF DAMAGE, THOUGH.
UHHHHH...
IT KINDA BURNT OUT WHEN WE TURNED IT ON. SPARKS AND LIGHTNING EVERY-WHERE.
IT WAS PRETTY WILD.
WELL, IT'S BASICALLY FALLING APART AT A MOLECULAR LEVEL. YOU SAID THIS STARTED AFTER A SHORT?
YEAH, KINDA?
YEAH. TACHYONICS CAN BE PRETTY UNPREDICTABLE. I'VE SEEN WEIRDER.
LEMME TAKE A LOOK IN THE BACK?

WE'RE GONNA HAVE TO TOUCH BASE ABOUT WHAT THE HELL THOSE THINGS ARE, BUT WE CAN'T DO *ANYTHING* UNTIL WE GET THIS THING WORKING. I'LL SWING BY THE GARAGE TOMORROW

COOL?

LATER.

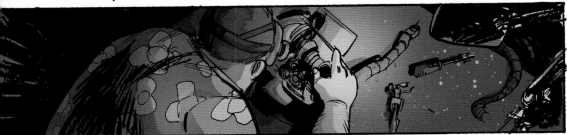

FSSSHH

SO YOU WANNA GO DICK AROUND?

SURE.

WE COULD MAYBE FIND A SPOT AND MAKE OUT--

DUDE, I ALREADY SAID SURE.

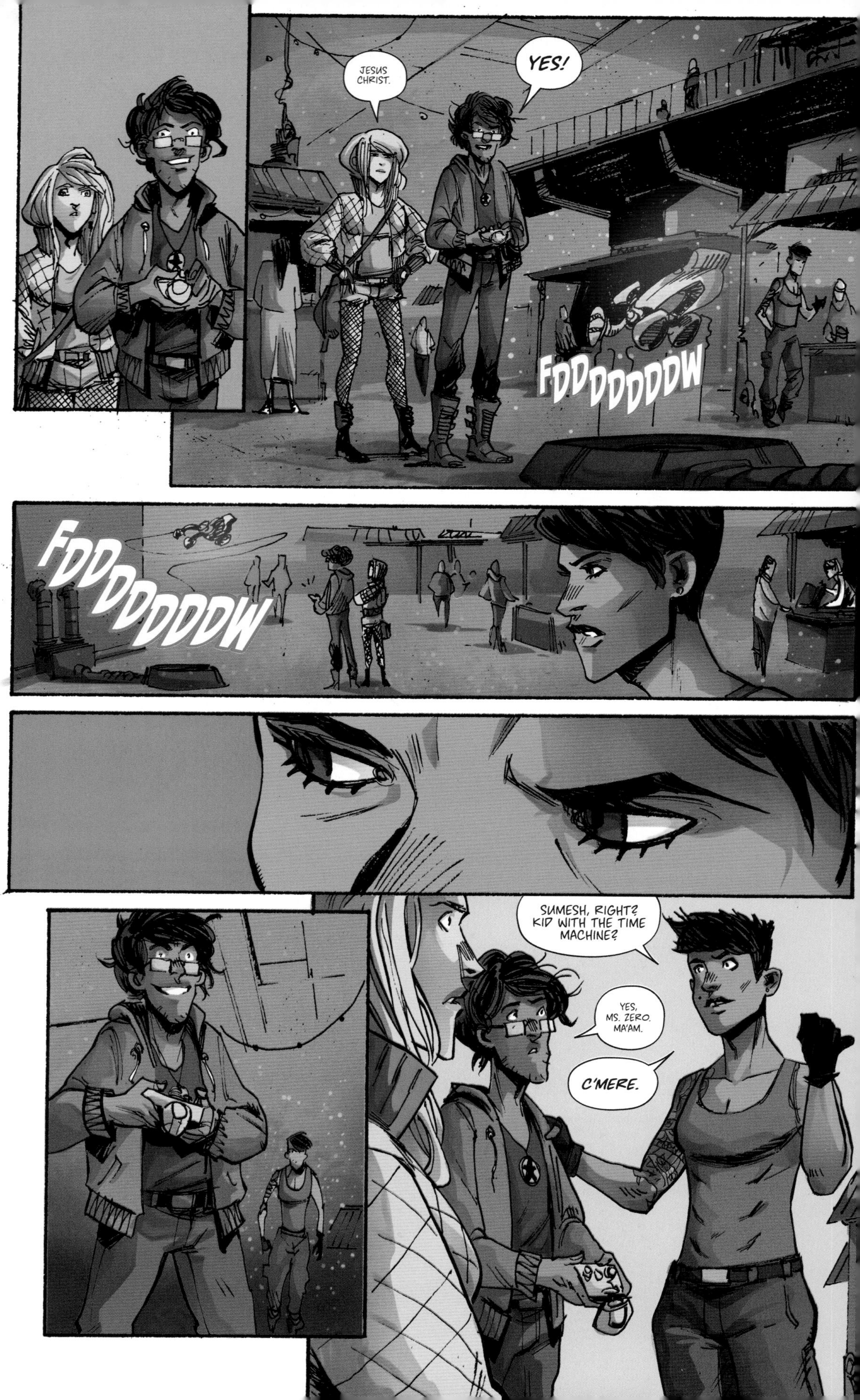
JESUS CHRIST.
YES!
FDDDDDDDW
FDDDDDDDW
SUMESH, RIGHT? KID WITH THE TIME MACHINE?
YES, MS. ZERO. MA'AM.
C'MERE.

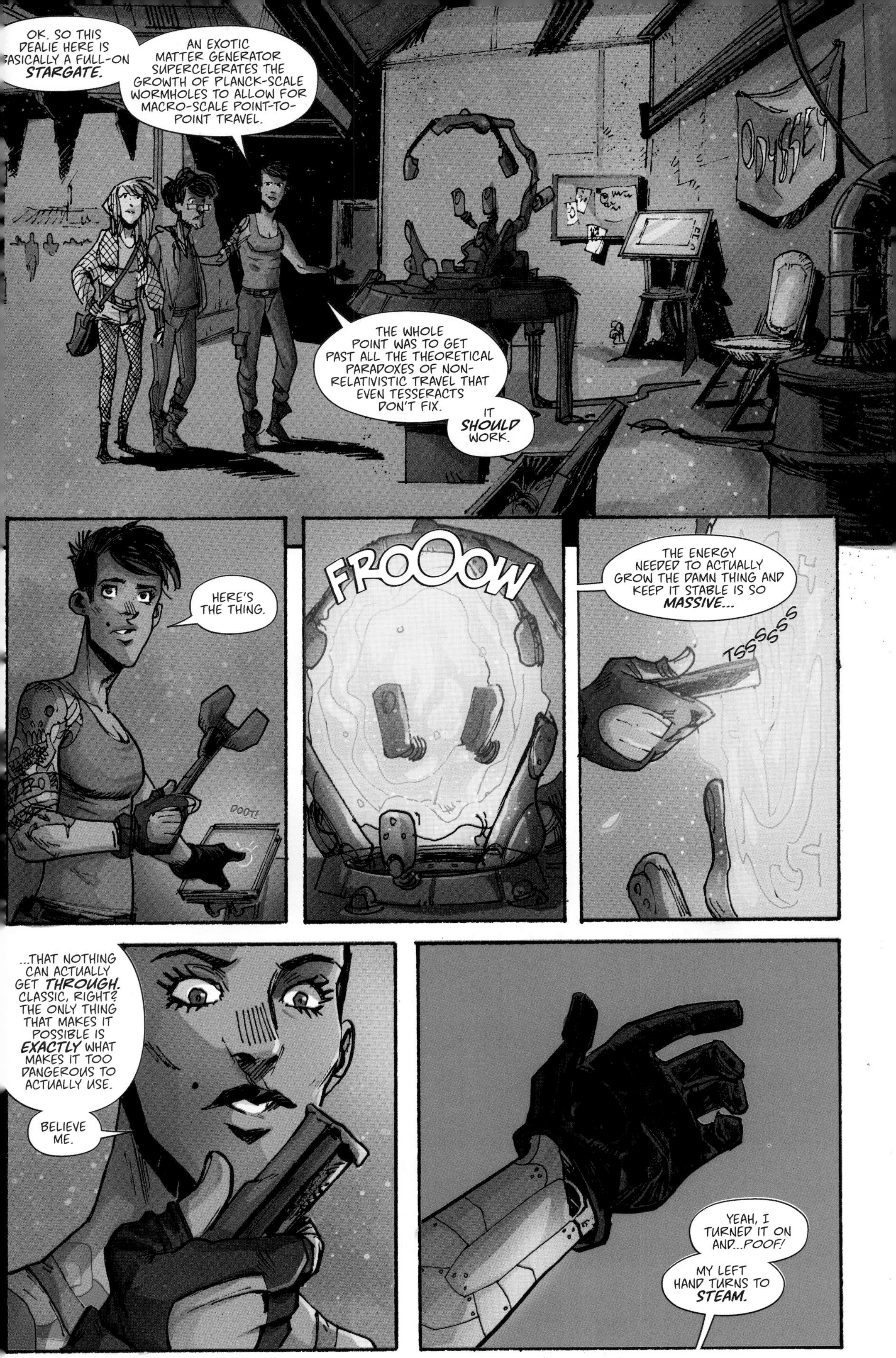
OK. SO THIS DEALIE HERE IS BASICALLY A FULL-ON **STARGATE.**
AN EXOTIC MATTER GENERATOR SUPERCELERATES THE GROWTH OF PLANCK-SCALE WORMHOLES TO ALLOW FOR MACRO-SCALE POINT-TO-POINT TRAVEL.
ODYSSEY
THE WHOLE POINT WAS TO GET PAST ALL THE THEORETICAL PARADOXES OF NON-RELATIVISTIC TRAVEL THAT EVEN TESSERACTS DON'T FIX.
IT **SHOULD** WORK.
HERE'S THE THING.
DOOT!
FROOOW
THE ENERGY NEEDED TO ACTUALLY GROW THE DAMN THING AND KEEP IT STABLE IS SO **MASSIVE...**
TSSSSSS
...THAT NOTHING CAN ACTUALLY GET **THROUGH.** CLASSIC, RIGHT? THE ONLY THING THAT MAKES IT POSSIBLE IS **EXACTLY** WHAT MAKES IT TOO DANGEROUS TO ACTUALLY USE.
BELIEVE ME.
YEAH, I TURNED IT ON AND...POOF!
MY LEFT HAND TURNS TO **STEAM.**

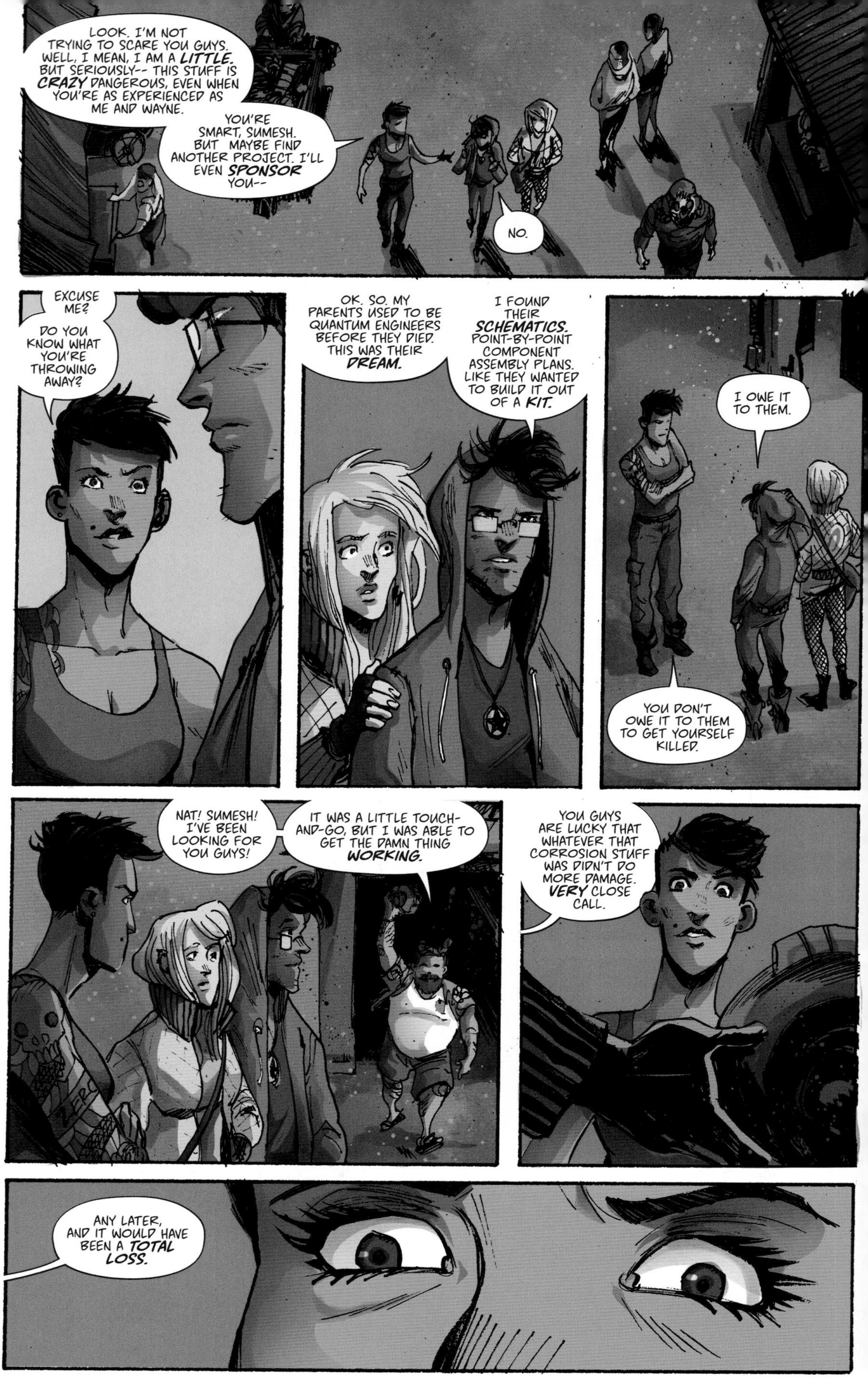
LOOK. I'M NOT TRYING TO SCARE YOU GUYS. WELL, I MEAN, I AM A LITTLE. BUT SERIOUSLY-- THIS STUFF IS CRAZY DANGEROUS, EVEN WHEN YOU'RE AS EXPERIENCED AS ME AND WAYNE.
YOU'RE SMART, SUMESH. BUT MAYBE FIND ANOTHER PROJECT. I'LL EVEN SPONSOR YOU--
NO.
EXCUSE ME?
DO YOU KNOW WHAT YOU'RE THROWING AWAY?
OK. SO. MY PARENTS USED TO BE QUANTUM ENGINEERS BEFORE THEY DIED. THIS WAS THEIR DREAM.
I FOUND THEIR SCHEMATICS. POINT-BY-POINT COMPONENT ASSEMBLY PLANS. LIKE THEY WANTED TO BUILD IT OUT OF A KIT.
I OWE IT TO THEM.
YOU DON'T OWE IT TO THEM TO GET YOURSELF KILLED.
NAT! SUMESH! I'VE BEEN LOOKING FOR YOU GUYS!
IT WAS A LITTLE TOUCH-AND-GO, BUT I WAS ABLE TO GET THE DAMN THING WORKING.
YOU GUYS ARE LUCKY THAT WHATEVER THAT CORROSION STUFF WAS DIDN'T DO MORE DAMAGE. VERY CLOSE CALL.
ANY LATER, AND IT WOULD HAVE BEEN A TOTAL LOSS.

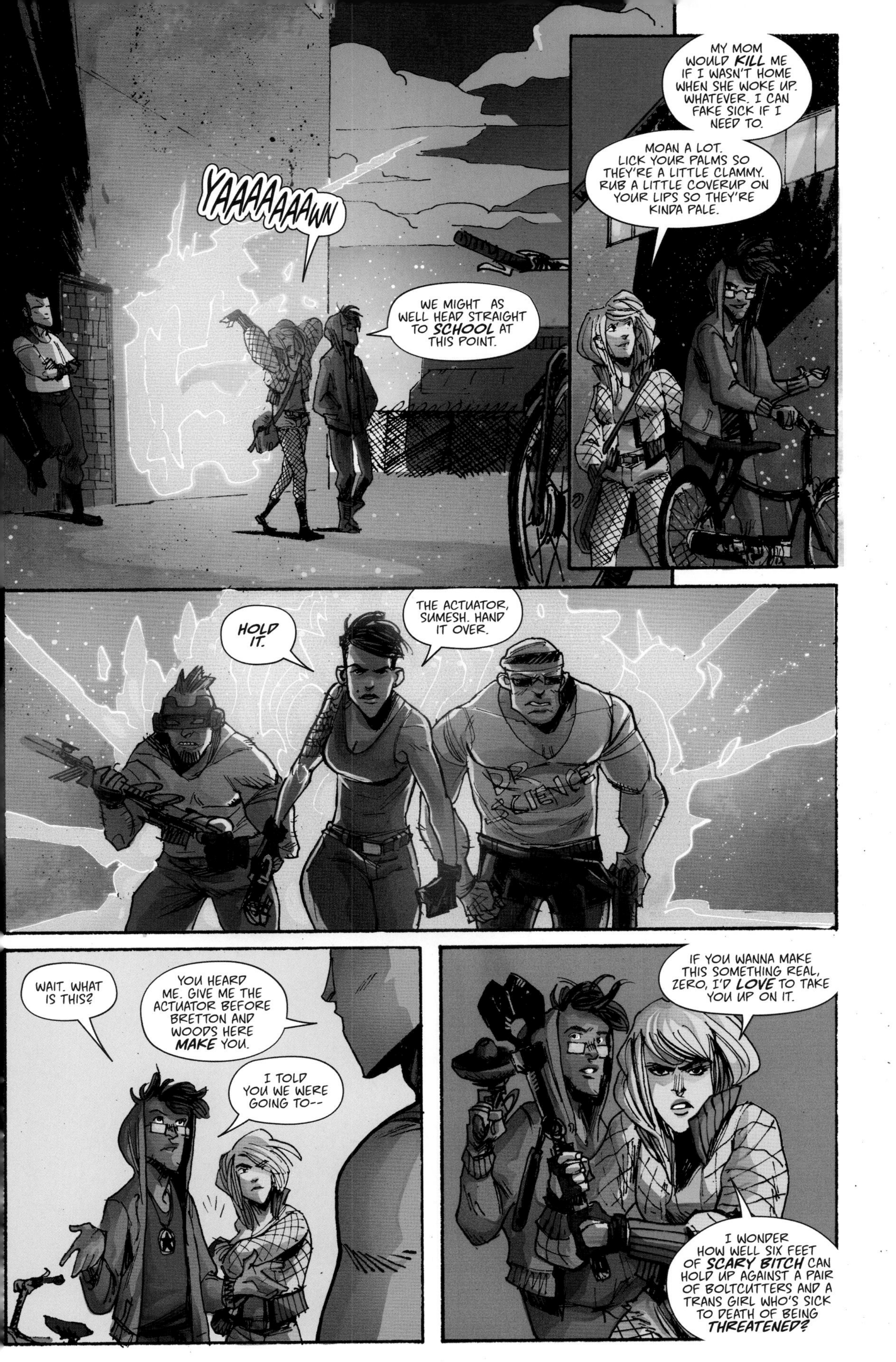
YAAAAAAAWN
WE MIGHT AS WELL HEAD STRAIGHT TO SCHOOL AT THIS POINT.
MY MOM WOULD KILL ME IF I WASN'T HOME WHEN SHE WOKE UP. WHATEVER. I CAN FAKE SICK IF I NEED TO.
MOAN A LOT. LICK YOUR PALMS SO THEY'RE A LITTLE CLAMMY. RUB A LITTLE COVERUP ON YOUR LIPS SO THEY'RE KINDA PALE.
HOLD IT.
THE ACTUATOR, SUMESH. HAND IT OVER.
DR SCIENCE
WAIT. WHAT IS THIS?
YOU HEARD ME. GIVE ME THE ACTUATOR BEFORE BRETTON AND WOODS HERE MAKE YOU.
I TOLD YOU WE WERE GOING TO--
IF YOU WANNA MAKE THIS SOMETHING REAL, ZERO, I'D LOVE TO TAKE YOU UP ON IT.
I WONDER HOW WELL SIX FEET OF SCARY BITCH CAN HOLD UP AGAINST A PAIR OF BOLTCUTTERS AND A TRANS GIRL WHO'S SICK TO DEATH OF BEING THREATENED?

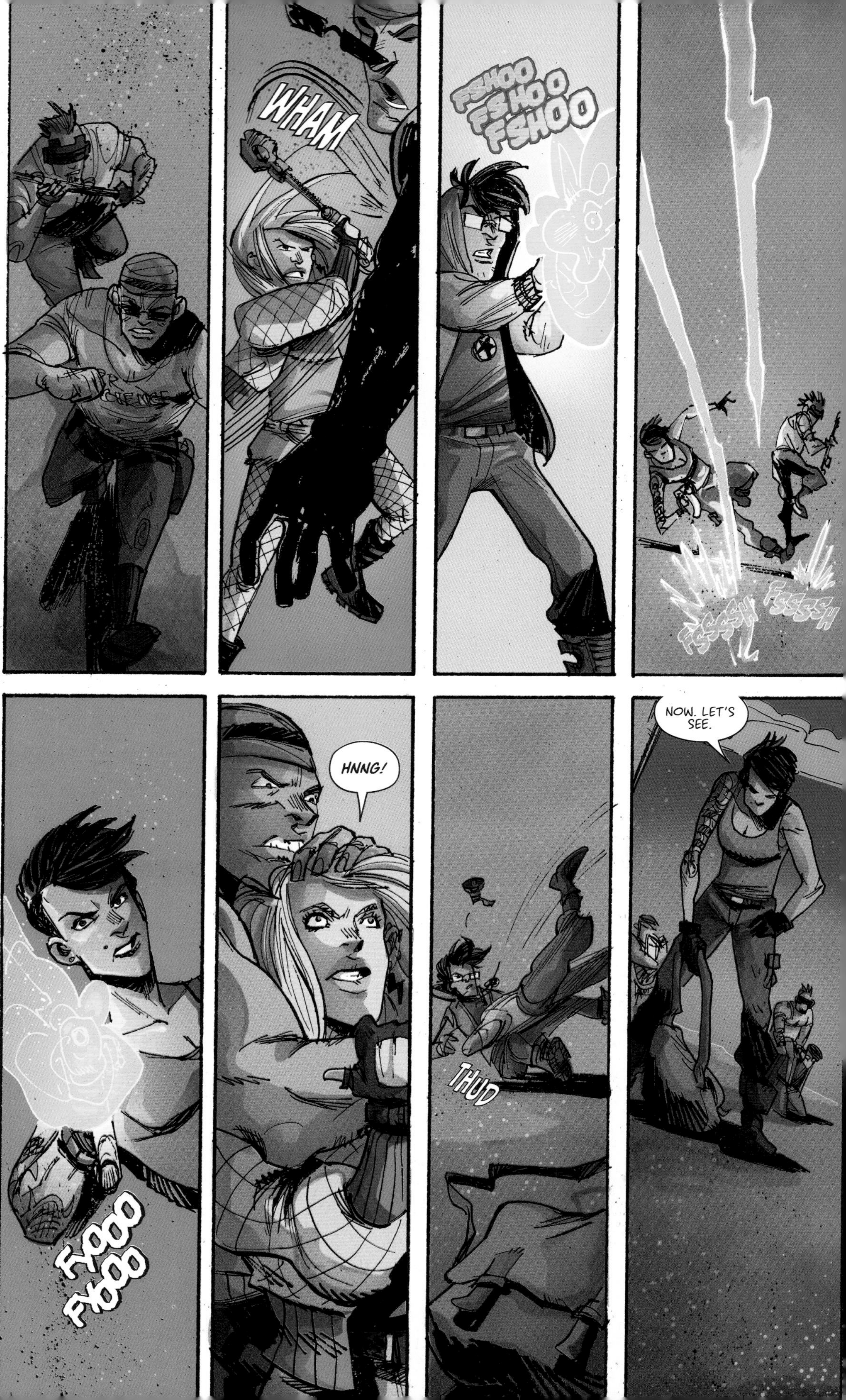
WHAM
FSHOO FSHOO FSHOO
FSSSH FSSSH
FYOOO FYOOO
HNNG!
THUD
NOW. LET'S SEE.

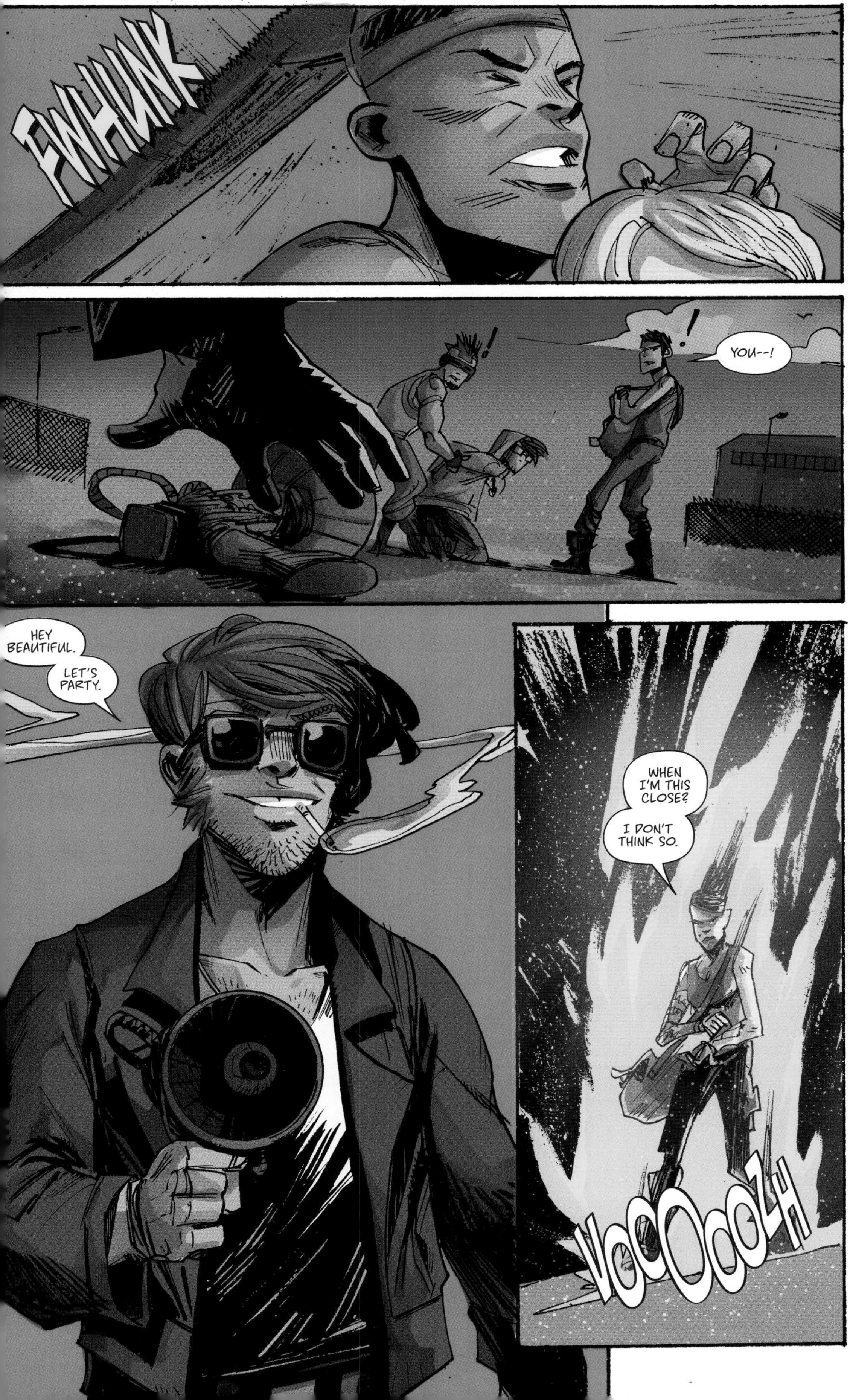
FWHUNK
!
!
YOU--!
HEY BEAUTIFUL.
LET'S PARTY.
WHEN I'M THIS CLOSE?
I DON'T THINK SO.
VOOOOOOZH

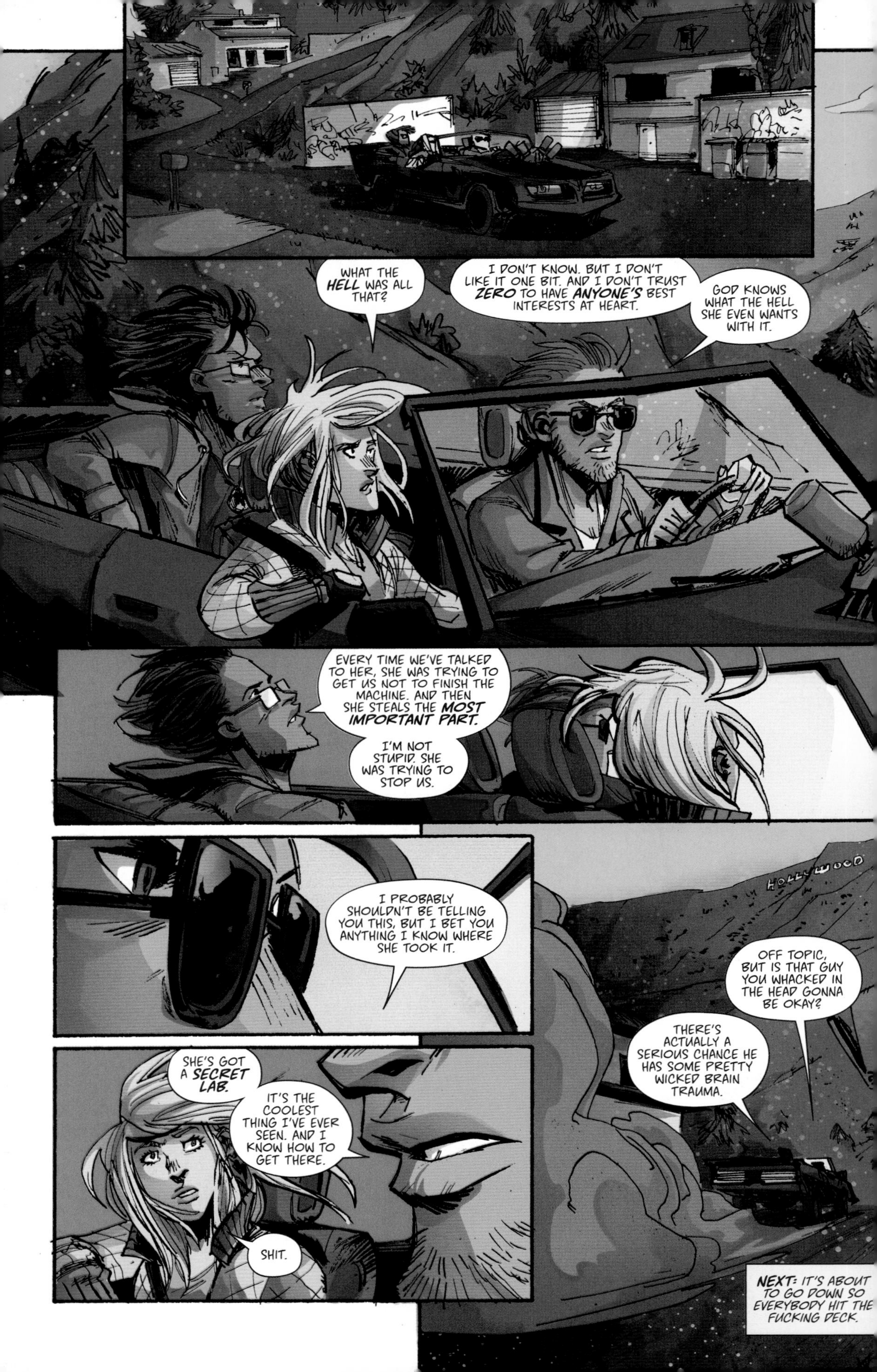

WHAT THE HELL WAS ALL THAT?
I DON'T KNOW. BUT I DON'T LIKE IT ONE BIT. AND I DON'T TRUST ZERO TO HAVE ANYONE'S BEST INTERESTS AT HEART.
GOD KNOWS WHAT THE HELL SHE EVEN WANTS WITH IT.
EVERY TIME WE'VE TALKED TO HER, SHE WAS TRYING TO GET US NOT TO FINISH THE MACHINE. AND THEN SHE STEALS THE MOST IMPORTANT PART.
I'M NOT STUPID. SHE WAS TRYING TO STOP US.
I PROBABLY SHOULDN'T BE TELLING YOU THIS, BUT I BET YOU ANYTHING I KNOW WHERE SHE TOOK IT.
SHE'S GOT A SECRET LAB.
IT'S THE COOLEST THING I'VE EVER SEEN. AND I KNOW HOW TO GET THERE.
SHIT.
HOLLYWOOD
OFF TOPIC, BUT IS THAT GUY YOU WHACKED IN THE HEAD GONNA BE OKAY?
THERE'S ACTUALLY A SERIOUS CHANCE HE HAS SOME PRETTY WICKED BRAIN TRAUMA.
NEXT: IT'S ABOUT TO GO DOWN SO EVERYBODY HIT THE FUCKING DECK.

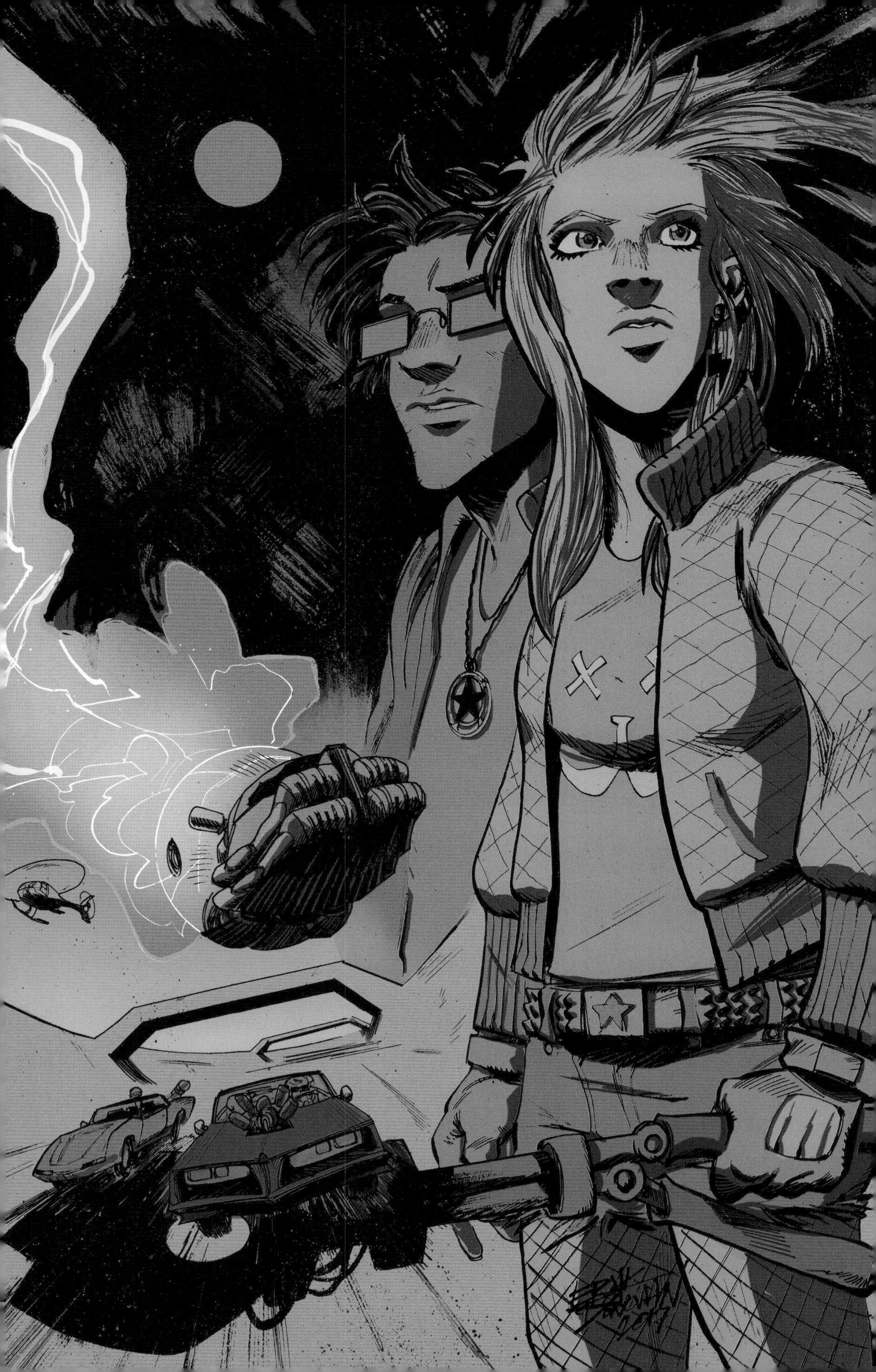

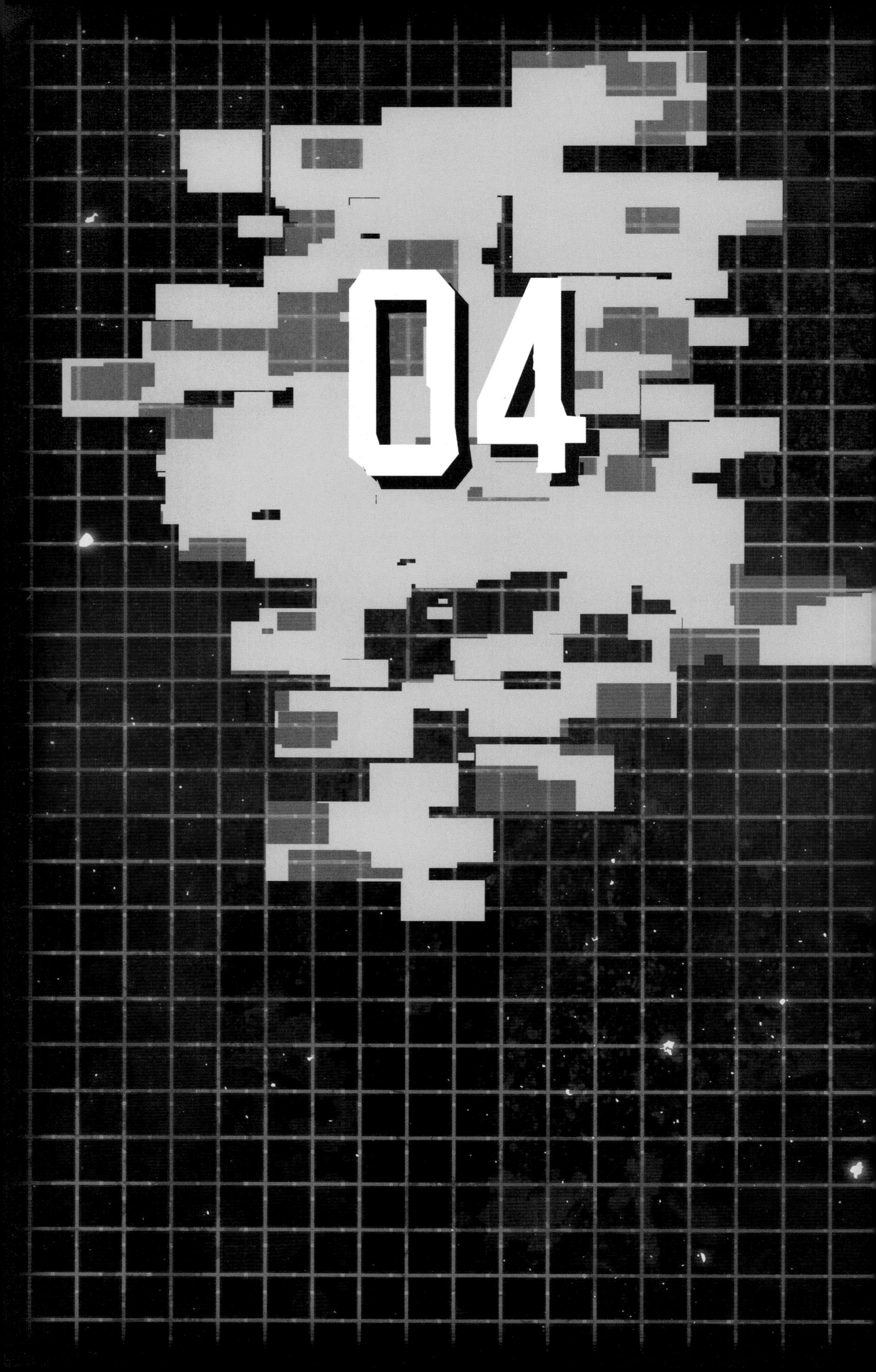
04

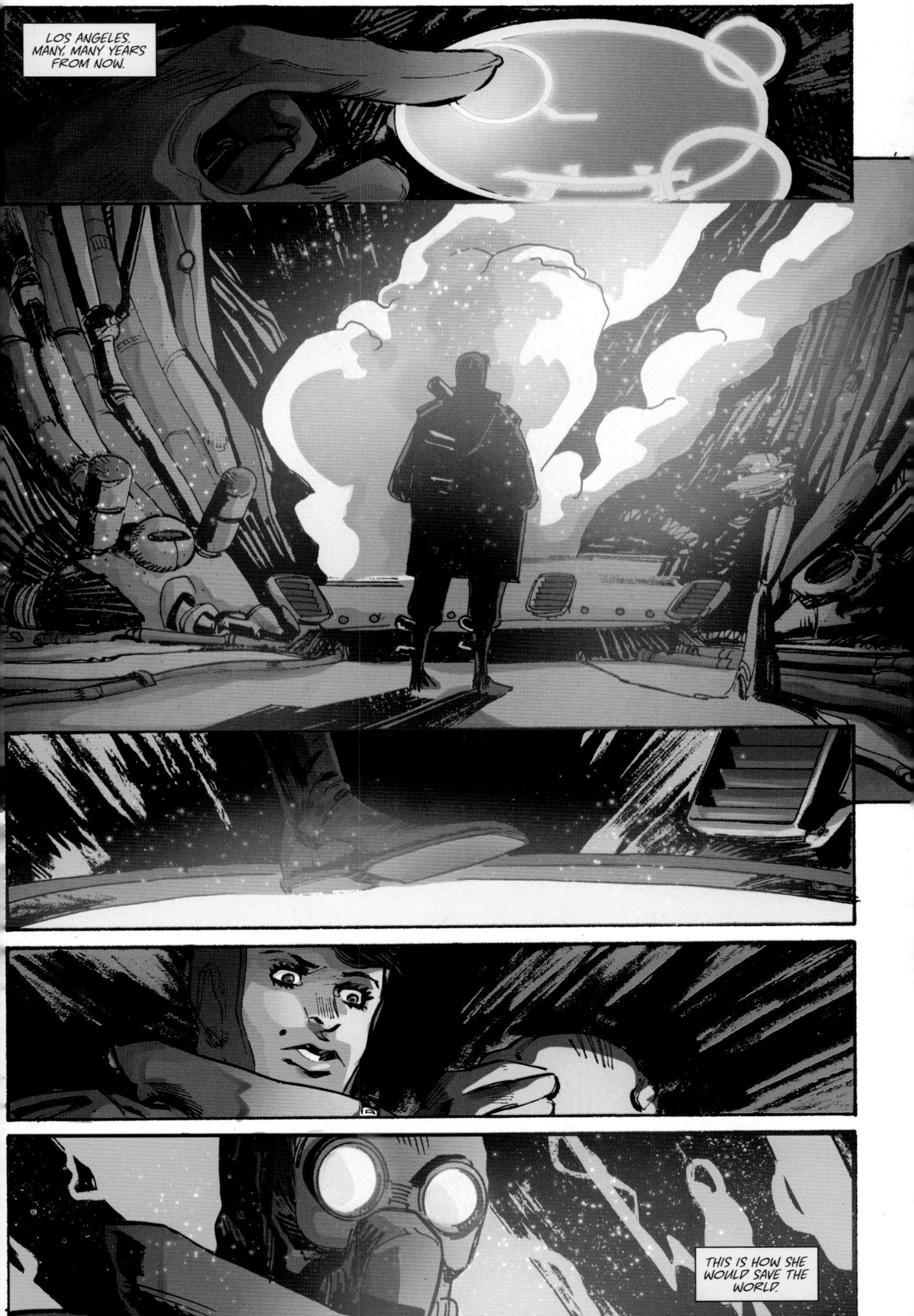
LOS ANGELES.
MANY, MANY YEARS
FROM NOW.
THIS IS HOW SHE
WOULD SAVE THE
WORLD.

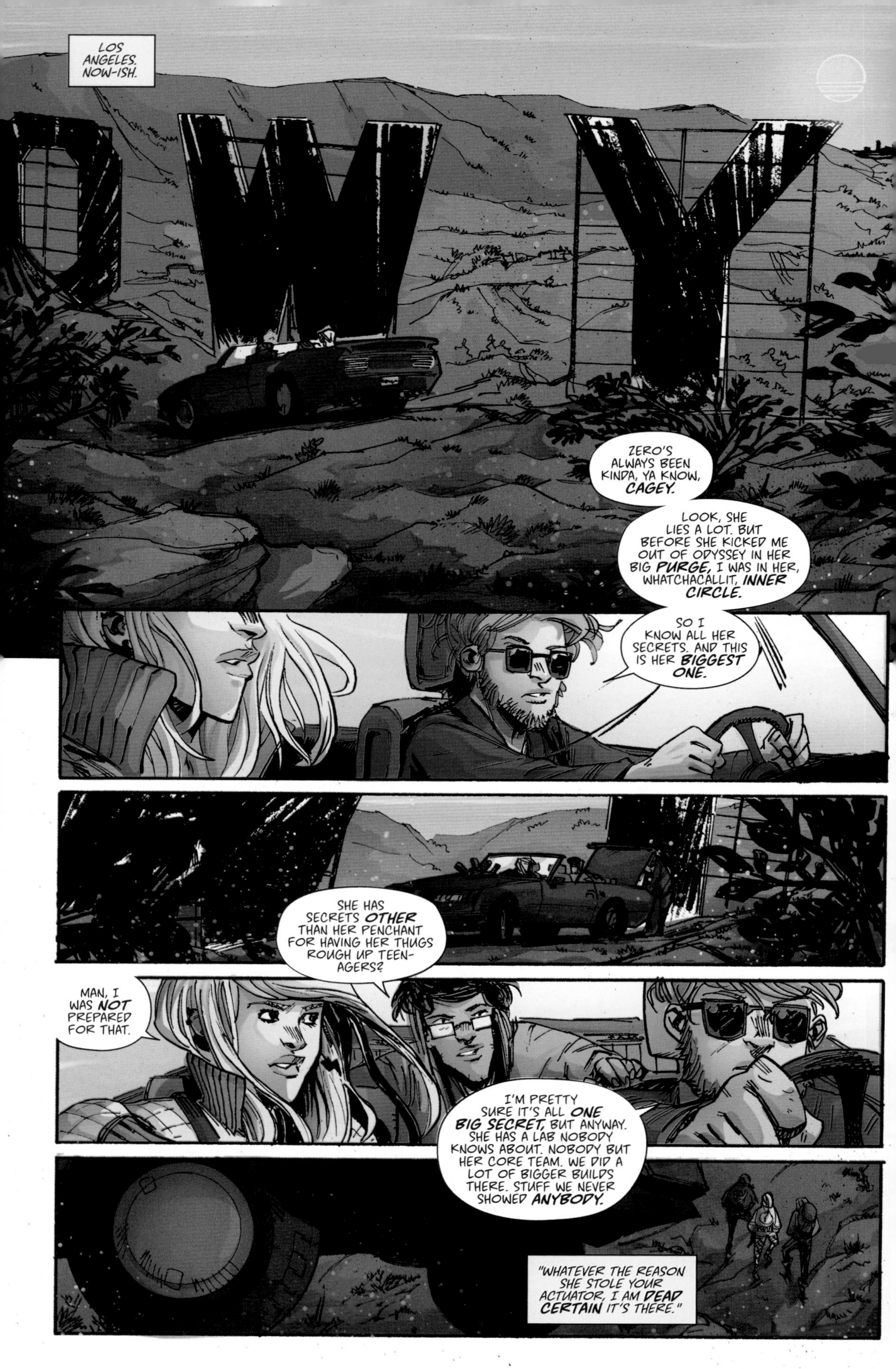
LOS ANGELES. NOW-ISH.
ZERO'S ALWAYS BEEN KINDA, YA KNOW, CAGEY.
LOOK, SHE LIES A LOT. BUT BEFORE SHE KICKED ME OUT OF ODYSSEY IN HER BIG PURGE, I WAS IN HER, WHATCHACALLIT, INNER CIRCLE.
SO I KNOW ALL HER SECRETS. AND THIS IS HER BIGGEST ONE.
SHE HAS SECRETS OTHER THAN HER PENCHANT FOR HAVING HER THUGS ROUGH UP TEEN-AGERS?
MAN, I WAS NOT PREPARED FOR THAT.
I'M PRETTY SURE IT'S ALL ONE BIG SECRET, BUT ANYWAY. SHE HAS A LAB NOBODY KNOWS ABOUT. NOBODY BUT HER CORE TEAM. WE DID A LOT OF BIGGER BUILDS THERE. STUFF WE NEVER SHOWED ANYBODY.
"WHATEVER THE REASON SHE STOLE YOUR ACTUATOR, I AM DEAD CERTAIN IT'S THERE."

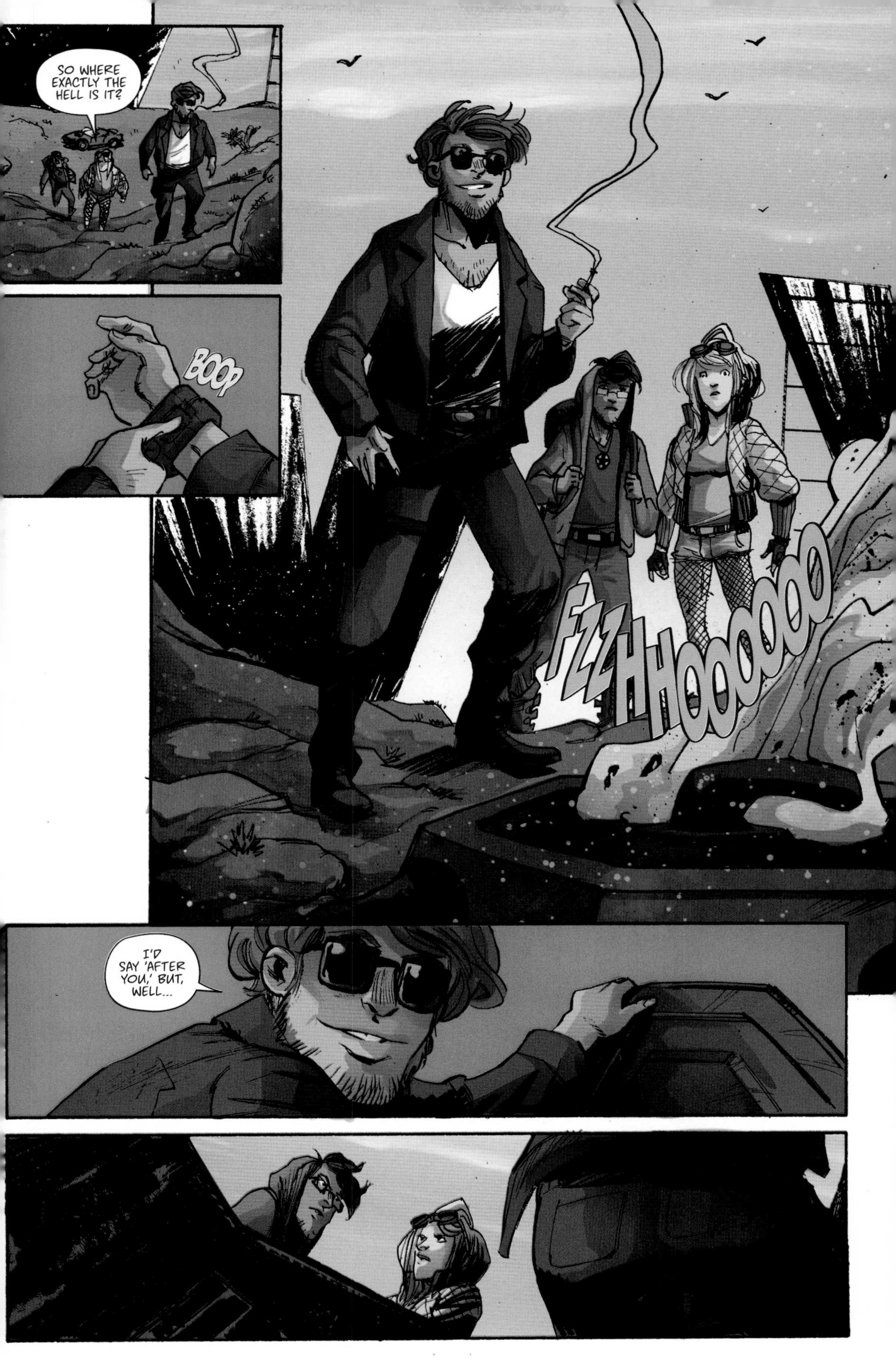
SO WHERE EXACTLY THE HELL IS IT?
BOOP
FZZHHOOOOOO
I'D SAY 'AFTER YOU,' BUT, WELL...

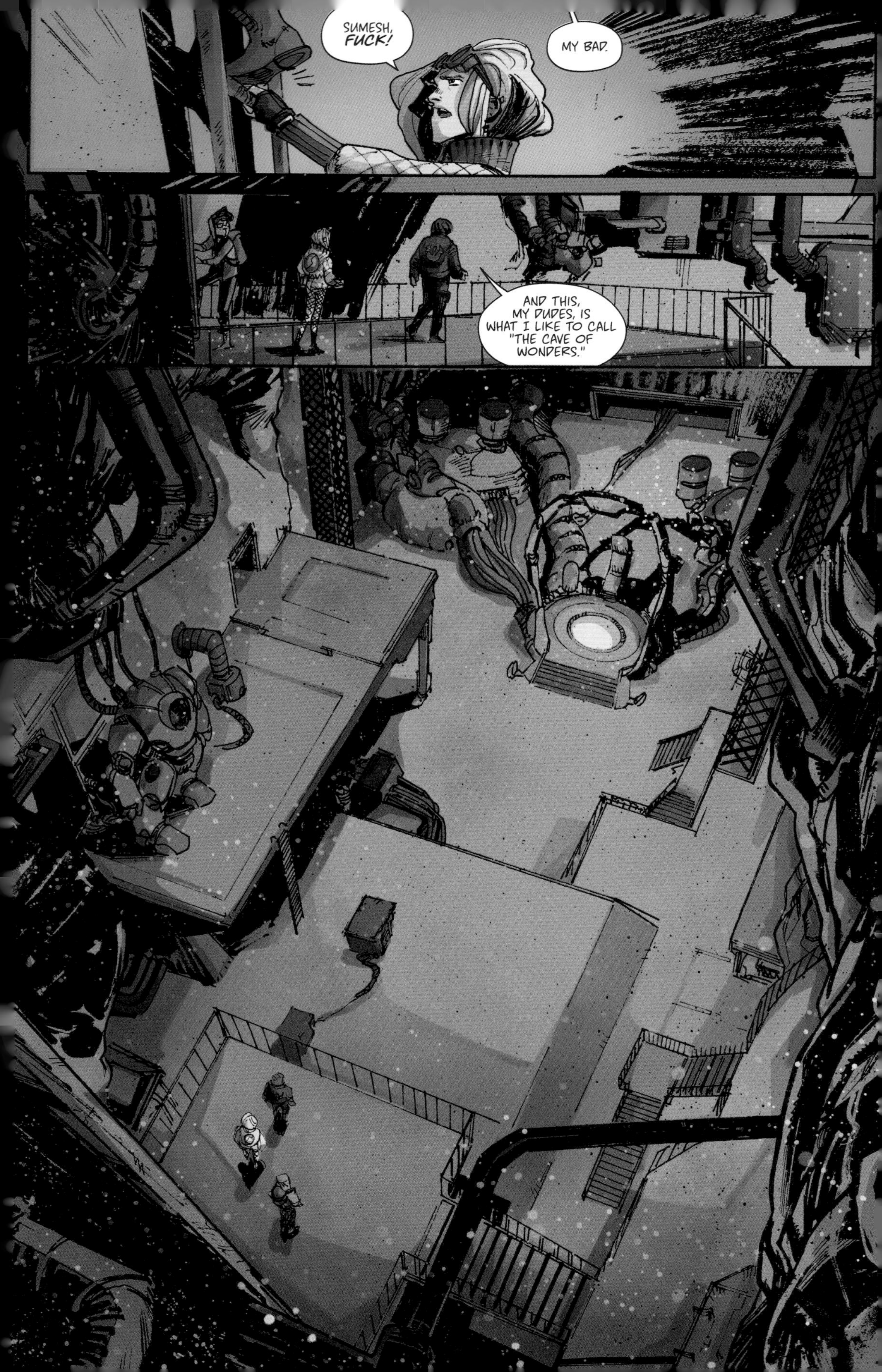
SUMESH, FUCK!
MY BAD.
AND THIS, MY DUDES, IS WHAT I LIKE TO CALL "THE CAVE OF WONDERS."

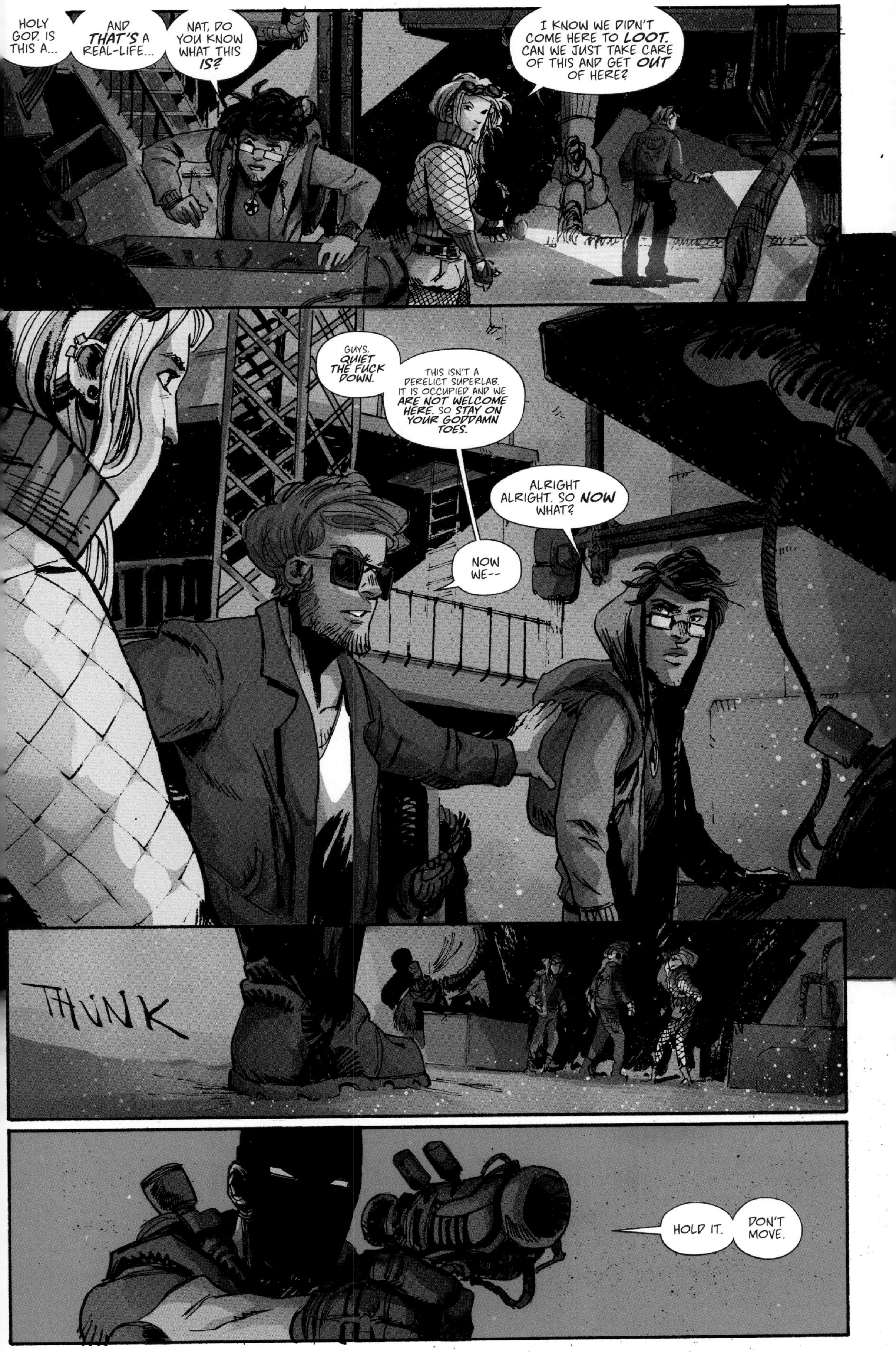
HOLY GOD. IS THIS A...
AND **THAT'S** A REAL-LIFE...
NAT, DO YOU KNOW WHAT THIS **IS?**
I KNOW WE DIDN'T COME HERE TO **LOOT.** CAN WE JUST TAKE CARE OF THIS AND GET **OUT** OF HERE?
GUYS, **QUIET THE FUCK DOWN.**
THIS ISN'T A DERELICT SUPERLAB. IT IS OCCUPIED AND WE **ARE NOT WELCOME HERE.** SO **STAY ON YOUR GODDAMN TOES.**
ALRIGHT ALRIGHT. SO **NOW** WHAT?
NOW WE--
THUNK
HOLD IT.
DON'T MOVE.

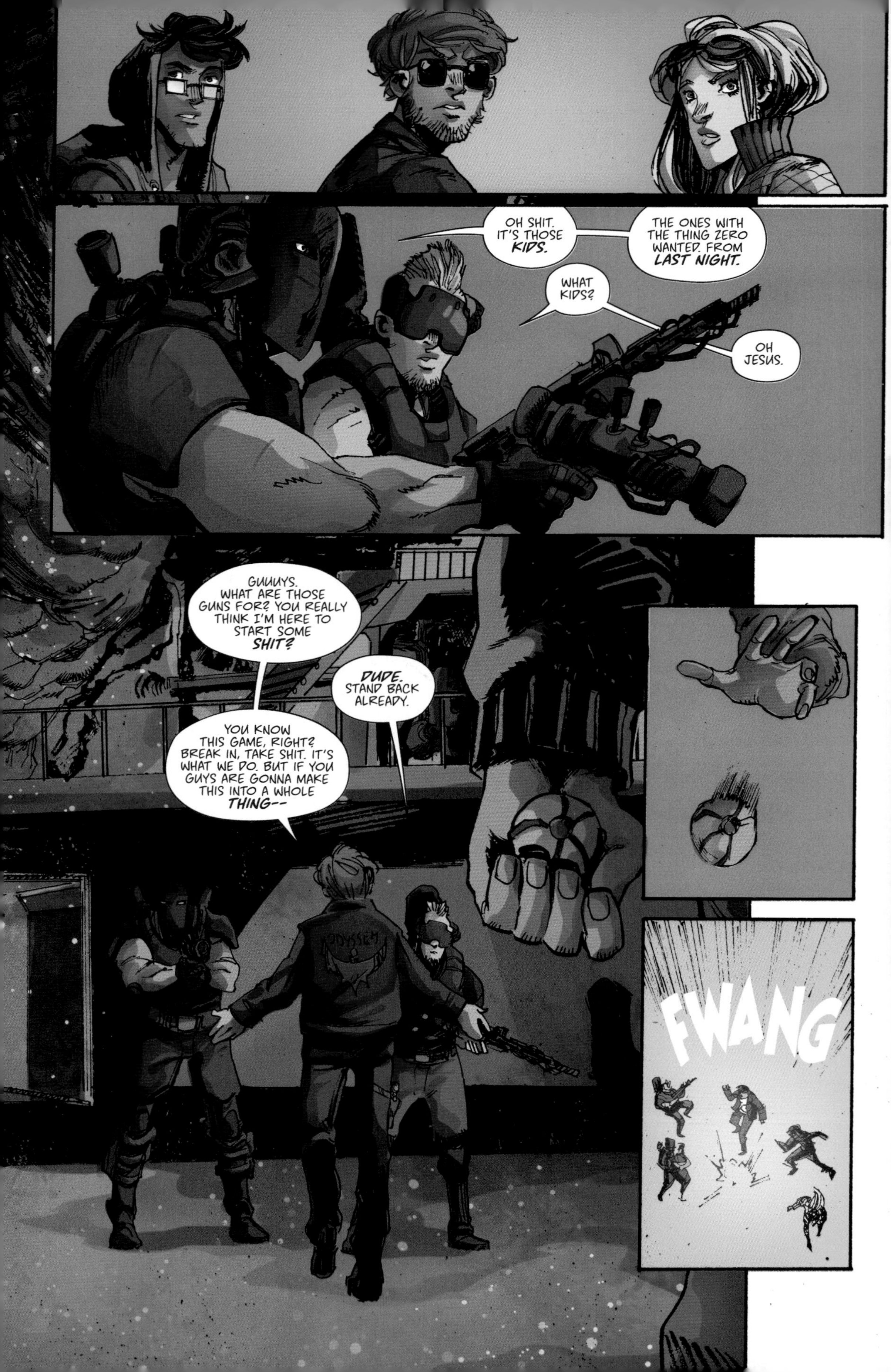

OH SHIT. IT'S THOSE KIDS.
THE ONES WITH THE THING ZERO WANTED. FROM LAST NIGHT.
WHAT KIDS?
OH JESUS.
GUUUYS. WHAT ARE THOSE GUNS FOR? YOU REALLY THINK I'M HERE TO START SOME SHIT?
YOU KNOW THIS GAME, RIGHT? BREAK IN, TAKE SHIT. IT'S WHAT WE DO. BUT IF YOU GUYS ARE GONNA MAKE THIS INTO A WHOLE THING--
DUDE. STAND BACK ALREADY.
ODYSSEY
FWANG

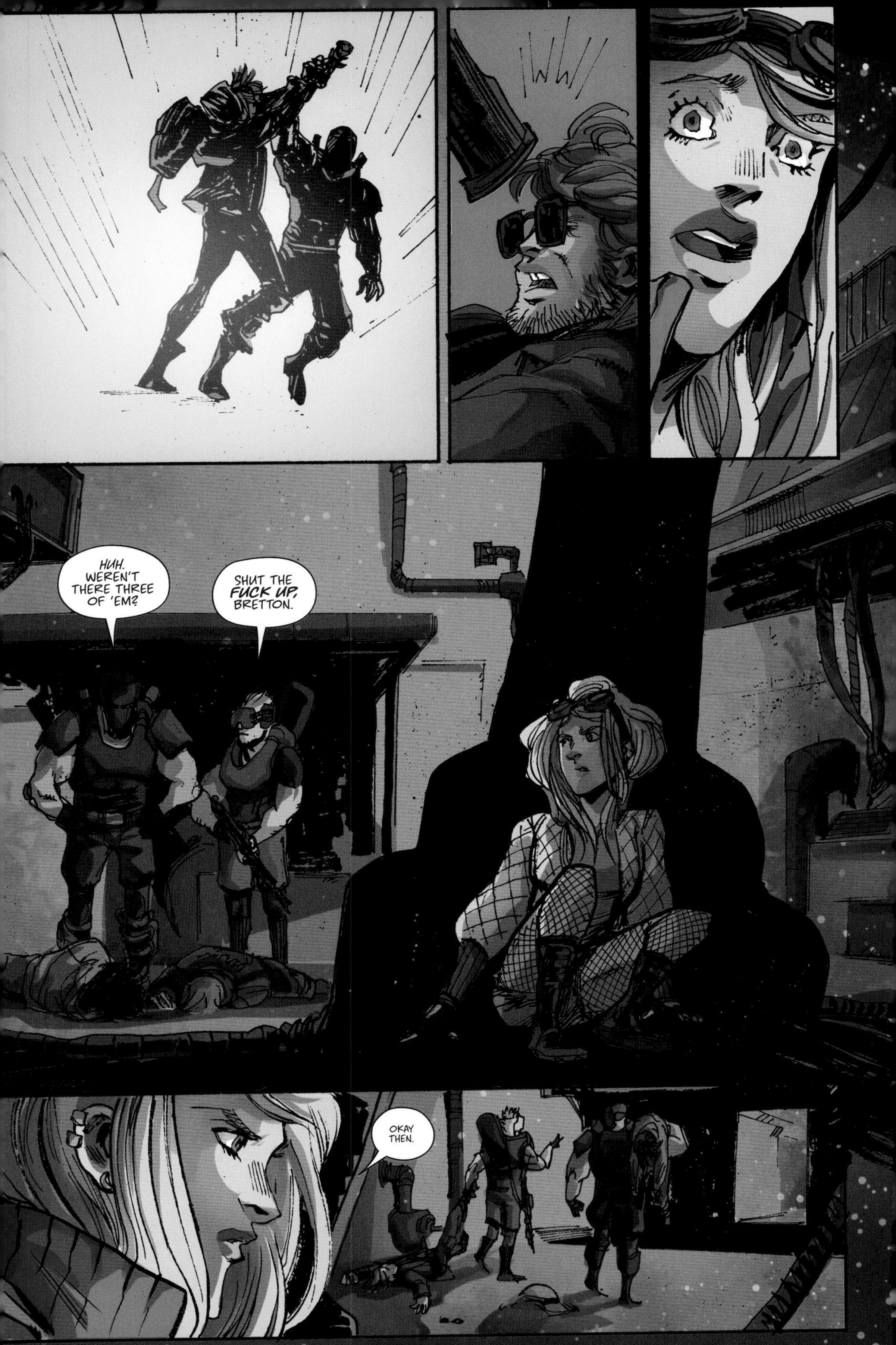
WHH
HUH. WEREN'T THERE THREE OF 'EM?
SHUT THE FUCK UP, BRETTON.
OKAY THEN.

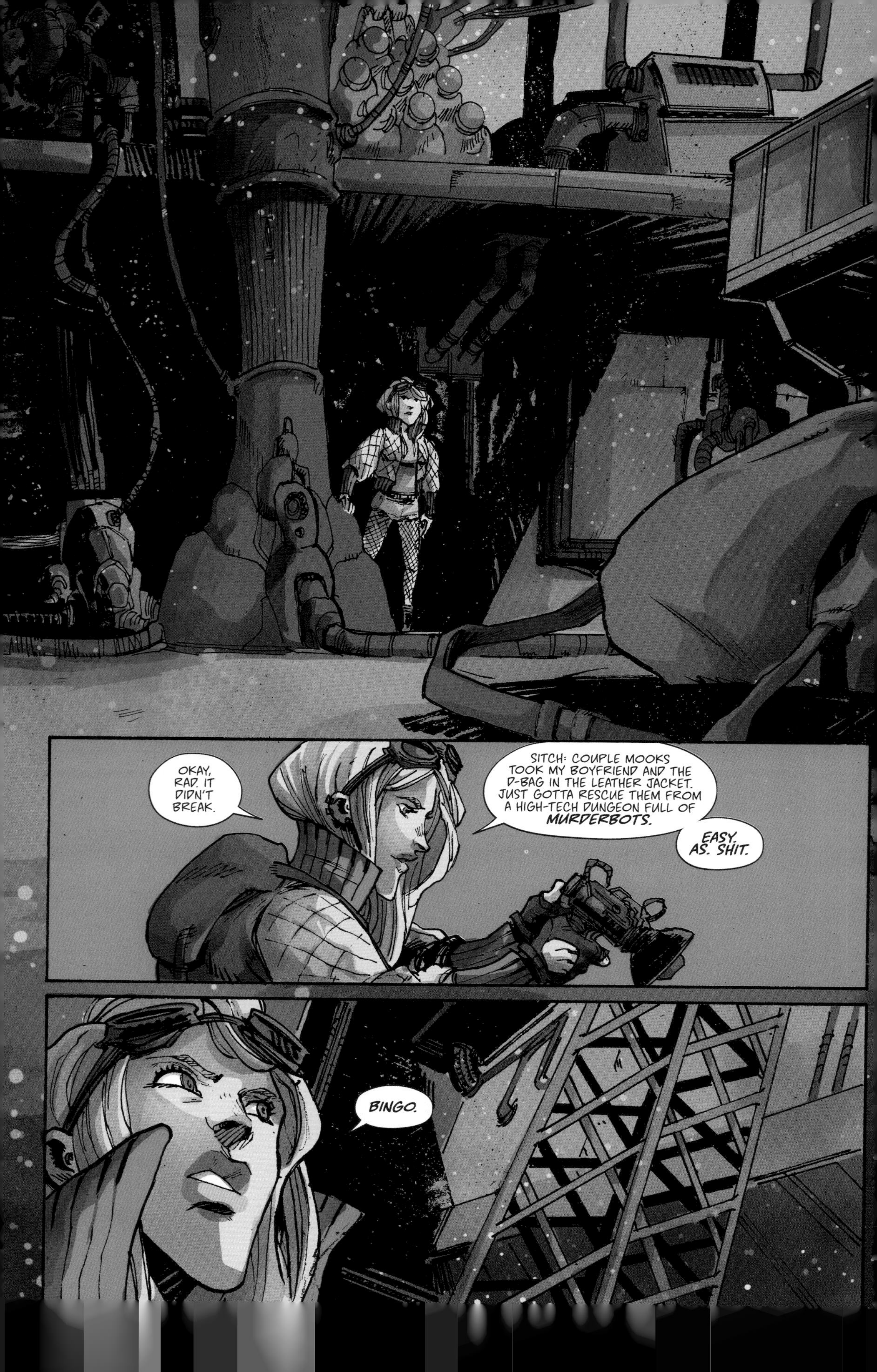
OKAY, RAD. IT DIDN'T BREAK.
SITCH: COUPLE MOOKS TOOK MY BOYFRIEND AND THE D-BAG IN THE LEATHER JACKET. JUST GOTTA RESCUE THEM FROM A HIGH-TECH DUNGEON FULL OF MURDERBOTS.
EASY. AS. SHIT.
BINGO.

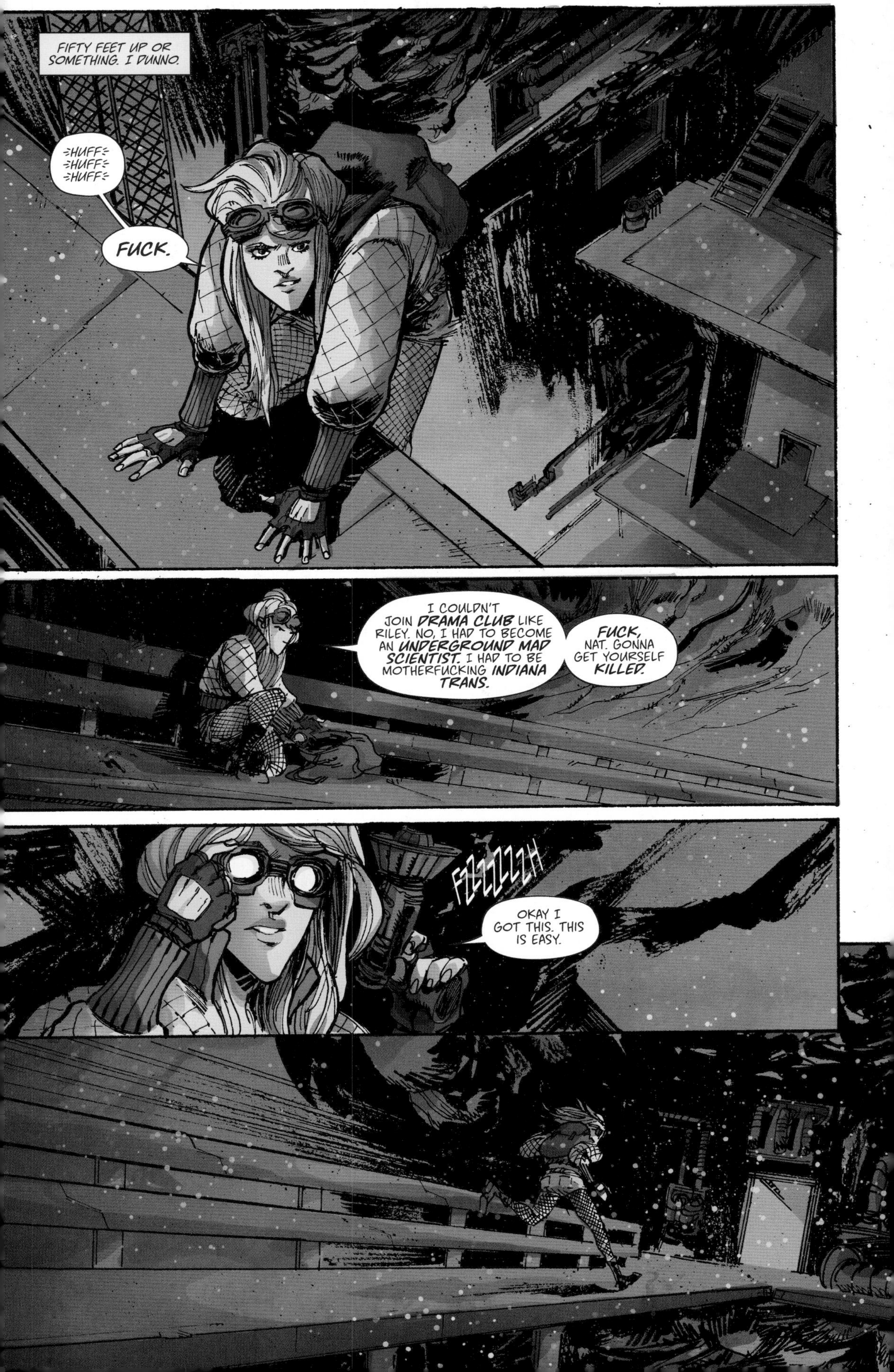
FIFTY FEET UP OR SOMETHING. I DUNNO.
=HUFF= =HUFF= =HUFF=
FUCK.
I COULDN'T JOIN DRAMA CLUB LIKE RILEY. NO, I HAD TO BECOME AN UNDERGROUND MAD SCIENTIST. I HAD TO BE MOTHERFUCKING INDIANA TRANS.
FUCK, NAT. GONNA GET YOURSELF KILLED.
FZZZZZZZH
OKAY I GOT THIS. THIS IS EASY.

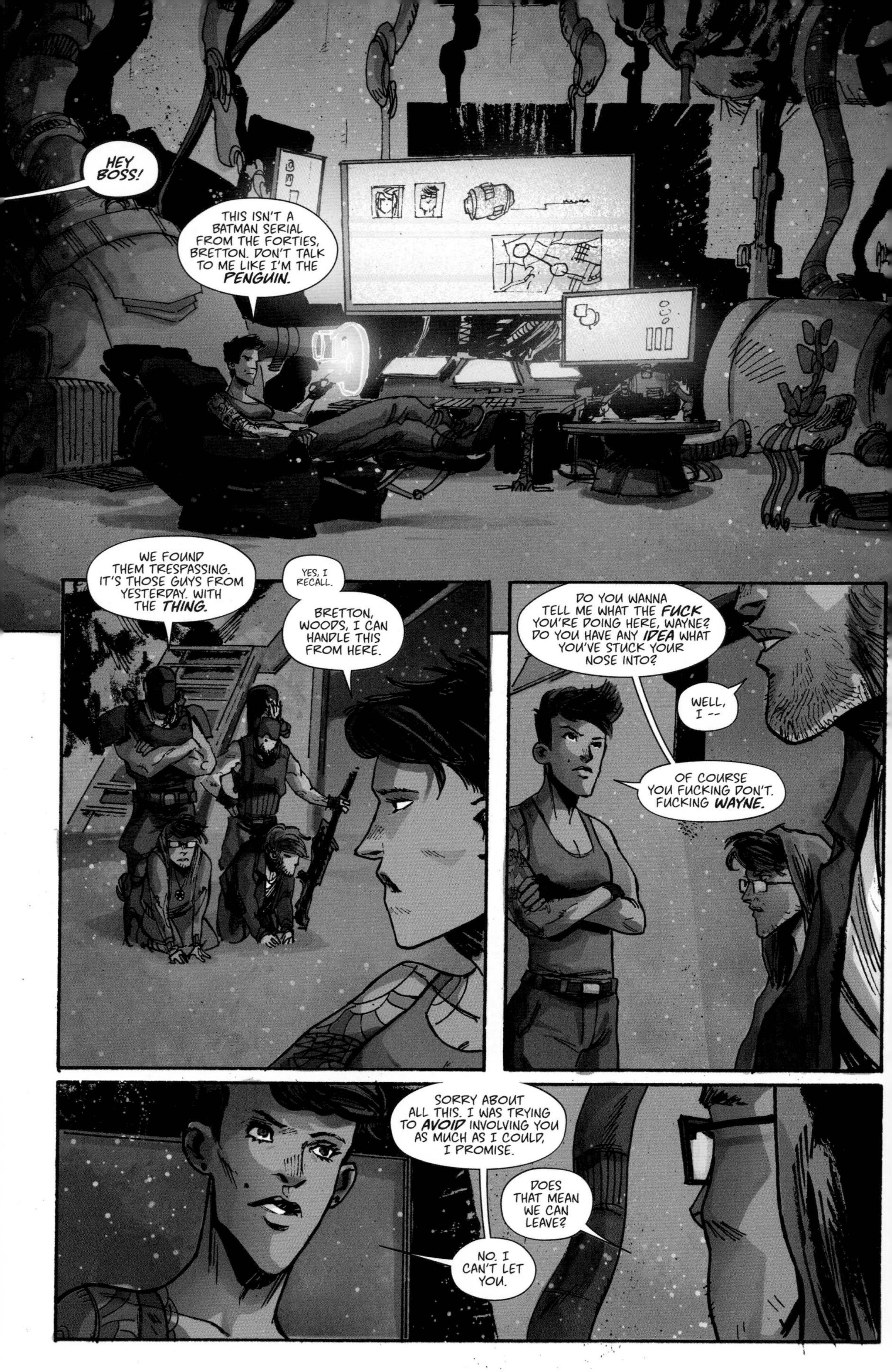
HEY BOSS!
THIS ISN'T A BATMAN SERIAL FROM THE FORTIES, BRETTON. DON'T TALK TO ME LIKE I'M THE PENGUIN.
WE FOUND THEM TRESPASSING. IT'S THOSE GUYS FROM YESTERDAY. WITH THE THING.
YES, I RECALL.
BRETTON, WOODS, I CAN HANDLE THIS FROM HERE.
DO YOU WANNA TELL ME WHAT THE FUCK YOU'RE DOING HERE, WAYNE? DO YOU HAVE ANY IDEA WHAT YOU'VE STUCK YOUR NOSE INTO?
WELL, I --
OF COURSE YOU FUCKING DON'T. FUCKING WAYNE.
SORRY ABOUT ALL THIS. I WAS TRYING TO AVOID INVOLVING YOU AS MUCH AS I COULD, I PROMISE.
DOES THAT MEAN WE CAN LEAVE?
NO. I CAN'T LET YOU.

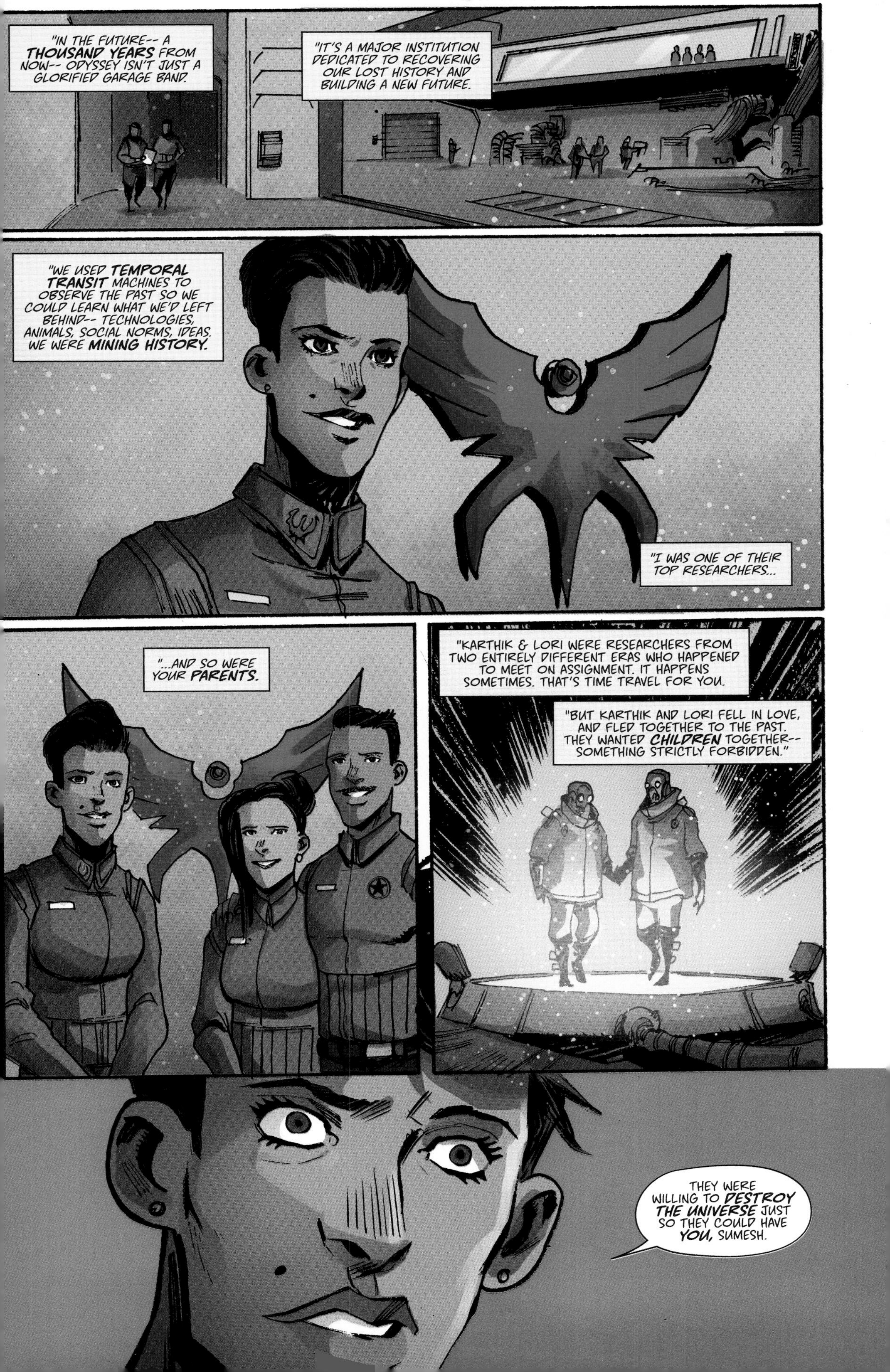

"IN THE FUTURE-- A THOUSAND YEARS FROM NOW-- ODYSSEY ISN'T JUST A GLORIFIED GARAGE BAND.
"IT'S A MAJOR INSTITUTION DEDICATED TO RECOVERING OUR LOST HISTORY AND BUILDING A NEW FUTURE.
"WE USED TEMPORAL TRANSIT MACHINES TO OBSERVE THE PAST SO WE COULD LEARN WHAT WE'D LEFT BEHIND-- TECHNOLOGIES, ANIMALS, SOCIAL NORMS, IDEAS. WE WERE MINING HISTORY.
"I WAS ONE OF THEIR TOP RESEARCHERS...
"...AND SO WERE YOUR PARENTS.
"KARTHIK & LORI WERE RESEARCHERS FROM TWO ENTIRELY DIFFERENT ERAS WHO HAPPENED TO MEET ON ASSIGNMENT. IT HAPPENS SOMETIMES. THAT'S TIME TRAVEL FOR YOU.
"BUT KARTHIK AND LORI FELL IN LOVE, AND FLED TOGETHER TO THE PAST. THEY WANTED CHILDREN TOGETHER-- SOMETHING STRICTLY FORBIDDEN."
THEY WERE WILLING TO DESTROY THE UNIVERSE JUST SO THEY COULD HAVE YOU, SUMESH.

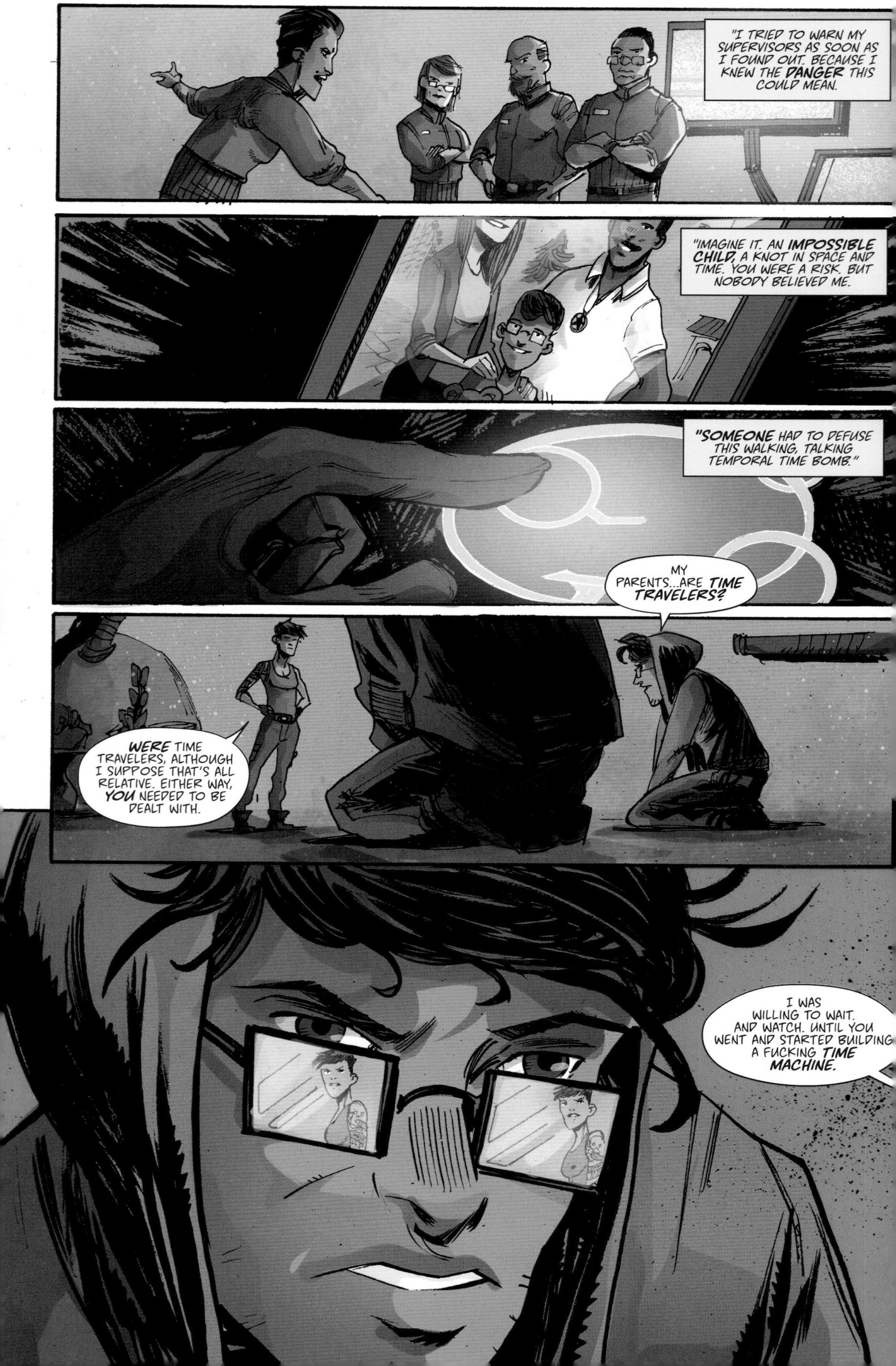
"I TRIED TO WARN MY SUPERVISORS AS SOON AS I FOUND OUT. BECAUSE I KNEW THE **DANGER** THIS COULD MEAN.
"IMAGINE IT. AN **IMPOSSIBLE CHILD,** A KNOT IN SPACE AND TIME. YOU WERE A RISK. BUT NOBODY BELIEVED ME.
"**SOMEONE** HAD TO DEFUSE THIS WALKING, TALKING TEMPORAL TIME BOMB."
MY PARENTS...ARE ***TIME TRAVELERS?***
WERE TIME TRAVELERS, ALTHOUGH I SUPPOSE THAT'S ALL RELATIVE. EITHER WAY, ***YOU*** NEEDED TO BE DEALT WITH.
I WAS WILLING TO WAIT. AND WATCH. UNTIL YOU WENT AND STARTED BUILDING A FUCKING ***TIME MACHINE.***

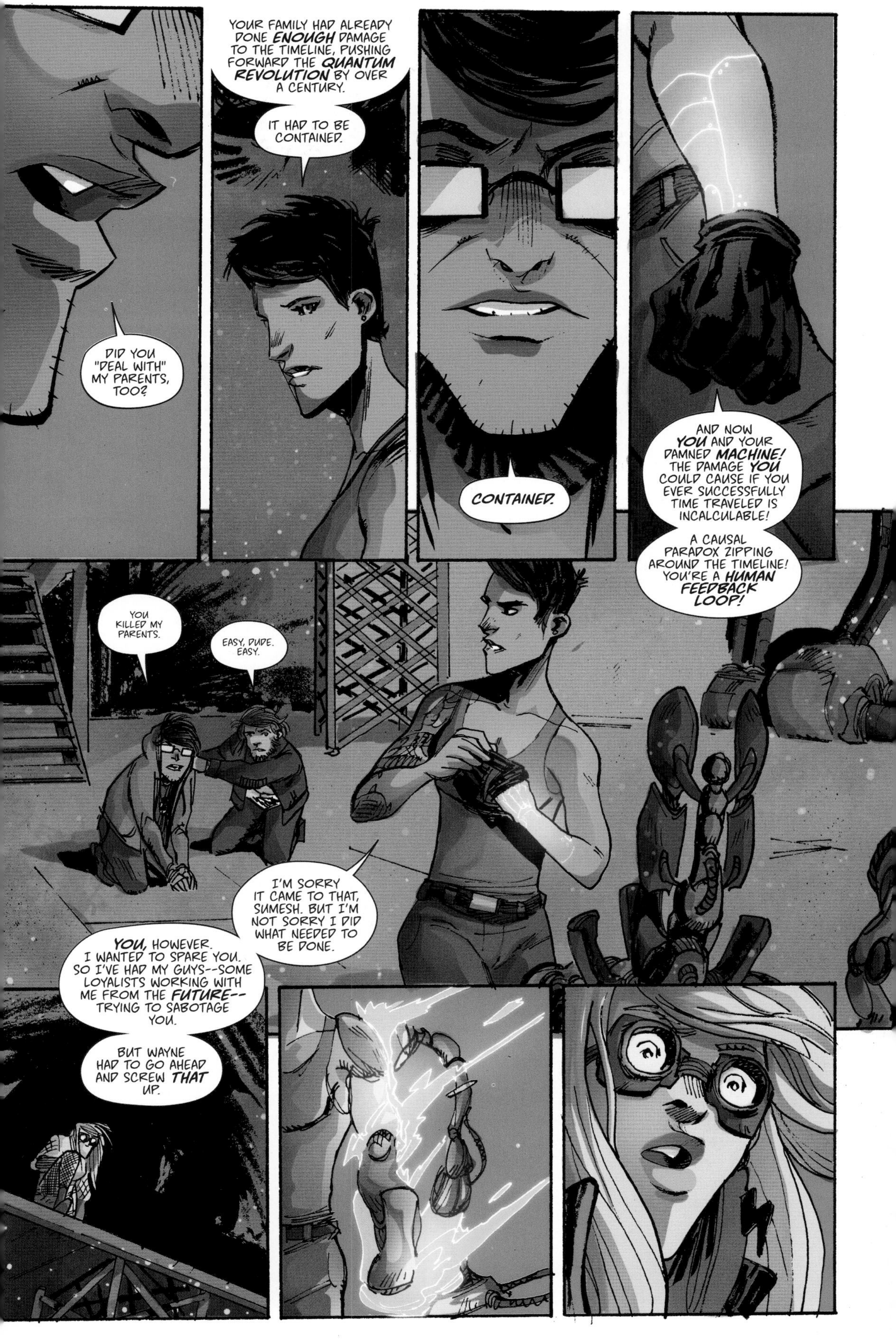
YOUR FAMILY HAD ALREADY DONE ENOUGH DAMAGE TO THE TIMELINE, PUSHING FORWARD THE QUANTUM REVOLUTION BY OVER A CENTURY.
IT HAD TO BE CONTAINED.
DID YOU "DEAL WITH" MY PARENTS, TOO?
CONTAINED.
AND NOW YOU AND YOUR DAMNED MACHINE! THE DAMAGE YOU COULD CAUSE IF YOU EVER SUCCESSFULLY TIME TRAVELED IS INCALCULABLE!
A CAUSAL PARADOX ZIPPING AROUND THE TIMELINE! YOU'RE A HUMAN FEEDBACK LOOP!
YOU KILLED MY PARENTS.
EASY, DUDE. EASY.
I'M SORRY IT CAME TO THAT, SUMESH. BUT I'M NOT SORRY I DID WHAT NEEDED TO BE DONE.
YOU, HOWEVER. I WANTED TO SPARE YOU. SO I'VE HAD MY GUYS--SOME LOYALISTS WORKING WITH ME FROM THE FUTURE--TRYING TO SABOTAGE YOU.
BUT WAYNE HAD TO GO AHEAD AND SCREW THAT UP.

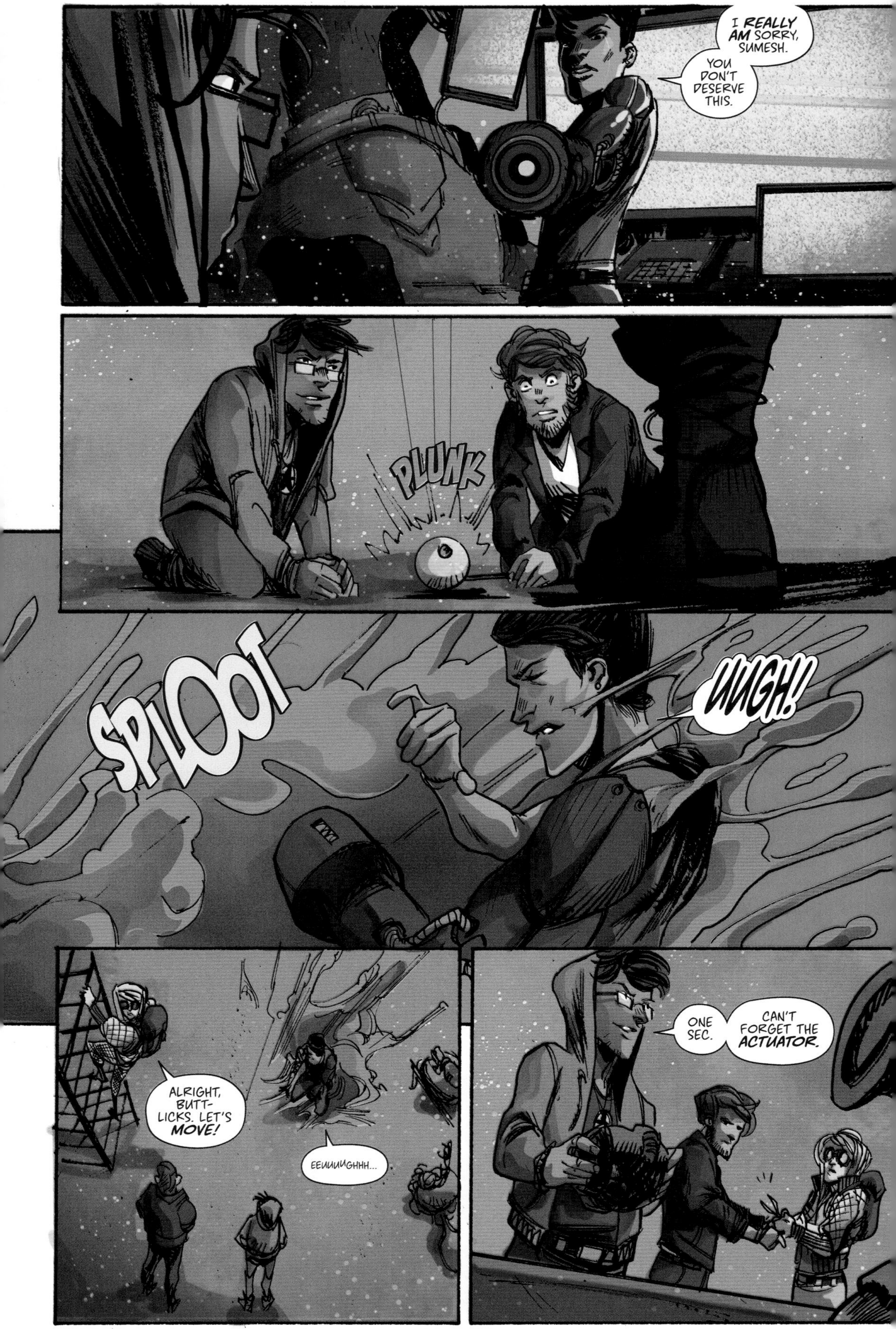
I REALLY AM SORRY, SUMESH.
YOU DON'T DESERVE THIS.
PLUNK
SPLOOT
UUGH!
ALRIGHT, BUTT-LICKS. LET'S MOVE!
EEUUUUGHHH...
ONE SEC.
CAN'T FORGET THE ACTUATOR.

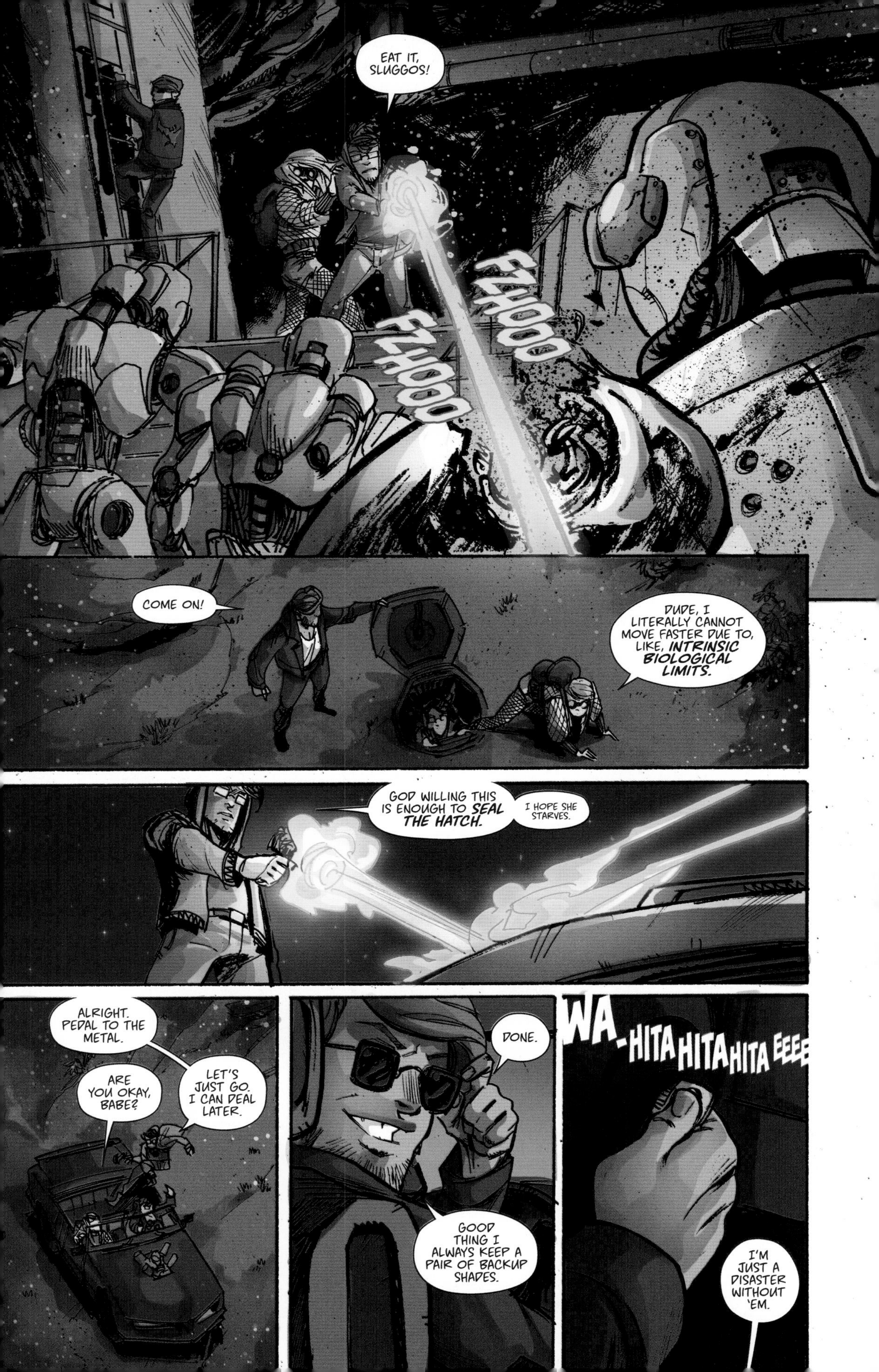
EAT IT, SLUGGOS!
FZHOOO
FZHOOO
COME ON!
DUDE, I LITERALLY CANNOT MOVE FASTER DUE TO, LIKE, INTRINSIC BIOLOGICAL LIMITS.
GOD WILLING THIS IS ENOUGH TO SEAL THE HATCH.
I HOPE SHE STARVES.
ALRIGHT. PEDAL TO THE METAL.
ARE YOU OKAY, BABE?
LET'S JUST GO. I CAN DEAL LATER.
DONE.
GOOD THING I ALWAYS KEEP A PAIR OF BACKUP SHADES.
WA-HITA HITA HITA EEEE
I'M JUST A DISASTER WITHOUT 'EM.

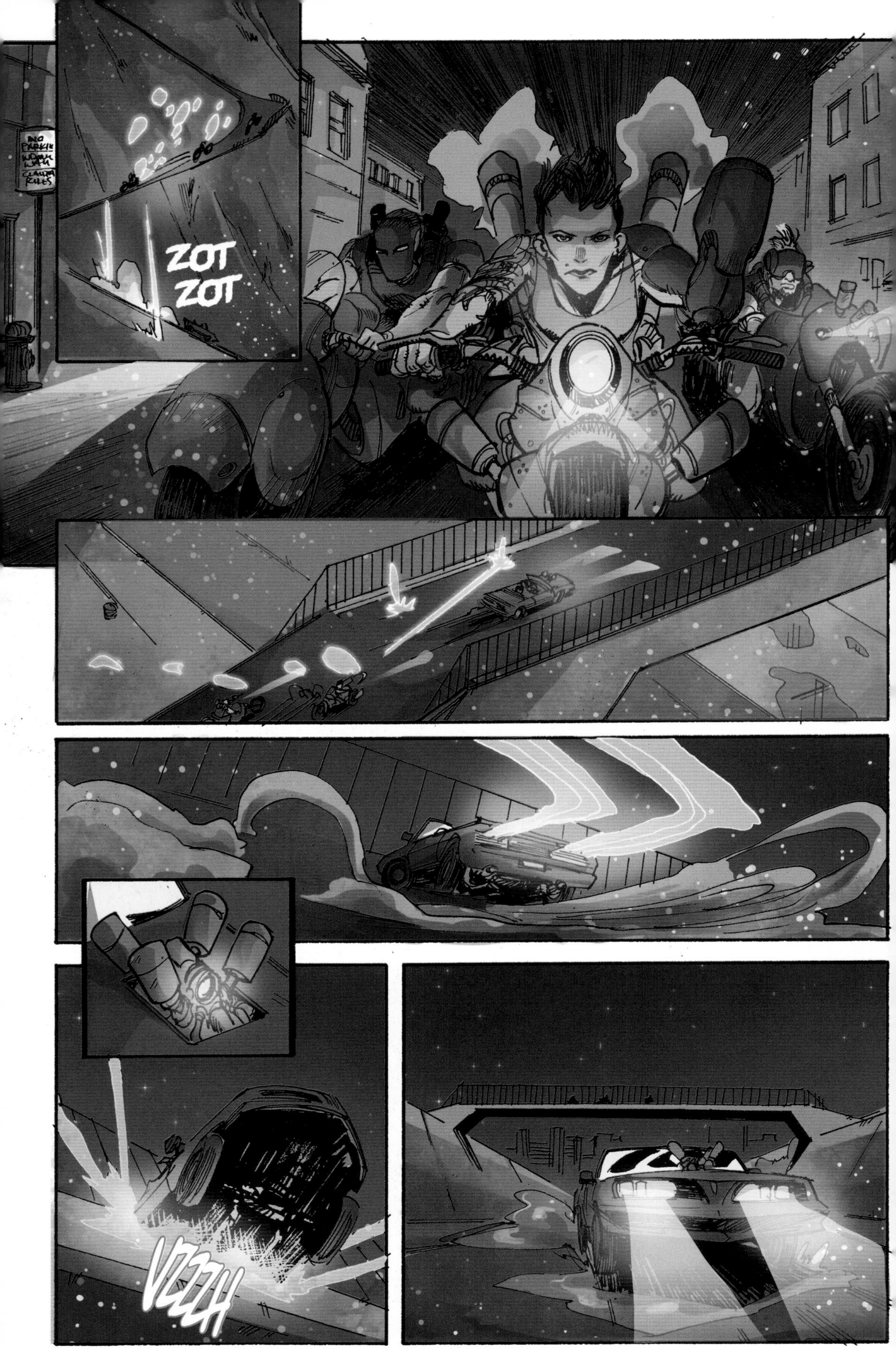
ZOT
ZOT
VZZZH

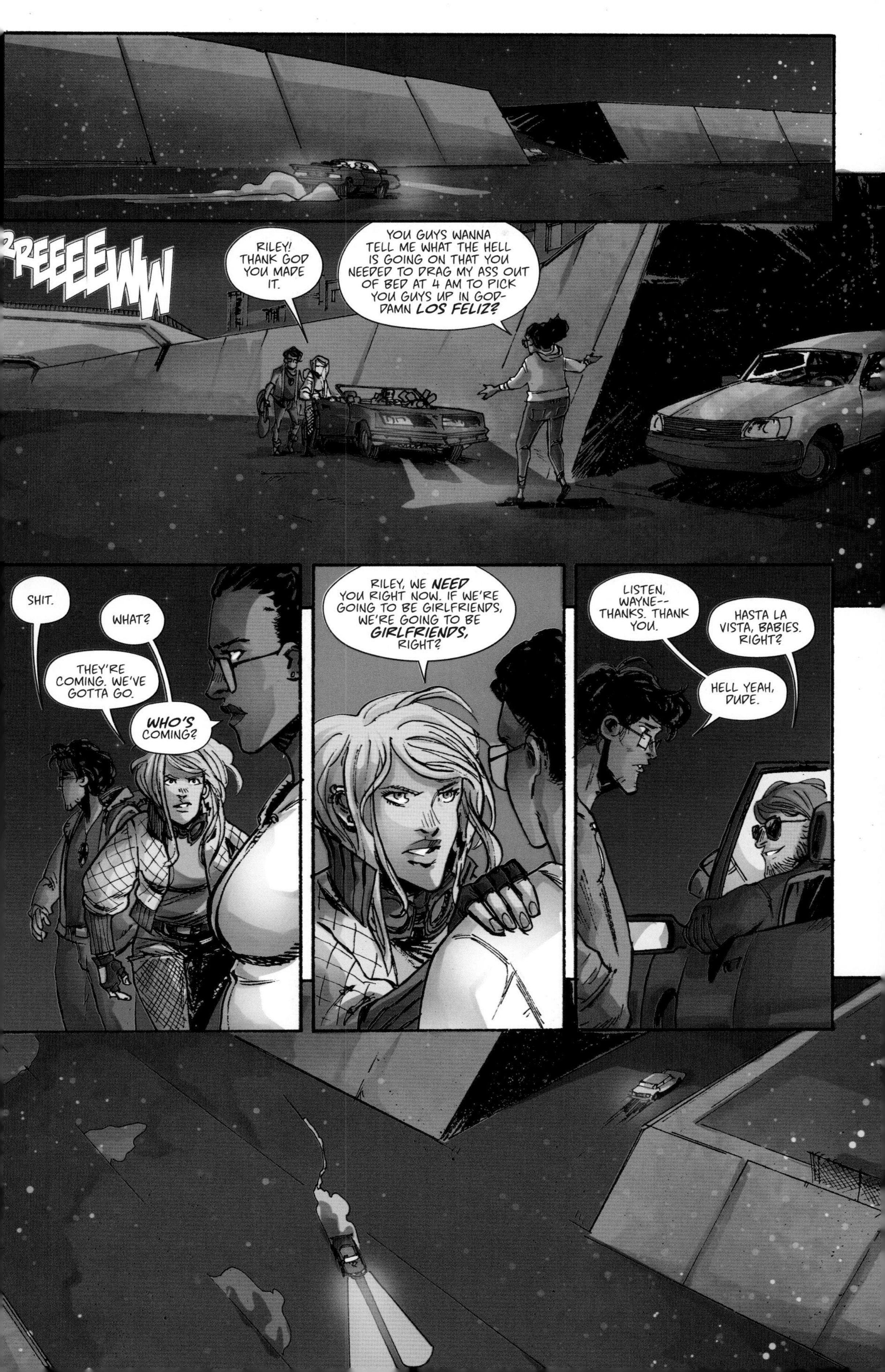

RREEEEWW
RILEY! THANK GOD YOU MADE IT.
YOU GUYS WANNA TELL ME WHAT THE HELL IS GOING ON THAT YOU NEEDED TO DRAG MY ASS OUT OF BED AT 4 AM TO PICK YOU GUYS UP IN GOD-DAMN **LOS FELIZ?**
SHIT.
WHAT?
THEY'RE COMING. WE'VE GOTTA GO.
WHO'S COMING?
RILEY, WE **NEED** YOU RIGHT NOW. IF WE'RE GOING TO BE GIRLFRIENDS, WE'RE GOING TO BE **GIRLFRIENDS,** RIGHT?
LISTEN, WAYNE-- THANKS. THANK YOU.
HASTA LA VISTA, BABIES. RIGHT?
HELL YEAH, DUDE.

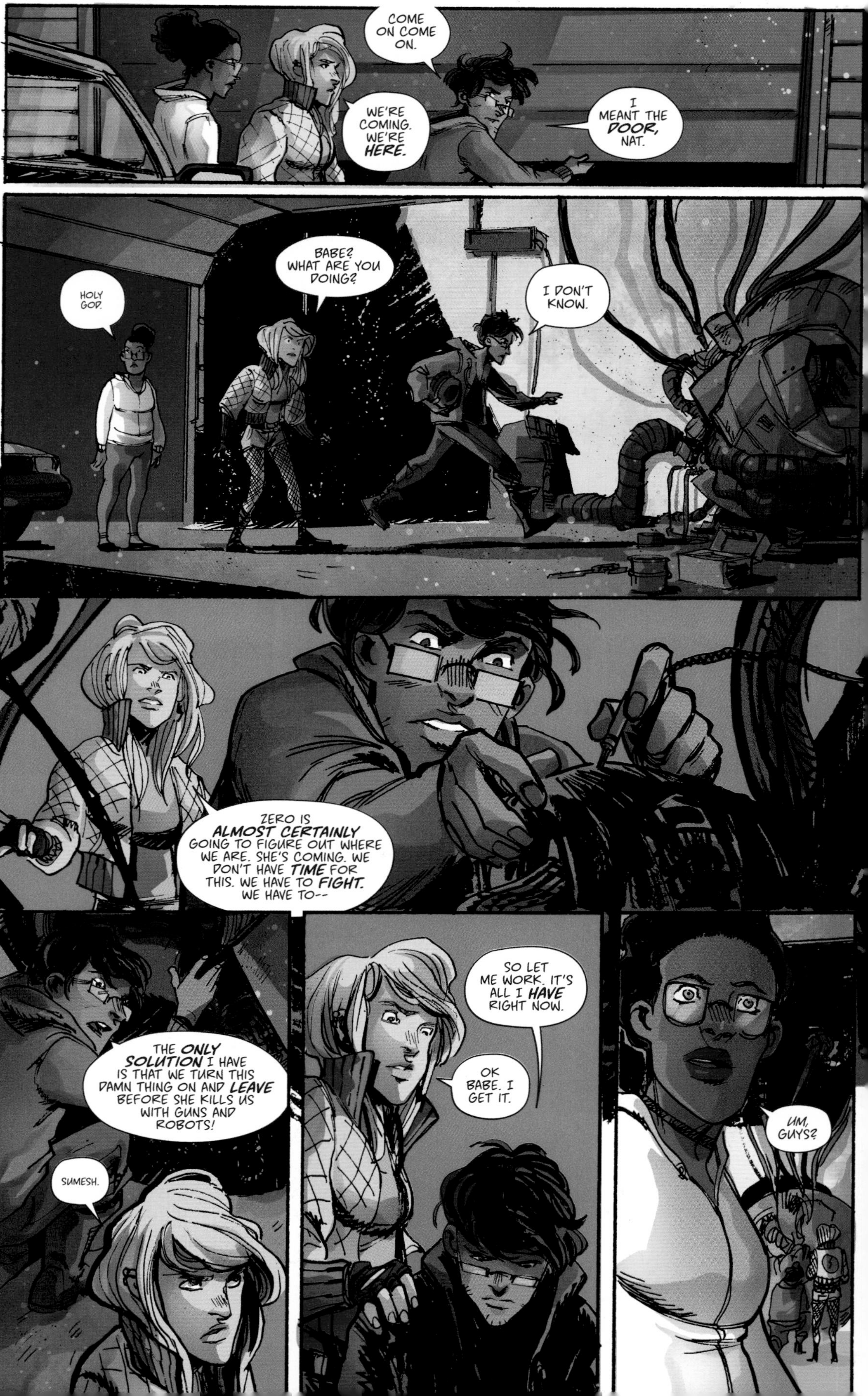
COME ON COME ON.
WE'RE COMING. WE'RE HERE.
I MEANT THE DOOR, NAT.
HOLY GOD.
BABE? WHAT ARE YOU DOING?
I DON'T KNOW.
ZERO IS ALMOST CERTAINLY GOING TO FIGURE OUT WHERE WE ARE. SHE'S COMING. WE DON'T HAVE TIME FOR THIS. WE HAVE TO FIGHT. WE HAVE TO--
THE ONLY SOLUTION I HAVE IS THAT WE TURN THIS DAMN THING ON AND LEAVE BEFORE SHE KILLS US WITH GUNS AND ROBOTS!
SUMESH.
SO LET ME WORK. IT'S ALL I HAVE RIGHT NOW.
OK BABE. I GET IT.
UM, GUYS?

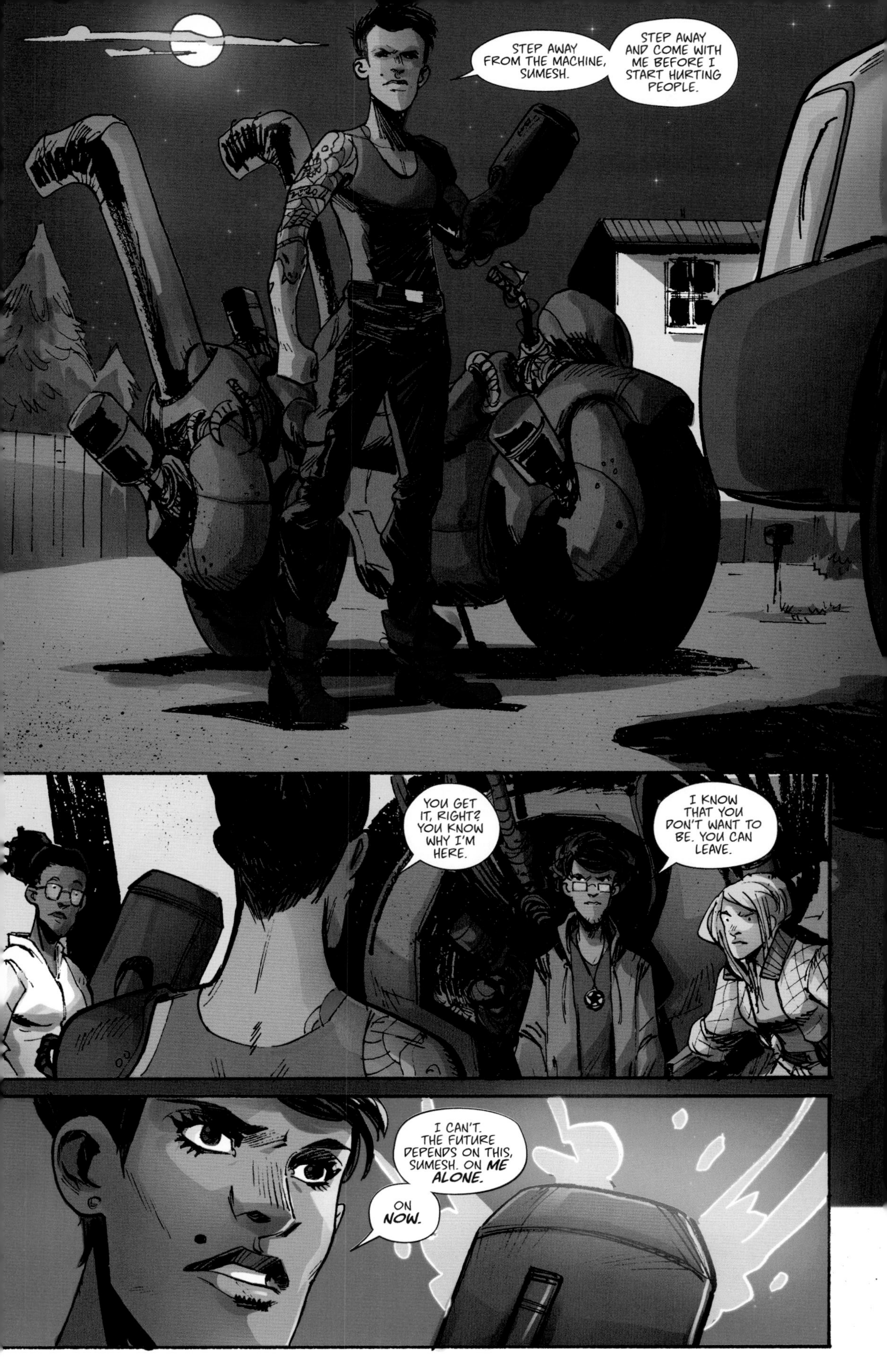
STEP AWAY FROM THE MACHINE, SUMESH.
STEP AWAY AND COME WITH ME BEFORE I START HURTING PEOPLE.
YOU GET IT, RIGHT? YOU KNOW WHY I'M HERE.
I KNOW THAT YOU DON'T WANT TO BE. YOU CAN LEAVE.
I CAN'T. THE FUTURE DEPENDS ON THIS, SUMESH. ON ***ME ALONE.***
ON ***NOW.***

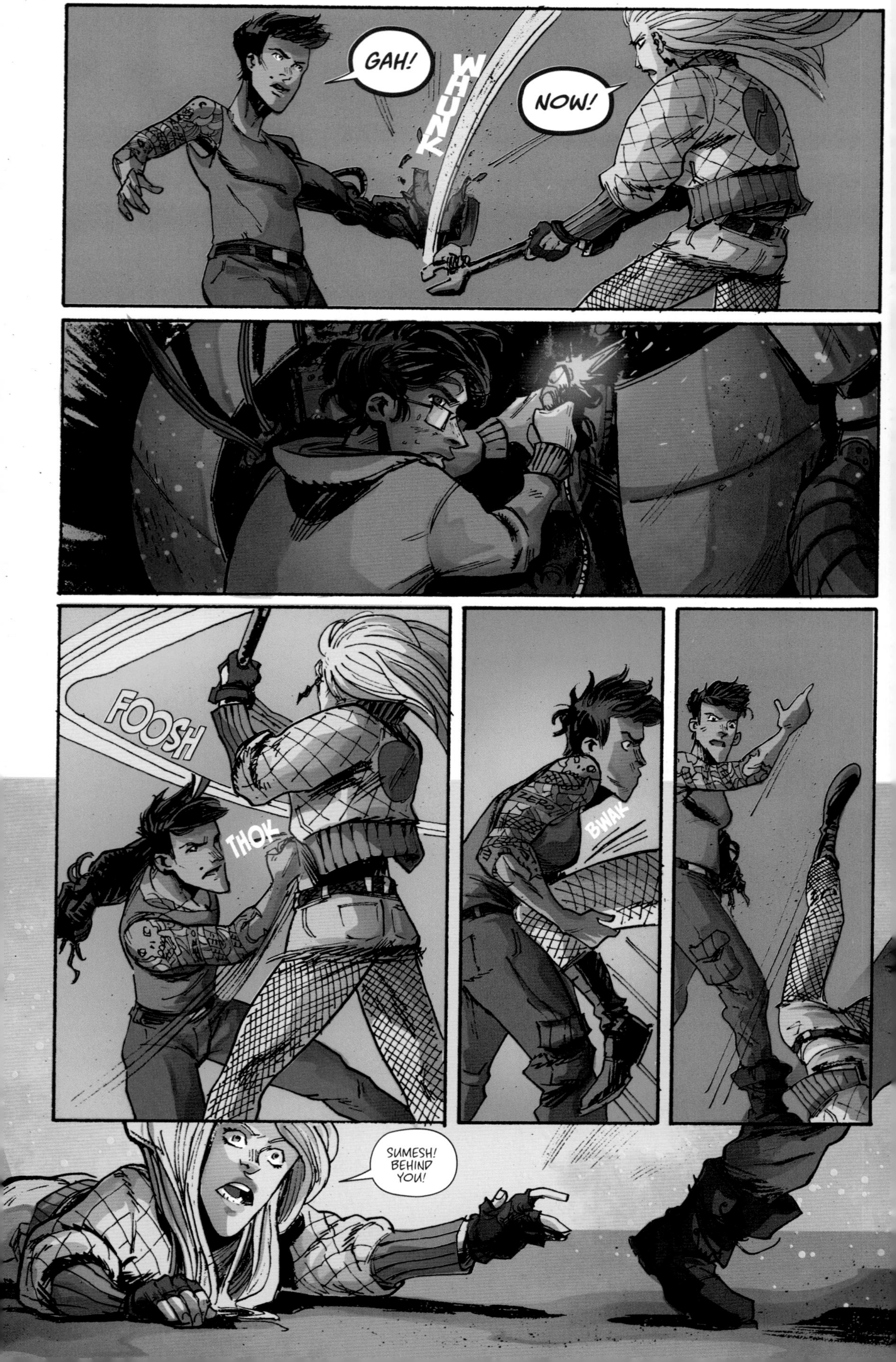
GAH!
WHUNK
NOW!
FOOSH
THOK
BWAK
SUMESH! BEHIND YOU!

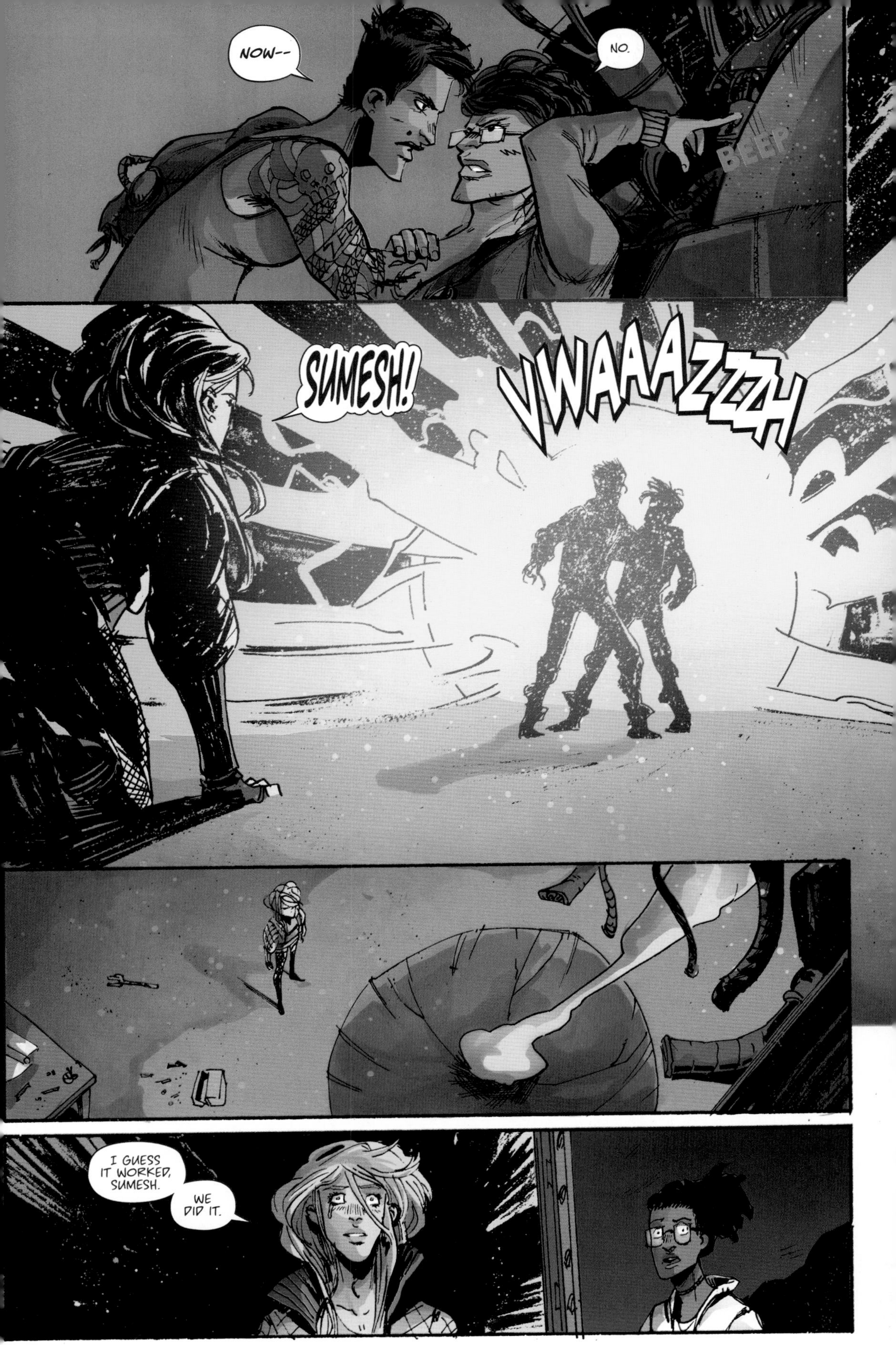
NOW--
NO.
BEEP
SUMESH!
VWAAAZZZH
I GUESS IT WORKED, SUMESH.
WE DID IT.

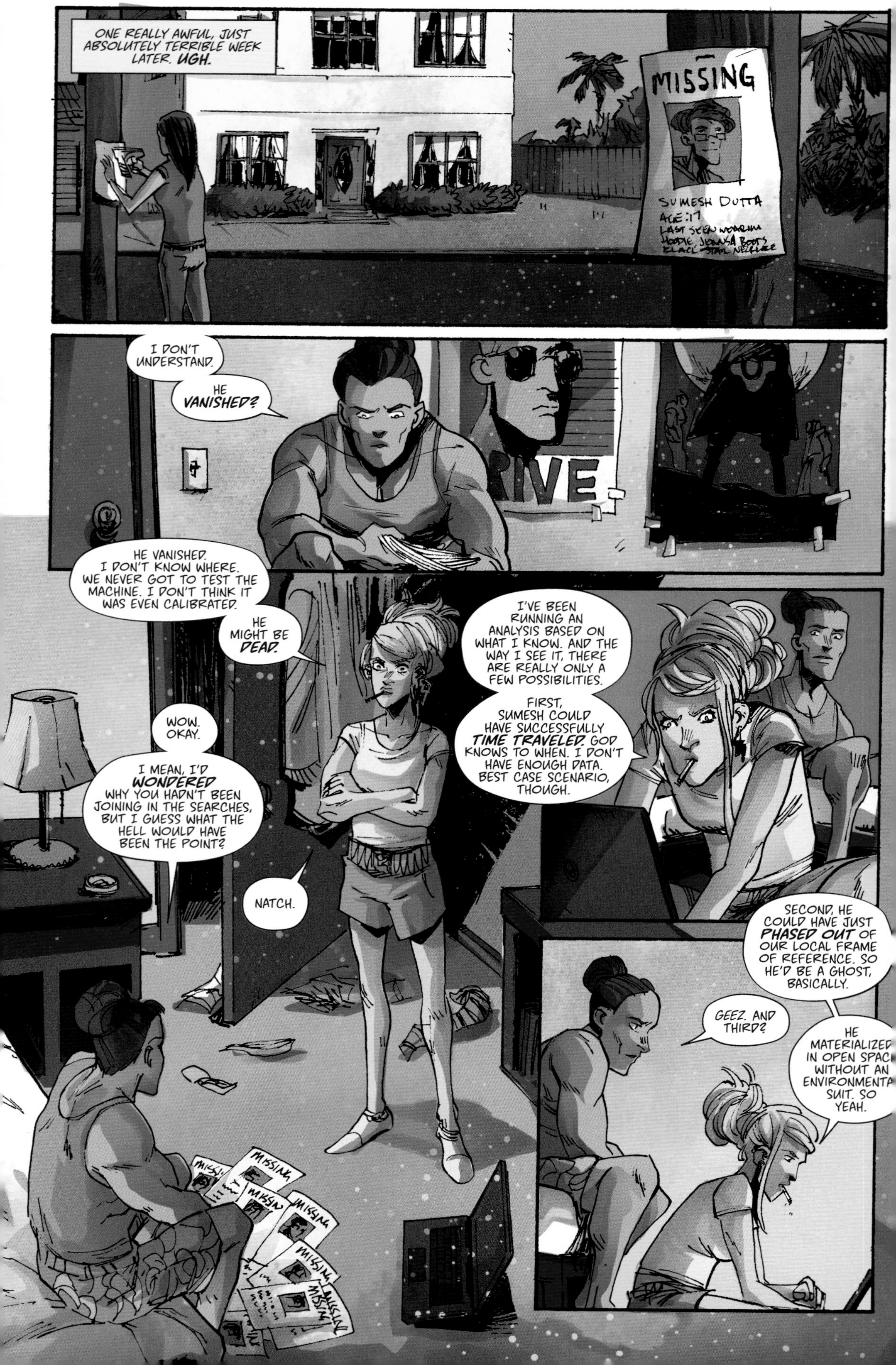
ONE REALLY AWFUL, JUST ABSOLUTELY TERRIBLE WEEK LATER. UGH.
MISSING
SUMESH DUTTA
I DON'T UNDERSTAND.
HE VANISHED?
HE VANISHED. I DON'T KNOW WHERE. WE NEVER GOT TO TEST THE MACHINE. I DON'T THINK IT WAS EVEN CALIBRATED.
HE MIGHT BE DEAD.
WOW. OKAY.
I MEAN, I'D WONDERED WHY YOU HADN'T BEEN JOINING IN THE SEARCHES, BUT I GUESS WHAT THE HELL WOULD HAVE BEEN THE POINT?
NATCH.
I'VE BEEN RUNNING AN ANALYSIS BASED ON WHAT I KNOW. AND THE WAY I SEE IT, THERE ARE REALLY ONLY A FEW POSSIBILITIES.
FIRST, SUMESH COULD HAVE SUCCESSFULLY TIME TRAVELED. GOD KNOWS TO WHEN. I DON'T HAVE ENOUGH DATA. BEST CASE SCENARIO, THOUGH.
SECOND, HE COULD HAVE JUST PHASED OUT OF OUR LOCAL FRAME OF REFERENCE. SO HE'D BE A GHOST, BASICALLY.
GEEZ. AND THIRD?
HE MATERIALIZED IN OPEN SPAC WITHOUT AN ENVIRONMENTA SUIT. SO YEAH.

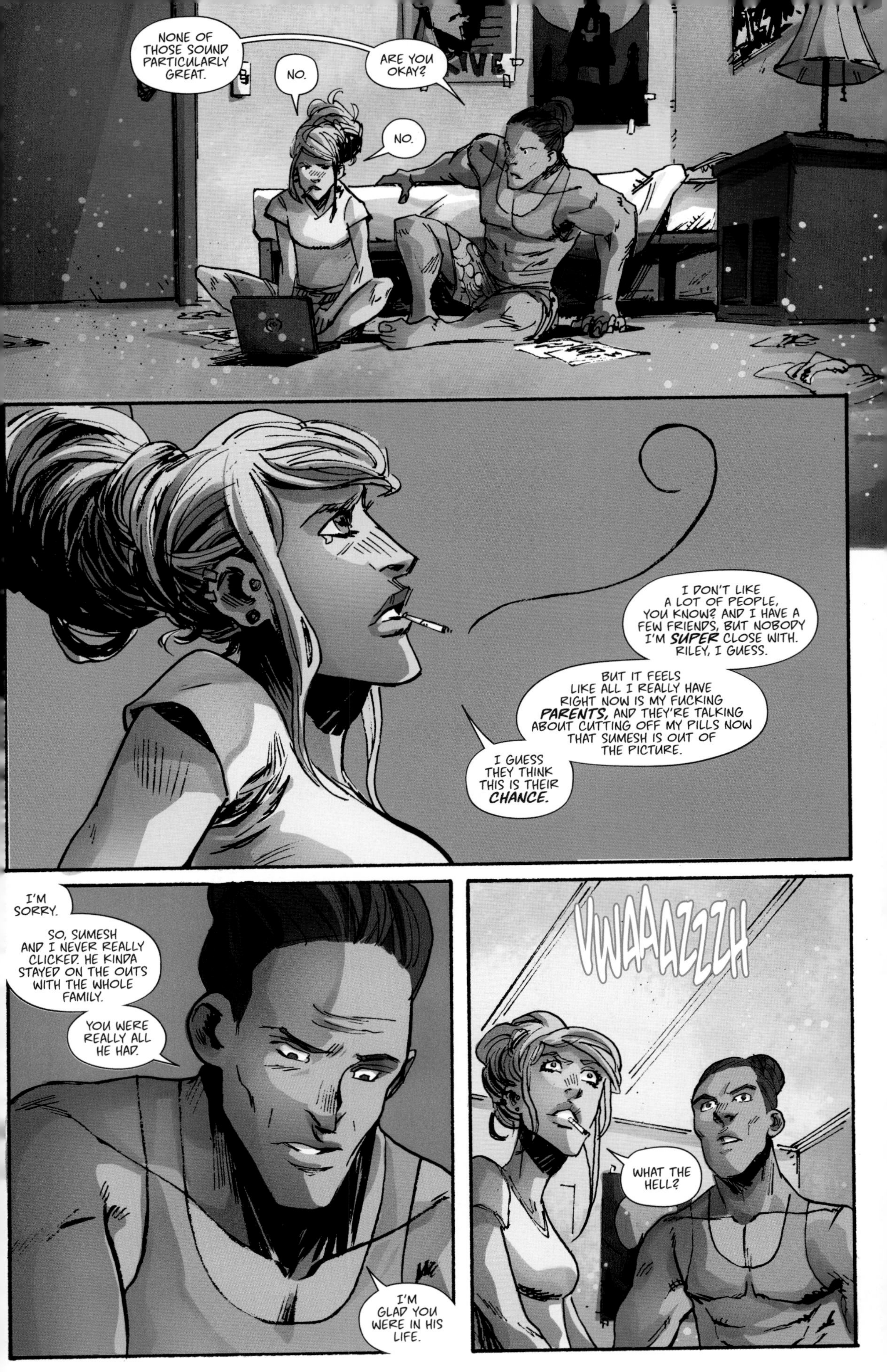
NONE OF THOSE SOUND PARTICULARLY GREAT.
NO.
ARE YOU OKAY?
NO.
I DON'T LIKE A LOT OF PEOPLE, YOU KNOW? AND I HAVE A FEW FRIENDS, BUT NOBODY I'M *SUPER* CLOSE WITH. RILEY, I GUESS.
BUT IT FEELS LIKE ALL I REALLY HAVE RIGHT NOW IS MY FUCKING *PARENTS,* AND THEY'RE TALKING ABOUT CUTTING OFF MY PILLS NOW THAT SUMESH IS OUT OF THE PICTURE.
I GUESS THEY THINK THIS IS THEIR *CHANCE.*
I'M SORRY.
SO, SUMESH AND I NEVER REALLY CLICKED. HE KINDA STAYED ON THE OUTS WITH THE WHOLE FAMILY.
YOU WERE REALLY ALL HE HAD.
I'M GLAD YOU WERE IN HIS LIFE.
VWAAAZZZH
WHAT THE HELL?

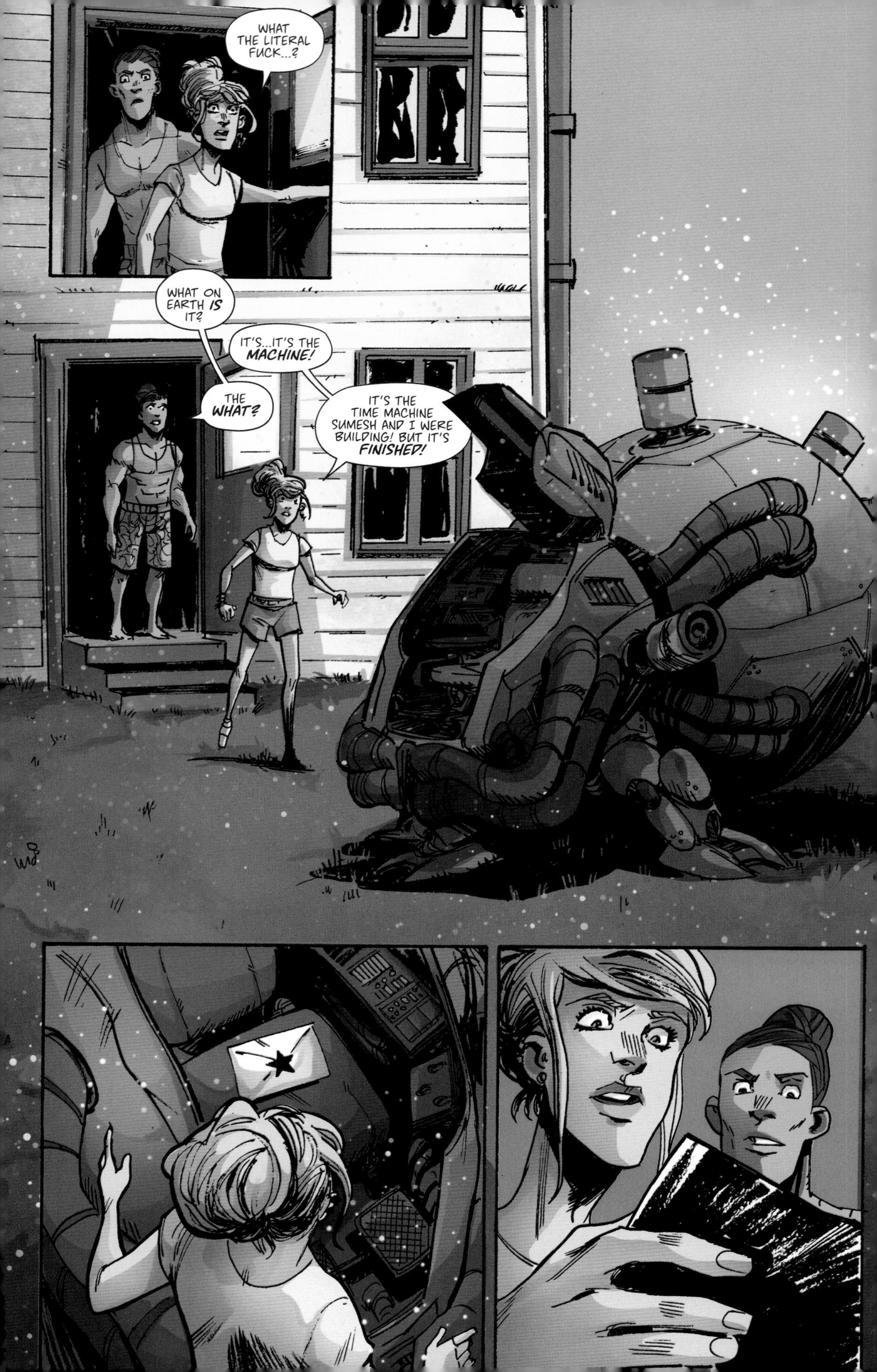
WHAT THE LITERAL FUCK...?
WHAT ON EARTH IS IT?
IT'S...IT'S THE MACHINE!
THE WHAT?
IT'S THE TIME MACHINE SUMESH AND I WERE BUILDING! BUT IT'S FINISHED!

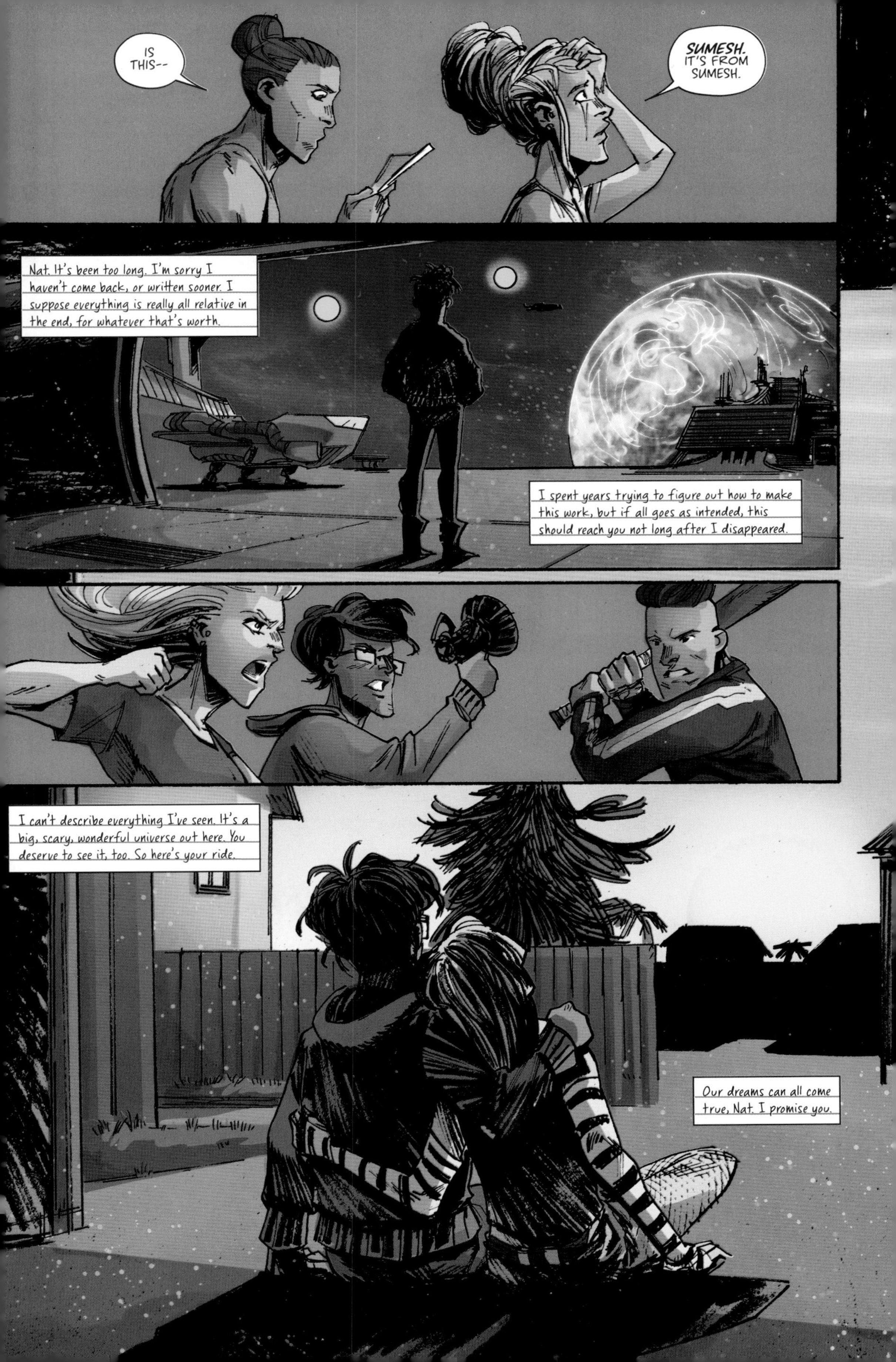
IS THIS--
SUMESH. IT'S FROM SUMESH.
Nat. It's been too long. I'm sorry I haven't come back, or written sooner. I suppose everything is really all relative in the end, for whatever that's worth.
I spent years trying to figure out how to make this work, but if all goes as intended, this should reach you not long after I disappeared.
I can't describe everything I've seen. It's a big, scary, wonderful universe out here. You deserve to see it, too. So here's your ride.
Our dreams can all come true, Nat. I promise you.

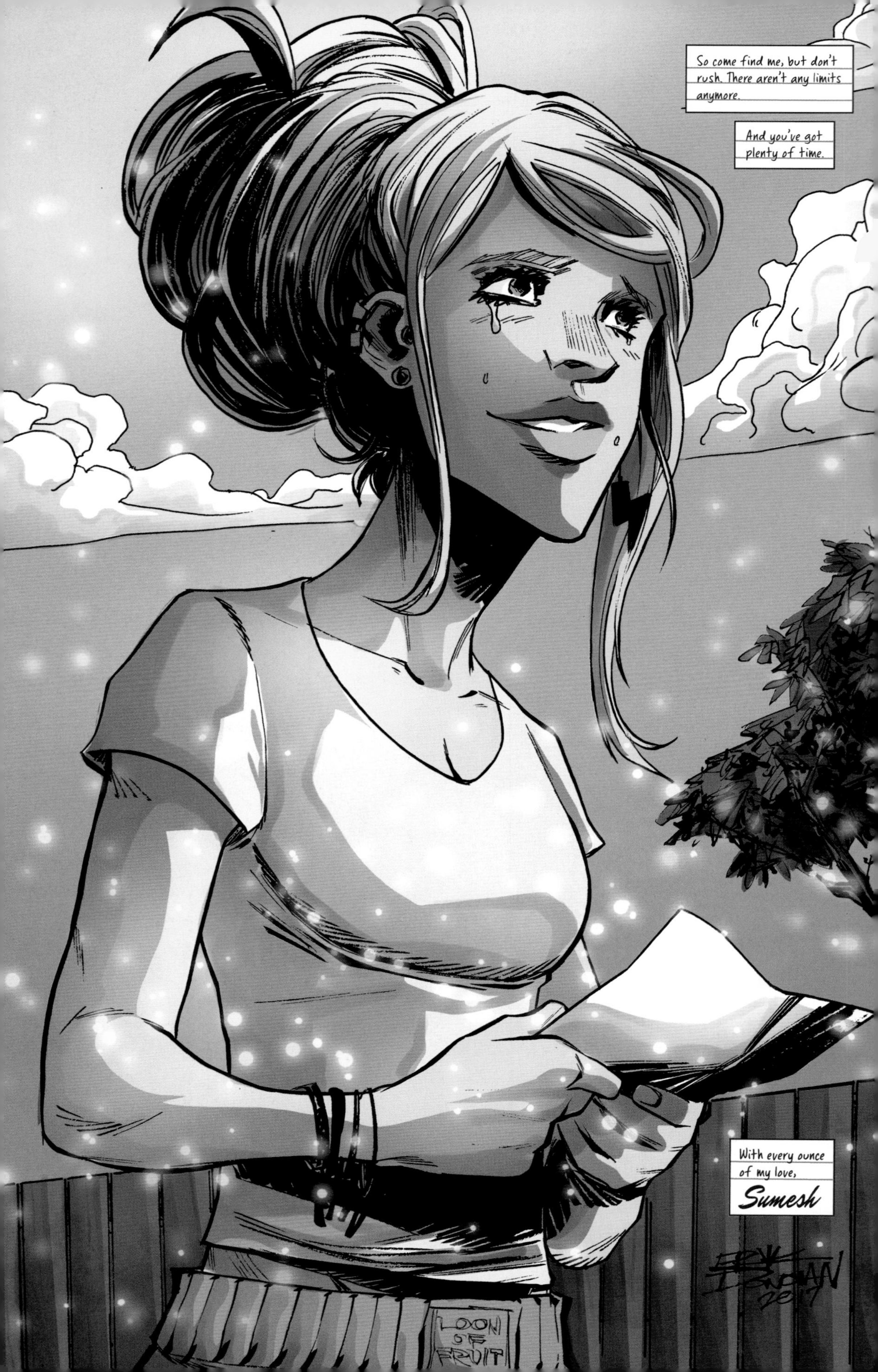
So come find me, but don't rush. There aren't any limits anymore.
And you've got plenty of time.
With every ounce of my love,
Sumesh
LOON OF FRUIT

EPILOGUE:

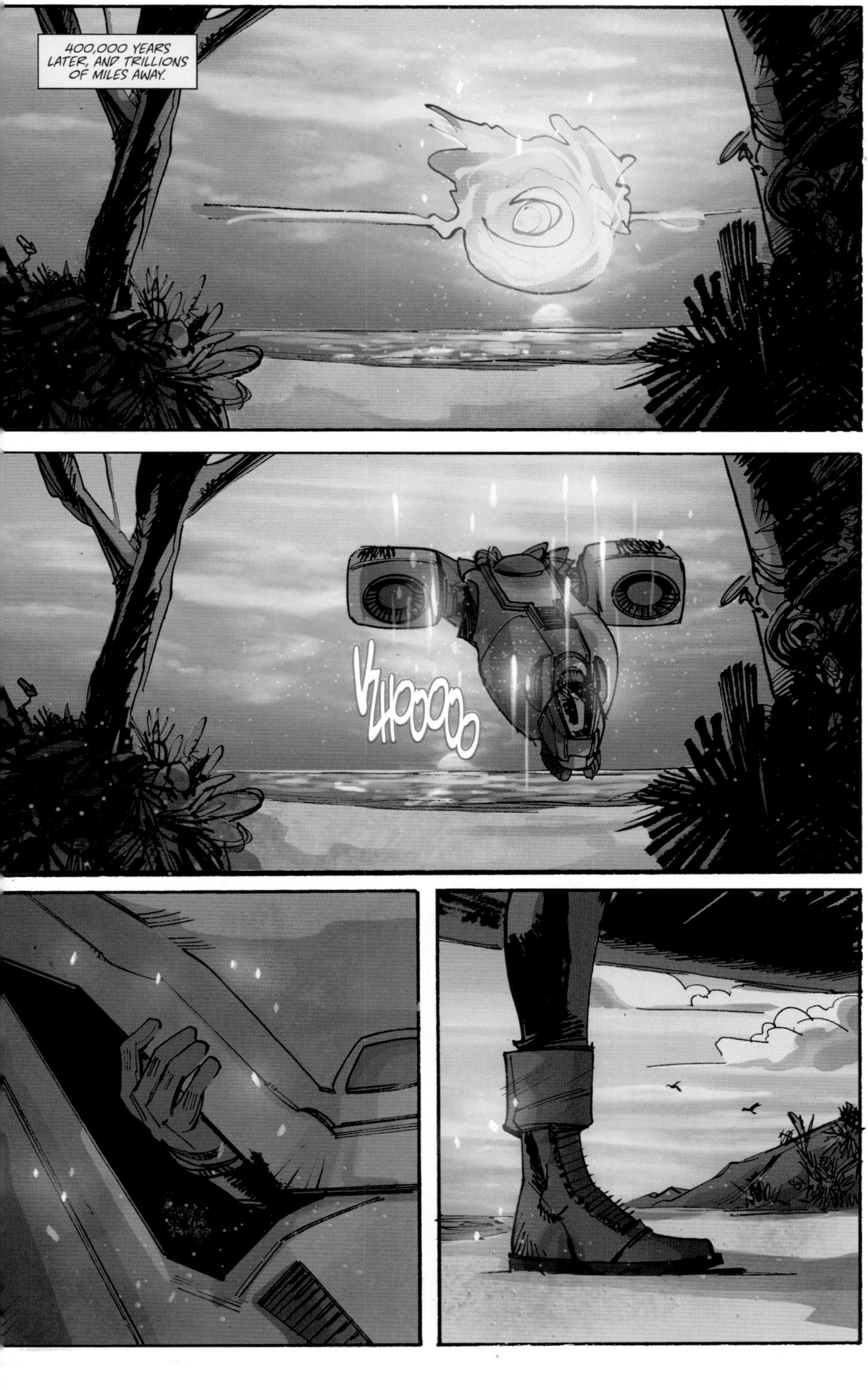
400,000 YEARS LATER, AND TRILLIONS OF MILES AWAY.
VZHOOOOO

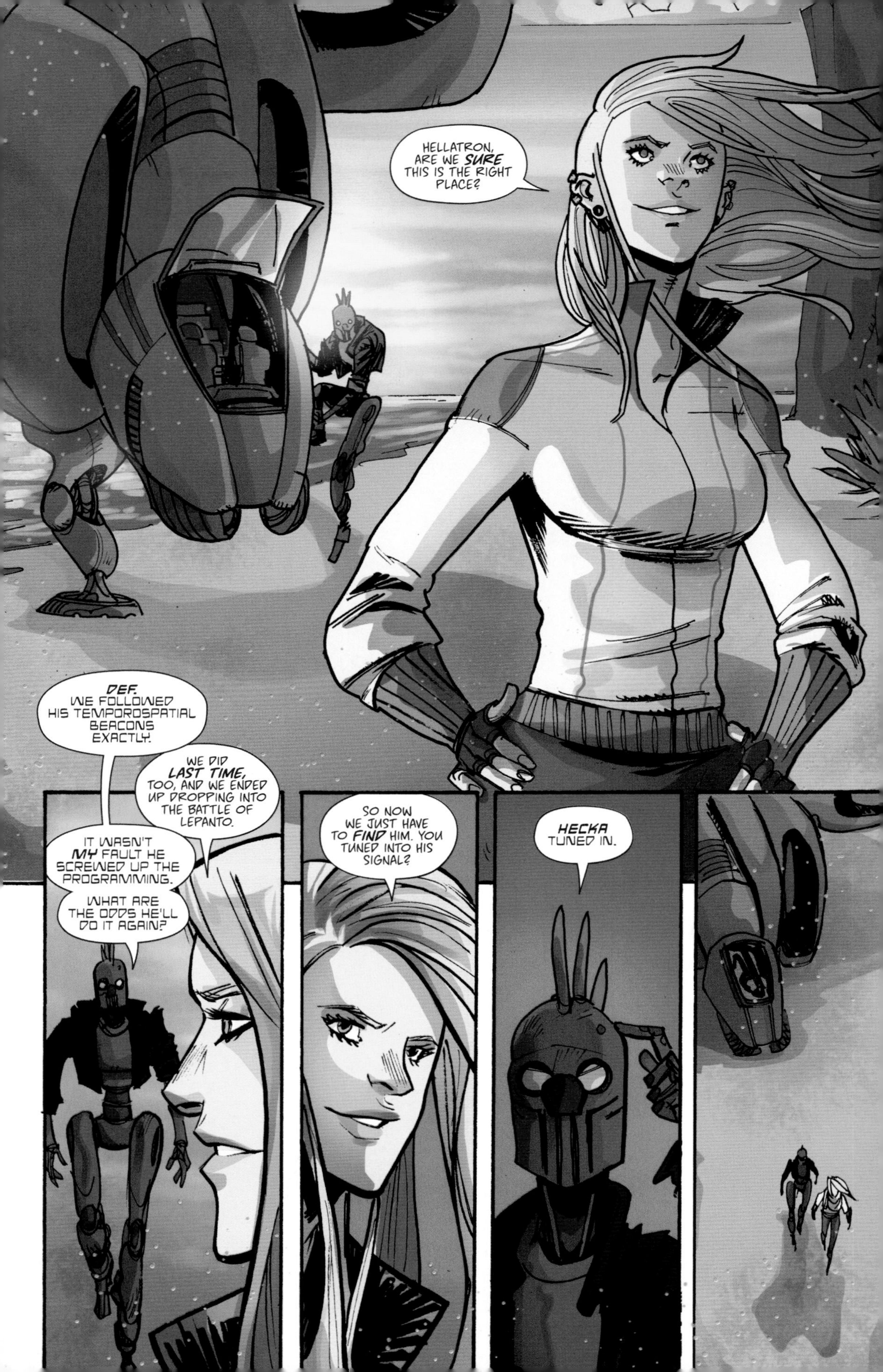
HELLATRON, ARE WE SURE THIS IS THE RIGHT PLACE?
DEF. WE FOLLOWED HIS TEMPOROSPATIAL BEACONS EXACTLY.
WE DID LAST TIME, TOO, AND WE ENDED UP DROPPING INTO THE BATTLE OF LEPANTO.
IT WASN'T MY FAULT HE SCREWED UP THE PROGRAMMING.
WHAT ARE THE ODDS HE'LL DO IT AGAIN?
SO NOW WE JUST HAVE TO FIND HIM. YOU TUNED INTO HIS SIGNAL?
HECKA TUNED IN.

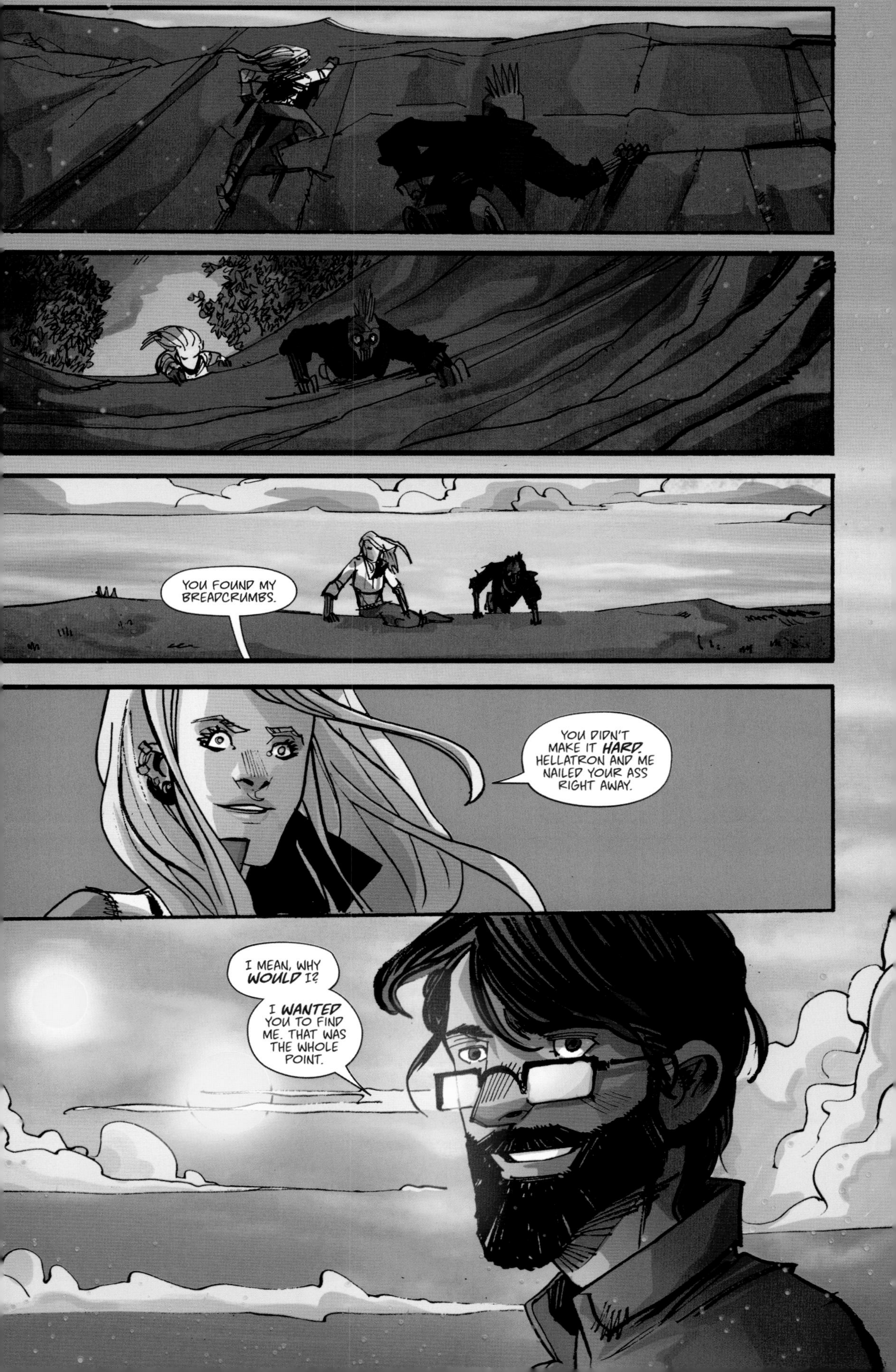
YOU FOUND MY BREADCRUMBS.
YOU DIDN'T MAKE IT HARD. HELLATRON AND ME NAILED YOUR ASS RIGHT AWAY.
I MEAN, WHY WOULD I?
I WANTED YOU TO FIND ME. THAT WAS THE WHOLE POINT.

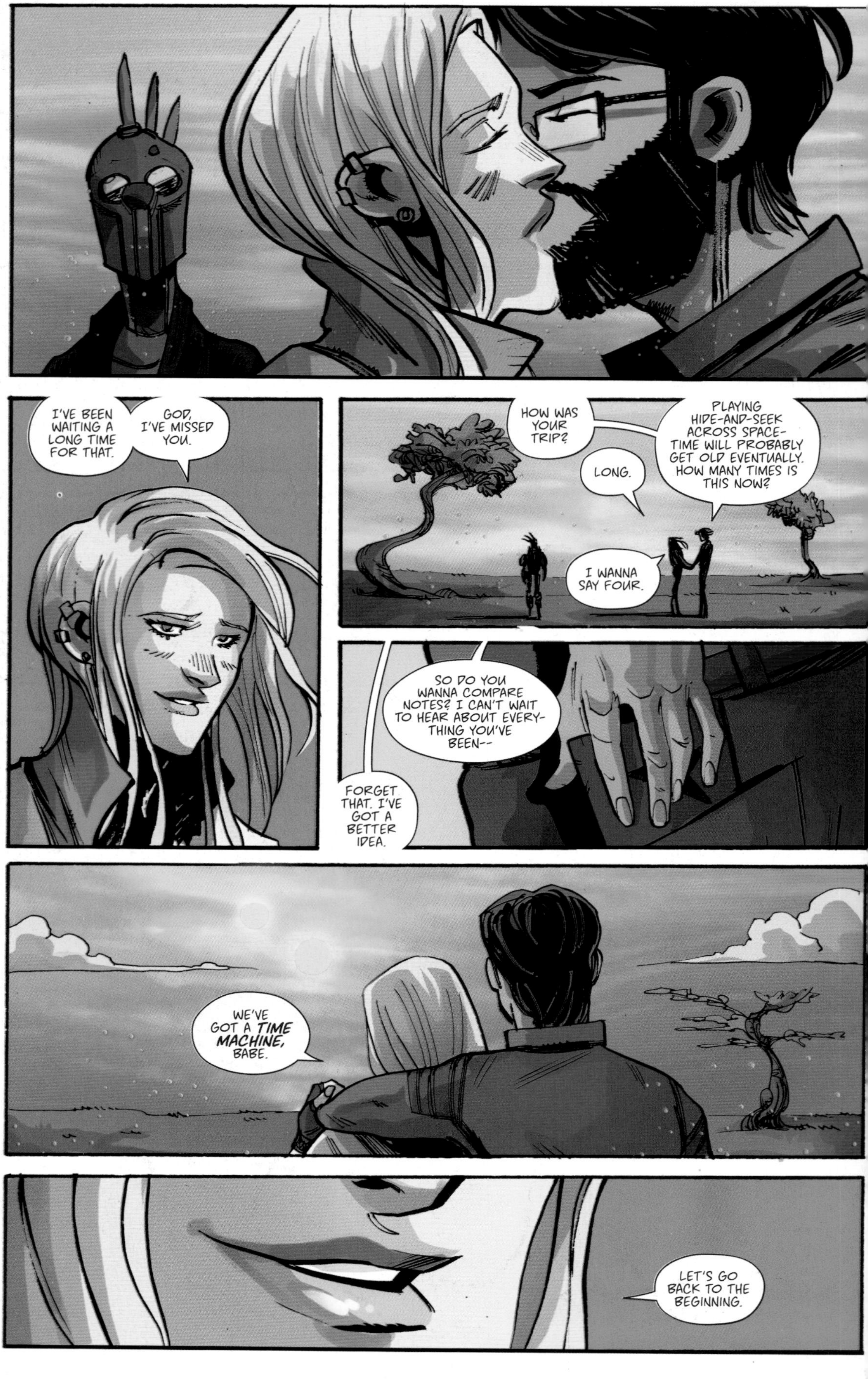
I'VE BEEN WAITING A LONG TIME FOR THAT.
GOD, I'VE MISSED YOU.
HOW WAS YOUR TRIP?
LONG.
PLAYING HIDE-AND-SEEK ACROSS SPACE-TIME WILL PROBABLY GET OLD EVENTUALLY. HOW MANY TIMES IS THIS NOW?
I WANNA SAY FOUR.
SO DO YOU WANNA COMPARE NOTES? I CAN'T WAIT TO HEAR ABOUT EVERY-THING YOU'VE BEEN--
FORGET THAT. I'VE GOT A BETTER IDEA.
WE'VE GOT A *TIME MACHINE,* BABE.
LET'S GO BACK TO THE BEGINNING.